# BLADES REFORGED

NOVELS BY **LIZ SAUCO**
available from Dark Waters Publishing:


*BLADES OF THE GODDESS*
LOST BLADES
BROKEN BLADES
BLADES REFORGED

COLORS OF MAGIC

# Blades Reforged

Blades of the Goddess Book 3

Liz Sauco

Dark Waters Publishing

Colors of Magic
Hardcover ISBN: 978-1-960723-14-7
Paperback ISBN: 978-1-960723-13-0
E-book ISBN: 978-1-960723-12-3
Audiobook ISBN: 978-1-960723-15-4

Published by Dark Waters Publishing
5600 Post Rd
Suite 114-PMB#307
East Greenwich RI 02818

First edition: September 2024
10 9 8 7 6 5 4 3 2 1



Cover design by Liz Sauco

lizsauco.com

*For Papa.*
*We miss you.*

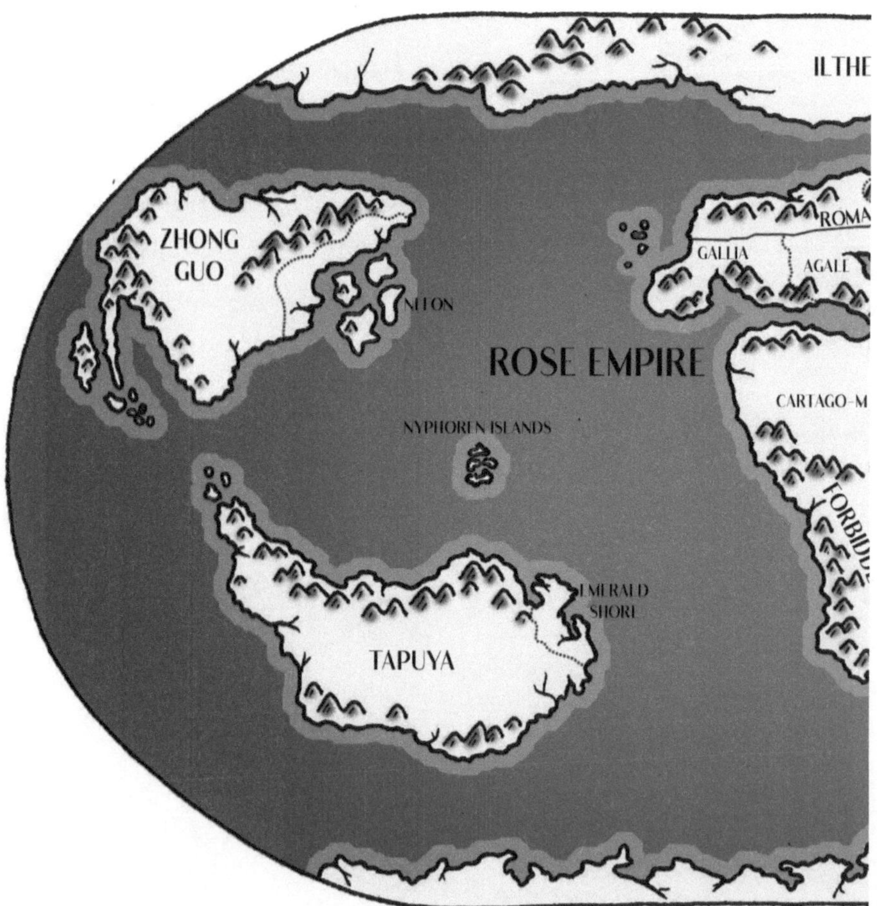

WORLD MAP
GAIA
COUNTRIES - 2026 AG
ILTHE
ZHONG GUO
ROMA
GALLIA
AGALE
NEFON
ROSE EMPIRE
CARTAGO-M
NYPHOREN ISLANDS
FORBIDDE
EMERALD SHORE
TAPUYA

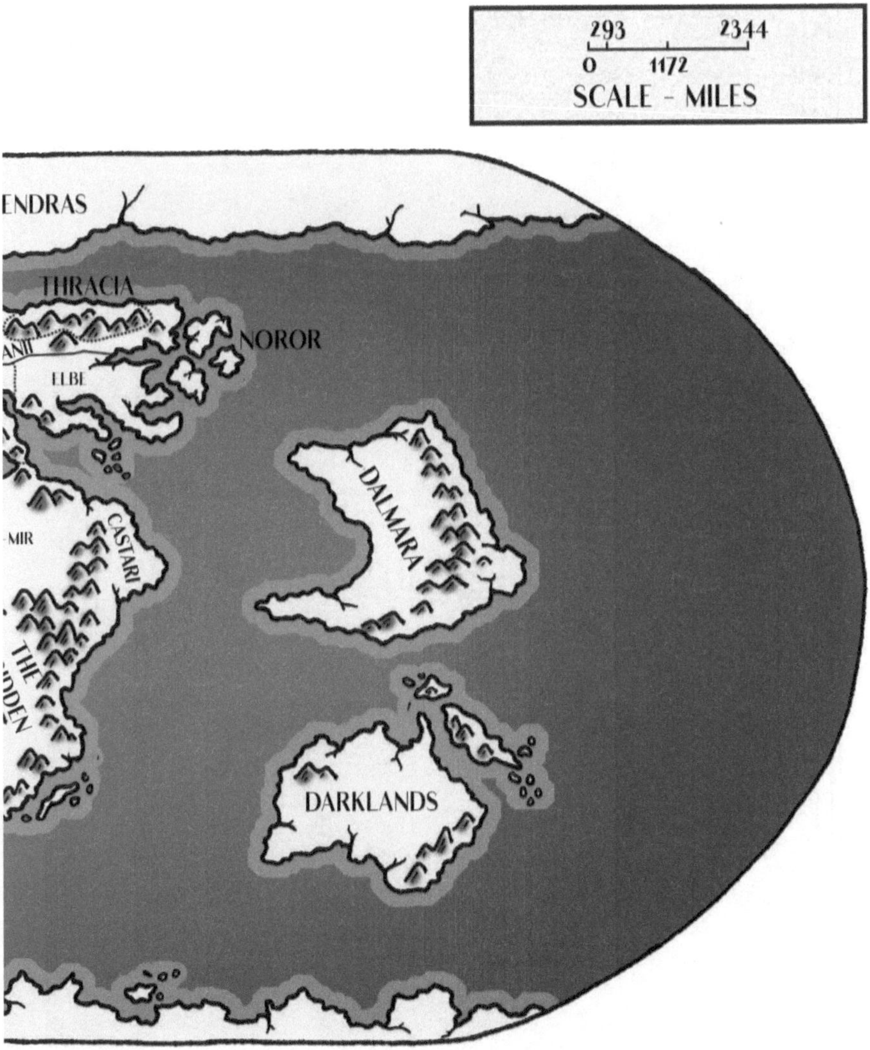

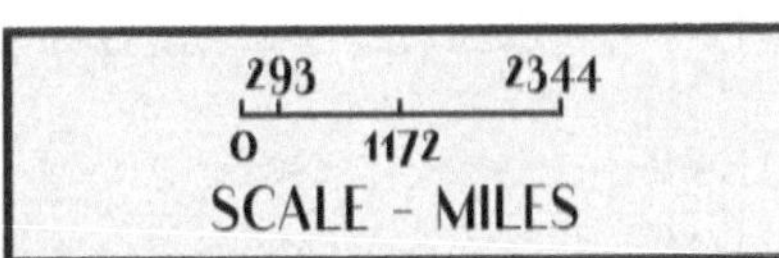

293
2344
0
1172
SCALE - MILES



ENDRAS
THRACIA
ANTI
NOROR
ELBE
MIR
CASTARI
DALMARA
THE
DEN
DARKLANDS

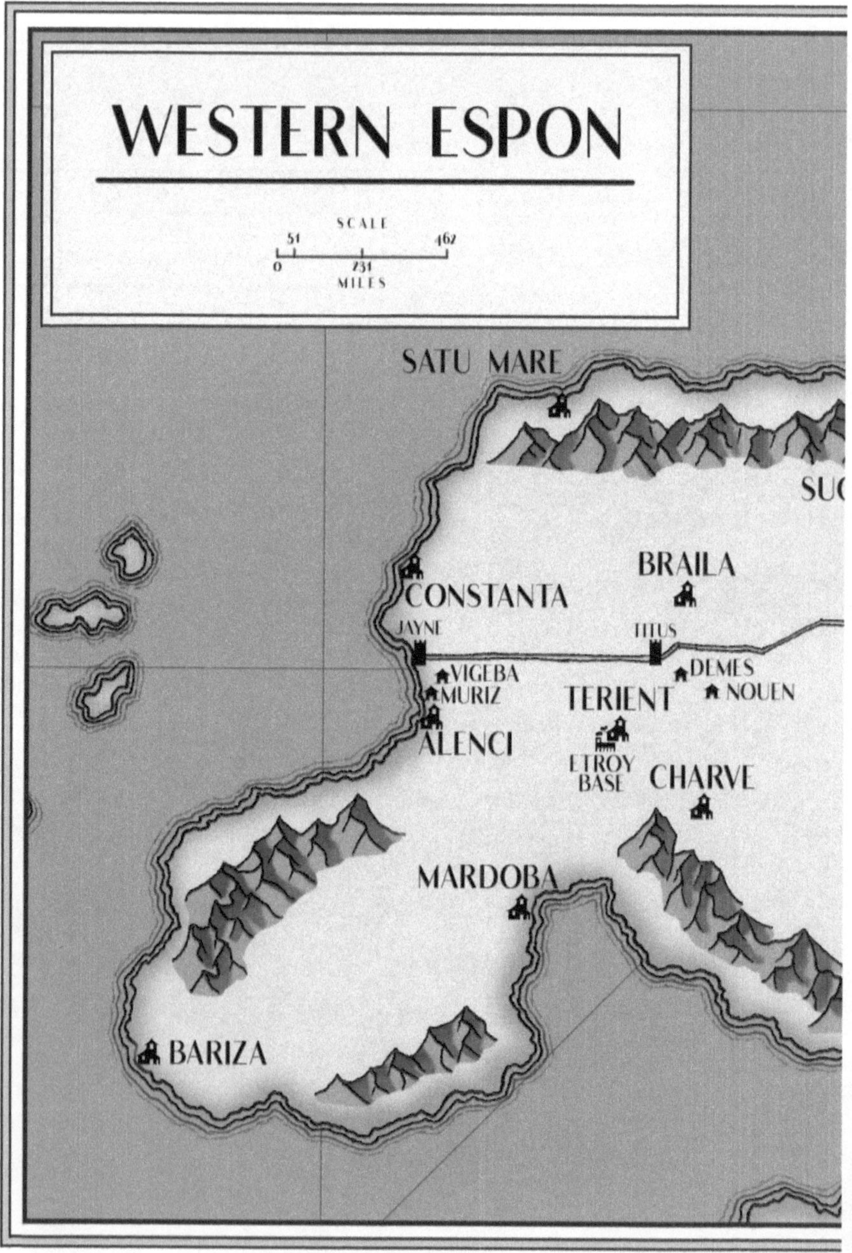

WESTERN ESPON
SCALE
51
462
0
231
MILES
SATU MARE
SUC
BRAILA
CONSTANTA
JAYNE
TITUS
VIGEBA
DEMES
MURIZ
NOUEN
TERIENT
ALENCI
ETROY
BASE
CHARVE
MARDOBA
BARIZA

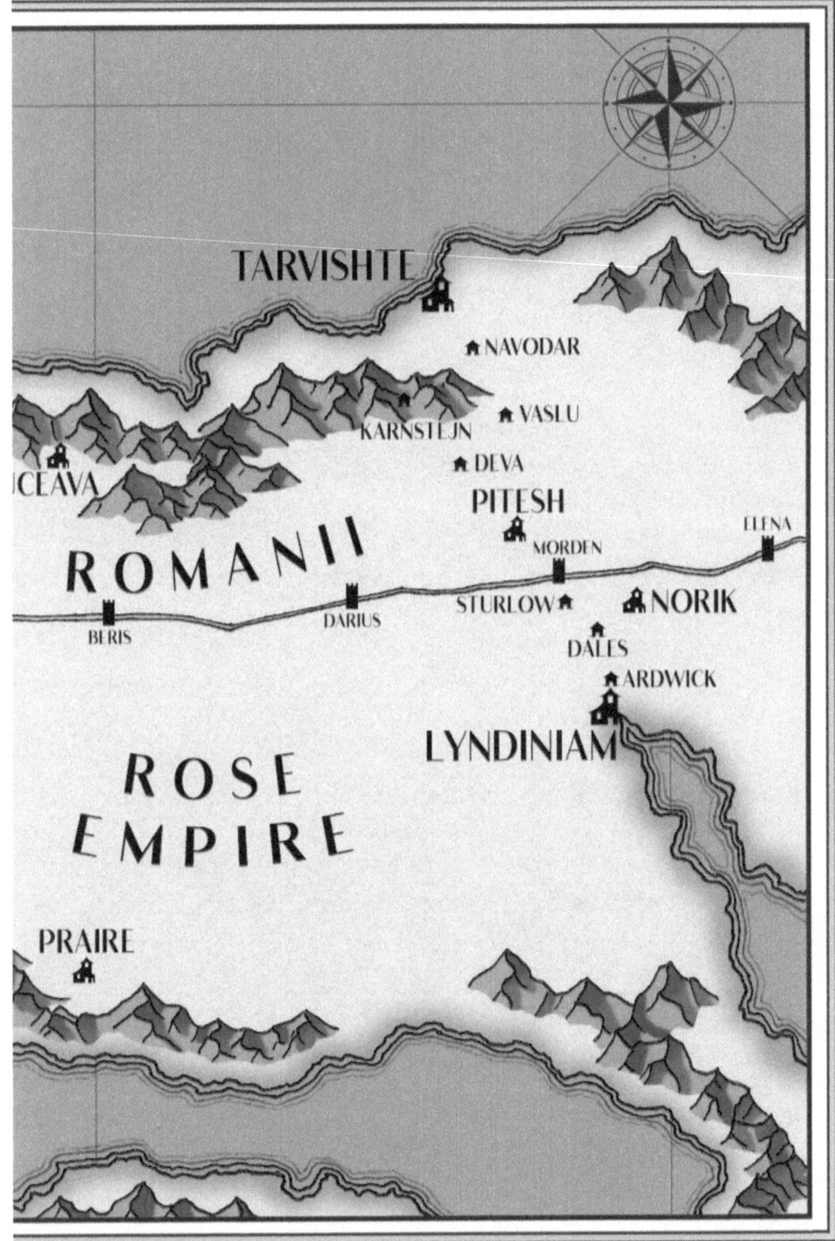

TARVISHTE
NAVODAR
VASLU
KARNSTEJN
DEVA
PITESH
ELENA
UCEAVA
MORDEN
ROMANII
STURLOW
NORIK
BERIS
DARIUS
DALES
ARDWICK
LYNDINIAM
ROSE
EMPIRE
PRAIRE

## Crescent Island

And also, not

Hades considered the remains of the Blade.

Magic still permeated the area, occasionally hemorrhaging in small bursts. Absently, she turned part of herself towards calming it, easing the pressure. Even with her help it would be a long time before this place recovered. The flooding of her power would have had little impact on its own, but then there had been the death of the Blade and the final strike of the Truth Seekers.

Self-sacrifice was something she valued.

But still, threads of power were running rampant as a result. She could sense Nyphora and Nyphore nearby, attempting to ease the pain themselves, probably to prevent it from affecting their mortals too severely. There was, after all, a city of various races nearby, and the Veren lived below.

They had yet to approach her. She knew they would not approve of the flooding of herself in an area they considered to be theirs, but she doubted they would confront her about it.

They must have sensed the stain of Abomination in their lands, but there was so little they could do. Even Hades herself had known – there had been so much death, here – but the rules were in place for good reasons, and she and her siblings had bound themselves to them long ago. Little manipulations, then, to bring one of her own to this place, to then tell the others.

Not even a single shard of blue crystal remained in the area. The only remnant of the Blade was a small piece of violet spell crystal: a piece of vanity, a part of herself she had added to the sword when she forged it. She gathered herself near it, considering the situation.

"Will you reforge the Blade?"

Hades allowed her attention to focus on Nyphora's presence.

Her sister danced away, unable to help herself, but still she spoke. "It's just that we are not sure we can create the required crystallization of power in this time. The Veren are devout, but they are few, and the cities above... well, even you must understand, surely?"

She turned her attention away from Nyphora to ease her. They did not rely on mortals for their existence – they had existed before them and would likely exist after them – but they had put much of themselves into the creation of Those who had come After. They relied on them to share back that power, and without it, they were weakened.

Hades was affected less than her siblings, though, and... well.

Not every family was a happy one.

Fear drove gods just as it did mortals.

Which brought her back to the current problem.

Nyphora was correct; it was unlikely any of the elemental twins save the Patoran and maybe the Faleri would be able to crystalize their essence strongly enough. And besides, a sword forged of magic was clearly not the solution to this expression of Abomination. Something else would have to be done.

Part of her sighed. So much effort, and the Blade had barely lasted a millennium.

"But we do not wish to be corrupted by our antithesis again," Nyphora added. "Surely you have some plan in place?"

Hades understood that, too. Her own being had remained unscathed the time Abomination had come closest to succeeding, but she remembered seeing her siblings begin their falls. She would do everything she could to prevent it from happening again.

She turned her attention briefly to the shards of herself that remained with her beloved priests. They were all hurting right now, unable to see past the crystal chrysalis. Even those truly devoted to her found it difficult to perceive the Cycle. But then, they were all very young. They lacked context, struggled to see the larger picture. They would learn. She sent them a wave of love and affection and offered hugs to those who would accept them; she basked in the feelings returned, was amused by the mild confusion from the youngest.

He would learn this, too.

Another minor detonation of elemental power occurred; she did her best to soothe it. The Nyphoren shuddered and redoubled their own efforts. She was impressed by how willing they were to come to a place so recently touched by Abomination, especially considering their fear of being corrupted by it – but then again, magic overwhelming had won this battle.

Carefully, she recalled the small piece of herself that had been in the Blade, reconsidering it and the possibilities. She would not reforge the Blade.

But she also rather thought the question was missing the point.

# Chapter One

Jamirh stared at the fancy drink Salisha plopped on the table in front of him. Silver eyes took in the thick, pale-pink liquid in a tall glass, topped with a swirl of whipped cream and a strawberry. A red-and-white-striped straw stuck out next to some thin curls of white chocolate. A strawberry milkshake. Probably spiked with some sort of alcohol, if he knew the twins at all. They added it to everything. Twice in the past month they had added it to soup, and once to a sandwich. He still wasn't sure about the salad.

Desha grinned at him from where she lounged in her chair, feet up on the café table. Her green eyes sparkled with mischief. "Ohh! That one looks good!"

"It is," her sister confirmed, putting two more milkshakes on the table and dropping into a third chair. She twisted and leaned far to the right so that the umbrella hid her face from the sun, ending up practically lying on Desha, who pushed her sister's sun-bleached blonde hair out of her face.

Jamirh cringed internally, seeing the disapproving glances of the other patrons at the sisters' display, but obediently tried the milkshake. "It's good," he agreed, taking another sip to savor the creamy strawberry flavor. There was definitely alcohol in there. And also little crumbs of cake, maybe? "Very, uh, strawberry." He tried to muster up some excitement for them, tugging on his short ruby-red ponytail as his long ears twitched.

The way the sisters glanced at each other made him think he wasn't successful. "Well, o' course!" Salisha laughed, stretching awkwardly to grab her milkshake while keeping her eyes out of the sun. The weather was warm for late March, and the sun was obnoxiously bright. "It be a strawberry shortcake milkshake! With rum."

That made him pause. "They have rum here?" It was a little café overlooking Tarvishte's port. They served little cakes and pastries, and a selection of teas and other sweet beverages. Rum wasn't the alcohol he would have figured they served.

In his Life Before Hel, he never would have believed that this would be possible – an Avari, hanging out with two Humans. In Lyndiniam, the city he had lived in for his whole life, such a thing was practically unheard of. But here, in Vampire-ruled Tarvishte, the only thing that made them stand out was the disrespect Desha was showing the café furniture by putting her shoes on the table.

Hel had changed everything when she broke him out of that jail.

"No." Salisha didn't even have the grace to look sheepish. "I supplied it."

Jamirh decided that wasn't his problem as the sisters high-fived each other. They *were* pirates, and the milkshake *was* good. And they'd been trying so hard to cheer him up over the past month. He looked down at his right hand, at the angry red lines still present, spiraling up his arm. Marcus had removed the stitches two weeks ago, but wounds caused by exploding magical artifacts apparently took longer to heal completely.

Everything that could have gone wrong in their raid of Tilden Base had. Bionics had followed them everywhere. The ghost of Ebryn Stormlight had appeared. The Crystal Light Blade had shattered. Truth Seekers had magically blown up the base. It was a miracle any of them were still alive – a miracle Jak, Hades' first High Priest, had paid for with his own life.

Despite the sisters' efforts, Jamirh felt lost. Takeshi and Ander had been busy doing something priest-related, since another priest was supposed to be coming to Tarvishte but had run into some sort of delay. Jeri, who'd been by his side since Hel had broken him out of jail, was busy as a member of the Black Watch trying to determine if the Emperor's death was going to cause problems for Romanii. Many of the other friends he'd made here were also members of the Watch and also busy. Hel had been clear that Abomination still existed somewhere and had to be destroyed, so everyone was trying to figure out how to track down the remaining bionics.

Everyone except Jamirh, it felt like.

He felt sad at the thought of Jeri. He understood why she was busy. Everything was uncertain right now. But the few times they had run into each other she had seemed uncomfortable, and quickly made excuses to leave. The only explanation Jamirh could come to was that she was avoiding him for some reason. Was it over his failure at Tilden Base? He'd thought they were closer than that, but maybe he was wrong. The thought made his stomach flip uncomfortably. He missed his friend.

He'd been mostly left alone since the Tilden Base disaster, and he guessed that made sense. It wasn't like he still had any use to them. He had been special because he was Ebryn Stormlight reborn and could use the Crystal Light Blade. Now that the sword was shattered, why should they bother with Jamirh? He was just a random, homeless Avari from Lyndiniam who was able to learn how to use weapons really fast.

The sisters, equally out of place due to being teleported with the rest of the strike team to Tarvishte, had stuck to Jamirh like burrs. Even once the *Sea Spirit* made port in Tarvishte and they'd reunited with the rest of their crew, they'd made an effort to keep Jamirh occupied. They made him take them on tours around the city and the palace, then made him give those same tours to other crewmates. They dragged him out to get dinner and breakfast, and generally made nuisances of themselves as they investigated the differences between Romanii's steam-based tech and their own.

Jamirh was thankful for it. It kept him from remembering those glassy, sightless silver eyes, staring back at him from within that tank–

"Hey!" Salisha was snapping her fingers in front of his face. "Attention on us! No need t' go far away like that."

Jamirh snapped back to attention, wrenching his mind away from the memory with sheer strength of will. There was no reason to think of that. None at all. It was gone now anyway. "Sorry." Neither of the sisters looked impressed, and his ears twitched down as he groped for an excuse. "I was just thinking about the Empire. I can't believe only Rikona has officially declared her province a separate nation."

Salisha shrugged. Jamirh couldn't tell if she believed him or if she was humoring him. "It's hard t' say, ye know?"

"It's kinda surprising nothing's happened yet," Desha added, "considering he didn't have an heir. Guess they wanted t' wait for the big funeral and all. Maybe one o' the dukes will take over?"

"Gods know they were ruling the joint anyway," Salisha snorted. "Poor guy was just a figurehead."

Jamirh shrugged. Even though he'd lived in the capital city, the Emperor had been a distant concept. What had his name even been? Beorn? Baldrin? Beren! That sounded right. "Maybe nothing will change, then? If they were already in charge, why does it matter if the Emperor is there or not?"

"Appearances!" Desha shouted, slamming her hand down on the table. They earned another round of dirty looks from nearby patrons, and even her sister looked at her in surprise. "In order t' have an Empire, ye *need* an Emperor! The whole thing falls apart without that role! Having someone t' do all the non-important social bits while *they* do all the real work! Mark my words – if one o' them takes over, they won't stand for being a figurehead. They'll want *real* power, and that means taking power from the others. That's where the real problems are going t' begin."

"Oh," Jamirh squeaked, unwilling to question that in the face of such zeal. "I guess I hadn't thought of it that way."

"It's what all the top meetings be about, I bet," she continued. "The king and his advisors be trying t' figure out if the Empire is going t' hold or collapse, and how either option will affect them. Personally, I think Duchess Tyra's going t' see that Rikona's getting away with Ni Fon's independence and ask herself why the Emerald Shore can't do the same. They're even farther from Lyndiniam than Ni Fon is, and they're going t' see it can be an easy break. Johen might then consider how the Islands could be their own thing, and then it'll just be Gallia, Elbe, Agale, and Cartago-Mir t' battle it out for the mainland. Who knows? Maybe all four will break apart completely, and we'll go back t' how it was waaaaaay back when in Ebryn's time!"

"I think there were more countries then," Salisha said, eyeing her sister warily. "The provinces would have t' break apart t' go back t' that."

Desha just shrugged, looking pleased with her analysis of the situation. "Doesn't matter, really. The important thing be – I bet there won't be an Empire in two years' time. Not the way we know it, certainly. And that'll affect the bureaucracy."

Salisha looked confused, but then her eyes widened in understanding. "Oh. Oh! But then *that* means–"

Desha was grinning. "Yup. Piracy is about t' be *way* easier for the next few years."

"Sweet!" Salisha exclaimed. "Imagine all the loot!" She paused. "But then again, Cap'n's been talking about trying the Dead Seas."

Her sister grinned like a shark. "Yeah, even better, because everyone else will be up here. Less competition fer the *real* prize."

Salisha snorted. "That no one else even seems t' know about."

Jamirh found himself smiling at their excitement, even though he wasn't sure he followed the logic. Then again, he had never really cared about how governments worked, and he couldn't find it in himself to start caring now. In his opinion, if the Empire fell then maybe the Avari would be able to carve out some better spaces for themselves among the wreckage. Good riddance to the useless institution his illustrious predecessor had helped create. "Then this is just... the calm before the storm, you think?"

He found himself the subject of two beaming grins. "Yup!" they chorused.

He took another sip of his milkshake. "What about the Truth Seekers?"

Desha shrugged. "Hard t' know, since they've been trying t' scrub any mention o' them out o' the news. The Empire's trying t' pretend they don't exist or something."

"That ship's sailed," Salisha laughed. "The assassination happened during a live broadcast. And there's not a person in the Empire who didn't know about the Truth Seekers."

Jamirh frowned. "I never would have believed it could happen. Truth Seekers..." He paused, trying to fit his thoughts into words. "They are – or were, I guess – indistinguishable from the law. I never would've even considered that they would betray it."

"It's hard t' know what's going on in someone's head sometimes. And ye can't see the Blind Ones' eyes – lets them hide their true thoughts pretty easily," Salisha observed.

Her sister nodded. "Goes t' show – just because ye create something t' be loyal t' ye doesn't mean it won't turn around and bite ye if ye don't treat it right."

"What do you mean?" Jamirh asked. "They were, like, the most prestigious rank."

The sisters shook their heads. "Empire wanted it t' look like that, yeah," Desha said, her voice dropping to a dramatic whisper. "But I talked t' the wizard, and if ye really think about it – they were using magic, the thing the Empire was trying t' wipe out. How long do ye think they had before the bigwigs found ways t' replace them? I don't know how involved they were in actual decision-making up there either. And *then* the whole Abomination thing becomes... a thing."

"Wizard says it doesn't feel right t' mages," Salisha said thoughtfully. "Didn't really feel right t' me, either. No reason not t' believe that's part o' what set off the Blind Ones."

"Exactly!" Desha agreed. "And lucky for them, the Empire didn't believe they could rebel either, so they were in a lot o' good positions t' really hit hard. Boom." She leaned back in her chair, arms sweeping open. "Dead Emperor, everyone's taken by surprise, the balance o' power at the top is destabilized, and they can do what they want."

"But... can they?" Jamirh asked. "The rest of the military isn't just going to let them walk off like that."

Salisha shrugged. "What can they do about it? Their only anti-magic force just walked off. Sure, they can try t' bring them back in line, but how?"

It didn't sit right with Jamirh, but he wasn't sure why. He finished his milkshake as he tried to gather his thoughts. "I think–"

"Yer right! We should grab some snacks!" Desha interrupted.

"What?" Jamirh asked, thrown by the change in topic.

Salisha drank the rest of her milkshake down in one long gulp. "Hm, what'll we go for? There were those tasty little cakes at the place we went t' last week."

"Or those odd little cereal things from that other place!"

"Or the cute breads from the *other* other place!"

"Let's get some chocolate from the little stand thing on the palace grounds!" they declared together, turning to look at Jamirh hopefully.

"Sure," he agreed carefully, having decided some time ago not to get between them and chocolate. And it wasn't like he was going to turn down food of any kind.

They cheered, and Desha finished her drink. The waitress hovering nearby looked relieved to see them go as they waved at her in goodbye.

Jamirh took a moment to appreciate the beautiful weather as they wandered through the cobbled streets of Tarvishte. It was nothing like the clean, sterile look of white lester and glass that the Empire favored. Brick was the overwhelming material of choice here, heavily embellished with copper or brass and wood framing. Large pipes traveled up buildings, passing the trailing plants spilling out over ornate balconies. Glass windows had thick metal frames and dividers. No two buildings were the same, and unlike his home district of Blackfields everything was well-maintained. If there were slums in Tarvishte, he hadn't found them on any of his excursions.

The streets were a little more crowded than usual, Avari, Humans, and Vampires all taking advantage of the nice weather. Far up above, the sky shimmered with the magic that kept out harmful UV rays and allowed the Vampires to enjoy some sunlight. Now and then they passed a warg, creatures similar to large wolves, but far more friendly. They liked to lie in sunny spots like furry rugs and hope people would give them food.

Wargs were the scavengers of Tarvishte, Jamirh reflected. At least they were cuter than Lyndiniam's pigeons.

They passed one of the many goddess statues as they entered through the ornate metal gates onto the palace grounds proper. Unlike the palace in Lyndiniam, the Palace of Dusk and its grounds were open to the public. In fact, one of the major city hospitals was on palace grounds, as well as the Temple of Night Rising – the main place of worship for Hades. The palace itself stole the view, however, with its large domes and tall spires decorated with ornate stone and metalwork. Well-maintained and cultivated gardens spread out on the west side.

Jamirh felt his ears sink a bit as they passed by the training grounds. He hadn't trained at all since they'd returned from the Nyphoren Islands. Takeshi was just too busy to train with him now. Jamirh knew the priests had been trying to figure out what to do now that Jak was a crystal statue. Or did Takeshi think there wasn't a need to train Jamirh now that the Crystal Light Blade was gone?

Maybe the former shinobi was right in that case. Maybe Jamirh should just accept that the reason he was brought here was gone and he was just dead weight now. Maybe he should be thankful everyone was leaving him alone, and not pressuring him into doing something he hadn't wanted to do in the first place. That was what he'd wanted, right? To just be allowed to be Jamirh? Leave his past – and Ebryn's – far behind him?

Where was Ebryn, anyway? The ghost had shown up once and that was it. Even when Jamirh tried to talk to him there was no answer. Maybe the destruction of the Blade had made him disappear permanently. And what about poor Ryn, the incarnation between Jamirh and Ebryn? He'd died fighting the bionics nearly twenty-five years ago, but he'd been talking to Jamirh for weeks before they had attempted to destroy Tilden Base. He'd been silent since...

...blank silver eyes...

...since just before Ebryn had shown up. Was he okay? Jamirh found himself worrying.

What was wrong with him? Why was he fighting this? He hadn't wanted any of it to begin with. He should be happy!

So why wasn't he?

"Oh, Jamirh!"

Jeri was standing a few feet away, looking as surprised as he felt. The Vampire's platinum-blonde hair was in its typical long braid and she was wearing her Watch Blacks. Which meant she was working. Jamirh tried to swallow the disappointment as he reached up to rub the old key hanging from a cord around his neck. "Jeri! Hi!"

"Hiya, Jeri!" the sisters chorused behind him.

Was it just Jamirh, or did Jeri's smile look strained? "Good afternoon," she greeted. "What are you all doing here?"

What were they doing here? Jamirh lived here. What sort of question was that?

"Getting those little chocolate things from the little cart thing near the entrance t' the gardens!" Salisha answered, oblivious to Jamirh's confusion. "Ye want t' get some with us?"

"It's been a bit since we were all forced t' hang out in poor Mara's little apartment!" Desha added.

"Was it even that girl's actual apartment? Never did get a straight answer on that."

"Props t' her for figuring it out before we got there if it wasn't."

Jeri was already shaking her head. "I am sorry, but... perhaps another time? I have to be in a, ah, meeting soon."

Something about the way Jeri was standing suddenly struck Jamirh as odd, like she was keeping herself slightly turned away. Why would that be?

"Oooh, some super-secret stuff?" Salisha asked, eyes widening with excitement.

Desha's eyes glinted like a shark scenting blood in the water. "Anything ye could share with some old friends?"

"She's got theories." Salisha jerked her thumb in her sister's direction.

Jeri took a step back, beginning to look alarmed. Jamirh wasn't surprised; the sisters had that effect on most people. "Sorry, sorry; it would all be incredibly boring to you I'm sure. You should continue to enjoy the city though, don't let me stop you. Enjoy the rest of your day!" She exploded into a cloud of bats that flew off in the direction of the palace.

"Wow," Desha snorted as Jamirh felt his ears sink even lower. "Talk about making a getaway."

"I don't know what's up with that, but something's wrong with that girl," Salisha agreed.

Jamirh bit his lip as he looked down, clutching his key tightly.

"But there's chocolate ahead for us!" Desha declared, grabbing Jamirh's arm to pull him along. "Can't be sad when there's chocolate."

"I'm not sad," Jamirh lied reflexively. "Why would I be sad?"

"Never said ye were," Salisha stated mildly.

"Cho-co-la-te time!" Desha stressed each syllable with each step she took. "Maybe they have waffles."

"*What?*" Jamirh asked.

"Oooh, we could add the rum to that!" Salisha enthused.

Gods, it was getting worse. "How do you add rum to a waffle?"

"I can think o' at least five ways, but the easiest is just t' pour it on top." Desha mimed pouring a bottle.

Jamirh was saved from having to ask what the other four methods were by the presence of two familiar figures at the chocolate cart. Vlad, the ruler of Romanii and king of the Vampires, was inspecting the offerings on display with Miravu, the Aradian ambassador to Romanii. Jamirh was always a little taken aback by the casualness Vlad showed around his subjects and how they treated him in turn. He couldn't imagine the former Emperor enjoying food at a random street cart in Lyndiniam.

Miravu brushed a long strand of violet hair behind an ear, catching sight of Jamirh and the twins approaching. "Jamirh, and sisters twain. Well met." The blue-green flames in her eyes flickered happily as her lips formed a gentle smile.

He found himself smiling back. "Hello, Miravu, Your Majesty."

Vlad sent him a dry look at the address. "Hello, Jamirh."

"Hello, King-sir!" Salisha giggled.

"And Ambassador-miss," Desha added.

Vlad just shook his head, long black waves of hair drifting gently in the breeze. Ruby eyes found Jamirh's. "How have you been? My apologies for being unable to seek you out sooner; national security has been and continues to be in question."

"Okay, I guess," he deflected with a shrug. "Keeping busy."

A delicate black eyebrow rose.

"Yeah, we've been doing all sorts o' things!" Desha agreed. "Exploring and eating and more exploring!"

Miravu smiled, clearly amused. "You have been having much more fun than we, then."

Vlad winced. "I think everyone not involved in the daily meetings is having more fun than we are purely on principle. Has your captain decided when the *Sea Spirit* will be casting off?"

Jamirh swallowed hard. Everyone leaves eventually, he reminded himself. A lesson learned long ago.

But Salisha surprised him. "Nope, not yet!"

"Cap'n says he's going t' wait and see what we can do," Desha confirmed.

"And besides, we're greatly enjoying our vacation here!" Salisha finished.

"I'm glad to hear that," Vlad said. "You are welcome to stay in my country for as long as you like." His eyes slid to Jamirh. "The political situation is likely to be tense for some time moving forward, but I would like to find time to meet with you. I have no idea what my schedule looks like for the coming week – probably something that will make me contemplate running off into the wild and becoming a hermit – but my secretary Elise does. Could you book yourself with me for a meeting? I will make sure she knows to expect you."

"Uh, sure," Jamirh stuttered. Vlad wanted to talk to him? Why?

"Good, thank you. If she asks you for a secret password, there isn't one. She just likes to make people work for it," the Vampire explained.

"Ah, I have been using 'emerald sands,'" Miravu laughed softly.

The sisters giggled.

Vlad just shook his head. "We should be getting back." He sounded regretful. "Everyone will be cross if I'm late because they cannot start without me."

"But it's Saturday," Jamirh protested.

"There have been meetings every day of the week since the Emperor's assassination," Vlad said, pained. "And running a country does not usually come with weekends, unfortunately."

"It was very nice to speak with you again, Jamirh," Miravu said. "May the Fires light your path."

They exchanged goodbyes, and Vlad and Miravu left to return to the palace.

"I wonder why he wants to speak with me?" Jamirh wondered as he gazed after them.

"Well, duh – yer special," Salisha said like it was obvious.

"Yeah, maybe he wants t' talk with ye about the whole Base thing!" Desha added.

Jamirh shuddered at the memory. He hoped not. He had already talked about what had happened at Tilden Base a lot when they first returned. And besides – he wasn't special, not anymore.

Now he was just Jamirh.

# Chapter Two

Takeshi was a hairsbreadth away from throwing something at the wall. Preferably something breakable. Something that could shatter in a satisfying way. If his soul crystal would stay outside his body for more than two milliseconds he would probably throw that.

Jitsu gave a hesitant whine from where she lay on the couch in Takeshi's quarters. She didn't think those crystals broke like that. They weren't supposed to, at least.

Takeshi shot the white warg an unimpressed look before taking a deep breath to calm himself. The anger wasn't helping. Then he took another. Then a third.

He decided after the tenth breath that it wasn't going to happen today. Annoyed with himself all over again, he unfolded from the couch into a stretch. Anger he couldn't squash added a sharp edge to the movements that only succeeded in annoying him further.

Jitsu lifted her head from her paws and gave one tail wag. She was sure he would get it soon! Takeshi was her Human, after all, and that made him special. And if the Lady said he could then he could.

He sighed, running a hand over the top of her head and offering a scratch behind one of her ears. "Being able to do something isn't the same as knowing how to do something," he pointed out tiredly.

It was an unfortunate reality of high-level magics – those who could do them struggled to explain how they could. There were numerous people for Takeshi to talk to in Tarvishte who could soul-forge; Vampires made up the vast majority. He'd spoken to many. No one seemed to have a good explanation for how they did it; they just did.

*:You can access it just fine, it just retreats almost immediately. Maybe it's scared?:* the goddess wondered.

Takeshi snorted to himself. Hades' view of magic and magic theory was a little sideways of how he and every other mage he knew conceived of it. The gods did not perceive things the same way as mortals. "Isn't it representative of me? I'm not scared. Certainly not here, in my rooms in the Palace of Dusk in the center of your capital. And from what I understand, not much would be able to harm it anyway."

The goddess merely hummed.

Takeshi waited another moment to see if she had anything to add, then gave up. He checked the time. He still had another two hours until yet another meeting about what could be gleaned from Takeshi's short time connected to the Truth Seeker mental collective. He wasn't sure what more they were expecting to find after a month of going over everything he remembered with a fine-toothed comb. The answer was always "no" – no, he didn't know where the Seekers were; no, he didn't know what their long-term plans were; no, he didn't know what they were doing now.

Then there were the never-ending meetings about the status of the Empire, which were also contributing to his failing mood. Everyone wanted to know Takeshi's opinions on what Rikona was likely to do. In theory he should be a great source for that information, but considering how thoroughly she had manipulated him in the past he didn't think they should rate his opinion too highly. The only person who knew what Rikona would do was Rikona. Everyone else was just along for the ride.

He felt a pang of regret. Hotaru would have understood.

He could see if Ander was willing to discuss the soulforging problem, but... since Jak had miraculously gated them all back from Tilden Base and subsequently become a crystal statue, Ander had withdrawn almost completely. He never left the Temple. Takeshi wasn't entirely sure he was leaving his office. Each time Takeshi had been there, the door was closed and visibly locked with unfriendly looking magic. He hadn't been at any of the meetings Takeshi was at, either. Hades would only say the other priest was busy.

Takeshi accepted that, but he had also seen the look on Mara's face at that response and he wasn't sure how much longer Ander was going to be able to hide. It was a look that spelled doom for whatever was in her way, and Takeshi had vowed to not be that thing.

Restless, he left his rooms with Jitsu in tow. He wasn't sure how he had gone from being a high-ranking official in one country to a high-ranking priest in another, but he missed being able to go out on missions. Even when he had been Captain of the Imperial Guard in Ni Fon he had always had tasks to complete, a way to move forward. Here, everyone seemed paralyzed with uncertainty, an entire nation paused in the middle of a deep breath.

He wondered how explosive the release would be.

Jitsu jumped in front of him, almost toppling him with her three-foot-tall bulk when he failed to stop in time. She bumped him with her nose in apology, but he was scaring people. He should try to be less scary.

Takeshi stared at her, before realizing that while the navy mask over the bottom half of his face hid most of his expression, he was probably radiating discontent to anyone with a brush of Empathic magic. Which was a fair number of people here. He felt his mood sink further at the evidence of his lack of control. This was why he tried to meditate every morning.

Maybe he should try to meditate in the Temple. Sometimes a change of scenery helped. And if he bothered Ander enough, maybe the man would come out and Takeshi could ask him what the hell he'd been doing for the past month while Takeshi was being interrogated over and over again about the events of Tilden Base–

Jitsu's nose bumped into his arm. The Temple was a good plan. They should go to the Temple. Maybe Takeshi would feel better there. And the wargs wouldn't mind if her special two-foot was in a bad mood!

Takeshi took a deep breath, running his fingers through his messy black hair. "Okay," he agreed after he was sure he could keep the snap out of his voice. Jitsu hadn't done anything to deserve his ire.

She brushed against him reassuringly with a friendly tail wag, then pushed him in the right direction. Time to go!

Takeshi almost lost his balance again, looking closely at her as he obediently began moving. "Are you bigger than you were when we met?" That was just over four months ago.

Jitsu pranced. She was, which was a good thing – she'd seen the things Takeshi could get into, and the extra bulk would come in handy. She expected to keep growing for another few months. She wanted to end up on the larger side.

Takeshi blinked. "How much larger do you intend to get?"

She huffed in amusement. It was impossible to know until she got there. But she was hoping to be a little larger than Thorn.

Takeshi hid a wince. Thorn was the gray warg that had chosen Primrose, the Captain of the Guard here in Tarvishte, as his "special two-foot," and he was massive – nearly four feet tall. "Do you think you'll still fit on the bed at that size?"

She snorted. Takeshi fit on the bed. So would she.

He patted her on the head. "I'm shaped a little differently than you."

Not a problem. If her Human fit, she would also fit.

He decided not to argue the limits of physical space with her. He wasn't certain he could win. Wargs seemed to exist by their own rules anyway. Sacred to Hades, the wolf-adjacent creatures had magic of their own. Takeshi had no idea how it worked but couldn't deny the evidence. Wargs also believed they were always correct, and trying to change those furry minds was like trying to stop a moving train with bare hands and no magic. Takeshi found it infinitely easier just to agree.

As they exited the palace, Takeshi heard music drift by and frowned. It was the same ethereal music that had been haunting him since Hades had encased Jak in the chrysalis. No one else was able to hear it. Sometimes it was loud and clear; other times it was quiet, just a soft background hum.

*:Hades–:*

*:Still not Abomination,:* she soothed immediately. *:I promise, it is just the World Sound, though I still do not know why you can suddenly hear it.:*

Takeshi had asked her about it when it was clear it wasn't going away, afraid that it either had to do with Abomination or that it came from his brief connection to the Truth Seekers. Hades had been quick to reassure him that this was not so, but no other answer had emerged.

*:The World Sound is just the ebb and flow of existence. It has always been there, though very few mortals ever hear it. Those that do are usually bards, though even they do not usually hear it with such clarity. Do you have any proficiency with Voice magic?:*

*:No,:* he answered, perplexed. *:The inherent isn't terribly rare in Ni Fon, and all shinobi are tested for inherents, so it wouldn't have been missed.:* He shook his head to clear it, but the soft sounds remained. He felt his mood souring again, and Hades tactfully withdrew. "Come on," he sighed to Jitsu. "We are almost there."

As he crossed the courtyard he felt a shiver work its way through him, which he grimly ignored. Though the weather was warm for late March, he always felt chilled. One last gift from his homeland – a microchip placed in the base of his skull without his knowledge before sending him to Espon to scout for information about a rebellion against the Empire. The chip had been able to take the information he learned directly from his brain and transmit it back to Ni Fon. An expression of Abomination, it had been removed when its existence was discovered, but a persistent chill remained.

Takeshi was thankful that at least the migraines it had caused were gone.

The Temple of Night Rising was a three-story building made of smokey-gray marble with black and silver trim. It was more modest in design than many of the larger structures around it, boasting only one dome and one tower, with a large clock hanging over the front door. Oddly, there were no wargs in sight. The Temple was one of their favorite places; Takeshi had expected to see at least three lounging outside.

Jitsu shook herself with a snort. Many had retreated into dens for the spring. They would be back in a month or so. Some were still out and about, though.

"Why would they only den in spring, and not winter?" Takeshi took the single step up to the door and pushed it open.

Jitsu huffed. Her Human was new to Tarvishte. She didn't want to ruin the surprise. It was a *good* surprise. She was excited.

Takeshi's eyebrows rose as he entered the Temple. That sounded more foreboding than he would have preferred.

Ander's office was immediately to the left, and as Takeshi had guessed, the door was tightly shut with lines of bright-green magic warning off any trespassers. Takeshi considered pushing his luck and knocking, but decided he wasn't quite sure what the glyph for fire was doing in a locking pattern and he preferred not to find out. He passed through the short hallway, ignoring the stairs leading up to the priests' living quarters to reach the sanctuary proper.

The domed space was large and open, black, gray, and white marble cut into decorative patterns evocative of Hades' sigil and the spell glyphs associated with her domains – death, destruction, healing, and rebirth. Silver scrollwork and cut gemstones in various shades of purple added delicate detailing. The altar sat on a raised dais at the center back of the room, a small statue of Hades the centerpiece surrounded by candles and offerings of wilted or dead plants. There were a few marble benches with soft lavender and cream cushions scattered about for people to sit on.

Then there was Jak.

An explosion of crystal took up the center space, shimmering in transparent pale blues and purples. In the center of the formation stood Hades' first High Priest, now made of the same crystal. After teleporting over five thousand miles from Tarvishte to the Nyphoren Islands and then teleporting back with seven people, Jak had been so close to death that Takeshi wasn't sure how he had still been speaking. Hades had sung, and Jak had turned into this crystal statue. The goddess called it a chrysalis and reassured the rest of her priests that Jak would be able to heal, though she was vague on how long that could take. Months? Years? Decades?

The other priests had been thrown into complete disarray. As Takeshi understood it, Jak was older than even Siva, the second High Priest, by thousands of years. There had never been a priesthood without Jak. Even though he had been a fairly distant leader, he had always been there if they had needed him. Now they were looking at possibly centuries without him, and no one was sure what to do about that. Siva herself was on her way to hopefully come straighten out the mess. He hadn't met her in person yet, only spoken to her through a mirror once, but she gave the impression of someone who knew what they were doing.

He glanced back at Ander's closed office door. Maybe she'd be able to drag him out.

:He's... alive,: Hades offered. :Just very focused.:

Takeshi rolled his eyes. :"Alive" is the best you can do?:

She didn't answer.

He decided on one of the benches close to the wall and made himself comfortable. It was near the door to the Temple's inner courtyard with a large goddess statue; the door had been left open and Takeshi could just see the tip of a warg's tail lying across the threshold. At least some of them were still around.

His dark-blue eyes traveled back to the form of Jak. What did this mean for him? He was potentially the ninth priest of Hades, though he was currently treating it as a trial period. He'd never considered being a member of a priesthood as a possible life-path, and Hades' priests were far more haphazard in their organization than the religions he was familiar with. As it was, he felt he was being treated more like a soldier than a priest, and he had yet to successfully soulforge – something all Hades' priests could do as well as her children, the Vampires.

:You bring much to the table, beloved. Do not sell yourself so short. We are in no rush.: Her voice was kind.

:Ander told me he soulforged successfully moments after becoming your priest.:

:I wouldn't use Ander as a metric. He's... unique,: Hades rebuffed wryly. :Jak took a long time to learn to soulforge,: she added after a moment. :Almost two centuries, if I remember correctly.:

Takeshi blinked in surprise at the crystal. "Two centuries?" he repeated in disbelief.

*:And I wouldn't use Jak as a metric, either. He is also unique. But my point is just that – everyone is different. Everyone learns at their own pace. Take the time to find yours.:*

*:You say that, but my failure to soulforge has already cost us,:* he reminded her, nodding at the statue. *:If I had been able to–:*

*:Perhaps, perhaps not. You might have been able to cast an aegis capable of shielding your group from the Truth Seekers' final strike, but I doubt Jak would have waited to see if you could. That's the sort of thing he would never leave to chance. He saw many ways for your party to die, and one where you all lived. He would choose that one again without hesitation, no matter the cost to himself. And besides, as I keep telling you all, he's not dead! Just resting.:*

He shook his head and closed his eyes, preparing to clear his mind and try meditating again. He needed to be more centered.

"Takeshi!"

Or not.

He prevented himself from sighing through sheer force of will as the seventh High Priest darted into the sanctuary. "Good morning, Mara."

She stopped a few feet away from him, waiting for his nod of acquiescence before giving him a tight hug. "Trying to find patience for the morning news hour?"

"Trying to find patience for everything," he admitted. "Is it really necessary for *us* to be at the daily recounting of the Empire's activity for the previous day?"

The Avari shrugged. "I think they're hoping something will jog some sort of memory from the Truth Seekers." She looked up at him through her severely cut bangs, the rest of her nearly floor-length dark-blue hair held back in a high ponytail that Jitsu was sniffing at interestedly.

Jitsu gave a short tail wag when she noticed Takeshi watching her. She liked the happy-water priest! Her hair was almost as long as the Lady's!

He decided he didn't want to know, returning his attention to Mara. "It's been over a month," he pointed out. "We aren't likely to find any new information that way."

"Maybe they just want our fabulous insight?"

Some part of him was impressed with her positivity. "Perhaps." He glanced towards Ander's office. "Any word, or...?"

She shook her head. "Hades swears he's eating–"

*:He is!:*

"–which is good, because if he wasn't there wouldn't be a door there anymore, but She refuses to comment on the quality of the food."

Takeshi got the impression of a shrug from the deity.

"So I was thinking about it, and we could stake it out," she added, completely out of nowhere.

Takeshi blinked at her. "Pardon?"

"You know" – she waved a hand in the air, trying to indicate something Takeshi was not getting – "stake it out! Maybe he only comes out super late at night. We could lie in wait here, in the sanctuary–"

"Where?" he asked, looking around. Where were they supposed to hide? Under a bench? Behind the transparent statue of Jak?

"I don't know, you're the stealth expert! You can come up with something!" She pointed a finger at him sternly. "And then, when he comes out–"

"Do we know he's coming out?" he interrupted again, not surprised when Hades didn't chime in. "I was under the impression he was living in there."

"But he can't be!" Mara stomped a high-heeled foot. "He's got to come out sometime, right? It's just an office! Right?"

*:There are some amenities in there,:* Hades offered meekly. *:And it is technically a lab and an office.:*

Mara's lips thinned. "We'll see about that," she muttered, clearly displeased, fists coming to rest on her hips as she glared in Ander's direction. Takeshi resolved again not to get in her way. Then her mood flipped completely and she smiled cheerfully at Takeshi again. "Have you heard from Jamirh lately?"

Jamirh? Takeshi tried to think back through the haze of constant meetings and failed soulforging attempts. Jamirh was luckily not required to be present at those meetings. "Not recently, no. I believe he's been entertaining Salisha and Desha while the *Sea Spirit* remains in port." He was also probably reveling in his newfound freedom. With the Crystal Light Blade gone, Hades' contract over Ebryn and his reincarnations was void. Jamirh was finally free to do as he pleased. "And Jeri is likely keeping an eye on him, anyway." The female Vampire was a little too protective of the Avari, who was an adult in his own right and, in Takeshi's opinion, did not require a babysitter.

Mara raised an eyebrow. "Have you spoken to Jeri lately? And I don't mean in the meetings. I mean have you actually spoken to her?"

"I feel like the only ways I spend my time are the meetings and my attempts to soulforge, so no," he admitted.

"Uh huh. Still not going well?" Her expression turned sympathetic.

"No," he said shortly.

She shrugged. "It can take a bit."

"How long did it take you?" he asked.

"Depends on what you mean," she answered thoughtfully after a moment. "I learned it maybe fifty years or so after becoming a priest, but I also didn't start trying until around that time. I think once I started working at it, it took me a month or two, but I already had decades of living with Hades under my belt."

"I see." The answer was both helpful and not. "It would be better if I had a larger sample size to work with."

She laughed at him. "Oh no! Now you sound like Ander. One of him is enough, though I love my little brother dearly." She patted his arm. "And you are one of my precious siblings too, now. Don't worry, Takeshi – I know you'll figure it out! You're really smart!" She paused for a moment, considering that. "It's probably why Ander gets along with you so well. He respects intelligent people. Intelligent by his standards, not everyone else's."

He glanced back at the closed office and the unfriendly lines of green magic.

"I'm pretty sure he's just sulking," she said, following his gaze. "He'll come out soon. Or I'll make him. Or Siva will. When she gets here... eventually. Why can't anything be on time? She should have been here *ages* ago."

"Miravu has also been worried about the disruptions to the shipping routes the Empire is causing," Takeshi said. "But at least with Hades we know Siva is coming. She's delayed, not... absent." His eyes slid towards Jak.

Mara gaze grew thoughtful. "And she's too far north for... eh, that's not the point." She shook her head. "This is just how Ander gets sometimes, you know? He's not doing it to slight anyone, he's feeling down about himself. Happened when he first came here, too."

Takeshi frowned. "Oh?"

Mara shook her head, long navy ponytail swaying side to side. "It's not my story to tell. You'll have to ask him. After he *removes himself from this self-imposed isolation!*"

No response from the door.

She shrugged. "Was worth a try. Anyway, we've still got like an hour before news time; we should spend it doing something relaxing instead of something that's stressing you out. Let's go grab coffee. Or tea; you drink tea, right?"

Jitsu agreed with the happy-water priest. A break would be good. Her Human was trying too hard.

He sent a weary glance at the statue of Hades on the altar, but when no answer came he decided to concede. "Very well. You know this city better than I; where shall we go?"

She grinned. "Just follow me! Relaxation break, here we come!"

# Chapter Three

Ander was busy.

People did not understand that.

Not that he was checking in with people; they were a distraction. And he didn't need distractions. Not if he was to improve on the process significantly enough to result in a forty percent increase in speed. But Hades could not be convinced that he did not need to know if someone was outside his door. That was what the lock was for. To keep them out and away so he could focus.

*:I just don't think that this is the best way to deal with... anything, really.:*

He shushed Her automatically as he slowly and carefully manipulated the molecular compound he was working with. It had to be done right, or he'd be set back five hours and twenty-three minutes.

*:They are worried about you.:*

He took a deep breath as it reformed as he wished it, the green glow of his magic fading and leaving the room dim. He made a mark on his to-do list and shifted a note from one column of his process mapping board to the next.

*:And it's not that I'm not thankful for this. I am. I'm actually really excited! But I don't want it to come at your expense.:*

"I'm fine," he murmured reflexively as he reviewed his notes on the next step in the process.

*:Please eat something.:*

He grabbed a granola bar from the right top desk drawer, unwrapped it, and shoved it into his mouth, chewing mechanically without stopping his reading. He made a note – this could be changed, here, and this would have to be scrapped and re-processed – but he judged that he was still ahead of schedule. It was amazing what a few uninterrupted days of work could do.

*:Beloved, it's been weeks, not a few days.:*

Even better. Productivity was at an all-time high. He spared a glance for his timer, but it was still fifteen hours before he'd have to check on the aquarium. Excellent. He could get a lot done in fifteen hours.

*:You could take a break? Talk to people?:*

Absolutely not. He was more useful doing this. The faster they got the Lady into a physical body again, the better. They didn't need him going out there and theorizing; his talents clearly lay in a lab environment and so this was where he would stay.

*:No one foresaw that the Blade would break when it came into contact with tech–:*

"But I should have," he snapped with a flash of anger before he brought himself back under control. His voice was dull when he continued. "It's been well-documented that tech and magic do not interact well, often having unexpected or explosive results when the two are forced to mingle. That sword was one hundred percent a magical artifact, created from divine sources. The bionics are upward of eighty-two percent tech, with slight variances based on the individual Avari used for the process. It was the logical outcome. As the person with the most expertise on the subject, I should have been able to foresee this conclusion, but I did not. The fault is mine and mine alone." He rubbed at the scar that ran from his hairline down the left of his nose, almost reaching the corner of his mouth.

*:No one else sees it that way.:*

"Because they're all too stupid to realize it!" He couldn't help but lose his temper. He pulled himself back together again. "Some of them will figure it out eventually, I'm sure. At that point I'd like to have something else to offer them."

He couldn't repair the damage he had caused, but... a divine being in place of a priest was close, wasn't it?

*:Ander, you originally estimated completion of the avatar body to be reached in fourteen years. Even at a forty percent reduction, that's... eight years.:*

"Eight years, four months, and twenty-four days." She was right, that was still too long. He frowned, considering some of the improvements he had already implemented. Was there a way to iterate on those to speed up the process even further? Or was he really bound by the speed of growth? He grabbed a notebook and began scribbling formulas down.

*:That's not really what I— oh, I suppose it doesn't matter. Siva will hopefully be arriving soon. You can't possibly think she'll be okay with this. I can barely stop Mara from breaking your door down.:*

"Mara? What does she want?" he asked absently, considering two of the variables.

*:To make sure you're eating, for one.:*

"I'm eating." He pulled another granola bar out of a different drawer and took a bite to prove the point.

*:I've asked Vlad, and he tells me that neither Humans nor Avari can live on granola bars.:*

He swallowed. "I've gone much longer than this before."

*:Right, but I thought we were going to try prioritizing yourself over the experiments?:*

"I'm eating. And sleeping. What more do they want?" he asked, mildly offended.

*:You've slept four hours over the past three days.:*

"It counts. I slept." He eyed the small coffee brewing setup on the table under the shuttered window. It was probably time for more coffee. "Thank you for reminding me."

*:What? Oh.:* There was a pause while he started heating the water with a handy little spell circle. *:That's... not what I meant. Have you considered that you might be overdoing it on the coffee and underdoing it on the sleep?:*

"I'm still functional and my work is not suffering, so no." He set the first few ounces to filter through the little bag and grabbed a set of notes to flip through while he waited. "You are thinking too hard about this. I am fine."

*:It makes me quite sad that you believe that.:*

There was blessed silence while he finished brewing his coffee. He tossed the filter and coffee grinds into the little waste basket under the table, noting that it was rather full and he would have to dispose of it soon. He made a mental note to do so on his next fish break.

*:You know, if you took a bit of a longer break, maybe got a solid eight hours of sleep – or twelve, considering how little you've gotten recently,*

*maybe even eighteen – you could help Takeshi? He's floundering with soulforging. He still can't get his soul crystal to remain in the physical world for more than a few moments. I think you could help.:*

"He doesn't need my help; he's one of the only smart ones. He'll figure it out," he said dismissively. "Has a good grasp of the theory; it's all practice from here on out."

*:Yeah, that doesn't seem to be working.:*

"Do you still want the body to be Avari? This is the last chance to change your mind."

She sighed. *:Yes, Avari is fine.:*

"Keep the coloring the same, too?"

*:Yes, please.:*

There was something odd about Her tone there, but Ander decided he didn't have the time or resources to look more deeply into it. "Excellent, that allows me to eliminate these three variables..." He trailed off as he stared at the equation and took a sip of scalding hot coffee. "Hm. Perhaps..." He edited two numbers, pausing as his vision swam.

Damn. He'd waited too long on the coffee.

That was fine, he consoled himself. He could finish the coffee and then catnap while the caffeine kicked in. That was a solid plan.

*:I do not like that plan.:*

"Well, if efficiency were your strong suit, maybe our current situation would be different."

The answering silence felt like it was judging him as his brain caught up with his mouth.

"That's not… well. It's still my fault, anyways." Green eyes drifted in the direction of the sanctuary, where the proof of that mistake stood, having somehow been turned to crystal.

Ander had examined it; it wasn't spell crystal, which he would have expected. Instead, it almost seemed to be Jak's soul crystal. It had similar properties in strength and its ability to rebuff any sort of magical probe. But how could one's soul crystal be used in this way? Jak wasn't encased in the crystal, as the term "chrysalis" seemed to suggest; he *was* the crystal. Or more precisely, the crystal was *him*. How did that work? What was the crystal doing to heal Jak? How did *being* crystal heal Jak, when it meant his body was currently composed of completely different elements compared to its natural state? Jak didn't even have usable magic in the first place; he always used Hades' power to cast. But Hades insisted it was a chrysalis, and also insisted that there was no way to know how long whatever process was happening would take. Her predicted timelines were insultingly vague.

Therefore, their priesthood was going to have to last an uncertain amount of time without their first High Priest. Ander was thankful Siva was coming; she'd be able to sort everything out. She was good at that.

*:I am not sure you are going to like that process.:*

And Siva had every right to blame him for Jak's situation. Ander wouldn't disagree with her. And then he could continue to work on what he did best – research and development of a synthetic body a metaphysical being like Hades could inhabit. That way, She could help them guard against future iterations of the Abominations directly, and hopefully sidestep all of the problems they had run headfirst into this round. He took another sip of coffee.

*:We haven't finished dealing with* this *iteration of Abomination.:*

"We blew up the base," he pointed out, then paused. "Then the Truth Seekers wiped it off the map. Is the island still there?"

*:There are still some bionics out there. I can feel them,:* the Goddess insisted.

"That is... unfortunate," he said slowly. "But I'm sure the Black Watch can deal with whatever's left."

*:They can't find it, and I can't pinpoint it for them. The feeling is vague, but there.:*

He took one last long swallow, putting the empty cup back on the table and turning to the little couch against the far wall. "Sounds like they have work to do. Maybe Takeshi or Mara could help them."

*:Takeshi and Mara* are *helping them. They've been to countless meetings about the bionics, the Truth Seekers, and the Empire since you all returned.:*

"Sounds like they have it under control then." He lay down on the couch, mourning that it was just an inch too short for him to lie down comfortably. Perhaps he should consider replacing it.

*:I wouldn't describe it that way, exactly.:*

He shrugged, trying to scrunch himself into a semi-comfortable position, and set the alarm on the small end table by his head for thirty minutes. By that point, most of the caffeine would be absorbed by his system, he'd have the refresh from the nap, and he'd be able to work again. Perfect.

He shot up as the alarm went off, adrenaline racing through his system. Why? Was there a threat? Where?

*:I think the alarm startled you.:*

Oh. He glanced down at the inconspicuous little thing, still merrily ringing as he tried to get his heartbeat under control. He rubbed at his eyes, pushing long white bangs out of his face. Only after he was more in control of himself did he turn the alarm clock off.

Then a thought occurred. "Did Jamirh's stitches get removed?"

*:Two weeks ago, yes. Marcus took care of it.:*

"Good." He remembered the large gashes inflicted on the kid's arm from when the Blade had shattered. "Someone should keep an eye on that; wounds caused by magical artifacts can act strangely."

*:Ander...:*

"And Jeri probably isn't doing that because she's still trying to keep her missing arm secret, unless I miss my guess?"

Hades didn't answer.

"Or she is, but from a distance, which means she might as well not be doing it."

*:Jeri is also taking part in the meetings about... everything.:*

"How's she avoiding Jamirh, then?" He went to brew himself a cup of coffee, picking up his notes as he passed by.

*:Jamirh is not part of the meetings.:*

That actually made Ander pause, then he burst out laughing. "All of that about how it wasn't the Blade that was special, that it was him, that there's more to him than we know – and when the Blade breaks, he gets dropped immediately. Perfect." He shook his head, floored by just how hilarious that was.

*:Jamirh never wanted to be a part of this, and without the Blade he is no longer bound by Ebryn's oath. He is free to do as he wishes, now.:*

"So you just cut him loose?" He couldn't stop the laughter that was bubbling up. "I'm curious – did anyone talk to Jamirh about that? Wait, no, I know! Everyone's caught up in the meetings that he's not invited to anymore. Never mind that he lived in the Empire and – you know what? It doesn't matter. I hope his arm is fine!" He set the coffee to brew.

*:If you are that concerned,:* Hades said slowly, as though She were picking Her words very carefully, *:you could check on him.:*

He snorted, downed the whole cup of coffee in one go – that one didn't taste right, for some reason – and returned to reviewing his notes.

The aquarium timer went off. Ander carefully checked that the current process would be able to continue without him for a few minutes, then went to the corner of the room furthest from the door. A spell array had been etched into the floor. He stepped onto it and activated it with a flex of power.

It deposited him in the communal space for the priests' quarters above his lab. The lights were off, but the full moon filtering through the large windows gave him plenty of light to see by. He went through the motions of feeding his fish and checking the water temperature and salinity with the ease of long practice. Certain that experiment was continuing on as planned, he stepped back onto the faintly glowing temporary array created by his arrival and was transported back to his lab.

He reset the timer for two days, then went back to observing the brightly glowing liquid traveling through the numerous vials and tubes.

He woke up from another nap, this time just before the alarm went off. Pleased with himself, he made sure to shut it off before it could startle him again. Perhaps he should look into a different alarm, one with a less shrill tone?

He set another cup of coffee to brew, noting his progress so far. He was making good time. More could be saved if he tweaked one or two things.

He drank the coffee, barely even tasting it, though the heat was pleasant.

*:That was mostly water. You used the same coffee grounds as the last three cups. They don't have anything left to give. They're dead.:*

"You would know," he agreed absently, checking his notes from before the nap. He was on step 42.6b, process iii. Perfect.

*:Eat something, please.:*

He chewed the granola bar from the bottom drawer of the filing cabinet as quickly as he could. He needed to get back to work.

*:I think we should discuss this whole... living in the lab thing. It is making me uncomfortable at this point.:*

"You are a metaphysical expression of magic. Can you even get uncomfortable?" he asked as he meticulously recorded the results of that last fusion attempt.

*:I can, and I am. Ander, I – and a number of others – are growing concerned. What if you took a full day off? Just twenty-four hours. It wouldn't set you back that much, and I know you have a section coming up where you will have to wait at least that long before you continue anyway.:*

"On the contrary; it will set me back twenty-four hours," he corrected. "There's no reason to delay for that long."

*:I am baffled by how you believe that.:*

He frowned. "I'm not lying."

*:You... don't think you are, no. It's impressive.:*

He decided he didn't have time for Her riddles and started setting up the next round.

He frowned at the muddy red color of his most recent concoction. That was not the correct color. It should have been much brighter, and with a shimmer to it. This was useless.

*:Beloved, the last four rounds have all failed. Perhaps it's time to rest, and you can come back to it with fresh eyes?:*

He rubbed at his scar. "I just took a nap an hour ago. I'm fine."

*:You are tired. You need rest. Eat something.:*

He grabbed a granola bar from the top drawer of the side table, scarfing it down quickly.

*:What about six hours? Six hours of uninterrupted rest, and then–:*

"No." His voice was firm. "If Jak gets to make his choice, then I get to make mine. You can't make me do otherwise."

*:I cannot,:* She conceded. *:But I am not who you should be worried about.:*

"I keep telling you. That's why there's a lock on the door."

He held back a yawn through sheer strength of will as he delicately finished connecting the new line of tubing. He took a step back to double check that everything was set up correctly, then fed the line into the starting solution. He waited just long enough to be sure the process was starting before going to brew himself another cup of coffee.

A different set of notes caught his eye, the corner of an array poking out from underneath a stack of papers. That didn't belong there. Gingerly, he pulled it out without disturbing the other sheets.

It was one of the attempts at recreating the array on the Truth Seekers' blindfolds. He frowned, realizing that they never had figured it out. Except... Takeshi had interfaced with the Truth Seeker hive, even if only briefly. Maybe that was knowledge he had gained?

*:That's an interesting theory. Let's go ask him! It's almost one in the morning, but I'm sure he won't mind! Once I explain, anyway.:* The last bit was muttered under Her breath.

Except She didn't have breath. Ander absently wondered how She managed that. "No need. I'll ask once the avatar is complete. It can stay over here for now." He placed it under the alarm he was using for naps.

The aquarium timer went off. Ander went to take care of his fish.

The liquid this time was a non-homogenous cross between yellow and purple. Ander had no clue what had caused this. He reviewed the last few sheets of notes, truly perplexed. Everything seemed to be in order.

*:Um, beloved?:*

He put the notes down on the table and checked over the configuration of vials and tubes. He cross-checked it with the annotated sketch he had made, then cross-checked that with his original notes. All correct.

*:Beloved?:*

The yellow-and-purple sludge was mocking him. How on Gaia had this happened? By all accounts, it didn't make any sense. He took a sip of cold coffee, though it barely even tasted like it, as he narrowed his eyes at the mess.

He needed more coffee. And maybe another short nap. Then he'd try again. Surely, the... fourteenth time was the charm?

*:Ander!:*

"What?" he asked as he cast an array to dispose of it. He needed to start fresh. He'd start by re-sanitizing the equipment.

*:You have a pair of witches demanding access to your lab.:*

"That is the whole. Purpose. Of the lock. Tell them to come back in a few years." He started disassembling the structure so he could wash it.

*:I have relayed your answer, though it's only fair to inform you that it wasn't a request. Did you really have to shield the room from telepathic communication, too?:*

"Yes, I'm trying to remove distractions. People needing my attention are distractions. Giving them an avenue through which to contact me defeats the whole point." He placed the first of the beakers into the sink.

He paused. Something in the air didn't smell quite right. Like lava mixing into the sea. He glanced around the lab, but there was nothing that could be making that smell. Maybe the yellow-and-purple mixture could have, but he'd already destroyed it.

*:I did warn you.:*

The door groaned, green lines of power – his own magic – being forced into the wood grain from the other side. As he watched, the green shifted to an angry dark red streaked with orange, and the door began to crumble into chunks of ashy rock. Mara was on the other side, looking downright murderous with her arms crossed and her hips cocked to the side. In front of her was an Aradian woman with long, pin-straight, pinkish-orange hair, and violet flames tinged with gold burning in her eyes.

Siva smiled at him, deceptively pleasant. "Hello, Ander. I think we should have a chat."

Sherri Cole, formerly a major of the Rose Empire's military, took a moment to close her eyes and feel the plant life around her.

"Are you well?"

She turned to her sister. Madine was a Truth Seeker and they didn't show emotion well at the best of times, but there was a slight frown on her blindfolded face.

Sherri nodded reassuringly. "Yes, I'm fine. Just enjoying the feel of nature."

Madine inclined her head. "The military did not allow us much time to do so before, though chasing ghosts around the Nyphoren Islands must have been a pleasant experience."

For almost two weeks Colonel Rhode had dragged the sisters around the Nyphoren Islands trying to find information on a former captive, a being that was magic in the shape of an Avari. He hadn't understood that she was a god.

He'd been one of the many casualties of the Truth Seekers' first strike against the Empire that had birthed them.

Sherri adjusted her glasses. "How did the meeting in Nouen go?"

"Well. The group there will suit. By attempting to suppress so many people, the government made their own internal enemies."

"As long as we are able to hold Muriz, the rest of the Empire doesn't matter," Sherri said with a shrug. The town in north-west Gallia was ideal for their purposes – a small corner of the map, backed up against the Waste and the Warcross War. "If other groups disenchanted with the Empire's rule happen to have goals that align with ours, that can only help."

"It is only a matter of time before one of the dukes makes a move," Madine agreed. "Few of them are known for their patience."

Her blindfolded head shifted towards the left. "Our visitors have arrived." She turned and began to walk towards one of the sentry sites.

Sherri frowned as she followed. "They were told to find us here?" She wasn't sure letting a group of rebels know the location of the headquarters was a good idea. They didn't know what kind of people Crimson Shadows would be sending, either.

"Yes. We won't be able to keep the location secret for much longer anyway," Madine warned. "Someone will realize the communications are wrong."

"Yes, we need open war to break out so the dukes target each other." It was a miracle they had managed to work together as long as they had under the Emperor without anyone being assassinated. "Our survival depends on it." The sisters fell silent as they approached the sentry post.

Perra and Axtion were standing a few feet away from an Avari stranger. No more than twenty-five years old, he had long white hair tied back in a braid, olive skin, and messy bangs that didn't quite hide his red eyes. His hands were stuffed into the pockets of his jeans, but he straightened out of his slouch when he saw them coming.

"This is Madine and Sherri. Madine, Sherri, this is Gren," Perra introduced dispassionately.

"Gren is the leader of Crimson Shadows," Madine said for Sherri's benefit.

Scarlet eyes studied her closely. "I see the rumor that you all can talk to each other no matter where you are is true, then." He grinned. "That's a neat trick. Maybe you can share how it's done?"

Sherri glanced around, ignoring the question. They didn't know how much longer knowledge of magic would remain a secret, but they weren't going to be the ones to open that can of worms. "You came by yourself?"

He nodded. "Yup! We're all friends now, right? At least until we strip that base of all its weapons and stuff."

"The Truth Seekers do not seek to harm the Avari," Sherri explained. "Even after our contract is through, your people have nothing to fear from us."

The way his eyebrows raised said he didn't agree, though he didn't give the thought voice. Sherri decided that was good enough. The Avari had plenty of reason to doubt their word considering how the Truth Seekers had been wielded against them in the past. And while she wasn't lying, that didn't mean other things wouldn't threaten the Avari.

That was part of the plan. A failsafe, just in case.

"Come, we have detailed plans for Etroy Base." Sherri turned, heading for the hotel they had been using as their headquarters.

"And you'll really let us have our pick of weapons and tech?" he asked. When she nodded, he added, "What's in it for you, then?"

Madine smiled, sending a chill down even Sherri's spine. "There is something there that must be destroyed."

# Chapter Four

*Takeshi?:*

Takeshi felt the gentle mind touch drawing him from sleep. *:Mm?:*

*:Good morning, beloved. Siva has arrived.:*

Takeshi forced his eyes open, looking for the bedside clock. Six thirty in the morning. He sighed, sitting up and relinquishing the warmth of his cocoon of blankets.

Jitsu's head shot up, and she gave a cheerful tail wag as her eyes met Takeshi's. They were getting up early today! That was fun. Unless Takeshi just wanted to do more of the sitting thing. That was boring.

"Siva has arrived in Tarvishte. We should probably be ready to receive her, especially since she's so late?" He made it a question.

*:I am directing her to make Ander her first priority. You do not need to rush; I'm sure she will seek you out at some point today.:*

Something about her tone made Takeshi pause. "Ander?"

*:Yes.:*

When no further explanation came, Takeshi decided it didn't have to do with him. He considered trying to get another hour of sleep but dismissed it as a lost cause. He could just take his time with his morning routine. "I'm sorry, Jitsu. There will probably be more of the sitting thing after all."

The warg huffed and jumped off the bed, but made sure to bump him with her nose so he knew she loved him before going to nap in the sitting room.

Takeshi readied himself for the day, adding an extra shirt when a glance through the large windows showed a gray and threatening sky. He hoped it would be a good storm; the past few had been middling at best.

He settled himself on the couch and closed his eyes, starting to clear his mind and focus on his breathing. Jitsu huffed and curled her massive form into a ball. He ignored her.

*:Uh, Takeshi?:* The goddess's voice sounded strained.

He frowned. *:Yes?:*

*:Slight problem, heading your way–:*

She was cut off by the door to the apartment sparking green for a moment, then slamming open. Takeshi kept himself from attacking only by virtue of the fact that he recognized the color of Ander's magic. Jitsu bounded between him and the door, hackles raised.

"Hide me!" the half-Avari demanded.

Takeshi was taken aback. Ander was disheveled, completely out of character with the man Takeshi had come to know. His clothes were askew, his hair a mess, puffy bags under his eyes so big Takeshi's face hurt in sympathy. He seemed to have lost weight and his face was pale. He was clutching a stack of papers to his chest as though his life depended on them.

"From whom?" Takeshi asked, feeling a little out of his depth. It had been three and a half weeks since they had last seen each other, but Takeshi very much doubted that anyone in Tarvishte seriously meant Ander harm.

"The witches!" Ander hissed, shutting the door behind him as he skittered into the sitting room, looking around wildly. "They want my notes!"

:*Mara and Siva,*: Hades clarified, sounding exasperated.

That did give some context to this situation. Not a lot, but some. :*The intervention didn't go as planned?*:

:*You win some, you lose some.*:

:*Usually when people say that, they didn't lose a whole person.*:

Jitsu sat. Tall-white priest was not a threat. Though he did look terrible for a two-foot. Had some interesting smells on him, though. Maybe he would let her sniff them a little closer?

Takeshi decided to point out the obvious. "If Hades knows where you are, so do Mara and Siva."

Ander narrowed bloodshot eyes as he processed that. "They won't barge in here if you don't let them, though." He hugged his papers a little tighter.

:*The irony of that is completely lost on him at the moment,*: Hades said with a sigh.

Takeshi distinctly remembered thinking just a few days ago that he did not want to be the thing keeping Mara from Ander. Had he cursed himself?

:*I won't let them take your door down the way they did Ander's,*: Hades reassured him.

:*Do I want to know?*:

:*Probably not. But the good thing is that he's not hiding in the lab anymore. This is technically an improvement.*:

Takeshi wasn't sure he agreed with that, but let it pass.

Jitsu was still studying tall-white priest closely. He didn't look so good. She could probably take him in this state, if Takeshi needed her to. She could sit on him. Maybe lick his face a bit.

Takeshi gave a subtle shake of his head, and she shook herself and went to lie on the couch. He eyed the way Ander was clutching the papers. "Would you like to put those down?"

"*No!*" The half-Avari's green eyes were wild. "They want to take them!"

"I see." Takeshi groped for something else to say. He figured at this point he was just buying time for Mara and Siva to arrive. "Would you like to sit, then? You look tired." Exhausted was more accurate, but he wasn't sure how receptive Ander would be to that. He was like a wild thing, skittish and untrusting, and Takeshi wasn't sure what would make him bolt.

Ander glanced at the chair Takeshi had gestured towards and shook his head. He took another step away from the door. "The notes are important," he tried to explain. "Surely you at least know the notes are important?"

*:He's been working on creating another avatar body for me, like the one that died in Charve,:* Hades offered. *:It's been... consuming him. He's been stuck because he can't tell he's making mistakes.:*

*:I see that,:* he replied, eyeing the way the dirty coat hung off Ander's frame. "The notes are important," he agreed, and was rewarded by some of the tension leaving Ander's body. "Would you like some tea? I'm afraid that's all I have on hand at the moment."

Ander's expression brightened. "Caffeine?"

"Yes," Takeshi lied effortlessly. The last thing the man in front of him needed was a stimulant. He looked like he needed to sleep for the next week.

Ander's eyes jumped to the door again, but when nothing happened, he nodded. "Caffeine is good."

Takeshi hummed in agreement and fetched his supplies, grabbing a decaf tea blend from his growing collection and setting aside two cups.

Ander watched him with an uncomfortable intensity, still hugging his papers, but slowly he began to lose some of the manic energy. As the tea steeped, he moved so that both couches were between him and the door, but at least he seemed less wary of Takeshi.

He wasn't sure what to think about the fact that Ander thought him an ally against two other priests.

Hades snorted. :*He thinks you are smarter than they are, and so naturally you will side with him. Since he seems to be calming down, think you can handle him for a bit? Siva doesn't want to set him off again. He really needs to sleep. Hopefully, now that he's not in the lab and can't actually work on the project, he'll crash soon.*:

Takeshi studied the steeping tea, hoping to find serenity. Or at least sanity. After another minute he removed the tea strainer from the pot and filled both cups. He took one and sat back down on the couch, taking a deep breath of the fragrant steam. This blend was new and contained passionflower, oats, and raspberry leaf, as well as a small amount of chamomile. Hotaru would have enjoyed it. He hoped it would help calm Ander, who was stepping towards the table warily while still facing the door. The other priest grabbed the cup and downed the whole thing at once, turning his head so his eyes were still firmly on the exit.

Takeshi suppressed a sigh and took a sip, placing the cup on the coffee table in front of him and closing his eyes. Maybe meditation would help.

"What are you doing?" Ander asked, sounding suspicious.

Takeshi was unmoved. "Meditating."

"You are just going to sit there... thinking of nothing?"

"More or less."

"What on Gaia is that like?" The priest sounded horrified. Ander did not strike Takeshi as the kind of person who slowed down enough to be introspective.

"It helps center me and gives me focus." He opened his eyes and gave Ander a pointed look. "It helps me start my day with less stress."

The white-haired man looked at Jitsu. "Does he do this often?"

Jitsu snorted. Not even tall-white priest liked the sitting thing.

"I try to do it every day," Takeshi informed him.

Ander's eyes narrowed and he tilted his head as though seeing Takeshi in a whole new light. "You didn't do it while we were on the mission together."

"I most certainly did," Takeshi corrected, closing his eyes again. "You just weren't present for it."

"We stayed in an apartment the size of a postage stamp for a week and a half with five other people. How was I not present?"

"I had a different sleep schedule than the rest of you because I was scouting at night. I would meditate in the bedroom before coming out in the evening," Takeshi explained. Ander didn't respond, and the shinobi stole a quick glance to see the other man thinking very hard. "I'd offer you something to eat but I don't have anything here. Is there anything else I can provide? Water?" Thinking about it, Takeshi realized Ander was possibly dehydrated. "You can use my shower if you'd like." He ignored the feeling of disappointment from Jitsu, who had been attempting to inch closer to the smells.

*:He was kind of drinking water,:* Hades said thoughtfully. *:He thought it was coffee, but I think after you use the same coffee grounds so many times it stops qualifying.:*

Takeshi shuddered.

"I'm fine," Ander replied in a way that sounded like he'd said it a lot recently. "I'll just review these notes while we wait."

"While we wait for what?" Takeshi asked, voice bland.

Ander didn't answer, though Takeshi could hear the shuffling of papers.

They stayed like that for ten minutes before he heard Ander finally sit in one of the armchairs. Takeshi wondered how Ander expected this to end. Did he think he could hide in Takeshi's rooms until Mara and Siva lost interest?

"This is excruciating," Ander declared after another twenty minutes had gone by. "How much longer?"

Jitsu huffed in agreement.

Ander was cranky, Takeshi decided. "I usually meditate for an hour. Would you like to try?"

"Try thinking of nothing?" Pure bafflement. "I think too much to think of nothing."

"It doesn't have to be that way. Hades said you were having trouble with part of your experiment," Takeshi explained patiently. "Meditation can help you gain a different perspective on a problem."

It wasn't helping him make progress on his soulforging, but maybe it could help Ander. At the very least, he'd probably fall asleep if he tried.

"Hmm." The other priest didn't sound convinced. "I would prefer actually working on the problem in my lab."

"If you'd like to leave–"

"No!" Ander interrupted frantically. His voice dropped to a whisper. "They're out there. Waiting." A pause. "They want to take my notes from me."

Takeshi thought that was probably true, though he would hazard a guess that they would also give the notes back after Ander had slept. "Then you have the same options as before."

Ander made a sound of disgust, but didn't protest. "Do I have to hum?" he asked after a moment.

"Hum?" Takeshi asked, confused. "No, you don't. Why do you ask?"

"You were humming," Ander said.

"What? No I wasn't." He opened his eyes to look at Ander, concerned that the other man had started hallucinating.

Jitsu made a soft sound. Her Human had been humming, just a little. It was nice.

He stared at her, completely taken aback.

*:The World Sound,:* Hades informed him.

He'd been humming the World Sound without even knowing it? He couldn't even hear it right now. What the hell did that mean? This problem was getting worse.

*:The World Sound by its nature likes to synchronize with things. I don't think it's too bad a thing,:* Hades tried to reassure him. *:Music is good after all, right? I like music.:*

*:I like music too, but I don't want to be humming without knowing it,:* he countered. He took a deep breath. He couldn't deal with that right now. "Humming is not required, no." The last thing Ander needed was for Takeshi to have an existential crisis.

Ander shifted in the chair and looked down at his notes again. "Do I have to put the notes down?"

"You should, but you don't have to," he said patiently. "Sit in a way that feels comfortable."

Jitsu sighed. Why did everyone want to do the sitting thing?

Ander looked down at his notes, around the room, at Jitsu, then back at Takeshi.

That was probably the best he was going to get. "Close your eyes, and try to relax." He waited for Ander to follow the directions before continuing. "Focus on your breathing. It should take a slow count of three for you to inhale, then a count of three to exhale. I will count aloud. One..."

Takeshi kept an eye on Ander's breathing as he counted. It only took three repetitions before Hades said with great relief, *:He's out.:*

Takeshi waited a few minutes to ensure that he'd stay asleep, then got up and opened the door. Mara, Siva, and Marcus were all waiting a little ways down the hall. Mara waved, a huge grin on her face. Takeshi gestured into the room. "Are you collecting him, or...?"

As Marcus slipped past him into the apartment with a wry smile, Siva bowed her head. "I greet you, Shuurai Takeshi."

He returned the bow. "Well met, Siva of the House of Shadows."

Mara sighed in disgust. "Why's everyone so formal? We're family! Don't be like that."

Siva's smile was kind as the flames in her eyes flickered merrily. "Respect shown at first meeting sets the precedent for a good relationship, no?"

Takeshi nodded as Mara hmphed.

Jitsu padded out into the hallway, tail wagging as soon as she saw the fire-eyed priest and the happy-water priest. Now Takeshi wouldn't do the sitting thing!

*:Marcus took Ander to the hospital, Takeshi. Your rooms are free,:* Hades informed him.

"The hospital?" He frowned. "Is he really that badly off?"

*:He's malnourished,:* she explained. *:He'll probably be allowed to return home tomorrow as long as he promises to eat real food.:*

"Oh, he'll be eating real food," Mara said darkly.

"I'm certain we can figure something out," Siva agreed. She gestured towards the staircase. "Perhaps we could return to the Temple? I would like a chance to see what has become of Jak, now that we have dislodged Ander from his lab."

"I have never seen anything like it," she admitted as the four of them stood in front of the statue. Takeshi and Mara had done their best to explain the circumstances surrounding Jak's transformation. "And I have lived a very long time."

*:He did not wish to die. This was the only other option, given how he drained his own life-force to gate so far,:* Hades said.

Siva shook her head. "I'm not blaming you. Jak is old enough to make his own choices. And, to be perfectly honest, it is well within his character to go off and leave us with a mess to clean up."

"What are we going to do, though?" Mara asked, gazing sadly at the first priest's frozen form.

Siva was silent for a long moment. "We are priests of death, of loss. Who would know better than we that we carry the memory of those gone with us, and the knowledge that an end is not *the* end. We know that we will meet again one day. Jak is not the first priest of Hades to be lost to us; both of you are too young to remember Timon and Geshen." Her hands fisted in her long skirt. "We are blessed with the knowledge that his absence will be temporary. Death brings change; it is the responsibility of the living to finish the work left undone. We should endeavor to ensure that there is a world for him to come back to."

Takeshi felt bolstered by her words. That was a clear goal. "We hunt down the remaining bionics, then."

She nodded. "Yes. The Lady is correct; Abomination cannot be allowed to fester, lest the wound sour. I deeply regret that I could not get here any earlier."

"With the assassination of the Emperor, everything is a mess." Mara winced. "Why'd the Seekers have to do that? Not like I liked the guy, but still."

"It was difficult to find a ship that was willing to attempt the journey at all," Siva admitted. "I knew we could communicate through Hades if there was an emergency, but we did not realize Ander would spiral into such a condition."

*:It worsened considerably only a couple of days ago.:* Hades sounded miserable. *:Before that he was functioning fairly well.:*

"He probably hit the limits of what he was physically capable of," Takeshi said thoughtfully.

Mara huffed. "He could have asked for help."

"That has never been Ander's strong suit," Siva pointed out. "I find myself weary after my journey. Why don't we continue this upstairs?"

A few minutes later found them settled into the sitting room in the priests' apartments, Jitsu cuddled as close to Takeshi as she could after he fought back a shiver. He stroked her head, thankful as always for her warmth, especially after the walk through the rain.

"How have you been faring, Takeshi?" Siva asked. "I understand you had been under a great amount of stress even before this occurred, and suffered near corruption from Abomination? Please do not just say 'fine'; I believe Ander has used up all of our allotments for that word for the month."

He kept his eyes on Jitsu's ears. "The microchip left its mark. I get cold very easily now, but it could have been much worse. The migraines are gone."

She nodded. "And are there any aftereffects from being connected to the Truth Seekers?"

"There don't seem to be. It was so quick, and there was so much information that I don't think any of it stuck, except what they wanted me to know." The memory of all those minds, working together as one, still disturbed him for reasons he couldn't pinpoint.

"No, I do not mean information. I mean you, the person." She smiled. "Have you experienced anything odd? Anything that could be left over from having been in mental contact with them, or any feelings that you do not believe to be yours?"

"Oh." He considered that. "I have no desire to join them, if that's what you mean. I like being myself too much, and they lost most of their individuality in whatever process linked them together. But..." He trailed off, trying to decide if he should mention it or not. "I've been hearing music when there isn't any. Hades says it's the World Sound."

"What?" Mara exclaimed. "You didn't tell me this!"

Takeshi blinked at her. "I told Hades."

"Well, yeah, but, maybe I could have helped?" Her ears sank.

*:It is the World Sound,:* Hades insisted firmly. *:I know the World Sound intimately. It is not harmful to hear it, just strange.:*

"But why can I hear it?" he stressed. "I couldn't before we went to the Nyphoren Islands. I don't know if touching their minds did something to mine."

*:That's not impossible, but I still wouldn't be concerned.:*

"That is a lot to ask of someone," Siva corrected the goddess gently. "Something major has changed in his life, and he does not know why. That will cause stress. You say it is not harmful. How do you know? Are there others who can hear this?"

*:It is rare, but not unheard of. Those who can hear it usually become bards, though Takeshi is hearing it with... unusual clarity.:*

"Do we know if there is anyone in Tarvishte who can hear it?" Siva asked.

*:I am uncertain. Though the World Sound is part of all living beings, it is not related to my domains.:*

"Maybe we could just ask around? There are a number of bards here in Tarvishte," Mara pointed out. "Even if none of them can hear it, maybe they've heard of it!"

Takeshi felt dumb. "I didn't even consider that. I've been... rather focused on soulforging, I'm afraid."

"And that is why you should ask others for aid," Siva reminded him. "The Lady is a wonderful being, but she is not mortal and does not think as we do. She is also only one mind. Different perspectives on a problem are always to be valued."

That was a good point. He dropped his gaze. "I understand."

"I do not mean to scold you," Siva said gently. "But we are stronger together than apart. There are so few of us. It is imperative that we support each other in all things."

"Right!" Mara interrupted. "That's what I keep saying – we're all family!"

Even when Ander had been exhausted beyond the point of rational thought, he had still fled to another priest, Takeshi reflected. And the concept of the many being stronger than the one was familiar to him as well. Shinobi often combined their spell weaves for more powerful effects, though he hadn't seen such spell work here.

Siva smiled, the flames in her eyes dancing. "Indeed. Then, since you have brought this up as well, I will ask – soulforging?"

Takeshi's mouth twisted in disgust. "I've been trying for two months now and have made no progress on that front. I've dedicated the entirety of my free time to learning it, but I cannot keep my soul crystal outside my body for more than a heartbeat."

"Soulforging is a tricky, personal thing. In theory, it should not work at all." The flames in Siva's eyes flickered thoughtfully. "Yet the Vampires and the priests of Hades are capable of it."

Takeshi was tired. "I'm all too familiar with how it is different for everyone. I have tried to get advice, but none of it seems to work for me."

"Then I suggest you stop trying. For at least a week. Possibly longer, though."

"Just stop?" Takeshi blinked at her, trying to wrap his head around that.

"Not to give up, but to give yourself distance," she explained. "Let your subconscious mind consider the problem for a time, while you allow yourself to do other things. There is no need to rush soulforging. Have you considered what it is you wish to do with yourself as a priest?"

"Oh, well, I took over warg duties from Ander." Which he had been neglecting, he realized with a sinking feeling.

Jitsu huffed, then stretched up so she could lick his face. The wargs understood that the two-feet had a lot going on right now. They were purposefully not bothering Takeshi. He did not need to worry. If they needed him, they would let him know. Most of them weren't in the city right now anyway.

That made Takeshi feel worse.

"Ander must be thankful for that," Siva mused. "He's not one for canine companions."

As one, they all turned to look at the giant saltwater aquarium Ander kept in the sitting room. A variety of brightly colored fish and coral were on display.

*:He was still taking care of the aquarium!:* Hades blurted out.

Takeshi did not know much about fish, but they all looked fine. At least Ander had some priorities.

"That's good, but maybe we could redirect some of that energy towards himself," Mara said wryly.

"Indeed," Siva agreed. "As it is, after Ander recovers I would like to meet with those who were involved with the incident at the Nyphoren base. I believe it would be prudent to gather all information on the Abomination and look at it with fresh eyes. And I would very much like to meet Jamirh. I never had a chance to meet Ebryn of Storms and Light, but I came to know Sukra very well after she returned to the desert and began her own House. I would honor her memory."

"Ah," Mara started with a wince, "he's not overly fond of Ebryn. Or of being Ebryn. Or of being reminded of his predecessor's existence at all."

Siva raised an eyebrow. "Oh?"

"From my understanding, he wants to be able to live his own life without being reminded of someone who lived a thousand years ago," Takeshi explained.

*:He feels that his life has been dictated by the choices and wants of others, including Ebryn,:* Hades added. *:And us.:*

"Has it not been?" Siva asked.

Takeshi realized he didn't know the answer to that question.

# Chapter Five

"Come in!"

Jamirh hesitantly opened the ornate wooden door to reveal a comfortable office. Dark wood furnishings and gold-and-black decor created a warm space. Expensive, but tasteful. Two plush armchairs sat in front of a heavy desk, and a cream-colored couch with embroidered pillows rested against the wall. Above the couch–

Jamirh snapped his eyes away. He didn't need to look at himself in the mirror.

Vlad sat at the desk, red eyes watching Jamirh. "Thank you for coming," the Vampire king said. "Feel free to sit wherever you'd like. I know we were supposed to have tea, but would you like some hot chocolate instead?"

Jamirh gingerly took a seat in one of the armchairs. "Uh, sure, that's fine."

"Excellent!" He strode across the room to a large hutch, pulling out two mugs before opening a drawer and starting to pull out far too many things for a simple cup of hot chocolate.

Jamirh eyed him warily. "What did you want to see me about?"

"Two reasons. One, you've been fairly absent from my court for the past few weeks, and I wanted to check in to see how you've been doing. Two..." He grimaced. "Did you know all of my time is booked and budgeted right now due to a certain political situation happening right across our border?"

"You wanted a break," Jamirh realized, ears twitching in amusement. "You had me schedule myself with you so you didn't have to do work."

"Yes," Vlad agreed easily. "I am very interested in not working right now. So, how have you been?"

Jamirh watched him add ingredients to the mugs. "I've been hanging out with Salisha and Desha, mostly."

"The pirate sisters you were with last Saturday, yes?" Vlad waited for Jamirh's nod. "You could bring them to the dining hall for meals, you know. You don't need to eat out every day."

The Avari shrugged. "I don't usually choose where we go, but I'll mention it to them."

Vlad made a gesture and twin red circles of magic appeared under the mugs, which promptly began to steam. "They do seem to have opinions."

"Yeah." No denying that. "But mostly I've been showing them and their crewmates around."

Vlad hummed. "Have you continued training at all? Not that you have to, I'm just curious."

"No. Jeri is busy every time I run into her, and I've barely even seen Takeshi since we got back," Jamirh said glumly.

The Vampire frowned as he handed Jamirh a cup. "Surely there have been others around the training grounds? I know many of the Watch are busy, but they should still be training at some point. Surely one of them would be willing to spar with you? They were doing so before; I saw some of the bouts. It is impressive how fast your technique develops."

The warmth of the cup seeped into Jamirh's hands. "Oh, I guess I didn't consider that. I only ever went to the training grounds with Jeri or Takeshi." He tried to hide a wince. "I didn't think I could just... go on my own."

"The training grounds are for everyone. You do not need permission from someone to use them." Vlad added blood to his cup. "If it is something you enjoy, you should continue it, even if you just keep to daggers. I seem to recall those were what Jeri was teaching you to use?"

"Yeah. I actually do miss those," he admitted. It was something he was good at that was just his, not Ebryn's.

"Then you should continue using them. The world is a dangerous place; it is helpful to be equally dangerous."

Jamirh took a sip of his drink. Rich chocolate combined with cinnamon and another spice he couldn't place melted together in a delicious explosion of flavor. He took another sip. "This is amazing."

"Thank you. I am surprised, though, that you don't seem to be spending time with Jeri anymore?" Vlad raised an eyebrow.

"Like I said – she's busy." It was hard to keep the bitterness out of his voice. "Every time I run into her she's on her way to somewhere else."

Vlad hummed thoughtfully. "It's true the Watch has been on guard since the Emperor's assassination, and Jeri is a senior member. She's in almost as many meetings as I am. But I would have thought…" He trailed off. "Hm. Maybe I will speak to Prim about adjusting some of the shifts. No one should be being overworked that much. We aren't at war; we're just being cautious."

Jamirh wasn't sure how to explain that he thought Jeri was avoiding him. Surely that would come across as clingy or selfish. Everyone was working hard right now; it wasn't fair of him to demand Jeri's time if she had none to give. "Do you think that's a possibility? War, that is?"

"Anything is technically possible. War will likely break out south of the Wall as soon as one of the dukes feels they have enough of an advantage to make the first move, but our hope is they will be too preoccupied with each other to look north," Vlad explained. "And even if they did, they would have to find a way to cross the Wall."

"Most people in the Empire don't even know Romanii exists. They think it's all wasteland up here." That was what he had believed, before Hel had turned his life upside down. "Do the dukes know?"

"Yes, they do," Vlad assured him. "Though they usually prefer to pretend like we don't exist."

"Then why is everyone so concerned about what's going on in the Empire?" Jamirh asked, frustrated. "If Romanii is going to be safe, why's everyone so busy and walking on eggshells?"

Vlad sighed, putting his mug down and folding his hands in front of him. "Politics can be a tricky thing, and a volatile political climate can result in things no one has foreseen. The current stalemate between the dukes is placing tension on all international relations because the Rose Empire is so large and politically interconnected that it affects everyone. Should it break into multiple countries, it becomes more likely *someone* will try to involve us. And through all of that, we still must try to track down the remaining bionics."

Jamirh winced at the reminder, ears twitching down as his hand found his key. He rubbed it, but the familiar gesture didn't offer any comfort. "Do we know how many more there are? Or where?"

Vlad shook his head. "No. My mother has confirmed that Abomination does still exist, but she cannot tell where."

"So what can we do?"

Something flickered in Vlad's eyes, but it was gone before Jamirh could pin down what it was. "Believe it or not, it will be easier to hunt them down once war has broken out in the south. With the dukes fighting each other, our agents will be able to move more freely and will hopefully be able to determine likely locations. There's even the possibility some of them will be destroyed for us. The bigger problem is actually Ni Fon."

Jamirh blinked. "Ni Fon? What do they have to do with it?"

"We know they are able to manufacture chips like the one we found in Takeshi. Those chips are also Abomination, according to my mother. We have no idea how Ni Fon is utilizing them. However, the chips have terrible side effects; our best-case scenario there is that they abandon the idea entirely."

"That sounds awfully risky, to hope they just... stopped," Jamirh said, frowning.

Vlad shrugged. "So as you see, we do not currently have many good moves to make. This is why everyone is waiting with bated breath for the other shoe to drop."

Desha wasn't far off in her assessment. Jamirh made a mental note to share all this with her later. "That sucks."

That drew a laugh out of Vlad. "You are not incorrect. But this is something I wanted to take a break from." His eyes caught on Jamirh's hand. "Is that the wound from when the Blade shattered?"

"Oh, yeah." Jamirh rolled up his sleeve so Vlad could see the rest of the angry red lines. "They're not really getting better, but they're not getting any worse, either."

Vlad was frowning, eyebrows drawing together. "May I take a look? I am a healer by trade."

Jamirh vaguely recalled that. "Uh, sure? If you want. Marcus said that wounds from magical artifacts can sometimes do weird things. And it's not like it hurts or anything. Sometimes it gets a little sore, but that's it."

"He's not wrong," Vlad said slowly, coming around the desk to Jamirh's side. "When was the last time he checked this, though? Has Ander seen it? No, probably not," he answered his own question with a sigh.

"The last time I saw Marcus was when he took the stitches out two, two and a half weeks ago," Jamirh answered. "Was I supposed to see him again?"

"If it still looks like this, I would recommend it." Vlad ran a hand just over Jamirh's arm, a red glow following that coalesced into runes. Jamirh felt a chill travel down his spine. The Vampire hummed. "Nothing appears to be wrong, per se, but I do not like that color." He gently touched one of the marks. "Would you be willing to check in with Marcus or Ander so they can look at this? They have more knowledge of this type of wound than I do."

Jamirh felt a sinking feeling in his gut. "I thought you said nothing was wrong?"

"Nothing is showing up to me, but the fact the wounds still look this... angry tells me something isn't right. I would feel better knowing someone was monitoring this. It might just be healing very slowly – you were in the epicenter of an explosion of elemental magic, and that could have affected your body's natural ability to heal – but I would not leave that to chance. Do not worry too much," Vlad soothed, seeing Jamirh beginning to look panicked. "If it doesn't hurt then that's a good sign. It's just better to be safe than sorry."

Jamirh strangled down the desire to scream. It figured. "It had to do one last thing to make my life a living hell, didn't it?"

Vlad winced. "I find most magical artifacts are like that. The ones with 'higher purpose,' anyway." He studied Jamirh closely. "At least the Blade is gone, now."

Jamirh looked down, uncertain. "Is that good, though? Like, I didn't want it, but... it was supposed to help against the Abomination. Now that it's gone, doesn't that... I don't know, make our side weaker?"

"From what I understand of what happened in the Nyphoren it was not going to be terribly helpful against the bionics in the long run anyway." The Vampire shrugged, then returned to his seat. "As soon as the Abomination took a form that involved tech, it negated the advantage of the Blade. We were just late to that realization. It would not be so terrible if it hadn't almost killed you and six other people."

"I still feel bad that I broke the Blade," Jamirh said quietly.

"Don't," came the flat reply. "You are not responsible for that. No one is. If Ebryn himself had been wielding it, it still would have shattered. Be glad you are all still alive."

"Ander saved us," Jamirh remembered. It was hard to think back through the shock, but Jeri had gotten him away from the bionic and then... "He made some kind of shield. Layered, I think. As the blasts were breaking the inner layers he was throwing more around them."

Vlad nodded. "Ander is very talented when it comes to spell casting, and very powerful. With my mother's backing he is only more so, though he chooses to put his talents towards science and medicine more than battle. He is second to none when it comes to shields, though." His eyes flickered behind Jamirh, and he sighed. "Speaking of my mother..." He nodded his head towards the wall.

Jamirh hesitantly turned, unwilling to see himself in the mirror and remember, but it wasn't his reflection he saw. Hel was in the mirror instead, somehow? And she was waving at him, a big grin on her face.

Vlad sighed. "This is my Jamirh time. Go away."

She gave them both an offended look.

"Jamirh, she'd like you to meet her in her temple after you leave here. She says she has something for you," Vlad relayed.

Jamirh shot her a confused look, but she just grinned. "Uh, sure, I guess?"

She waved again, then faded from view, leaving–

Jamirh snapped around again, face paling.

Vlad frowned. "Are you okay?"

"Yeah, fine," Jamirh lied. How on Gaia would he explain that he just couldn't look at himself in the mirror anymore without seeing Ryn's... no. He wrenched his thoughts away from the memory.

"Okay," Vlad said slowly. "If you're sure?"

Jamirh nodded.

Vlad glanced at the mirror again, then sighed. "Very well then. Where were we?"

Jamirh hadn't been to the Temple of Night Rising since Jak had teleported them there over a month ago. As he entered, pausing at the entrance to shake off some of the unseasonably cold rain, he noticed the door to Ander's office was gone, charred debris lying on the ground in its place. He wondered if one of the priest's experiments had gone wrong.

In the sanctuary, Jak's statue commanded attention. If Jamirh hadn't known any better, he'd have thought it was a temple to Jak, not Hades. Her own statue, set back on the altar, was small and unimpressive by comparison.

"Hi Jamirh!"

He turned. Mara grinned at him from the doorway to the courtyard, ears twitching up in joy. He returned the grin. "Hey, Mara. How've you been?"

She made a sound of disgust. "Busy. Way too busy. Feels like everyone's waiting for who even knows what, you know?" She strode over, heels clicking against the marble floor. "And what have you been up to?"

"Nothing," he snorted. "Feels like I've been spinning in place ever since we got back."

Mara pursed her lips before her expression smoothed out. "Well, at least you get a chance to relax! But anyway, the Lady told me she wanted to speak to you?"

Jamirh nodded. "That's why I'm here."

"Ah, well, no worries! I'm going to be just in the courtyard over there; the Lady just needs one of us nearby to make manifesting on this plane of existence a little easier." The older Avari winked.

Jamirh eyed the doorway. "In the storm?"

"What's wrong with a little water?" She feigned an exaggerated look of offense. "But nah, the whole side is covered. But feel free to stick around a bit after, you know? You're not a stranger; don't act like one!" And with that, she flounced out.

Jamirh watched her go. Maybe he would. He hadn't seen Ander or Takeshi in a while either; maybe they were around too?

"Jamirh."

She was standing next to Jak's statue. In this form, her white hair was far longer than it had been as Hel, pooling on the floor around her. Her black dress had lavender accents and pearl detailing, much fancier than the Watch Blacks she'd been wearing when he met her. But her violet eyes still sparkled with the same mischief he'd seen back in that jail cell.

He cleared his throat. "Hey."

She grinned at him before her expression softened. "I know you're wondering why I wanted to speak with you."

"You could say that," he agreed.

"It's just that – well. I've been working on something for a while. I had hoped it would be ready before you had to put yourself in danger, but it wasn't." She held out an arm, and black fabric coalesced into being. "Here. Take this."

Hesitantly, Jamirh touched the material and was surprised to feel leather. He held it up to get a good look at it.

It was a coat.

Cut in Romanii style, the coat was long and single-breasted. Black leather on the outside, a soft, warm material on the inside with a lot of pockets. It was the nicest piece of clothing Jamirh had ever laid hands on. "What's this?"

"When we first met, you were deeply saddened by the loss of a coat. We weren't able to get it for you on the way out – running was of utmost importance – but I remembered. I've been working on it since I lost the avatar in Charve."

"You made me a coat?" he repeated, baffled. "But... why?"

Violet eyes blinked slowly. "You needed one."

"I needed one? You mean months ago?" Suspicion rose. "The Blade is gone. Is this a new contract?"

"No." The answer was swift and firm. "This is a gift. Perhaps even more useful now that the Blade is shattered. I've saturated it with spell work. It will keep you warm in freezing temperatures but will be comfortable to wear in warmer weather. It's nearly impossible to rip or damage, and it will protect you from most physical harm. It has some ability to rebuff spells. I added a ton of pockets for you – I remember one of the things you liked about the other coat was its numerous pockets. Some of them are deeper than they look."

"But I didn't tell you about the coat. Did I?" He tried to think back, but he'd had a concussion at the time and it had happened months ago.

"No. But you were thinking about it very hard," she admitted. "I am a god. When the emotion is strong enough, we can hear things like that. That's basically what praying is, if you think about it."

He stared at her. "But I wasn't praying to you."

"You were in close proximity. It helps." Hel shrugged.

"You made me a coat," he repeated after a moment, still stuck on that thought. Why would the goddess of death make him a coat?

She tilted her head sideways. "This does not have a price, Jamirh. The coat is yours. You may do as you wish with it. It is not bound to you like the Blade was, if that's your concern. There are no chains here. It is a magical artifact, and if anyone looks for magic on your person it will light up like the sun, but magical artifacts do not need to be bound to an individual. You could give the coat away, if you like, or try to destroy it. But it is my hope you take it with you when you go."

He didn't know what she was talking about. "When I go?"

"The Blade is gone, and with it, our contract." She was silent for a moment. "I had thought you would take this opportunity to be rid of the lot of us and forge your own path."

They thought *he* was leaving *them*?

A part of him pointed out that while no one had been talking to him, he hadn't made any real effort to talk to anyone else, either. Except for the twins, he'd been keeping mostly to himself. Vlad had said Jamirh was absent from his court. Mara had told him not to be a stranger. He'd been avoiding the places he associated with the Blade, but those were also the places the people he was missing were bound to. He had let this stalemate continue instead of trying to break it.

Maybe they all had to try a little harder. Maybe he should try Vlad's tactic of officially booking "meetings" with them.

"I don't know what I'm doing yet," he admitted to her. He looked down at the angry red lines spiraling down his arm. Then he ran a hand over the supple leather of the coat. It was hard to believe she was giving such a thing to him. "But thank you. This is the nicest thing I've ever owned."

Her face lit up.

"What about you, though?" he continued. "Are you going to remake the Blade? You could give it to someone else if you remade it, right?" That seemed like the best option to him.

But she shook her head. "No. Its time has passed. Let it now fall into legend. It is unfortunate that it could not be used against multiple cycles, but new threats require new strategies. We will adapt." She smiled. "You truly are free to do as you wish."

"What about Ryn? And Ebryn?" he asked.

"What about them?"

"I haven't heard from either of them since the Blade shattered." He looked back up at her. "Are they... gone?"

"I'm not sure I follow." She looked confused. "You were able to speak with Ebryn? I mean, it does make sense since you could talk with Ryn, but... when was this?"

He shuddered. "Right before we found..." He trailed off, unable to finish. He could still see those sightless eyes boring into him.

She made a soft sound of understanding. "Takeshi, Ander, and Mara flooded the area with my power. It is possible that's what made him strong enough to manifest that way. Or it could simply be that you share the same soul." She thought for a moment. "The Blade shattering should not have been able to affect that. If the Blade breaking were to destroy them, it would have destroyed you, too. You three are one. In fact, I would go so far as to say that it was more of a threat to you than to them, as you are still alive, and it could have killed you. But it could not destroy your soul."

"But then, where are they?" he asked, perplexed. "I've tried to speak with them. Even Ebryn! But no one ever answers."

"I don't know," she admitted quietly. "Well, they are likely still where they've always been – inside you. But I don't know why you can't reach them."

Jamirh felt his ears sink. If even the goddess of death didn't know, what chance did he have?

# Chapter Six

---

Ander did not want to be here.

Siva and Mara were doing something with food over in the kitchen area of the priests' apartments. Jeri had slunk in and placed herself on the window seat so the shadows making up her missing arm were out of sight. So that was somehow still a secret; great. Salisha and Desha had come in with Jamirh and were oohing and aahing over the aquarium while Jamirh stood nearby, silver eyes darting all over the room.

Ander himself had been placed by Siva in one of the armchairs and told in no uncertain terms that he was to stay there until this meeting was over. She refused to acknowledge his point that she already knew everything he could possibly say and therefore his presence was superfluous. So he was wasting his time here when he could be replacing his door or making progress on the avatar. Though that would be tricky; Siva had confiscated his notes and told him he wouldn't be getting them back for at least a week.

Thoughtfully he eyed Jamirh. The kid was a thief, right? Maybe Ander could hire him to steal his notes back?

*:First of all, Jamirh is twenty-three. Not a 'kid' by Avari standards. Second of all, no.:*

Ander sighed. Hades had now become a babysitter on Siva's behalf.

*:Maybe if you hadn't completely run yourself into the ground we'd be having a different conversation.:*

Ander's expression darkened. So he had slightly miscalculated how much sleep he needed. That was fixable. There was no need to treat him like a child.

*:You didn't even realize you were drinking water instead of coffee.:* She was definitely judging him.

He had noticed something didn't taste right. He just hadn't figured out why. If he threw an extra hour or two of sleep in there—

*:No.:*

He sighed, disgusted. No one valued productivity.

*:How was that being productive?!? You set up the same experiment incorrectly almost twenty times. Wouldn't it have been better to sleep for six hours, then get it right once?:*

There was something to be said for that, he supposed. But he was sure he had set it up incorrectly using a different method each time, so he had still been iterating on the problem. And it didn't give them the right to take his notes. They hadn't let him go look at his lab either. He was concerned about the shape it was in. At least they had let him leave the hospital.

"Good morning, Ander."

Takeshi and Jitsu had arrived. Great. Now it was a party. Ander huffed a greeting as the shinobi and warg took a seat on one of the couches. The traitor had handed him over to the witches. Though... Ander *had* passed out in the other man's rooms.

"Are you feeling any better?"

Ander turned his attention sharply to the other man, but his tone was mild and his masked face only showed polite interest. He wasn't laughing at Ander, at least. The half-Avari didn't think he could take that.

"Much," he responded shortly.

Takeshi inclined his head. "That is good to hear."

For all that he'd given Ander to Siva, Takeshi was still one of the smartest people in the room. He hadn't threatened to take Ander's notes, even though it would have been pathetically easy in the state he'd been in. Surely he could see the value in the avatar's existence. Maybe Takeshi would consider stealing his notes back?

*:No.:*

From the corner of his eye Ander saw Jamirh's gaze settle on him and Takeshi. The Avari hesitated, then squared his shoulders as he came over. Ander's brows drew together as he watched Jamirh exchange pleasantries with Takeshi. Something was different about the Avari, but he wasn't sure what.

Jamirh turned to Ander. "Hey, it's been a while. What have you been up to?"

"I've been trying to rebuild the avatar," Ander sniffed. "Though everyone appears to be determined to get in my way."

Takeshi's eyebrows lifted slightly. "Including you?"

Ander stared at him, stung. How rude.

Jamirh's eyes grew wide. "Oh, you're making that body for Hel! Didn't you say it would take fifteen years or something, though?"

"I think I have brought it down to just over eight," Ander explained. "However, there is more room for improvement. Which is why I should be working on it instead of being here."

Jamirh nodded slowly. "Ah."

Jitsu huffed in the warg equivalent of a laugh, and Ander shot her a glare. He didn't need the opinion of three hundred pounds of fur.

"I wanted to say thank you," Jamirh blurted out.

Ander blinked. Takeshi looked equally confused. "For...?" Ander prompted.

"Shielding us when the Blade broke. You saved our lives. I just wanted to let you know I appreciate it."

"Oh." Ander wasn't sure what to do with that. That night had been full of so many mistakes on his part. Even that shield hadn't been able to hold long enough; the final pulse of elemental magic had broken it.

"I was talking to Vlad, and he mentioned that kind of shield is really hard to pull off. And you were exhausted afterwards, so it must have taken a lot of magic, right?"

Ander had completely drained his *crystallus* and a not insignificant amount of his own magicore to maintain it as long as he had. "Yes, but it still was overcome by the remnants of the Blade."

Jamirh shrugged. "But we didn't get hit by the brunt of it, and I think we would have been dead if we did. So thanks."

"You're welcome," Ander said reflexively. "Takeshi helped as well," he added. Credit where credit was due; Takeshi had helped him hold out longer.

Takeshi inclined his head. "I merely supplied additional power. The spell work was all yours."

Siva and Mara were passing out cups filled with a deep-red tea he recognized as being from Dalmara. Siva also placed a dish with hummus and flatbread chips in the center of the table. The regional cuisine reassured Ander that Siva had done the majority of the preparation. Mara's cooking was usually just this side of edible.

As everyone settled down, Siva asked for everyone's attention. "Thank you everyone for coming. For those who do not know me, I am Siva of the House of Shadows, second High Priest of Hades. In the wake of Jak's temporary displacement, it is my duty to ensure that what has been begun is finished. The Abominations must be destroyed." She paused to take in the nods the words garnered. "As of now, I've heard Mara, Ander, and Takeshi's perspectives on the events of Tilden Base. I would like to hear from everyone else. We need as full and as clear a picture as possible."

Ander tuned out the following recitations. He had been there. He did not need to relive it another four times. Instead he turned his mind back to the problem of his lab. A new door was paramount. He should arrange for that first. Then he needed to–

*:Have you noticed anything strange about Jeri?:* Takeshi asked him.

Ander blinked, previous thoughts derailed. Did *no one* know? How the hell had she managed that? *:Why do you ask?:*

*:There's something odd about the way she's positioned herself,:* Takeshi explained. *:And now that I'm thinking about it, it's similar to how she's been in most of the meetings we've been to. Even when she gave her accounting of events, she didn't turn to address the group more directly. It just feels off for some reason.:*

*:Maybe she's just comfortable that way,:* he deflected. While he would have liked to put an end to this farce, she had come to him in confidence, and even he knew that wasn't something you just threw out.

Takeshi glanced at him sharply, and Ander felt a sinking sensation. Perhaps he was still more tired than he thought if he was unable to redirect such suspicion.

*:I arrived last, so perhaps I missed it, but I don't believe she and Jamirh have interacted at all today?:* The shinobi's observation was devoid of inflection.

*:Maybe, maybe not. I'm not watching them. Maybe they had a spat of some sort.:*

*:I see.:*

This was squarely Jeri's problem. She had made the decision to hide it, not Ander. She could deal with the inevitable fallout when it was discovered. Why did everyone keep dragging Ander into their problems?

*:You want to pay attention again,:* Hades informed him.

Siva was thanking the sisters for their information; apparently they had given one account instead of two. Ander wondered if there was anything they didn't do together. "And so, with these things in mind, we can begin to formulate a plan for how to track down that which remains."

"Romanii is already trying to find a solution," Jeri spoke up. "I'm not sure what this group is supposed to do differently?"

Siva took a sip of tea. "Romanii must divide its resources due to the current political climate. Vlad cannot dedicate his forces fully to this problem. Abomination is not a political issue; it is a metaphysical one that threatens life. Thus we, as Hades' clergy, must step in. I've already requested our siblings be available if required."

Siva had contacted the other four? Interesting. To his knowledge, Kade and Fen were somewhere in the Darklands, Daiyu was in

Zhong Gou, and Yafen was doing something with the Lowkeef in the Forbidden. It would be difficult for any of them to respond in a reasonable amount of time without Jak's gates.

Siva continued, "Additionally, there are several people here who have not been included in the previous discussions and may have valuable insight, as their familiarity with the Empire is greater than our own."

Jeri made a sound of protest. "Many members of the Black Watch, myself included, have spent years spying from within the Empire."

"And not to discount those missions," Siva agreed, "and the risks taken to ensure their success, but there are some things native members of a community will always notice that even the most well-trained spy may miss, for the spy will always be 'other.'"

Ander wished he could tune out again. None of this was going to affect him.

"We have come to no solid conclusions after a month of discussion, brainstorming, and bickering," Takeshi pointed out. "Fresh eyes could catch something that has been missed."

The sisters glanced at each other before the one on the right spoke. "We've been keeping a closer eye on the politics o' it all t' be honest."

"Weren't even really thinking o' the bionics," the other concluded.

"Well, not much," the first conceded.

"Yeah, maybe a bit, but not anything helpful."

Goddess, Ander hated them.

"Are we sure that was the only factory that was producing the bionics?" Jamirh rested his chin on his fist.

Jeri shrugged. "It was the only lead we had, and even then Mara found it more by accident than anything else. It does not seem likely there were many factories that were somehow kept completely secret."

Jamirh looked down. "It's just that... one of the first times I talked to Ryn, he said he died fighting in the factory that was producing them, but it was in Gallia, not the Nyphoren."

Takeshi hummed. "There was something–" He cut himself off, then tried again. "The Truth Seekers did have a few other military bases marked as targets. I assumed it was more for strategic purposes to aid in their break from the Empire, but... they *hate* the Abominations. That was something I picked up on while joined to them. It's possible that those locations were actually being targeted for that reason."

Jeri perked up. "Do you know which bases? Or even general locations? Anything at all would give us something to start with."

The shinobi shook his head. "Nothing concrete. I can try to poke at it a bit and see what comes up, but I haven't been able to pull much from those memories before."

*:Actually... I might be able to help.:*

Ander exchanged surprised glances with the other priests.

*:When the avatar was captured, I was moved between several bases before being relocated to Charve. Some of those bases felt far more strongly of Abomination than others. Though for what it's worth, I do not think there are any new bionics being created. The amount of Abomination in the world has been going down, not up, though it is still present.:*

Ander considered that while Siva relayed the Lady's words to the others. "It might be that some of those bases were involved in the construction of parts," he said slowly when she finished.

"What do you mean?" Mara asked.

Ander took a deep breath, trying to get his thoughts in order. "The bionics are extremely complex constructions, requiring many pieces of tech to successfully integrate with an Avari host. The base the Truth Seekers destroyed in the Nyphoren was where everything was assembled into its final form, but I don't remember seeing the necessary facilities for fabricating the parts they needed. Therefore, the parts must have been constructed off site and shipped to the Nyphoren."

"What about the base in Gallia, then?" Jeri asked.

"Ryn died attacking that base?" Ander asked Jamirh, waiting for his confirmation before continuing. "So twenty-five to twenty-six years ago, I would bet that was the main production facility for the Empire. But then some Avari kid with red hair and silver eyes shows up and attacks it. The attack is unsuccessful, but it spooks the Empire – someone who looks like Ebryn Stormlight, hero of the Avari, showed up out of nowhere and threatened their pet project."

"The Truth Seekers had some sort of prophecy about Ebryn, too," Takeshi said with a glance at Jamirh. "Depending on when it was made, that could have caused them to outright panic."

Ander nodded. "Very likely. So they move production off the mainland to the Nyphoren Islands. They don't need to move the other facilities producing mechanical parts, just the final assembly location. While we should make some effort to get rid of the information those bases have, I'd bet the most dangerous info is held in that original base, as they probably had a number of prototypes and all of their experimental and production notes. Additionally, we now have a very important data point – Hades says the amount of Abomination in the world is decreasing."

"Wait," Jeri interrupted. "Are you suggesting that the Truth Seekers might actually be hunting down the bionics?"

"It is the most likely conclusion," Ander agreed. "We know because of Takeshi that they hate the bionics, and it makes sense. Truth Seekers are mages, no matter what the Empire tells its citizens. Mages are always more sensitive to the presence of Abomination. And the Truth Seekers, being the strongest troops the Empire had, were made to guard these places. The bionics, if you think about it logically, were probably supposed to be their replacements considering how much the Empire hates magic."

Mara raised an eyebrow. "No wonder they snapped."

"The Empire's mistake was thinking they had complete control over the Truth Seekers," Ander continued. "So they would have been given access to every bit of information we are currently looking for – locations of bases, personnel, where the remaining bionics were stationed. Even if they weren't directly given that information, they would have known where to look. So yes, I bet they've been successfully hunting down the bionics in the Empire while the majority of us have been sitting here twiddling our thumbs."

*:And you thought you shouldn't be at this meeting,:* Hades snorted.

He ignored Her. "Which means I'm the only one who hasn't been wasting their time. We need the avatar. In a physical body, the Lady is able to better locate where the Abomination is. While the Truth

Seekers take care of the bulk of the remaining bionics, She can make sure we catch anything that might slip past them."

Jamirh cocked his head. "Didn't you say eight years?"

Ander nodded firmly. "Yes, though possibly less." Maybe if he had the help of one of Tadurin's priests it could be sped up even faster? Except... weird, unexplainable things often happened when the creator god's magic was directly involved, so maybe not.

The red-headed Avari squinted at him. "You know this is a 'now' problem, right?"

"Of course. That's why it is imperative I get back to work quickly." What was he getting at?

"Jamirh's point is valid," Siva agreed. "Eight years from now, or even six, is too late. We should focus on more immediate solutions."

Ander wanted to throw up his hands in disgust. "It's already been here for almost fifty years! Numbers *now* are the lowest they've been in decades. We have only fragments of useful information, the Blade is gone, and many of us are still recovering from our most recent jaunt into the Empire." He saw Jeri flinch out of the corner of his eye. And Jamirh? What was wrong with him? Takeshi was also looking away. Honestly, this just proved his point. "The Truth Seekers are a hive mind with a mission. They are better positioned to take care of this for now. I say we let them."

"How would they know they got them all?" one of the sisters questioned.

"They can probably hack the records and see how many were produced, if they don't have that information already. They can probably hack the locations, too. Some bionics might slip through the cracks, but that's what we need the avatar for." He shrugged. "There, problem solved."

"No, not problem solved," Siva said firmly. "A few counters to your arguments, Ander. While I agree it is a good thing that the bionics are being destroyed even without our interference, we should still be keeping a close eye to ensure complete destruction. Hoping the Truth Seekers will be successful is not good enough. At minimum, we should attempt to make contact and offer our support."

Takeshi coughed. "I do not know where they are."

Siva inclined her head. "No, but attempting to find a group of mages might be a better use of our time than doing the same to an unknown number of bionics scattered across an Empire. Second, Ander, I disagree that you were using your time wisely, having seen the toll it was taking on you."

"Because you don't understand–"

"I understand very well what you thought you were doing," she cut him off, the flames in her eyes dancing angrily. "And I understand that you were neglecting yourself for no real reason. Sacrificing yourself in that way is a waste, Ander. It is not necessary. We have already lost one priest; would you make us suffer the loss of another?"

He pulled back, stung. That was low. And untrue – he'd been in need of sleep and nutrients, but he hadn't been near *death*.

*:You had to be hospitalized for a day,:* Hades pointed out unsympathetically. *:And you specifically told me that if Jak could make his choice, you could make yours.:*

*:That wasn't what I meant and you know it,:* he snapped back. *:You of all people should have understood.:*

*:I'm not going to sit back and watch you waste away. Alice wouldn't have wanted that, either.:*

For a moment his vision went red.

"Ander!"

He realized the tea cup he'd been holding was broken. Mara was kneeling in front of him, holding his hands in hers, blue eyes fierce, but when her mind touched his it was only full of concern. *:There you are. Are you okay?:*

The looks being leveled at him ranged from stunned to concerned to afraid. Wonderful. He wrested himself back under control. He'd known this whole thing was a bad idea. "My apologies. Perhaps I should take my leave."

Mara's grip tightened before releasing. "That's enough. Let me take care of this." She pulled the spilled tea out of his clothes with a small but complicated blue array and tossed it in the sink. Then she began gathering the fragments of broken porcelain. "Don't you dare move until I have bandages on those cuts."

Jamirh snorted. "Hey, we kind of match." He pulled up his right sleeve.

Ander stared at the angry red lines traveling up the Avari's arm. "What in the world– is that from the Blade?" Hades had said the stitches were removed... how long ago?

*:A little over two weeks ago.:*

"Uh, yeah?" Jamirh asked, suddenly hesitant. Possibly because almost everyone was now looking at him in alarm. Even Jeri had twisted away from the window to get a better look.

Ander deeply regretted having broken the tea cup, as his hands were now being bandaged and he could not inspect Jamirh's wounds. "Did it look like that when Marcus removed the stitches?"

"Yeah, basically. It doesn't look any worse," Jamirh reassured him. "Marcus said that sometimes injuries from magical artifacts act weird."

"Not incorrect, but after two weeks I would expect to see improvement. Are you in pain?"

Jamirh shook his head wordlessly.

Well, that was good at least. He probably wasn't in any immediate danger, but still. "And Marcus is keeping an eye on it?"

The Avari hesitated, and Ander felt like banging his head against a wall.

"As soon as we are done here, go find Marcus. I want him to take a look at that." Ander would prefer to do it himself, but now he couldn't. He made a mental note to confer with Marcus later as Mara finished tying off the bandages around his fingers. There was a disproportionate number of hand and arm injuries amongst this group, he reflected wryly.

"If we could return to the matter at hand?" Siva gently reminded everyone. Ander wondered if she had made the pun on purpose.

Takeshi rubbed his eyes. "So you believe we should be focusing our efforts on finding the Truth Seekers? How do we know they will accept our help? They seemed... more mildly annoyed with our presence at Tilden than anything else. I think they thought we were in their way."

"That does not mean we should not try diplomatic avenues first," Siva said. "Should those avenues fail, then we can reconsider. In the meantime, perhaps you and the Lady could work together to come up with a list of potential locations of interest?"

"The Black Watch keeps a list of known military bases as well," Jeri added. "You could cross-check with what we know." Despite the offer, she sounded unsure.

Takeshi inclined his head in agreement. "Jamirh, did Ryn ever give you the exact location of the base he raided?"

The Avari shrugged. "Not so much in words, but I could point to its rough location on a map, maybe."

"Is this really the right way to go about this?" Jeri asked.

Siva turned to her. "What do you mean?"

The Vampire hesitated. "Bypassing the Watch entirely. We saw what happened the last time we put together a strike team. We are alive only due to Jak's sacrifice."

"You are a member of the Black Watch. We are hardly 'bypassing it entirely,'" Ander pointed out.

"But I am not... I cannot make decisions for the rest of the Watch," Jeri argued. "We should bring the plan to Vlad and Prim. Let them vet it, or at the very least make them aware."

Siva brushed back a lock of orange-pink hair. "Certainly we will ensure Vlad knows what we plan to do, but he does not command us. I do understand though if you feel this puts you in a difficult position." She nodded at the twins and Jamirh. "I appreciate your insight, but participation is completely voluntary. Please do not feel that you must involve yourselves further."

"We're not really sure why we're here at all," one of the twins said, laughing awkwardly.

"Maybe Cap'n should've been here instead?" the other mused.

"Or Ben."

Siva smiled. "By all means, please feel free to share this information with your crew, though you are free to make whatever decision you please."

Jeri made a pained sound. "I will certainly do what I have to in order to ensure the destruction of the bionics, but I do not know that these... backroom deals are the way to go about it."

Takeshi's eyebrows rose. "'Backroom deals'?"

"You are talking about working with Truth Seekers," Jeri said. "A group that has been responsible for the deaths of many Vampires south of the Wall. Believe me, they are aware of us. I do not think working with them is even possible. They have their own agenda, as the Empire found out too late. Who is to say we wouldn't be walking into a trap they laid using Takeshi?" She gestured at the shinobi to emphasize her point. Her voice was getting more and more frantic. "He does not even know what he knows because of them. This whole thing is probably a mistake!" Her eyes settled on Jamirh. "Hell, forget Vampires; do you know how many *Avari* they have killed?"

"She's not wrong," one of the twins said, folding her arms in front of her chest. "The Blind Ones've been a thorn in our side for years."

Her sister nodded. "They're always where ye don't want them."

"They're the boogeymen," Jamirh agreed. "But... everything they did they did on the orders of the military, right? Do we know how they are going to act now that they're their own thing? Don't get me wrong," he hastened to add as Jeri's gaze turned incredulous, "I don't like the idea of working with them. They have a very...

uncomfortable feeling about them, and I don't think that's going to go away. But isn't the enemy of my enemy my friend?"

"Even if we work together to destroy the bionics, it doesn't mean we are going to form lasting diplomatic bonds," Takeshi pointed out. "We merely need to agree on a common goal."

Jeri's face darkened. "I do not think you understand. They are not people, as such. They are one mind filtered through various bodies. They do not think the way we do."

"They don't," Takeshi agreed. "That was made very clear to me. But they do still carry some remnants of individual personality. They discuss among themselves constantly. That wouldn't be the case if they were truly melded into one mind."

Jeri folded her arms in front of her chest. "I am not sure if that is better or worse. Either way, I would be extremely cautious if you are committed to doing this. Don't trust them."

"Don't trust the Truth Seekers; they might lie," Ander chuckled. "That's kind of like us. People think that because the Lady can't lie, we are bound to the truth."

"I would be so dead right now if I couldn't lie," Mara mused. "Many times over."

Jeri shot Ander a disgusted look. "Mock it if you will. But do not say I didn't warn you." She leaned back against the wall, done with the conversation.

Her arm flickered.

Ander fought to hide the wince, glancing around at the others. Maybe no one had noticed? Oh, why did he even care?

Takeshi's eyes were glued to Jeri. "Is your arm okay?"

Jeri froze. "Pardon?"

"Your arm. It almost... wasn't there, for a second," Takeshi said calmly.

"Of course it is here!" She waved her good arm at them.

Takeshi didn't blink. "The other arm."

"That one is here, too," she snapped, waving it towards them as well.

She must have been concentrating very hard because it didn't waver this time, but Takeshi had caught the scent. "That glove looks new. Any reason you are only wearing it on one hand? It must be very thin, to avoid adding bulk like mine do."

Everyone was staring at Jeri now, though Ander had to wonder how Takeshi had noticed that Jeri's "glove" didn't have any thickness to it.

"Why the sudden interest?" she tried to deflect, turning back towards the window.

Takeshi tilted his head slowly, eyes flickering from Jeri to Jamirh, and then back again. Ander wondered what pieces he was putting together. "Ah." At least he didn't seem inclined to share whatever he'd decided, though everyone else was still confused.

It was, perhaps, too much for Jeri though. "If this meeting is adjourned?" she asked Siva.

The Aradian looked around briefly, then nodded. "Yes, I think that is enough for today. Thank you all for coming."

Jeri nodded and took the chance to flee. As she passed by Jamirh, he reached out to stop her. "Wait, I thought maybe we could–" His hand went through her arm.

Everyone froze.

"Rikona has no interest in helping us."

"That's not surprising," Sherri answered her sister as they made their way to the hotel the Truth Seekers had been using for lodging. "But it is unfortunate."

"The current state of affairs suits her well. Should war break out on the continent, it will suit her better," Madine agreed.

Sherri nodded. "She has what she's always wanted. Freedom for Ni Fon. Can't fault her for that, though her support would have been nice. What about Valeth and Merin?"

"They will attempt to remain in Ni Fon for the time being. Better that we have a presence there before we need one, considering the travel time." Just before they entered the hotel, Madine paused. "Gren has returned." Sherri could feel her sister's gaze on her through the blindfold. "You do not mind, that we use you thusly?"

"No," Sherri hastened to reassure her sister. "Not at all. If he's more comfortable dealing with me, then it's no trouble. And it's practice, for after."

Madine's lips twitched into a smile. "We know you will represent us well."

Gren was waiting for them in the nearby park, a large cardboard box sitting next to him on a picnic table. Though he said he trusted the Seekers, he still preferred not to be in enclosed spaces with them. Sherri understood and acquiesced. After all, she was more powerful in natural spaces, though Gren had no way to know that.

And perhaps it was better to keep non-Seekers from the hotel, anyway. Sefera was old and deserved her privacy.

The Avari greeted them with a wave. "Yo!"

Sherri took the lead. "Gren. We did not expect you back so soon."

"Yeah, about that." The Avari hooked a thumb at the box. "I brought some stuff you might be able to use. See, I noticed you guys had a set watch – like, you have actual people out in the woods and stuff."

It wasn't a secret, so Sherri nodded. "We do, yes."

He pulled the flaps of the box apart and started pulling out little round devices. "You can set these things down in their place." He hit a small button, and a little yellow light turned on. He flipped it over and set it on the table, grabbing another device with a screen. "Once it's on, if it detects movement in a hundred-foot radius it'll send the information here, along with a rough image of what's doing the moving and the number of the triggered device."

He handed her the screen. It was dark green, with the silhouettes of her, Madine, and Gren flickering in a bright green each time they moved. "Fascinating. Where did you get these from?"

"Oh, I cobbled them together out of all sorts of stuff. We use them around our base; thought they might help you guys out." He grinned at her.

"You made these?" She inspected it closer. This was good crafts-manship, and complicated work, no matter how he brushed it off.

Madine was holding another one. "What does it actually detect? Would it work on something invisible?"

"Invisible?" Gren raised an eyebrow, but considered the question. "It detects motion. If something couldn't be seen, it wouldn't be able to notice it, but it would detect the movement of things affected by it. You might see a reverse image, or a partial one. It wouldn't work as well, but in theory it would still work."

Madine hummed, putting the device down. "These would be helpful."

"What are you looking for in exchange?" Sherri asked.

"Oh, these are just some extra ones we had lying around. No charge for our new friends." He grinned.

Sherri wasn't sure she believed that, but Madine's whispered thought through her mind confirmed that while they hadn't just been "lying around," they were meant as a gift. "Thank you. Surely we can give something in compensation, though?"

The Avari shook his head. "No, really, we don't need–"

Madine cut him off with a gesture as her head snapped to the left, clearly alerted by something. She stared into the distance for several long moments, both Sherri and Gren watching her. Finally, she turned back to them.

"Duke Stefan Belian of Agale has declared himself Emperor," she said dispassionately. "Duke Johen Cade of the Nyphoren Islands is dead. Dukes Latif Hisham of Cartago-Mir and Mila Hlozer of Elbe have declared war on Belian."

Sherri felt a smile bloom across her face. "So it begins."

# Chapter Seven

---

Jamirh and Jeri were both staring at each other like startled cats, eyes wide and bodies tense. "You... what happened to your arm?" One minute, he'd been wondering if he could convince her to get lunch together or something, talk about whatever was bothering her, the next... his hand had gone through her arm.

His hand had gone through her arm.

How did that even work?! Was her arm not real? But if the arm wasn't real that would mean...

"It's not important." But the words tumbled from her too quickly.

...That would mean she didn't have an arm.

"Is this... is this why you've been avoiding me?" he asked, trying to figure out what was going on. Why didn't Jeri have an arm?

"I haven't been avoiding you," Jeri denied, beginning to look panicked.

"You have been!" Jamirh wasn't having it. "Every time I've seen you since..." His voice trailed off as a sick feeling washed over him.

Ever since Tilden Base.

Jeri took a half-step back, then pushed past him before he could react, fleeing out the door.

Jamirh stood in the stunned silence. He didn't even know what he was feeling. Hurt and upset? Confusion? Concern? Surprise?

Relief that the reason she was avoiding him wasn't him?

Guilt for feeling relief?

Anger?

He glanced around, seeing a mix of expressions – wide eyes, narrowed eyes, piercing eyes, all looking at him. Another feeling rose up.

Embarrassment.

He felt the heat rise to his face as his hand groped for the comfort of his key. "I... um..." He tried to clear his throat of the lump that had formed. "I... I'll just..."

He turned and fled after her, almost tripping down the stairs in his haste.

The evening air hit him as he burst out of the Temple door, cooling his face. He darted around to the side of the Temple and leaned his back against the marble, putting his face in his hands while he tried to sort out... everything now that he no longer had an audience.

Jeri had lost an arm. Probably at Tilden Base. She didn't want him to know about it, apparently.

Why?

He didn't remember much after the Blade shattered, if he were being honest. Being on the base at all had made it difficult to focus, but after seeing Ebryn, after seeing...

...after seeing empty silver–

–after the Blade had shattered, it had been nearly impossible to keep his mind on anything else. He tried to think, but it was all a blur. Knowing the bionics were closing in on them, knowing they had to get out, and knowing they couldn't.

When had Jeri been hurt so badly that she had *lost an arm*?

"Okay," he said out loud, trying to ground himself. Maybe that wasn't the important bit at the moment. No matter how it had happened, Jeri had been avoiding him because it had. That was... hurtful. He'd already acknowledged that, though. One hand dropped down to hold his key again.

She was hurting too, wasn't she?

Connection went both ways. He'd already resolved that he was going to try harder.

He pushed himself off the wall and set out in search of her.

Jamirh found her sitting on the same balcony he had once fled to, staring out over the harbor below. Dusk was just beginning to fall, the sky turning to soft blues and purples, clouds just beginning to gather on the horizon. The city was lit by a soft glow as lights sparked to life one by one. She had her legs drawn up to her chest, her chin resting on her knees, and her arms hugging her legs. Well, her one arm. The other one wasn't real, apparently.

"We just keep messing things up, don't we?" Jeri asked softly.

He took a seat on the bench next to her. "It happened at Tilden Base." It wasn't a question, but he waited for her nod. If felt easier to start here than anywhere else. "When? How on Gaia did we not notice you were *missing an arm?*"

Jeri heaved a sigh, holding her left arm up. Now that Jamirh knew what he was looking for, he could tell it wasn't quite right – the arm wraps and the gloves were too inky black to be fabric, and if he looked closely enough he could see the shift of the shadows that formed them. "Just after the Blade broke. A bionic was bearing down on you, and I had to make a decision. I would make it again," she added defiantly. "But it was also a very bad time to be down an arm. Some Vampires use shadow manipulation to create extra limbs for themselves. My control is... usually very good, so I used shadows to fill in for what was missing."

"That must've hurt, though." Jamirh thought back to when he'd broken his arm. He couldn't imagine having it cut off.

She shrugged. "I am a Vampire. It did not feel good, I can assure you of that, but it was not as debilitating as it would have been to you, or one of the priests. And everyone had enough to deal with as we fled."

"And after?"

The Vampire was silent for several long moments. "I did not want you to blame yourself."

Jamirh felt his eyes sting. "Because you were protecting me."

"Jamirh–"

"I'm tired of everyone treating me like a child," he whispered. "Or like I'm made of glass. I'm supposed to be the reincarnation of the great Avari hero, but..." He trailed off.

She shifted her weight. "You do not like to be reminded of Ebryn. You did not ask to be his reincarnation, and you weren't prepared for what that even meant."

"Yeah, but you can both treat me like Jamirh and like an adult who can make decisions." Not that he had made a lot of decisions for himself since coming here. He'd let other people make decisions for him, then complained about them without actually doing anything about it, content to coast. He'd hoped things would work out for him without doing anything to help himself.

But he had chosen to take up the Blade and learn swordsmanship. And he had chosen to go to the Nyphoren Islands.

"That's true," she agreed. "I would blame it on being a Vampire who is a thousand years older than you, but that would just be an excuse, and not a terribly good one. I am sorry."

"Is that the only reason you were avoiding me?" He wanted to be sure.

She nodded. "For what it's worth, the arm will regenerate over time. Using shadows this way is only temporary, though it will probably take a couple of years. It just... takes a lot of concentration to hold everything in the correct configuration. So it is harder to be around people, because there is always the possibility that I could get distracted." Her arm blurred, shadows writhing in the air before returning to being an arm. "And it is even harder to get them to be solid enough to interact with things. I mostly was not bothering with that."

He frowned. He'd gathered that Takeshi hadn't known, but... "You were doing it all the time?"

"Only Ander knew I had lost it." She sounded miserable. "I did want someone to look at it to make sure it was healing as it should."

Well, at least it hadn't just been him. She'd been keeping the secret from everyone. "Vlad and Prim didn't know?"

"No." She sighed again. "I am going to be in so much trouble when they find out, too."

All because she hadn't wanted to upset him. "I didn't need that, though. I missed you. I wanted my friend."

She stilled. "You had the sisters. You were not alone. I checked in on you when I could."

"And they're great, but they aren't you. I thought you were upset with me because I had broken the Blade, or because of any of the other things that happened at Tilden. Ander and Takeshi were both busy all the time too. It felt like everyone was ignoring me," he confessed. "Like I lost all worth after the Blade broke."

"Don't ever think that. Magic artifacts do not determine our worth, no matter how they came about. Though I thought you would be happy, with the Blade out of your life?" she asked, puzzled.

His ears twitched down. "If you'd asked me before Tilden? Yeah, I would've agreed with that. The symbol of Ebryn finally gone, and me finally set free. But now... I don't know." He tried to gather all his thoughts from the past few weeks into something coherent. "I'm not happy, I can say that much. It doesn't feel anything like how I'd thought it'd feel. I guess... it does feel like a weight's been lifted, but at the same time, I feel even more adrift than before."

They sat in silence for several minutes, staring out over the city below. Jeri tugged on her braid. "You know... you were really great at Tilden."

He blinked. "What?"

She turned to look at him. "That was essentially your first real combat situation, you know?"

"Well, not really." He shook his head. "I had the encounter with the bionic in the palace not that long after the Festival of Night, and you, Hel, and I had that run-in with that Truth Seeker while trying to get to Romanii."

"Those were not real combat situations though. Not like Tilden," she stressed. "You were able to actually defend yourself this time – and you did! All your hard work paid off wonderfully. Not only that, but you also guided us efficiently through the facility, and in such a way that we were not running into bionics every three seconds. Yes, I know the Blade broke," she hastened to say when he opened his mouth to protest, "but that is not your fault. Really, you were doing well up to that point."

That was a lie, and he knew it. "I was a mess," he admitted. "It was hard to focus through that weird awareness of the base Ryn had, and then..." He forced the words out. "Coming face-to-face with Ebryn, and..." He couldn't finish.

But Jeri understood. "It was a bad situation that no one could have foreseen. If you had asked me for a list of things I thought had even the most remote possibility of going wrong, 'Jamirh sees the dismembered body of his predecessor' would not have even crossed my mind."

Jamirh flinched.

Jeri bumped her shoulder up against his. "It is okay to not be okay with that, you know. Put that together with seeing Ebryn – a person we all know you loathe – and the fact that it was your first combat experience, *and* the fact that you had the additional pressure of us relying on you to guide us through the base, and to be perfectly frank you were amazing."

They were remembering those events very differently. "It didn't feel amazing," he muttered, ears sinking.

"Combat rarely 'feels amazing,'" she pointed out. "A lot happens very quickly, and you have to just be able to react and go with whatever happens. Yeah, maybe you needed a little help after seeing Ryn, but that was really beyond what most people have to deal with in those kinds of situations. You just need to be able to push all that stuff aside and deal with it after everything is over. That is also a skill that takes practice. You survived to fight again, and so next time you will do better, but I must stress – *you were amazing*, especially given the situation."

He shuddered, and his hand found his key, gripping it tightly. "I still see him, sometimes."

"Who? Ebryn?"

"No, Ryn." He shook his head, trying not to picture those dead silver eyes, exactly like his own. "I can't look into a mirror without seeing him. He died so horribly. It wasn't fair!"

"Things rarely are," she soothed gently. "And even with that, he still wanted to help you succeed. You did well by him, Jamirh. No matter what happened in the moment, you were able to finish what he started twenty-plus years ago."

"But we didn't," he denied, voice soft. "They are still out there."

"Is that why you are still here?" she asked.

He closed his eyes and took a deep breath. "Everyone leaves eventually," he murmured. "I guess I shouldn't be surprised everyone thinks I'm leaving."

Jeri laughed, but there was little humor in it. "Here? Time might as well be frozen in Tarvishte. The mortals live, and they die, but overall everything remains the same. No one *leaves*, not really. So we don't deal with that well. You leaving would actually be quite the anomaly. But isn't that what you want? To be free of this place, and the burden of Ebryn's promise to Hades?"

That was not something Jamirh had considered. He guessed it made a certain kind of sense. He had even seen the effects of that kind of thinking with how slowly the Vampires had mobilized against the threat of Abomination. But still. "I really wasn't planning to go anywhere."

Her head whipped around to face him. "You weren't?"

"No." He shook his head. "Where would I go?"

She pursed her lips, looking down. "There are a number of Avari groups forming in the Empire. They'll probably form a full-blown rebellion of their own soon enough. You could join them, if you wanted to. I know how you feel about how Avari are treated there. I thought... maybe that you would want to help? Or maybe even go somewhere else entirely, out of the shadow of the Empire and the whole situation."

Avari were going to rebel? That was news to Jamirh. But it did make sense. The Empire was unstable and the Truth Seekers had broken away. If there was ever going to be a time to try to wrest back some power, it was now.

But that wasn't Jamirh's fight right now, was it?

"Maybe after," he murmured.

They sat in silence, both chewing on what they'd learned.

It still hurt, Jamirh decided. Her behavior had hurt both of them. He could acknowledge that.

But they were still friends. She didn't hate him, and that was a relief.

"When you said 'everybody leaves eventually,'" Jeri started slowly, "I did not make it clear, I don't think. But no one wants to just abandon you. Certainly not me or Takeshi. Vlad has supported your independence from the Lady since you arrived; he would hardly kick you out now. You have made a number of friends in the Watch who would be sad to see you go. Frir is an idiot but he means well, and Prim and Elena are both fond of you. You were everyone's favorite sparring partner for a while because of how quickly you adapt. Even Ander would... well, he would probably find your leaving to be 'an unacceptable loss of resources,' but that means a lot coming from him." Her eyes flicked towards him. "I know it is a sad excuse, but really, everyone has been busy. I think most immortals believe things to be more stagnant than they really are. A month passing is no time at all. The citizens of Romanii tolerate this sort of behavior from us because they grow up around Vampires. It did not even occur to me that you would not see it the same way."

Jamirh hummed, staring at a fixed spot on the horizon. More clouds were gathering in the darkening sky. He rubbed at his key. "Sorry, but I've never had anyone stick around. It's just how things are."

"What do you mean?"

"People leave. It isn't something anyone can control; it just happens. When I was about nine, my parents just... didn't come back one day. I never did find out what happened to them. Did they die? Or did they decide they didn't want another mouth to feed?" He shrugged, forcing down the lump in his throat that always formed when he thought about it. "I remember them being kind and loving, but what if that's just a child's memory? A skewed version of events, true only because I want it to be?"

"I..." She didn't seem to know what to say.

He refused to look at her. He didn't want to see the pity that was sure to be there. "No one else stuck around, either. Avari go missing. Who's going to look for them? Better to think that maybe they just decided to leave. Aether... Aether stuck around the longest, other than my parents." His fist tightened around the key, the teeth digging into his palm.

"Aether?" she prompted when he fell silent.

"Yeah." He managed to quirk a weak smile, remembering the periwinkle-haired Avari. "The two of us worked together to survive for years. I was good at pickpocketing, but Aether was able to convince people to give us stuff just by looking pathetic and begging. We had it pretty good for a while. It was always kind of odd how successful he was." Jamirh frowned as a thought occurred to him. "That was probably some sort of inherent, wasn't it?"

"That is certainly possible," Jeri conceded. "Though it is difficult to know for sure without talking to him."

"He died in a building collapse a few years back," Jamirh admitted, aiming for a disinterested tone. He didn't think he was succeeding. "There had been a lot of collapses, and... well." He looked down at the old brass key. He'd found Aether's body amid the flurry of people trying to find survivors. He'd barely had time to take the key before the Truth Seekers raided the area. He didn't remember a whole lot about the following days, hiding in the ruins of their home. "This was his. He told me that one day we'd have a proper home – one with a door that locked. This was our reminder of what we were working towards."

Green eyes studied the key and she bit her lip. "They did not want to leave you, Jamirh," Jeri said softly after a moment.

"Doesn't mean they didn't," he forced out past the pain in his throat. It was a long time ago. There wasn't any reason to be upset about it now. It was in the past.

He did not need his eyes to be acting up right now. Angrily he willed the gathering tears away.

"I'm still here," she added after a moment. "I have survived this" – she waved her shadow arm in his direction – "and can survive much, much worse. In all honesty, Jamirh, chances are pretty good I'll outlive you by hundreds, if not thousands of years. And I have no intention of abandoning you to be on your own." She paused. "I'm sorry if it came across that way."

Jamirh said nothing, still trying to get himself under control. He clutched the key tightly to his chest. How had this conversation flipped to her trying to comfort him?

"But... death is a part of life. Not even Vampires are immune from it, though the Lady's gift buys us more time than we might have had otherwise." Jeri heaved a sigh. "I've never thought of those who died as leaving me, I suppose. As a Vampire, I've had many, many friends die over the centuries. But they remain with me, in here." She placed a hand over her heart. "They are only ever a memory away. It's not the same as being able to speak to them, or hear them, but they are never truly gone, either."

He wasn't sure he agreed with that. The dead *were* gone.

Except... Ryn hadn't been gone, had he? Ebryn had been kicking around too.

But that wasn't the same!

Why was everything so complicated?

Jeri unfolded from her position and rose in one smooth motion, startling Jamirh. "Come with me," she declared. "I have something for you."

He stood and turned to follow her, throwing one last glance over his shoulder at the gathering storm on the horizon.

Jamirh had never been to this part of the palace before. He hadn't realized there was so much underground. Though if they hadn't gone down at least seven flights of stairs he wouldn't know it – the hallways were brightly lit, the walls plastered the same as above, and burgundy rugs covered the warm hardwood floors.

"What, did you think it would be dimly lit stone? We have to live down here," Jeri snorted when he asked her about it. "Might as well be the same as above."

They came to a door nearly identical to his own, with a small brass plaque numbered "-431." Jeri unlocked it and ushered him inside.

The apartment was a lot like his own, with plush couches and chairs and delicate wooden furniture, even though the color scheme was yellows and pale greens instead of his own reds and blacks. Instead of windows, the far wall had giant paintings showing a hillside in spring, framed by gossamer curtains.

Oh, he realized belatedly. These were Jeri's rooms.

He wandered over to the paintings as she disappeared into her bedroom, catching a glimpse of a pale-yellow coffin set into a dais as she returned. She held out a bundle of wrapped cloth, about a foot in length. "Here it is." She pressed it into his hands.

It was heavier than he expected. Carefully, he unwrapped it.

It was a set of four daggers. Six-inch blades with simple black hilts, sheathed in plain black leather with steel tips. Subdued but deadly elegance. Jamirh's mouth fell open. "What...?"

"I had these commissioned before you started using the Blade," she admitted. "You were doing so well learning how to use daggers. And you were excited! I wanted you to have something that was yours, in a way the Blade was not."

He touched an edge; it was very, very sharp. But since he had started training with Takeshi, they had let his dagger training fall by the wayside. And since they'd returned from the Nyphoren *all* of his training had been neglected. He'd never had the chance to consciously put his inherent ability as a Master of Blades to the test with daggers. He looked up at Jeri.

She smiled faintly. "Would you like to try them out?"

He began to nod, but then felt his ears sink as he caught sight of Jeri's arm.

She scoffed, catching his gaze. "It held against the bionics; I think it will hold against *you*," she teased.

Not even ten minutes later found them in a private room at the training grounds, squaring off against each other. Jeri had forged her soul crystal into a pair of daggers instead of her usual cutlasses, and to Jamirh's eye it didn't look like she was having any problem holding them.

She didn't ask if he was ready.

It was completely unlike their prior training. This time, she wasn't holding back. Slash, duck, attack, block. Jamirh felt himself shift into the strange awareness his inherent gave him while fighting and met her strike for strike. A deadly dance of metal and bodies. Swing and roll; an opening there– throw! He drew another dagger as she recovered from her dodge, and they met again with the shriek of metal on metal.

And as they moved, he watched, and he learned, and he absorbed.

Finally they called a draw. Jamirh wheezed from where he lay on the ground, collapsed in a puddle of exhaustion. It had been too long since he'd exerted himself that much. Jeri was out of breath too but standing, eyes filled with an emotion Jamirh couldn't quite name.

"This whole Tilden situation... it has not been handled well by any stretch of the imagination," she said, grabbing a water bottle and tossing it at him.

"Not by anyone," he agreed, though he wasn't sure why she was bringing it up again, or why now.

"We have all been struggling alone," she mused. "I withdrew because of my arm, Ander disappeared in his lab for almost a month and collapsed. Takeshi looks stressed every time I see him. Mara looks done with everyone. I honestly did think you were doing better than us because you had Salisha and Desha with you most of the time, and you seemed to be doing a bunch of fun things together."

He smiled faintly. "They've been great, but... it wasn't the same." He felt bad saying it, because they'd tried so hard, but it was true. "And they're pirates – it won't be long before the *Sea Spirit* leaves to go do pirate things."

"Maybe they also needed a break after Tilden," Jeri suggested.

"Yeah, maybe." He considered that. The pirates did seem to be enjoying themselves in Tarvishte. Maybe... maybe they'd stick around a little longer?

And what about him?

"I've never really known what I was doing with myself," he admitted, propping himself up off the floor. "Ever since Hel broke me out of that cell I've been coasting, letting others make the decisions for me. I don't like having to put too much thought into stuff, you know?"

Her eyebrows rose. "I think you made it pretty clear you did not want to have anything to do with Ebryn."

"And what did I end up doing? The same shit they wanted me to do anyway." He snorted. "And where did that get me? A shattered magical artifact and weird magic wounds. Great." He pulled his thoughts together, feeling more and more sure about them as he continued. "Everyone's been so sure I was going to leave, but I think I need to stop listening to what other people want for me – or what they think I want – and start trying to figure out what I really want for myself." He thought about Ryn – not the corpse from the base, but his earnest enthusiasm and surety about himself. It was something Jamirh had envied.

"No one wants you to leave," Jeri hastened to reassure him, tugging on her braid as she shifted her weight.

"No, no, that's not what I meant." He shook his head, trying to sort through the mess of his thoughts. Takeshi and Ryn had both told him that if he were going to fight, it should be because he felt a responsibility to help others. He'd thought he'd been doing that by going with them to Tilden, but he'd just been compromising on what he wanted by still going along with Ebryn's oath. In the end, he'd still felt beholden to the situation he'd found himself in.

But the Blade was gone now. The choice... really was his, wasn't it?

"I think... I think Siva is right. Something needs to be done about the bionics."

Because he'd thought he would feel set free, but all he felt was dread every time he remembered they were still out there. He glanced down at his hand and the angry red lines. Wasn't it odd, that he'd been harmed more by the sword he was supposed to wield than the things trying to kill him? And even with that, some part of him screamed that the bionics could not be allowed to continue.

"I'm going to fight, Jeri. I'm going to help destroy the bionics."

There was grim understanding in her eyes, though the tilt of her mouth said she didn't like it. Still, she nodded.

Then her brows furrowed as she stared at his arm.

"Uh, Jamirh? Were the wounds from the Blade *glowing* before?"

# Chapter Eight

"Has it done this before?" Ander asked, both fascinated and alarmed at the faint red glow coming off Jamirh's wounds.

The Avari shook his head. "Nope. Definitely not. I'd have noticed if my arm was glowing."

Maybe, maybe not. Ander wasn't certain how observant the Avari actually was. He considered the problem as he studied the wounds. Besides the glow, they didn't look any different than they had earlier. "And it doesn't hurt?"

"Not at all."

"Odd." Ander didn't like it. He ran a hand over the lines, casting a diagnostic spell as he did so. The green runes that followed indicated healing as normal, which it most certainly was not. Or maybe it was, and there was something else happening that they were missing? He scowled at the wounds, willing them to reveal their secrets.

Marcus snorted from where he was leaning against the counter taking notes. "That is one way to put it," the dark-haired Vampire said with a smile at Jamirh, whose ears twitched upward slightly as he shifted on the exam table.

Ander snorted. "I assume it wasn't doing this when you removed the stitches?"

"No." If the Vampire was offended by the question, he didn't show it. "The cuts are certainly healing slower than expected, but they have not shown any abnormal activity that I'm aware of until now."

"I swear it wasn't doing this before!" Jamirh shuddered as he glanced down at his hand.

"It could have done this before without your knowledge," Ander pointed out. "It's quite late. Perhaps it only does it at night?"

Jamirh stared at him, ears flat. "I've been awake past sunset many times since we returned from Tilden."

Ander waved a hand dismissively. "I said late, not after dark."

"It is quite late," Marcus agreed, shooting a glance at Jeri, who was leaning against the wall, arms folded. The blonde had come with Jamirh to the hospital but kept out of the way.

She shrugged in response to Marcus' challenge. "We were training."

Ander cursed his injured fingers as he groped around a cupboard for the supplies he needed for a blood sample. "At" – he glanced at the clock hanging on the wall – "one thirty in the morning?"

"We started earlier," she said, unconcerned.

Ander suppressed a sigh. While many in Romanii kept all sorts of hours due to the Vampires, he didn't think that included Jamirh, who kept a diurnal schedule.

*:You are not actually criticizing someone else's sleep schedule right now, are you? Certainly not after the last few weeks of trying to get by on less than an hour of rest a day.:*

He ignored Her. He refused to let Her make him feel bad for doing what he had to.

*:What happened to your hands?:* Marcus asked silently, eyebrows furrowing as he took in the bandages. He stepped over to help.

*:An incident with a tea cup. Unrelated to everything else,:* he added, disliking how everyone was keeping a close eye on his actions. Honestly, it was one misjudged variable. It wouldn't happen again. *:You'll have to draw, though,:* he admitted. *:It would be folly for me to attempt it with my dexterity hampered by the bandages.:*

The Vampire inclined his head as he pulled out the last few items. "Jamirh, I am just going to do a quick blood sample."

"Do you have to?" The Avari's ears sank as he leaned back slightly.

"Well, at this point we need to start ruling things out." Ander leaned back against the counter, mirroring Jeri's posture. At least both his arms were real. Actually, maybe it was a good sign Jeri and Jamirh had come in together? Considering how she had fled earlier in the day. Something must have happened between them in the meantime to smooth things out. Maybe they'd been fighting it out. "Marcus will be able to ascertain a lot of information from your blood."

Jamirh flinched, and Marcus hesitated. Ander recalled that the last time he had drawn blood from Jamirh he had needed Jitsu to be practically sitting on the Avari. That tactic wasn't going to work this time. Unless... He eyed Jeri speculatively.

*:No.:* The Lady's voice was firm.

"Have you done this before?" Marcus was asking gently.

Silver eyes darted in Ander's direction. "Once."

Marcus nodded. "Good! Would you prefer I walk you through it, or have Jeri distract you? I will be quick, I promise."

The Avari shuddered. "Maybe have Jeri distract me? I don't know."

The Vampire in question pushed herself from the wall and came to stand closer to Jamirh. "We can talk about something unrelated. Here, keep your attention on me, and ignore Marcus for the moment."

"Talk about what?" Jamirh reflexively glanced in Marcus' direction as the Vampire approached, but he just gave Jamirh a reassuring smile.

Jeri hummed. "How are Salisha and Desha doing?"

Ander immediately tuned out of that conversation, keeping an eye instead on what Marcus was doing. Not that Marcus wasn't an extremely accomplished healer in his own right, but Ander liked to be the one in charge. He considered the problem as he watched. The wounds had been caused by the shards of the Crystal Light Blade after it had shattered due to prolonged contact with tech. He knew there was no trace of the Blade left in Jamirh; he had been very thorough when he had provided the initial care. But the Blade had also been a unique magical artifact. There was no precedent for this kind of wound, no example Ander could point to for reference. Diagnostics were showing that there was nothing wrong, even though there was clearly something that wasn't right.

Maybe the presence of tech had caused something to go haywire?

*:The Blade contained high levels of concentrated elemental magic,:* the Lady observed as Marcus finished up. *:That alone could cause*

*problems. Mortal compositions can be easily disrupted with that level of influence.:*

Ander paused, then scanned the injuries for magic. Nothing. Except... that the wounds were glowing. How were they glowing if magic *wasn't* involved? There was absolutely no biological reason for Avari to glow at all, unless Jamirh was somehow part glow-fish. Was Jamirh part glow-fish?

*:I do wish you would get more sleep.:*

Probably not, then. But then why wasn't anything triggering? How was there a visible magical effect without the presence of magic? It was almost like...

Something was shielding.

Struck by the thought, he reached out to Marcus. *:Take a second sample, directly from the wound.:*

*:What?:* The Vampire glanced in his direction, curious.

He didn't know how to explain. *:A hunch.:*

Marcus hesitated but picked up a second vial, murmuring to Jamirh that it would be just a bit longer.

Ander was frowning as he glared at the offending arm. He didn't like this.

In the back of his mind, the Lady was watching, thoughtful. *:The Blade was never meant to shatter like that. This was never a possibility I considered.:*

*:Yes, well, tech does that to magic, unfortunately.:* If only they could understand why the two things were so antithetical to each other, then maybe they could understand the different interactions the two forces had when they came into contact. As it was, they just had to try different things and see what worked without knowledge of

the underlying principles that *must* be governing those interactions. There could not be a *truly* chaotic relationship between the two. Those did not exist. There was always an explanation, even if people didn't yet understand it.

Something to work on in the coming centuries. Luckily, he had time.

Marcus was drinking the first sample. *:I am not getting anything abnormal from this, either. He is in good health, obvious exception aside.:* The Vampire took a sip from the second sample.

Without wasting a single second, he turned and spat it out in the sink.

Ander straightened up in alarm, and Jamirh and Jeri fell silent as they stared at Marcus, who was rinsing his mouth out. That was not a normal reaction to a Vampire tasting blood. They only ever spat it out if it was harmful to them, and due to the magic that created them not much was. The maladies they could taste in mortal blood just were not a threat to them. Some even *liked* the taste of various illnesses or issues.

The Vampire took a moment before turning back around, expression impressively calm. "I have discovered either the cause or another symptom. More testing will be necessary to discover which it is. But those wounds are *flooded* with elemental magic right now." He looked to Ander with a frown. "You guessed."

"There is a visible magical effect," he pointed out, indicating the red glow. "Somehow magic must be involved."

Jeri was staring at Jamirh's arm in confusion. "I am not sensing any magic. It was the first thing I did, when we noticed it was glowing."

"Because it's the obvious conclusion," Ander agreed. "But we were too quick to rule it out."

"That much magic should be easily sensed." Marcus took another sip of water. "It is not a surprise to me that the effect is visible."

Ander considered the wounds. "Why red? The color of magic usually indicates the caster, but in this case it's likely caused by the magic of the Blade, which included four different elemental magics. So shouldn't the glow match the multi-colored light of the Blade?"

"We would need a magicolor specialist who had studied the Blade to determine if the shade of red is the exact color of the Blade's fire magic," Jeri pointed out.

Hades hummed. *:It is the color of my siblings' power.:*

"Hades says it is the Faleri's magic, so at least we can rule out a third party. But then... is the glow the shield? Or is it the magic being shielded against?" Ander frowned.

"Why would the Faleri be shielding it?" Jamirh asked, brow furrowed as his ears twitched.

"That is the far less likely answer, but then it begs the question – why doesn't the shield itself have color? Is the glow merely the magic that is seeping through the shield? That would be bad; Avari constitution handles magic overflow better than Humans do, but there's still a limit before it starts to negatively affect the body."

Jamirh blanched. "The magic is poisoning me? Or could be?"

Ander gave a single decisive shake of his head. "Don't be ridiculous. Magic isn't poison; it just... *is*. Poisons are chemical reactions. This is a magical one."

If anything, Jamirh's ears sank lower, and he rested a hand against his chest. "So... it's a magical poison? Is that worse? It sounds worse."

"Well, it's not doing anything right now." Ander rubbed at his scar. "We'd have been able to sense it." *Was* it a magical version of poison? That was interesting to consider, but impossible to prove while the effect remained shielded.

What was doing the shielding? Or who?

Marcus started putting supplies away. "The analogy may track, though. If the problem is an overabundance of magic, perhaps we need to find a way to drain it, similar to the way poison can be drawn from a wound."

"Ander is correct, though. Magic does not act in a way similar to poison. Not usually, anyway." Jeri shrugged as she laid a hand on Jamirh's shoulder. "How would one even begin to conceive of cleansing a wound of magic?"

"Using magic would be the logical answer, but it also seems counter-intuitive," Ander agreed. "Yet..."

"If the magic was introduced to his system via broken shards of the Blade, then perhaps it is more like venom than poison?" Jeri asked thoughtfully. "In which case, usually an antivenom is used, though what we would use for anti... magic..." She trailed off.

Ander could feel Hades' horror at the thought as he considered that.

"I do not believe we should go there," Marcus said with an awkward laugh after a moment.

It did seem unwise, and yet... it was an interesting thought.

:*Absolutely not.*:

Ander shook his head. Maybe the Lady was right about him needing more sleep. "There's no way to even know where to begin with something like that. Regardless, the magic isn't spreading right now due to the shield. And though elemental magic in high concentrations can be dangerous, the shield seems to be preventing any of the expected side effects of that, too. The most immediate problem is that without knowing its source, there's no way to know how long the shield can hold." He frowned at the red glow. Something was fighting it. But what? Jamirh's own body? That didn't make a whole lot of sense either. Jamirh didn't have magic of his own. Well, he was alive, so he had magic in that sense. But that sort of magic was passive, a proof of existence. It wasn't *usable* magic. If the body's ambient magic could contain magical overload like this they would have seen it in others before now.

So then what was shielding?

Ander sighed. "But as of now, that shield is buying us time. Jamirh, Marcus and I will look into possible methods of treatment." He met Marcus' eyes as the Vampire nodded in agreement. "In the meantime, you are to watch those wounds *very* carefully. If there is any change at all – how it looks, how it feels, *anything* – you are to come find either me or Marcus immediately. Is that clear?"

Jamirh nodded, ears still wilted and eyes glued to his arm. "Should I, like... I don't know, cover it, or something?"

"You can, if the glow bothers you, but I would check it often." Ander shrugged.

"The wounds may look nasty but they are not open," Marcus added. "They do not need to be covered anymore. At this point I think it is safe to say that the scarring is permanent; it should improve with time but the marks will not fade entirely. It is the magic that needs to be dealt with."

Jamirh slowly got off the table, clearly favoring his right arm.

Ander fought not to sigh. "You don't need to treat it like glass; just be aware of any changes."

Jeri shot him a sharp look as Jamirh's ears somehow wilted even further. "No one really understands what is going on with his arm; it makes sense he would want to be careful. You don't have to be rude about it."

Ander nearly threw his hands up in disgust. He wasn't being rude; he was stating facts. Whatever. His eyes caught on Jeri's arm; the shadows looked solid enough at the moment. He found himself eyeing the stump.

*:It is fine,:* Jeri sent quickly. *:You do not need to worry about it.:*

Okay then, he wouldn't. He stepped aside so they could leave, sweeping an arm towards the door.

Jeri scowled at him as she passed by for reasons he couldn't even begin to fathom, but Jamirh paused, hand hovering over the old key he wore under his shirt, and Ander squashed the part of him that wanted to touch his *crystallus* in the same way. The Avari looked up at him. "There's really nothing you can do?"

Had... had Jamirh been paying attention at all? "Not at the moment, no."

Hades nudged him mentally.

Ander sighed and added, "But I will be looking into it."

Jamirh looked down, biting his lip, then nodded. "Okay. Thanks."

Ander watched them go, feeling tired in a way that had nothing to do with physical exhaustion. Why did things always have to be difficult? Why did people have to be difficult?

Alice had never–

He wrenched his mind away from the thought, glancing down at his bandaged hands. Hades had no right to bring up Alice like that. He had no desire to dredge up old wounds, and yet she was closer to the surface now than she had been in decades. It was useless to dwell on it. He turned back to the room to collect his notes, only to find Marcus watching him. "What?" he snapped, not in the mood for more prying.

Why couldn't people leave him alone?

Marcus tilted his head slightly. "I wanted to apologize for waking you, but I thought you would be the best to consult, given the nature of his wounds."

Ander blinked. "Hm? Oh, that's..." He sighed, shaking his head. "You were correct to do so. I wasn't sleeping anyway."

Marcus raised an eyebrow. "I know for a fact you were told to get more sleep. If I were you I would do so, if only because of your current housemates."

Ander felt the fight go out of him. Marcus didn't deserve his ire, and he wasn't wrong about Ander's living situation, either. "I wasn't asleep, but I wasn't working, either. It's not so easy to just... shut down, after so long working. They don't understand. There was too much to do already, and now this on top of it..."

Marcus hummed. "The ladies have your best interests at heart. No one wants to see you work yourself into the ground."

"If they had my best interests in mind at all, Mara wouldn't be cooking," Ander muttered. "She doesn't even have to – we could get food delivered by the palace – but she's doing it anyway." Something about how home-cooked food was better? Ander didn't believe that for a second when Mara was the one doing the cooking, but Siva seemed to agree.

And he refused to cook for them.

"I have never had Lady Mara's cooking, but I *have* heard stories," Marcus mused as they left the room. "I believe it was described as 'dangerously exotic'?"

"That is... no. No, it's inedible," Ander corrected. "There is really no other way to put it. I don't even know how she manages to... ah, it doesn't matter."

"You could always go to the palace and get food there?" They paused outside Marcus' office.

Ander had already considered that. "There's no way to do so without hurting Mara's feelings."

"Oh." Both Marcus' eyebrows raised. "Does she not know her cooking could... use work?"

Ander shrugged, looking away. He had no idea how one would navigate that conversation, so he avoided it at all costs. He owed Mara too much for that.

"Ah, well, it could be worse," Marcus offered with a laugh. "Lady Daiyu could be present as well."

Ander shuddered. There was nothing more dangerous than a triad of witches. He ignored Hades' exasperation. "Thankfully she is not."

Marcus placed a hand on Ander's shoulder. "Most things pass with time. This will as well. Just hang in there. If the ladies get to be too much and you need somewhere to hide, you can use my office."

Ander smiled faintly. "They will always know where I am, but thank you for the offer."

They said their goodbyes, and Ander headed back to the hospital's main entrance, trying to think on what exactly could be causing the glow–

*:Beloved.:*

He suppressed a sigh. Or not.

*:Everyone truly does have your best interests in mind. No one wants you to be unwell.:*

*:And yet...:* He trailed off, not sure how to put it.

*:You feel trapped.:*

Yes, that felt accurate.

Hades was silent as he finally exited the hospital. The sky was full of clouds. There was a chill in the air, and the scent of rain, but the threatening storm hadn't broken yet. The trees and bushes were mostly recovered from their winter hibernation. He turned down the path that led to the Temple, but found himself hesitating.

*:Why not take a walk? You have not been outside in a while.:*

*:I had to go outside to get here,:* he pointed out, confused.

*:Correct. I mean you haven't spent a period of time outside in a while.:*

It would mean delaying returning to the Temple. He wasn't tired and had no interest in resting, which was what Siva was going to insist he do, and it made the alternative tempting. It wasn't as though he would be alone – Vampires would be out and about – but the gardens would be fairly quiet.

He turned in that direction, striding purposefully down the well-lit paths as he tried to return his attention to the newest problem at hand. His mind, however, did not wish to cooperate, instead jumping from topic to topic in a completely useless fashion. It was all too much, now. Where was his focus best placed? What was the correct path that would move them all forward? All he could see was a jumbled mess of strings that trailed off into a haze.

He didn't like being so uncertain. It reminded him of Alice's illness, and long, sleepless nights trying to find a cure, grasping at any opportunity that presented itself.

Magic had been the solution to that problem. He doubted it would work the same way for the current situation.

He found himself pausing beside an ash tree, not really wanting to remember, but–

"Ander?"

He startled, whipping around to see Takeshi standing a few feet away. Exasperated, he reached out to Hades.

*:I in no way even remotely suggested that he come here, or take a walk, or even leave his rooms,:* She said, equally exasperated. *:Coincidences* do *happen.:*

Not often, in his experience, but they were here now. "Takeshi."

The shinobi inclined his head. "What drives you to the gardens at two-thirty in the morning?"

Two-thirty in the morning? Was it really that late? "Everything," he answered, deciding that summed it up succinctly. "And yourself?"

Takeshi blinked slowly. "'Everything' is a decent enough answer for me as well."

"Ah." Ander looked around, but the white warg was nowhere in sight. "Where is your furry companion?"

"Sniffing something interesting, probably, or gossiping with the others. Though she often attempts to match my sleep patterns, I've noticed that wargs as a species seem to be around at all times. Did they evolve to be ideal companions for Vampires?"

"I'm not sure." Ander frowned. It was a good question. Certainly both species belonged to the Lady in some capacity, but did they mirror each other because of that, or by coincidence? "I haven't spent much time researching the wargs."

Takeshi shrugged. "Maybe I should? Though there is apparently something happening right now that I'm not allowed to know about just yet."

Ander was immediately alarmed. That sounded like trouble. "What? How do you know?"

"Jitsu will not tell me, just that I should wait until May."

Wait until–? Oh. Ander felt himself relax. That was normal. "Would you like to be informed?"

A single black eyebrow arched, and even though the face was masked Ander could tell Takeshi was studying him. "Should I be? Is it dangerous?"

Ander shrugged. "I usually like to know things, but no. It is not dangerous."

Takeshi hummed, but after a few moments said, "I think my knowing what it is would crush Jitsu. I will wait."

"As you wish." Ander did not understand why the warg's opinion mattered so much that Takeshi would deny himself knowledge, but then...

*"Vater, how did you get your scar?"*

*"I got it defending a kitten from a dragon."*

It wasn't so different, was it?

No, it was *completely* different. Those two situations did not correlate. What on Gaia was wrong with him tonight, that even the most tenuous connection would remind him of her? He rubbed at his scar.

"Are you all right?"

Ander realized he was scowling at the ash tree and tried to wipe the expression off his face. "I'm fine. Are you?" he snapped, annoyed all over again.

"Not really, no."

Ander found himself off-balance again, and he blinked at Takeshi, unsure how to proceed. No one answered that question with "no." It almost wasn't even a real question in his experience.

Luckily Takeshi wasn't as stunned as Ander. "It's this whole soulforging thing. I've been trying to summon my soul crystal for more than a few moments for months now, with absolutely no progress. How can that be? I have never struggled with anything magically oriented in this way before." The shinobi put his hands on his hips as he too glared at the ash tree. "And then there's the World Sound..."

Ander knew he didn't understand most people, but he did understand frustration. He hadn't realized it was upsetting Takeshi this badly to not be able to soulforge. Hell, when he'd originally suggested it Takeshi hadn't even seemed interested. What had changed?

What to even say that hadn't already been said? It would happen in time. Eventually something... would...

"When you were working with Jamirh to access his inherent, you said he needed to have a different angle of thought, didn't you?" Ander asked slowly.

Takeshi blinked. "I... yes?"

"What if this is similar?" Ander wondered, trying to work the problem through. "Jamirh didn't even believe magic existed, so he needed to open his mind to a different reality, if you will."

"But Jamirh *had* been using his inherent; he just wasn't aware he was doing so," Takeshi interrupted. "I don't believe it is possible for me to have been summoning my soul crystal unawares."

"No, of course not," Ander agreed, spinning on his heel and beginning to pace back and forth in front of the ash tree. "But you said that you've never struggled with magic in such a way before. But this isn't like learned magic. It's closer to inherent magic, but it's not that, either. It's not really magic at all the way we conceive of it. It's just a willing of effect."

Takeshi stared at him. "You are talking about... a Living Will?"

Ander could understand his disbelief. A Living Will was all but a myth – a person able to cast spells without actually casting, just by willing the world to do as they bade. "No, no, of course not. Could you imagine if the entire Vampire race were Living Wills? And I am certainly not able to cast in that way, though I can soulforge. But that is more the – to borrow your own words – 'angle of thought' required to utilize one's soul crystal."

"Not to cast, but to... *will* the crystal to do as I wish." Takeshi said the words slowly. "All magic involves will, or intent, if you'd rather, to cast. I am unsure how that could be any different to what I've been doing. Believe me, the intent has been there."

Ander tried to think back to what he'd seen of Takeshi's previous attempts. "Will is intent, yes, but it is more than that, too." He twisted a hand in the air and studied his own soul crystal. It shimmered placidly above his hand, pearlescent green. What *did* he do to summon it? How strange, to be able to do a thing but not understand the how.

Takeshi took a step closer, then paused. "May I?"

Ander shrugged. "You cannot harm it." He gestured, and it floated over to Takeshi. An odd feeling of detachment settled over Ander even though the distance was barely even a few feet.

"It would be ideal if I could achieve this before we go hunting the remaining Abominations," Takeshi mused. The shinobi's eyes flickered towards Ander. "Will you be aiding us?"

"No, I don't believe so. Not from the field, anyway." He'd had more than enough of that to last several lifetimes. "I think it's been more than proven that my talents would be better put to use here." He drifted over to the ash tree, looking up into its branches as he rubbed at the scar on his face.

"Do you really think so?"

Ander raised an eyebrow, turning back to Takeshi, who was staring intently at the soul crystal.

"Jamirh is correct. Your presence saved us when the Blade shattered." Dark eyes met green. "I could not have cast such a shield, and even if I could have, I would have been unable to maintain it long enough to matter."

Something about that made Ander distinctly uncomfortable, and he dismissed his soul crystal. "It would have been fine. Jak probably would have stepped in sooner." He looked away.

"Perhaps, perhaps not. The series of events we actually lived through involved you saving our lives, though. I'm not sure why you seem to think you wouldn't be welcome on any team with abilities like that." Takeshi shook his head. "But I will meditate on what you've said about soulforging. I am uncertain that I will be able to trick myself the way I tricked Jamirh, but anything is worth trying at this point. Good night, Ander."

The white warg materialized from the gathering mist and padded over to her Human, barely glancing Ander's way.

"Good night." He raised a hand in farewell and watched the shinobi walk back towards the palace.

Maybe it was the night, maybe it was the ash tree – Lady knew he'd been all but drowning in memories today anyway – but something about Takeshi suddenly reminded Ander of Fredrik.

The thought struck him as immediately ridiculous. Takeshi wasn't anything like Fredrik. Physically, they were almost complete opposites, Fredrik's wavy blond hair and blue eyes nothing like Takeshi's straight black hair and dark eyes. As far as magical ability and work ethic? Fredrik had none, whereas they seemed to govern Takeshi's life. Fredrik would have been all over the pirate women, but Takeshi had shown only disinterest. It would almost make more sense if Takeshi reminded him of Ida, with his quiet demeanor and foreign origin, but...

Still. Something about Takeshi reminded Ander of Fredrik.

Ander did not like remembering Elbe, and the people he had left behind there three hundred years ago.

But... what was the similarity?

Ander shook his head, deciding that maybe he *did* need sleep, and headed down the path that would return him to the Temple as the first drops of rain began to fall.

On his way, he reviewed the conversation and was struck by a thought. *:You were oddly silent through all that. Nothing to add?:*

A gentle feeling of a hug. *:The two of you seem to be managing just fine. Perhaps you can help each other?:*

Ander found himself chewing over that until sleep finally claimed him.

# Chapter Nine

---

Takeshi was just beginning his morning meditation when Hades hummed softly in his mind to grab his attention. *:Vlad has called an emergency meeting.:*

He unfolded himself from the couch, patting Jitsu's head when it popped up hopefully. *:What has happened?:*

*:They've just received word – Stefan Belian has declared himself Emperor, and two of the other dukes have declared war on him. Some in the Empire knew yesterday afternoon, but it broke to the public at large this morning.:*

Takeshi paused with his hand on the doorknob, then shook his head and headed for the council chamber, Jitsu beside him. *:I see.:*

It was earlier than had been expected, but not completely surprising. Duke Belian was one of the Empress's greatest political rivals, and they'd often tried to outdo each other. With the Empress finally claiming her rightful title to the public at large, perhaps Belian had decided he also deserved a crown. How unfortunate for him the other dukes disagreed. Though... only two? He wondered which ones. He couldn't see Duchess Strom of the Emerald Shores caring, and he assumed she would also be declaring her independence shortly. Duke Cade usually went along with the majority, despite the fact the Nyphoren Islands were also insulated by distance from the mainland. The remaining four usually presented a united front. What could have broken it? Just the fact Belian declared himself Emperor? If anything, that was the most obvious choice since Belian led Agale, and he would have assumed the four mainland dukes would have decided on that together.

*:Duke Hisham and Duchess Hlozer are the ones who have declared war. Duke Cade is being reported as dead.:*

"Being reported as dead"? Was he or wasn't he? But then, maybe it didn't matter. If it was made to look like Belian killed him, that could have been too much for the others. Though Duchess Leblanc seemed to be standing by him.

Takeshi had never liked the complicated web of power and the politics that arose from it. No one could be trusted, even if you thought they were your staunchest ally. He almost wished they could return to the days when if you disagreed with someone you just stabbed them and were done with it instead of playing these games.

He'd have made a terrible emperor for Ni Fon. Ni Fon loved those games.

The council room was packed full of people, many Takeshi didn't even know. He supposed war breaking out on your border would cause some degree of panic, but then, wouldn't the Wall prevent Romanii from being affected by it? That had been his assumption, but maybe it was wrong.

Jitsu opted to stay outside the room, and Takeshi slipped in alone.

Vlad was at the head of the table, deep in discussion with a Vampire Takeshi didn't recognize. Elena, the chief logistics officer in the

Watch, was speaking quietly to Jeri and Frir nearby. All members of Vlad's high council were present, and Takeshi recognized two guild leaders as well. Primrose was sitting next to Vlad. Siva had a tray of cups full of a reddish clear liquid she was delivering to those gathered; she smiled in greeting as she passed one to Takeshi.

He pulled down his mask and tasted it, pleased to discover it was the same tea she had served yesterday. The warmth helped ward off the chill he felt despite the number of people in the room.

He found a small section of wall to lean against as the meeting was called to order. Extra chairs had been brought in, but Takeshi was not the only one left standing. He listened with half an ear as Prim explained the situation at hand, scanning the crowd for red hair and frowning when he didn't see it. Then again, this meeting was centered around Romanii's security, so maybe it was acceptable to leave Jamirh out of this one? And Ander wasn't here either, though that was almost certainly for the best. They'd both been up very late the night before, and Ander needed rest. The man did not seem as well as he was pretending to be.

After Prim was finished, multiple people asked to be heard at once, and Takeshi was reminded of public council meetings in Ni Fon. He shook his head. People were concerned, and that was understandable.

But that made him think of Hotaru, and he felt a pang of sadness. What would she have done in this situation?

He was struck by a sudden mental image of those sharp gray eyes glaring at him fiercely. She wouldn't appreciate him ruminating over his loss. She'd have wanted him to move on, to live in the present.

Despite the warmth of the tea, he felt a shiver go through him, and he adjusted the blue scarf around his neck.

As the questions began to veer towards how this would affect the economy, he started reviewing the Truth Seeker memories he had of the bases they had marked for destruction. He could recall eight distinct targets. For a place the size of the Empire, that was a very focused operation, but then if making the bionics was as difficult as Ander said then it made sense. They wouldn't want to waste resources over-producing the parts. Or maybe there were other factories, and the Truth Seeker memories he had just didn't involve them. That was as likely as anything else.

Still, at least this could give them somewhere to start. War being declared in the Empire would be helpful in some ways and would complicate things in others. Regardless, it would be best to deal with the threat now, while there was confusion and uncertainty. Waiting for the Empire to re-stabilize would be a mistake.

Takeshi stared down into his cup, focusing on the warmth seeping through his gloves as he toyed with the idea of contacting the Seekers and just... *asking* which base had originally housed the bionic production. Would they answer him? Or would that be opening the door to other problems?

It was probably for the best that they hold off on that for now. While the Truth Seekers did loathe Abomination and were – from what he could tell – dedicated to destroying it, that did not necessarily mean they would be allies.

And the more he thought about it, the more it bothered him. Everything the Seekers did was meticulously planned out in layers. While they had ostensibly wanted him to see the death of the Emperor, was that really the *only* reason they had shared their mind with his? He didn't think they had wanted him to join them, which was what most of the others seemed to fear, but then... what other reasons did they have? Had they wanted him to see them targeting the bases? Why?

"Are you getting anything out of this?"

The quiet whisper so close to him startled Takeshi, and he nearly jumped out of his skin. He looked down to see Jamirh sitting against the wall next to him, arms resting on his knees in front of him and holding an empty tea cup loosely by the handle. The Avari's right hand was wrapped in bandages that disappeared under the arm of his black coat.

He blinked, trying to regather his thoughts. Jamirh *was* here. How had Takeshi missed that? And how had he gotten so close without Takeshi noticing? The Avari was more stealthy than some shinobi Takeshi knew.

He checked the conversation – now discussing impacts on trade – and shrugged to cover his surprise. "Not a lot, no."

Jamirh scowled at the crowd. "How is anything supposed to get done?"

Takeshi shrugged. "This is how countries are run."

The Avari's scowl deepened, ears flattening. Then he abruptly stood, putting a hand on Takeshi's arm and tugging him towards the door.

Takeshi found himself surprised yet again, and allowed himself to be pulled. On their way out he caught Siva's eye as they dropped their cups off at the door. *:I'm being kidnapped.:*

The Aradian's lips twitched as her gaze flickered to Jamirh. *:I will let you know if you miss anything important.:*

Excellent, though based on the way the meeting was going it did not seem likely either Jamirh or Takeshi would be of vital importance to it. He wondered what Jamirh wanted, though.

The Avari opened one of the large double doors to the room soundlessly and slipped through, waiting for Takeshi to follow before closing it just as quietly.

Jitsu padded over and bumped her head into his chest. The meeting wasn't done. Were they escaping?

*:That does seem to be the case.:*

Jamirh shuddered. "Okay, that was terrible. How many of those things have you gone to?"

"More than I'd like, though I've been more directly involved in most of the other recent meetings," Takeshi admitted. "That one does not seem to be... immediately relevant to the bionic situation, however."

The Avari nodded decisively. "Okay then. We need to figure out where the base is that Ryn... that Ryn died in." He winced.

Takeshi raised an eyebrow as he gestured for Jamirh to follow him. Interesting. This was definitely a shift in attitude. "How are you hoping to determine which base it is?"

"I'm, ah, actually not sure." The Avari laughed awkwardly, glancing back over his shoulder. "But anything's better than whatever that was. You said the Seekers were targeting some of the bases though, right?"

Takeshi hummed in agreement, leading them to one of the palace's many exits. He sighed at the deluge happening outside, but there was nothing to be done about that. At least both he and Jamirh were wearing coats, though he was already regretting this.

"I thought... maybe we could look at a map together, and see if anything stands out? Like, even just marking down possibilities is something." The Avari's ears flattened as they stepped out into the rain.

It was as cold as Takeshi had feared. "You still have not been able to communicate with Ryn, then?"

Jamirh shook his head. "Nope. Still complete silence. From Ebryn, too. I wish... I just wish I knew why."

Takeshi could sympathize with the frustration. He'd been feeling very frustrated himself lately. Perhaps working on this would be a good break from all the other things that weren't working. Mentally he nudged Hades.

*:I do not know why they have fallen silent.:*

"Hades doesn't know why either," he reported. "I can't even hazard a guess. I've never looked into anything having to do with reincarnation before." Maybe something to look into at a later date if he was going to be a priest of the goddess of death.

Jamirh shrugged. "It's fine, I guess. Ebryn being silent is no great loss, I just wonder if Ryn is okay. Or if I did something." He looked around as they passed through one of Tarvishte's market squares. "Where are we going?"

Takeshi nodded towards the ocean, visible up ahead through the buildings of Tarvishte. "To the *Sea Spirit.*"

"Here it is!"

Takeshi looked over from where he was drying himself off with a towel as Don flicked a switch, causing little holographic buildings to appear over the map of Gallia they had laid out over the table in the mess. They were all situated close together in the center of the province.

"Oh, wait, hold on a second," the youngest member of the crew muttered, fiddling with the device he had hung on the light. He pulled at the rope it was hanging from to raise it up, and the bases spread themselves out. "There we go, now the dots are lining up. These are the right spots."

Takeshi noted that all the towns and cities on the map now had little markers above them. Other places not marked on the map had pins as well.

"Wow, how does this work?" Jamirh asked, leaning in and poking at one of the little buildings. The blue light it was made of flickered. "How does it know where they are? This reminds me of the map Ander made once. Except that one was made of water."

"It's not a live feed or anything," Don explained, leaning on the table with both hands. "This little projector is something I bought a while back while at, ah..." He trailed off, glancing at Benjen, who was sitting on the other side of the table.

The first mate raised an eyebrow.

"Well, doesn't really matter, right?" Don laughed awkwardly, looking away. "It's technically a bit of salvage. Old, out of use as far as the Empire's concerned. They've got way better models now. But they show up every now and then, and I collect them. The tech in them is useful, yeah, but I like t' see the history, ye know? How things change over time and all that."

"How does this help us?" Takeshi asked. It was a little more detailed than the map on the table, but not by a lot.

"Oh, yeah. Let me just…" Don reached down and pulled out a small black box with colorful wires sticking out of it. He opened the side of the projector and started pulling wires out.

The image flickered and died.

"Shouldn't you attempt to do that while the projector is off?" Benjen asked with a wince.

"Nah, this is fine!" A pair of wires were connected between the two boxes, and with a shower of sparks the map flickered back to life.

Jamirh took a hasty step back, ears flicking down.

"Sorry, sorry! It's fine now." Don took the black box and pressed a button, causing a hidden lid to spring open, revealing a keyboard. He started typing. "We can use this t' filter the pins."

The vast majority of the markers disappeared, leaving nine on the map.

"Aha!" Don's face lit up in a grin. "There we go; those are the military bases that existed when this projector was made a couple of decades ago."

Takeshi frowned. "How does it know that?"

"Oh, this is a computer we took off one of the navy ships while we were engaging them off the coast of Crescent." Don indicated the black box. "The projector is cross-checking with the records in the computer."

Takeshi stared. "You stole things off the ships you were engaged in combat with?"

"Miss Mara was extremely helpful," Benjen said blandly. "Also – pirates."

Takeshi decided he didn't want to know.

Jamirh was nodding like that made sense. "Cool. All right then, there are these nine bases. Or there were." He paused, tilting his head to the side. "Which one was used...?"

They all stared at the map.

Well, we can eliminate the Charve base," Takeshi said slowly, shifting to get a better look. "That one has already been wrecked by Hades."

*:Don't sell yourself short – you helped!:* The goddess's tone was pleased. *And yes, there was no Abomination being created there.:*

"Huh, I think I can..." Don tapped on the little keyboard, and the marker above Charve winked out. "Yup, there we go."

A blonde head poked up from the stairwell. "Oh, what's going on up here?"

Takeshi stifled a flinch as Salisha and Desha made their way up. This was a common area; it wasn't as though they could be denied access. But still. Sometimes their presence made these things just a little bit harder.

Maybe that wasn't fair of him. They had been helpful in the raid on the Crescent Island base.

"The wizard and Jamirh be here!" One sister skipped over to the table, leaning over the map, while the other darted over to where Jitsu was lying next to the window. "And Jitsu!"

"Aw, did ye really brave the rain t' visit us?"

"How sweet!"

Takeshi frowned as Don explained. Jamirh got a name. Why did Jamirh get a name? He thought they came up with nicknames for everybody. Well, everyone not on the crew. And Jitsu. And Mara. Had they given Jeri a nickname? Or Ander?

Was it just him?

"Does that computer have a record o' any attacks on any o' these bases?" one of the sisters was asking.

Don shrugged. "If it did, I would need a lot more time to figure out how to access it."

Takeshi returned his attention to the map, trying to see if any of it triggered anything familiar from the Truth Seeker memories, but it was becoming harder and harder to remember them as time went by. Which was probably good for the sake of his mind, but not helpful at the moment. He glanced at Jamirh, but the Avari's face was scrunched up as he stared at the map. Probably nothing was coming from there either then. Oh well. It had been an idea.

"I wish I could see what the bases actually look like," Jamirh said. "I saw… flashes. Nothing clear, nothing concrete. Actually I mostly saw…" His voice trailed off, and he shuddered. "It was like the bionics, but not… not exactly the same. It's hard to pinpoint what's different, though."

"Probably an unrefined bionic, not yet at the form they are now," Takeshi reasoned. "And it is hard to sift through someone else's memories." He was having similar problems, after all.

"It's more like my memory of what he showed me, but I don't think he wanted me to see all that much." Jamirh frowned harder as his ears sank. "I wish I had thought to ask."

"Come on, now," the sister by the table said, gently bumping Jamirh's shoulder. "Ye had no way t' know that information'd be needed later."

"Yeah, don't be too hard on yerself," said the one petting Jitsu.

Jamirh sighed, rubbing at the old key he wore with his bandaged hand. Takeshi wondered absently if the wounds had gotten worse; it hadn't been wrapped like that yesterday.

Before he could ask, Jamirh went still, then his ears began to perk up. "Wait. Wait, maybe..." The Avari squinted at the map. "It's this one," he said, pointing to a marker about halfway between the Wall and the coast, a little northwest of Charve.

Takeshi blinked.

"That's sudden," Benjen observed, coming around the table to look at the indicated base. "Etroy Base. Are you sure that's the one?"

Jamirh nodded, eyes glued to the map. "Yes. That's it. That's where... where Ryn died."

"How do ye know?" The sister petting Jitsu got up and walked over to the table, to Jitsu's displeasure.

Jamirh bit his lip. "I don't... I don't know. But it *is* that one. I'm sure of it." He looked up at Takeshi. "It's like... looking at the memory of a memory of a map. He must have planned his attack at some point, had to have looked at a map, even if only to get there."

Takeshi nodded slowly as Hades hummed softly in the back of his mind. :*Some bleed-over of memory would be... expected, since he has made contact with the previous shard of himself before.*:

:*Shard?*: Takeshi asked. That sounded like a strange way to describe it. Like Jamirh wasn't whole, but fractured into different personalities.

The Lady took a moment before answering. *:No, Jamirh is a full being. A shard isn't a piece of a whole, it is just... an expression of a whole. I have many shards, for example. I am not split into many pieces, I am still cognizant of each shard and I am still each shard, but each is also a slightly different expression of myself.:*

That didn't make a whole lot of sense to Takeshi, but he could try to untangle it later. "We have a target, then." He considered the map. "We should strike as soon as possible. Do we know if that base is in active use? Don, you said this map was older?"

"The projector the map is stored in is older, yeah," he confirmed. "I'm not sure if it's in active use now, though. And something else t' consider – I've been able t' patch into the military communications with this thing every so often." He patted the stolen computer. "Signal's not great, and I don't get more than a few transmissions at a go, but there have been several reported attacks on Empire bases that I've heard chatter about."

"The Seekers," Takeshi murmured, staring at the map.

Hades shifted, and he was surprised to feel unease from her. *:It would be wise to check this one out regardless, I believe.:*

Well, that settled that.

Benjen cleared his throat. "Not to discount this mission, but what about the Nifoni?"

Jitsu heaved herself up and padded over to Takeshi, feeling his distress even though he was trying to hide it. She shoved her head into his side as she tried to wrap herself around him.

He petted her, thankful for the momentary distraction as he gathered his thoughts. He didn't like thinking about the microchip that had been embedded in his spine at the order of his Empress, and he didn't like how cold he felt whenever he did think of it. "Currently, it's something we are aware of, but the Lady has requested we focus here for now."

*:It could change, but... there did seem to be a sudden decrease in Abomination around there about a month ago. It is... very difficult to tell where it is located, but... it does feel like what is left is not that far from Romanii.:*

Takeshi thought about that. If she was really everywhere at the same time, then maybe locational confusion was to be expected. "After we can confirm this location is clear, we can check with her again."

A sudden decrease in Abomination. Was the Empress covering her tracks? How would she even know?

One problem at a time.

He waved off the offer to stay for dinner, though Jamirh accepted with a hopeful gleam in his eyes. Takeshi could understand – Caron's cooking was excellent – but he wanted to check in on how the other meeting was progressing and let Siva know what they had discovered. And while he could reach out and do so mentally, he would rather report in person.

They had a lot to do.

He said his goodbyes and thanked them for their help before heading out on deck, feeling a brief pang of regret about the weather. He liked watching storms; he didn't like to be in them. Before he took more than a step onto the gangplank, however, he was stopped by a voice from behind.

"Oh, by the way, wizard."

He turned to see the twins hovering in the doorway to the mess.

The one on the left grinned. "The humming is nice."

"Wonder what yer singing voice sounds like," the other said, singsong.

"If it's really good maybe we'll start calling you bard!" They giggled, waving and disappearing into the ship as he stared after them.

When the hell had he been humming?

Muriz was a flurry of activity.

Now that war was a reality, time was running out. They had to hit Etroy quickly, or it would become far more difficult to do what needed to be done. The base had a skeleton staff at the moment, but that would change soon.

Sherri shared Gren's uncertainty about why it was so imperative that Etroy be destroyed, even though she had more context. Sure, it was the last remaining place that had plans for the bionics, but with all the other factories having been destroyed no one would be able to create more for a long time. The Seekers were working hard to track down and destroy the remaining bionics as well.

It was not without cost.

Sherri's mouth thinned as Madine reported another three Seeker deaths. "Would it not be better to just leave the remaining ones alone?"

Her sister shook her head. "Their very presence is... staining the world. I know you could sense that something was wrong with them, but you cannot *see* it the way we can. This sacrifice is necessary to bring the world back into balance."

Sherri just shook her head. Sometimes she wondered how her sister perceived the world. It seemed very strange, and the Seekers themselves did not seem to know how to explain it any better. Even Sefera would just smile if asked.

"Bring what back into balance?"

Sherri turned to see Gren holding a large box full of the sensors he had offered them.

"The world," Madine said succinctly.

"Ah, okay, then." He gave them an uncertain look when neither explained any further. "The world, got it. Where do you want these?"

"I will take them," Madine said, stepping forward.

"You sure? The box is heavy; I don't mind carrying them a little farther." Gren frowned.

Madine paused and tilted her head ever so slightly. Sherri pressed her lips together to keep from laughing herself; Madine was more than capable of carrying a box. "Do not trouble yourself," Madine finally answered, taking the box from the Avari.

Sherri glanced at how full it was and wondered if he'd planned to give the sensors to them ahead of time. Surely he hadn't made all of those in one day?

"Can do," he said with a shrug.

They watched Madine go.

"How long before y'all are ready to head out?" he asked after a moment. "I've sent word to my headquarters; everything should be ready by the time we get there."

Sherri considered. "It'll be two or three days at least. The Seekers are preparing to completely destroy that base; your people had better be quick going in and grabbing what you want."

"All we need is an hour, tops," he said with a grin. "We appreciate the opportunity. No need to get in your way." The grin faded. "Why are you with them, if you don't mind me asking? Seems a little strange for a regular Human to be hanging out with Seekers. Not that it's a problem or anything," he added quickly. "I'm just curious."

She decided to be honest. "Madine is my sister."

"Oh." He placed a hand on her shoulder. "I get it. Family's the most important thing we got. I don't know what I'd do without my little sister." His face grew thoughtful. "I never really thought about it before. Seekers having families, I mean."

It made sense Avari wouldn't know. They were never selected to be Seekers. "They are taken from their families at a young age. Most die young; I don't think I've ever heard of them getting married or having children."

"Damn. The old order really was intent on screwing everyone over," he muttered. "Was that what she meant by bringing the world back into balance?"

It was as good a lie as any. "Yes."

He'd find out about magic somehow, but it wouldn't be from her.

# Chapter Ten

---

"**I** cannot believe you got invited to an important meeting and you just *left*!"

Jamirh shrugged, stuffing the rest of his corn muffin in his mouth.

Jeri's cranberry muffin was still untouched on her plate as she gestured wildly. "There were so many important people there, and I know you don't like how people equate you with Ebryn, but because of that people noticed that *you left*!"

He chewed slowly, savoring the taste. The muffins at this café were really good. Maybe he should get another one? They had a lot of flavors. Then again, it was hard to beat a good corn muffin.

"And you took Takeshi with you!"

He swallowed the rest of it and took a sip of his coffee. "Look, I want to know what's going on, but when they start mentioning taxes I'm out."

"But–"

"But nothing. What did any of that have to do with me? Or the bionics?" He frowned, looking down at his arm. "Besides, Takeshi and I figured out what base we should be investigating. That's got to count for something, right?"

She just stared at him for a moment, then dropped her head onto her folded arms.

"Besides, when I got the invite I was told I could go if I wanted to, not that I had to. Vlad didn't seem that upset."

"Vlad probably wishes you took him instead of Takeshi." She heaved a sigh, then sat up again. "Are you ready to go?"

He nodded, wondering if she wished he had taken her too. "It's not like we are supposed to pack or anything, right? Just a bag like last time?"

"Oh." She blinked at him. "No, I meant... are you *ready*? To go do it again?"

He looked away. It was a good question. Did he even know the answer? "I think I have to be," he said finally. "We can't really wait."

"No, but you could stay here," she said slowly. "There is nothing that says you have to go."

She didn't say it, but the words "the Blade is broken" hung in the air between them anyway.

He tried to squash the hurt that caused. She didn't mean it that way.

And...

...for just a moment, he saw Ryn's severed head floating in that tank, and his stomach rolled. He clenched his right hand into a fist, creasing the bandages wrapped around it. "It has to end," he said quietly. "I have to see it through."

How many others would suffer through that horrific process if it was allowed to continue?

She made a soft sound, but he couldn't tell if it was in agreement or not. Too bad, she would have to deal with his decision.

"How is the arm doing, then?"

He latched on to the change in topic with relief, though... "No change. It's still glowing. I don't think it's any brighter, but I've also been keeping it wrapped most of the time to avoid looking like a bionic myself."

She cringed. "Don't even joke about that, please."

He shrugged. "What else glows red like this? And, like... it *looks* nasty. Mean. Evil."

"It's pure elemental fire magic." She leaned back in her chair, folding her arms. "And many mages have magic in the red range. Vlad's magic is wine-red, Siva's magic is orange-red. There's nothing about the color that is inherently evil."

He eyed her doubtfully. "You can't possibly think this" – he waved his arm at her – "looks fine."

"Well, no," she conceded. "But that's because it is affecting your arm, not because it is magic. What about spell crystals? A lot of those are red." She paused, a strange look coming over her face.

Jamirh wasn't sure he liked that. "What?"

"Have you tried casting using the arm?" she asked after a moment.

He stared at her. "Have I tried– no. No I haven't. I wouldn't even know where to begin!"

"But what if you could use it like a spell crystal? It would even have the benefit of using up the magic that is infecting you." She was looking at his arm with an almost uncomfortable intensity now. "We should try this."

"Jeri, it took me forever to figure out how to use my inherent; I don't think–"

"Come on, let's go to the training grounds! Good thing we are leaving tomorrow; that gives us a little time to experiment."

He found himself staring down a training dummy in the salle in a private training room a short time later, despite his protests and without a second muffin. He felt his ears sink. "What, exactly, do you expect me to do?"

She hummed thoughtfully. "We can start by unwrapping the arm," she suggested.

He sighed but obeyed. His nose scrunched up involuntarily at the sight of the unnatural glowing lines etched into his skin. It was bad enough before they started glowing; why did he have such terrible luck?

"Okay," she murmured, studying the arm intently. "Glyphs are usually important for this kind of magic. Are any of the marks roughly glyph-shaped?"

"How would I know?" he asked, exasperated. "Wait, you don't even know this kind of magic! Your magic is inherent like mine!"

"That does not mean we are not on to something." She placed her hands on her hips and glared at the wounds as though they were personally offending her. "Try to throw a fireball or something at the target."

"How would I even–"

There was a knock on the door.

They blinked at each other, then Jeri went to answer it.

"My apologies for interrupting, but I was looking for Jamirh and was pointed in this direction." Violet flames tinged with gold burned merrily at him as Siva stepped into the room. "Are you training?"

He looked at the second High Priest of Hades in confusion. What did she want with him? "Not really," he said, ignoring Jeri's betrayed look. "What did you need?"

She frowned as her eyes caught on his arm. "That looks like the magic of the Faleri."

"It is. Ander thinks it's from the remains of the Blade," he explained. Then an idea struck him. "Hey, is there anything you could do about this? The Faleri created the Aradians, right?"

She smiled at him wryly. "True, but I follow a different deity." Still, she came over and studied the glowing marks. "How odd. It doesn't read as magic to me."

A thoughtful look came over Jeri's face. "Jamirh, I will be back in a few minutes." She waved as she darted out the door without waiting for a response.

Jamirh just shook his head as Siva continued to study the wounds. "Has Ander seen this?" she asked.

"Yes. I'm just supposed to keep an eye on it for now."

"Hmm." She took a step back. "Interesting. But I wished to speak with you for a different reason. I must admit it is convenient you are here."

He blinked. "Oh?"

She brushed a strand of pinkish-orange hair that had escaped from its loose braid behind an ear. "I would like to request a bout."

Jamirh shifted, feeling uneasy. "You would?"

She nodded. "You are a Master of Blades, but from my understanding, you are a new Master of Blades. I am interested to know... how your ability is coming along. And the best way to know this is to fight."

That all made sense, but there was something about the way she had hesitated in the middle that made Jamirh doubt it was the whole truth.

But she was also an Aradian. That probably meant a different style, and Takeshi had suggested he learn as many of those as he could. And he was curious. How would she fight? She was wearing heavy skirts; he had to think that would make it really hard to move around.

And besides, he wanted to get more practice in with the daggers anyway.

"Sure," he said, rolling his shoulders to loosen up. "Did you want to use practice weapons or real ones?"

She tilted her head. "Would you be opposed to my using soul-forged weaponry?"

He shook his head. "Jeri has practiced with me before like that."

She nodded. "So be it." She glanced around. "Is this an acceptable location, or would you prefer one of the outdoor rooms?"

"Oh, no, this is fine." He indicated his arm. "Trying not to spread the knowledge of this around too much. People already have enough reasons to think I'm something I'm not."

"Understandable," she said easily. "Have you ever worked against magic?"

Magic? "No, we've only used weapons. Since the bionics don't use magic, it didn't seem that important." But the idea was interesting. "What did you have in mind, though? Does my inherent even work against magic?"

Siva smiled and nodded. "While you will not learn any spells used against you, you will find that you develop ways of dealing with mages that are... not immediately apparent. It is simply another skill to learn, after all, and that is where Masters of Blades excel. But we need not attempt it if you have not progressed to that point yet."

He shrugged. It sounded like it was worth a try. "No idea if I've progressed to that level yet, but I'm not against trying it."

She raised an eyebrow, and the flames in her eyes flickered briefly. "If you'd like. I won't do anything excessive."

He took a few steps away, pulling his daggers from their sheaths. "Okay then. Uh... whenever you're ready, I guess."

If she was disappointed to see the daggers instead of a longsword, she didn't show it. Instead, she held her hand out to the side, and a flash of red threads formed the shape of a spear.

Hm. Jamirh hadn't fought against spears before, either. The reach could be a problem.

Then she charged forward.

Jamirh skipped back, taken aback by the speed. He knocked the spear aside and tried to step forward, but she spun in a strange way, and–

Oh. He should not have underestimated the dress.

It was actually made of four distinct panels, and when she spun the embroidery created a strange optical illusion that made it difficult to focus on her. They also were not moving the way fabric should move, flicking this way and that; he was certain she was controlling them with magic. He dodged another thrust of the spear and struck out at a panel, unsurprised when the fabric repelled his dagger like steel would.

Damn.

Well, he'd said magic was okay. Time to figure out how to deal with it.

He ducked away and down before dancing back, hoping to gain a moment to strategize, but she wasn't interested in letting him do so and followed aggressively with another spin. He blinked his eyes to try to clear them of the dizzying pattern, dropping and rolling past her to escape for a moment, but she stayed with him easily, and he found himself in a losing defensive position as she began to push him back again with quick jabs and sweeps.

If the spear's reach was long, though, and the daggers' reach was short...

He dodged forward, almost into her strike, trying to get into her reach. He twisted and brought his daggers up–

Only to be repelled by a shower of red sparks as the spear transformed into a scimitar.

A brutal push sent him spinning away, and the scimitar transformed back into a spear.

She didn't press her advantage, though, and he took a moment to catch his breath as he glared at the weapon.

She laughed, but it wasn't unkind. "It was a good attempt," she offered.

He shook his head and darted back in.

The sword had taken him by surprise, but he knew how to deal with swords.

She spun and stepped back, ceding ground, and he pushed forward. Trying to ignore the patterns of her skirts was difficult, but not impossible, and he wondered if she could make that much worse by layering illusions over them. In fact, considering her age and position, it was very likely she wasn't fighting at her full potential. Like how Ander had toyed with him that first time, though at least she was being more polite about it.

But Jamirh had come a long way since the match with Ander. And the longer a fight went on, the more he learned.

So he withdrew a bit, letting her take the offense. He focused on dodging, blocking only when he had to. His stamina wasn't infinite, but the more he learned of her style, the better off he would be.

He wondered what she was getting out of this.

After a few minutes of this, she frowned, and he darted forward with an attack. He didn't want her analyzing what he was doing too closely. He had to remember that she had fought other Masters of Blades before; the ability was most common among Aradians.

And she was old enough to have known Ebryn.

Was that what this was about?

He found himself twisting back and forth to avoid a flurry of quick jabs, and–

Opportunity!

He spun into a kick, putting as much force into it as he could. The spear was ripped from her grasp and clattered to the floor. He brought his daggers up–

And found himself dodging the stream of fire almost before his brain registered what was happening.

They spun apart. "Hold!" he called, needing to process that.

She dropped out of the defensive stance she had taken, her skirts falling around her like normal fabric as the spear re-materialized in her hand. "Are you okay?" she asked, concern clear in her voice.

"Did you just *breathe fire* at me?!" he asked, aghast.

She blinked, then smiled. "There's some debate over whether or not it is technically *breathing* fire, but that is the effect, yes."

He stared at her. "Can *all* Aradians do that?"

She hummed, shifting her weight so she was leaning on her spear. "It is an advanced technique to do that specifically, but every Aradian can call fire if they wish." She held out her other hand, and a ball of fire bloomed into existence above it. "We are truly the children of the Faleri."

That made sense, but... "Jeri!" he shouted as the Vampire slipped back into the room, holding a brown bag and looking between the two of them in confusion. "She breathed fire at me!"

Jeri looked at Siva, who nodded. "Oh. Did you try to shoot any fireballs at her?"

He'd almost forgotten the reason they had come here in the first place.

Siva's eyebrows furrowed as she looked back at Jamirh. "Do you have fire magic yourself?"

"No," he said with a sigh. At least the adrenaline was fading. "It's this." He held up his arm.

"Since it is the Faleri's magic that is visible, we thought that perhaps he would be able to use it," Jeri explained.

"No, *you* thought that was possible," he corrected.

"Oh, I see. That would make a certain amount of sense, I suppose, but I am uncertain how he would be able to cast without being a learned mage," Siva mused. Her spear dissolved into red threads that faded into the air. "To my knowledge, Ebryn did not have such an ability, so I do not believe Jamirh would."

Jamirh was reminded of his thought from earlier. "Did you know Ebryn? You were around then, right?"

But she shook her head. "I never met with him, no. He did spend a little time in Dalmara while earning the Crystal Light of Fire, but I was not present at the time. I did know Sukra, however, and–"

She stopped abruptly as they all stared at Jamirh's arm. The glow had flickered violently, fading to almost nothing before coming back bright as the sun, then returning to its original soft glow.

"Has it done that before?" Jeri asked, concern clear on her face after a moment.

Jamirh shook his head. "No, no, that was new." And he didn't like it. Why did everything have to be so weird? "It didn't hurt or anything, at least."

"We should let Ander know," Jeri said slowly. "He wanted to know if anything changed."

"Well, it's back to what it was now," Jamirh said with a frown. His left hand found his key, rubbing it comfortingly. What was going on with his arm?

"He is on his way," Siva said, stepping forward to examine his arm more closely. "I did pick up the feel of magic for just a second when it flickered. Very strong fire magic. Strong enough that I should still be able to feel it."

Jamirh frowned. "I didn't feel anything different at all."

Siva carefully took his arm in her hands, running her fingers over the glowing lines. Orangey-red glyphs were left in her wake, but the red glow of the wounds did not react at all. It reminded him of what Ander had done the other night. "Can you feel that?"

"Just feels normal," he admitted.

"I wonder what triggered it?" Jeri craned her head to see what Siva was doing.

"I don't think it was our match; it was a little too delayed for that," Siva murmured.

Jamirh felt his ears droop. "I was just standing there. I wasn't doing anything."

"It is not necessarily something you did," Jeri offered reassuringly. "Magic can have all sorts of odd triggers."

Siva frowned. "But if we don't know what's triggering it, is it wise for Jamirh to leave Tarvishte tomorrow?"

Jamirh flinched. "It's not doing anything but glowing. It didn't affect my ability to fight; you saw that."

"True. But a glowing magical effect..."

Jeri cleared her throat. "Actually, I have already thought of that." She held up the brown bag she had come in with. "Jamirh, this is for you."

Siva stepped back to let him take the bag. He frowned at Jeri. "You don't need to keep getting me stuff."

She folded her arms and cocked a hip. "You are about to go into a literal war zone to find and hopefully destroy Abomination. You *need* stuff. Proper equipment is a necessity."

Well, when put like that it made sense, but... "You shouldn't be spending so much money on me."

She blinked at him, and some of the attitude slipped away. "Oh. Don't worry about that, honestly. I don't spend a lot generally, and all of this has been well within my means."

He sighed and decided to pursue that later. He reached into the bag. "Arm guards?"

They were black leather with subtle detailing. Metal plates painted matte black were attached to the top. There was a pair of black fingerless gloves with them, also with plates to protect the back of the hand.

Jeri nodded. "Functional to protect your arms and also to prevent you from lighting up the night."

"Wow." He ran his fingers over the supple leather. "Thank you."

"Very practical," Siva agreed, "but that wasn't the entirety of my concern."

Ander swept into the room, white coat flaring dramatically behind him. "What's going on?"

Jamirh resigned himself to being poked and prodded even more.

Later that night Jamirh was finally able to escape to his rooms. Ander had determined that whatever had happened, it hadn't changed anything he could sense. And while he agreed that he would rather Jamirh stay in Tarvishte where he could keep an eye on it, he also didn't think it was grounds to forcefully keep Jamirh here if he really wanted to go.

"For all we know it could be a permanent effect," he'd pointed out. "As long as it's not causing any actual decay of the tissue or actively poisoning his system, it should be fine."

Ander had seemed very distracted, in Jamirh's opinion. He had a feeling he was getting off easy.

But Jeri had also agreed that Jamirh should be able to go if he wished, and so Jamirh found himself released to go get a good night's rest, arm freshly wrapped so the glow wouldn't bother him.

He checked his pack, leaning against the corner of the couch. A change of clothes, a few cereal bars, his daggers. The new coat Hel had given him was draped over the arm of the couch. He also had the spell crystal Jak had given him. A neat bit of illusion magic, wearing it would turn his hair orange.

He never intended to go into the Empire ever again without wearing it.

He frowned, thinking of Jak. Jak, who was now a crystal statue in Hel's temple. Another casualty of this craziness.

If he had been better sooner, would it have mattered? Could he have prevented it if he'd known what he was doing earlier? If he'd wanted to help earlier?

Would his arm forever be a reminder of his hesitance?

He bit his lip. He wished he were still able to talk to Ryn. Ryn had had good advice the few times they'd been able to talk.

A glint caught his eye, and he realized the corner of the mirror over the side table was peeking out from the sheet he'd thrown over it. He cringed. He still couldn't look in a mirror without seeing–

But what if that was the answer? He'd spoken to Ryn in the mirror before, right?

He gripped his key tightly. He didn't want to look, but... if there was a chance...

He looked away. Or he could just... not.

"Ryn?" he asked aloud, hoping against all hope that there would be an answer.

Silence.

"Ryn? Are you there?"

It felt really stupid to be talking to an empty room.

"Where did you go?" he whispered sadly, clutching his key tight. "Ebryn?"

Still no answer, though at least he hadn't really expected one from the Avari hero. Still, an answer would have been preferable to silence.

He looked at the covered mirror again and swallowed hard.

He could try it. Just a little peek, right? If they weren't there he could cover it again.

Slowly, he made his way over to the mirror. He'd tucked the sheet around it at the top and let the rest of it hang, so it would be easy to just reach out and lift the sheet. Very easy, in fact. Which was why he was standing in front of it doing nothing.

This was ridiculous. It was a *mirror*. Nothing in it was real.

Right hand clenched around his key so tight he could feel the teeth biting into the fresh bandages, he reached out with his left and gently lifted the corner of the sheet.

His own frightened reflection looked back at him, an eerie red glow just barely seeping from the wrappings around his arm.

But then his vision swam, and it was Ryn's severed head, floating in that tank.

It's not real, he told himself as his heartbeat began to race. It's gone. It was destroyed along with the rest of Tilden Base.

"Ryn?" he asked quietly.

But all he could see was that lifeless, empty gaze that looked so much like his own. That *was* his own.

No!

It was just a memory. It wasn't the same.

He threw the sheet back over the mirror and cried.

# Chapter Eleven

"Y ou're not going to come to the train station to see us off?"

Ander sighed. All he wanted to do was finish his coffee in peace. "No."

"Mara..." Siva tried to interject gently.

But the water witch was not interested in what Ander wanted. "Come on! It won't take that long and you have nothing better to do anyway. In fact, it is the *least* you could do since you're not coming with us!"

Ander failed to see what one had to do with the other. "I'm saying goodbye to you here. Why do I need to go to the train station?"

Mara pouted, folding her arms. "Us, sure. But what about the others? Takeshi? Jamirh? Jeri? The pirates?"

The pirates? They were getting involved with this now? Why? The target was nowhere near water. "I really don't see the need for long, drawn-out farewells. If Takeshi needs me, he can reach me through Hades. I very much doubt my presence will be missed by the others." He took a sip of coffee and flicked open the morning paper.

"*Ander.*" She drew his name out in an exasperated sigh. "Of course they'd like to see you before they go!"

He stared at her, silent.

"Okay, I think we need to go now," Siva said dryly, trying to usher Mara out of the kitchen. "We don't want to be late and miss the train."

Right. Because without Jak, they would have to take a train to Braila. It would take two days. That was Ander's fault, too. He was negatively affecting the mission and he wasn't even going on it.

"But–"

"Ander is an adult," Siva reminded her, "and can make this decision for himself. If he does not want to see them for what could possibly be the last time, then he certainly does not have to."

He turned his glare on Siva.

Mara was aghast. "Siva! Why would you– oh. Oh, yeah." She turned back to Ander. "Wouldn't you feel bad, then?"

He took a deep breath and counted to ten. *:Lady.:*

*:Strictly speaking, anything is possible,:* came the unhelpful but undeniably truthful answer.

This was one of those things where it was just... *required* that people do it, regardless of how little it actually accomplished, wasn't it?

*:It accomplishes connection between people,:* Hades observed absently. *:Most people like to be connected to each other in some way.:*

Was he actually connected to any of those people?

Maybe. He was often not the best judge of that, and even he knew it. Usually he preferred to have the other person tell him how they would define the relationship.

He hadn't been able to say goodbye to Alice and Fredrik. Those circumstances had been... bad.

He did regret that.

He sighed and put down his coffee.

It was bitterly cold for an April morning, which was not making this any more pleasant. Ander pulled his coat closer around himself as he hovered at the edge of the group gathered outside of the train station. They were drawing looks from people passing by. What a circus.

It wasn't even that there were that many people; it was just that the people who were here were loud. The whole crew of the *Sea Spirit* was present, though from what he could tell it was just the twins, the youngest, and the doctor going. Prim and Frir had also come to see the group off, though why, he wasn't sure. The two Vampires hadn't come to see anyone off when they'd left to go to the Nyphoren Islands.

He scanned the group and frowned as his eyes landed on Jamirh. The Avari was wearing a new black coat that was practically singing with Hades' magic, and he was armed with daggers instead of a longsword. He looked far more prepared for this mission than he had for the last one. But he also looked exhausted. Had he slept at all last night? The bags under his eyes looked like *they* had bags.

Ander hesitated, then went over. "Jamirh."

The Avari looked up at him, ears twitching. "Hey, Ander. You're really not coming with us?"

"No." He thought he'd made that clear enough earlier. "How is your arm?"

"Oh." Jamirh looked down at it. "It's fine. Hasn't lit up any more since... whatever it was that happened yesterday."

"That's good." It was something to work on, but since it didn't seem to be doing the Avari any harm, it could wait for the moment. He had thought that maybe that was the source of Jamirh's exhaustion, but more likely it was just nerves. "Let Takeshi or Mara know if anything changes, and they can alert me, though I don't think that's terribly likely."

Jamirh made a quiet sound Ander couldn't identify. "Thanks. I'll let them know if anything weird happens."

*:Why do you think nothing will change?:* Takeshi's mind touch almost startled him. *:It started glowing suddenly without warning. What if the stasis-like effect fails in the same way?:*

Ander considered the question. *:It is an overflow of magic. This place – which is* saturated *in magic – is likely a far worse environment for it than the Empire, where most magic has been stomped out. Stay away from Truth Seekers and he'll be fine. Maybe even better than here.:*

He caught Takeshi's eye. The shinobi looked thoughtful. *:Should we be careful about casting around him?:*

*:I think the greater issue is how much magic is just in the air here. He should be fine if you need to cast an illusion or something.:*

*:I see. I will keep this in mind.:*

"Ander?"

He blinked, returning his attention to Jamirh. "Hm?"

The Avari looked down, ears sinking. "You summoned Ryn once, right? But you said he didn't speak to you?"

"That's correct," Ander agreed, wondering where this was going.

"Did he seem…" Jamirh paused, shifting his weight from one foot to the other while he toyed with his key. "Did he seem like he was… upset, or anything?"

Ander tilted his head. "No. If anything I would describe him as distracted, or merely uninterested in me. It made sense at the time, given what I knew of Ebryn. Why?"

"It's just…" He trailed off before shaking his head and trying again. "He died really horribly."

Ander abruptly remembered that they had found the second Ebryn's dismembered corpse in the Tilden facility. He'd taken a data pad, meant to review it, but had forgotten about it in the aftermath of the destruction of the base and Jak's sacrifice. It was probably in his lab somewhere. "He very likely did," he admitted, remembering that Jamirh had been nearly catatonic immediately after finding the remains. "But his suffering would have been brief. Only the restless dead continue to suffer; the Lady's grace prevents the same from befalling the true dead. The dead rest, Jamirh."

Except that wasn't technically true in this case, was it? The soul had been reborn, had become Jamirh.

Reincarnation complicated things. Either way, Ander was certain that no version of Ebryn had ever become restless dead.

*:That is certainly true,:* the Lady affirmed. *:Neither Ebryn nor Ryn became restless dead.:*

"And the Lady has confirmed that, as well," he added for Jamirh's benefit.

Jamirh perked up a little at that, ears lifting. "That's… really good to hear. I was worried because he sort of went silent when we entered the base."

Ander considered that. "You did not have a good reaction to seeing the body. Which is understandable," he added quickly at Hades' sigh. "But it would not be unreasonable to believe that he also had a bad reaction, since he and you are the same person."

"I hadn't thought of it that way," Jamirh said, looking thoughtful. "And Ebryn did try to stop me from entering the room, but... Ryn would have already known what was in there?"

Ander shrugged. They were rapidly leaving known territory with this scenario. Reincarnation was not that common; one had to feel a burning desire to continue the work they had started in life, and once dead most souls just did not feel that way anymore. "It's possible even being near the body made him uncomfortable. Sometimes that happens with ghosts." Which were definitely not the same thing, but that was as close as he was going to get.

"Huh." The Avari looked down again, but then looked back up at Ander, a small smile on his face. "Thanks, Ander."

Ander inclined his head as Takeshi walked up to both of them. "Jamirh, we have to be on the train in a few minutes."

Jamirh nodded. "Yeah, got it. Bye, Ander. See you later!" He darted over to the pirate group. He still looked exhausted though. Luckily they had a very long train ride; he'd be able to rest before they crossed the Wall.

"Have any life-changing advice for me?" Takeshi asked when the Avari was out of earshot.

Ander turned to Takeshi. "I don't think anything of what I said counts as 'life-changing.'"

Takeshi shrugged. "He looks far happier than he has at any other point this morning. I was beginning to wonder if he was regretting asking to come along."

Ander hummed. "I try not to wonder what people are thinking," he said, suddenly reminded of Ida. He didn't think he'd ever understood her, and they'd lived together for years.

Had he ever understood Fredrik? They'd lived together even longer.

He shook his head, annoyed with himself. He turned his attention back to Takeshi and said the only thing that came to mind. "Good luck."

Takeshi's eyes crinkled over his mask as he clasped a hand on Ander's shoulder. "Try not to return to near-catatonia in our absence. Remember – your fish need you." He followed after Jamirh.

Ander squinted after him, trying to figure out if that was supposed to be a joke, when Mara cleared her throat behind him.

"I have said goodbye to people," he defended himself, uncertain why she was looking down with her hands clasped behind her.

"Yes, yes, I know!" She started playing with her hair. "I know we have an agreement about only once a century, but..."

Oh. She wanted a hug. He looked away. "It's fine."

He staggered as she threw herself at him, squeezing like an octopus that had found prey. He patted her on the back weakly.

She pulled away, and he was astonished to see tears in her eyes. "You take care of yourself, okay?" Her voice wavered.

"I'm not the one going into the Empire to hunt down Abomination," he said, confused. "I will be very safe here."

She wiped at her eyes. "That's not what I said, but that's okay."

"Goodbye, Ander. We'll be in touch," Siva said, drawing Mara away.

He waved.

And then they were gone.

And he was standing outside a train station. Staring at it as the others who had come to see the group off dispersed.

It was even colder than before.

Ander returned to a quiet temple for the first time in months.

He went upstairs and made himself a new cup of coffee, sipping it slowly as he worked out what he wanted to do now that no one was looking over his shoulder. He could continue work on the avatar, if he wanted. He could look into the mystery of whatever it was that was shielding Jamirh from the overflow of magic from the Blade. He could find that data pad and try to determine what exactly the Empire had been trying to do with Ebryn's corpse. He could inquire with Caelessa about bards and the World Sound for Takeshi, if he felt truly altruistic.

He finished his coffee, washed the cup and put it away. Then he tidied up the common area, deciding partway through that it needed more of a deep clean. He hadn't done that in a while, and it would be nice for everything to be back in its usual pristine condition. He dusted; he vacuumed. He sprayed the windows and freshened up the furniture.

There was a new crocheted blanket hidden under the pile of pillows in the corner of the room. He folded it neatly and draped it over one of the armchairs.

He fed his fish and updated the logs. Then he went downstairs to the main sanctuary and decided that could also use a good cleaning. He shooed the wargs outside, wiped down the surfaces, and swept the floor. He neatened the altar and replaced the dead flowers with more recently deceased ones. He stared at Jak for a few minutes before deciding that since he was currently made of soul crystal or something similar, it was probably fine to leave him alone.

Then he meandered to his office.

Some of the destruction had been removed, but he'd been adamant no one touch anything in the office proper without his oversight, so most of it remained. He still needed a new door, but at least he could remove the chunks of the old one that were strewn about. And there were things he had been working on that would need to be disposed of now. That was as good a starting point as any.

"Ander, what in the Lady's name happened to your office?"

He turned to see Marcus looking in over the ruins of the door, a brown paper bag in hand.

"The witches did," he said absently, wondering if he should bother with a dustpan and broom or just get a trash bag and put the debris directly in there. "Did you need something?"

Marcus held up the bag. "I thought you might like lunch."

Ander blinked and looked at the clock. Half past one. "Ah." He hadn't realized he'd been at it for so long. "Thank you. You can put it over there." He indicated a relatively empty table by the door.

"What if," Marcus said slowly, glancing around, "we eat lunch together, and then I help you with... whatever this is. Why do the remains of your door look like volcanic rock?"

That was fine, he supposed. Then a thought struck him. "How did you know I haven't eaten?"

"Just a hunch. I did not know for sure, but it seemed likely. I have noticed you often forget to eat when you're on duty at the hospital, too." He leaned against the crumbling door frame. "And the others all left this morning, right?"

"Mm hm." There was a lot to do, but he strangely just felt... apathetic towards it all at the moment. Maybe food would help. And more coffee.

The Lady hummed softly. *:You've been busy all morning, a short break won't hurt. You have nothing that is immediately pressing, and you are still supposed to be taking it easy anyway.:*

Yes, that would work. And now that he was taking a minute, his fingers were beginning to ache. They weren't completely healed from the incident with the tea cup. "I'm going to make coffee," he declared. "You can follow me."

"Did you see them off this morning?" Marcus asked as he followed Ander up the stairs.

Ander knew seeing people off was something people did, but he hadn't realized how expected it was that he do it, apparently. "I did."

"At the train station, or at the palace gates?"

Ander paused as he was opening the door to the apartments. He hadn't even realized the gates were an option; that would have saved him some time. "I went to the train station." He looked around as he entered the common space, pleased at how neat and clean it looked, before heading to the kitchen.

Marcus closed the door behind them. "You don't often leave the palace grounds."

Ander pressed his lips together as he gathered coffee implements. He'd been leaving the palace grounds far more in the past few months than he had in the last few centuries.

This was where he belonged. He didn't need to go any farther.

"Mara demanded I go." He paused mid-setup. "Would you like any coffee?"

"Yes please, thank you. Coffee sounds excellent." Marcus put the bag on the table and took a seat. "Do you wish you were going with them?"

"Absolutely not. There's far too much for me to do around here." Which was why he had spent the morning cleaning. To set himself up for success later. "I was away for long enough when we went to the Nyphoren Islands."

The Vampire leaned back in his chair. "It was a good thing you were there, though, from what I heard. But now that you have a break from everyone, what are you planning on doing? Besides cleaning, that is."

Ander watched the coffee drip down into the cup through the filter. "I haven't decided where I should focus yet. The creation of the avatar needs to be continued, and there's the mystery of Jamirh's arm, and…" He trailed off, not completely sure if Takeshi's problems had been told to him in confidence or not. "There are a few other options, as well."

"And you are still supposed to be taking it easy," Marcus mused. "How long are they supposed to be gone for? Can you get all that done before they come back while still taking care of yourself?"

Ander had not considered that, but Marcus was correct – when they returned, the quiet would be interrupted again, and the witches would be back to watching his every move like a pair of Lorn stalking prey. Could he actually restart work on the avatar if he wasn't sure that he wouldn't have to pause whatever he was doing when they returned? That would be inefficient. If only Hades had Tadurin's temporal abilities – then maybe he could stretch a short bit of time into a longer one. Though everyone would probably tell him that was "unwise," too. "It will take them a few days at least to get there, and then I'm not sure what their plan is. It did not seem like they planned to be gone for longer than a week or two." And while he could get quite a bit done in that time, could he get enough done? Hm.

"Well, if you would like an extra pair of hands, or someone to bounce thoughts off of, I can be available," Marcus offered. "I am also very curious about the situation with Jamirh's arm. Do you have any theories yet?"

That could work. "Only that being here surrounded by Tarvishte's ambient magic could be causing adverse effects." He paused. "What about your shifts at the hospital?"

Marcus waved the question away as he accepted the mug of coffee Ander handed him. "I do not have any long-term patients at the moment and thought it would be a good opportunity to use some vacation time. I am still working mornings, and if they really need me I can be available of course, but it seemed prudent to take a break before everything potentially goes sideways with war being declared in the south. The ambient magic, though? Is that why you think the wounds started glowing after a month here instead of immediately after they were inflicted?" He took a small vial of blood out from a pocket and poured it into the coffee.

"It is a better explanation than anything else I have come up with. Do you really think the war will affect us overly much here? I thought the plan was just to let the Empire restabilize or break apart on its own efforts." There hadn't even been any actual fighting that he was aware of yet, just people making loud announcements and posturing.

Marcus shrugged. "You would know more than me. I just get things trickling down through the hospital gossip vine."

"I've... not been paying much attention to it. The Abomination is the larger threat," he admitted.

The Vampire nodded, opening the brown bag he had brought with him and pulling out two containers, which he set on the table. "That's why so many of your order left this morning, right?"

Ander nodded. "I am the relay to Vlad, if necessary."

"I am surprised Lady Siva went. Aradians are very rare south of the Wall."

"She is only going as far as Braila. Another relay." Ander looked over at the containers: stuffed bell peppers. He grabbed a pair of forks and knives and sat at the table with his own blood-free coffee. "Things have become... slightly more difficult, without Jak."

Marcus inclined his head, taking the silverware and one of the containers. "Jak was older than the entire race of Vampires. It is odd to think of a world without him."

"The Lady says he isn't dead, just healing." Ander took a bite of the food and was surprised to find himself ravenous.

"Oh, that is excellent news!" Marcus took a bite, chewed. "It must be a little strange to suddenly be by yourself again after having so many other priests around. Plus Lord Takeshi is new."

Ander took another bite himself, considering. "I have spent almost three centuries mostly by myself here, with only occasional visits from the others. Is it strange that after only a few months that seems to have become the norm?"

Hades hummed soothingly in the back of his mind, offering wordless support in response to the discomfort he was just now beginning to realize he was feeling.

He had Her. Why would he ever need anyone else?

*:A god cannot be your only support.:*

His previous mortal supports hadn't worked out.

*:That just means you should try again.:*

"I do not think it is so strange," Marcus offered. "Most people want to belong to a group. Humans, Avari, Veren, Gini, Vampires... no matter the species, people tend to form connections. Even if an individual prefers to be alone, most of the time they still need some interaction or they... stop functioning effectively."

He didn't like how they were agreeing without actually communicating. Well, Hades could hear Marcus, just not the other way around. "That's terribly inefficient."

"Is it?" Marcus asked, finishing his coffee. "Often I've found my efficiency has increased when working with another."

Ander mulled that over. "That's not quite the same thing though, is it?"

Marcus shrugged. "One usually leads to the other."

An interesting hypothesis.

Maybe one he should consider.

# Chapter Twelve

---

J amirh was in the Empire.

Again.

He really, really did not want to be here. But unfortunately this was where the bionics were. As long as they continued to exist, chances were good Jamirh was going to have to keep coming back.

But once they were gone...

What did he want to do once the threat of Abomination no longer hung over his head?

Jamirh rested his head on the palm of his hand, elbow on the table in front of him as he stared out the large window of the hotel they were staying at. Rain pattered against the glass, only partially obscuring his view of the quiet city below. The faint orange reflection of his hair and blurry features of his face were easy enough to ignore, dissimilar enough from Ryn's that it didn't remind him of...

Well. It was nice to know that once he was dead his suffering had ended, but Jamirh himself was still struggling with mirrors. Jak's crystal was proving surprisingly helpful, though; the orange color was different enough from Jamirh's normal ruby red that stray glances of himself didn't make him want to run.

Terient was not a place he had ever heard of before. They had arrived yesterday evening, after having made yet another walk through the Waste and then taken a bus from Demes. Takeshi had found them a hotel, he'd led a short briefing on what their plan was, and then everyone had gone to sleep.

It was strange, watching the small figures bustle about below. Jamirh and everyone else knew that war had been declared, but no one seemed entirely sure what to do with that knowledge. No actual fighting had broken out yet, and no one seemed to know where or when it would break out, leaving everyone in a state of uncertainty. Belian had entrenched himself in the palace in Lyndiniam and was acting as Emperor. One duke was dead, another was supporting him, two were against him, and the remaining two were seceding from the Empire entirely. But no one seemed sure what "war" meant. Had the military chosen a side? Was the military in each province siding with their duke? Jamirh wasn't sure.

And he didn't really care, either. Once this was over, Jamirh intended to never step foot in this place ever again.

Maybe he could travel? He and Aether had never really considered going much farther than just beyond Lyndiniam one day. But there were so many places that had been beyond his ability to even consider as destinations before. Going to the Nyphoren Islands could have been interesting and fun if he'd been allowed to leave Mara's apartment. Maybe he could have met a Veren? Or he could visit Miravu's country and look for others like him who were Masters of Blades. Or he could just go explore somewhere completely different, like Patoran or the Darklands.

The *Sea Spirit* traveled places. He had enjoyed traveling with the pirates to the Nyphoren, even if that trip had turned out to be a disaster. Being out on the ocean was a completely new experience, too – one that Jamirh thought he might like to repeat without the threat of the world ending hanging over his head.

He hummed, thinking about the possibilities. When this crisis was over... if he stayed in Romanii, what would he *do*?

What had Ebryn done? Had the Hero left for some far land, looking for something different, and simply never returned?

His left hand gripped his key. He'd never really thought about more than his immediate future, except for when he'd spent two years planning to rob the casino. And even then, it didn't seem like the same thing.

What was everyone else expecting him to do?

Did that even matter?

"Jamirh?"

He sat up and turned. Takeshi was leaning on the doorway to the small kitchen, arms folded. Don was just visible in the shadows behind the shinobi, wearing a large backpack.

"You look like you are deep in thought." Dark eyes studied him carefully as the shinobi tilted his head.

Jamirh shrugged. "It's nothing important." He could mull that over more later, when they weren't about to go scout an active military base. "Is it time to go?"

Takeshi nodded. "Are you ready for this?"

Jamirh stood up.

Two and a half hours later and Jamirh was fingering the gun Desha had given him, not really sure what to do with it. It was holstered on his belt under his coat, but he'd never actually used a gun before. The sisters had given him a quick crash course, but he didn't feel as connected to it as he did to his daggers. There was no flash of insight, no understanding when holding it, even after watching them use theirs. A gun was technically tech, right? Perhaps his inherent would be useless with it.

It was a good thing he didn't expect to have to use any of his weapons tonight.

The rain had let up but been replaced by a fine mist, making it difficult to see in the dark with the moon barely a sliver in the sky. Jamirh was thankful for the new coat, which was keeping him warm and dry, but there was something about the dark tonight that had him on edge.

Don was squinting down at the complex as he dug around in his backpack. "Looking at the landscape, this feels like a stupid place fer a military base."

Jamirh, Takeshi, and Don were on a ridge about half a mile away from Etroy. The base was in the middle of a dusty plain, with a small, sad river winding its way past. There were fences and floodlights surrounding the complex, but the location was kind of in the middle of nowhere without any natural defenses. Even through the fog Jamirh could see that there were areas of the base that faded into the darkness – likely buildings without any lights on. The mist made it difficult to see if there were any people moving around. This late at night, on a partially abandoned base? Who knew.

"It was a manufacturing plant, originally," he said absently as he studied it. "The military took it over. Maybe that's why they don't seem to care about it now. It looks mostly empty."

Takeshi hummed as dark eyes shifted in Jamirh's direction. "It does seem odd that, as the country is gearing up for war, this one base has been ignored. I wonder if there are others in a similar situation, or if perhaps they have simply decided this one is indefensible. Were there any particular defenses that Ryn had to deal with?"

Jamirh blinked. How else would he have known this base's history? It must have come from Ryn's memories somehow. He tried to think, pulling his coat closed a little tighter as a cold wind blew past. "Nothing stands out," he said after a few minutes.

Don raised an eyebrow as he paused his digging. "The guy who hit the base over twenty years ago? What makes ye think the base has the same defenses? Tech changes a lot faster than that."

Takeshi inclined his head. "Certainly, but I'd rather have more knowledge than less. It is always better to prepare for something that won't happen than be surprised by something you didn't foresee."

Don shrugged and went back to searching the backpack. "Can't say it would be that useful, but sure." His face lit up as he pulled out a gadget shaped like a partially flattened circle with a row of colorful buttons along one edge.

The shinobi looked back at the base for a moment, silent, then turned back to Jamirh and Don. "Remember that this is *just* a scouting mission. Do not engage with anything or anyone. We only want to confirm if there are any bionics in the base. Listen for Jeri and Jitsu; they are prowling around in the mist and will howl if they think we should withdraw. Don, is that...?"

"Yessir, it is." He handed the object to Jamirh; it was about the size of his palm. "I've been working on these fer a long time. Ye just need t' hold this just under an electronic lock and press the yellow button, here" – he pointed – "t' send an EMP int' the door that'll disengage the lock."

"Except that we aren't going into any doors. We are going to be scouting along the fence," Takeshi reminded them both patiently.

"Right, right," Don agreed, though his face fell a bit. He perked up again quickly. "The blue button here will scan in a radius for the bionics. If it senses one, it will turn red. Has a range of about fifty feet, maybe; hard t' tell without the real thing to test it on."

Jamirh frowned, ears sinking. "How do you know it can sense the bionics at all, then?"

"There's this really odd alloy that's used in the bionics," Don explained. "There was one on one of the ships we tangled with in the Nyphoren, and Marjori managed to steal a little bit of it fer me."

"Ander discovered that as well when he studied the corpse of the bionic that attacked you in Tarvishte," Takeshi agreed. "Apparently it is some form of magic-resistant alloy. What else did you 'acquire' from the Empire's navy?"

Don shrugged, but the grin on his face said enough. He pulled out a second device and shrugged the backpack back on. "And fer what it's worth, if ye *do* come upon a bionic, the EMP can disrupt them just like the doors – but it takes about five minutes t' recharge, so use it wisely."

Well, at least the little thing could hopefully sense and interrupt the bionics. Jamirh slipped it into a pocket. He glanced at his arm, but he'd wrapped it in bandages in addition to covering it with the bracer and the coat. No light was getting through all that. But he felt jittery, like he needed to get it over and done with. "Meet back here in an hour?"

Takeshi nodded.

Jamirh sketched a sloppy salute and took off into the mist, heading slightly to the right of the hazy lights of the compound. Takeshi and Don would go left, and they'd see what they could find.

At least this base did not call to him the way Tilden had, though that was likely because of Ryn's... presence at the latter. Still, there was an odd sense of familiarity about this place, as though he'd been here before. Well, he guessed he had in a way, but still. There was something... they had been looking for something. What?

He paused, considering that thought. "They." Ryn had attacked the base with others. He felt like he could almost see them moving through the mist with him, Avari, though their colors were dull and muted. A girl and two guys. Yes, that made sense; Ryn had told him he'd had the help of three friends. Had they died here too?

Once again, he wished he could speak to Ryn. He could have helped Jamirh make sense of the almost-memories that were drifting by just out of reach.

He pushed the thought aside. He had a job to do; Takeshi and the others were counting on him.

He slowed as the lights got closer, trying to see if he could spot any cameras or personnel, but what he could see of the yard appeared deserted. Was that normal? Tilden Base had been busy even in the dead of night. Maybe they really had given up on this place. Maybe all who were left were ghosts.

He shuddered. Ghosts and bionics, probably, haunting empty halls, unaware that the living had long gone. He could almost see it now, dark corridors lit only by emergency lights, and the lone red eye on a bionic blinking at the far end…

Jamirh blinked, then shook himself, trying to fight back his unease. His imagination wasn't usually so good he could get lost in it. A memory, then?

He crept forward, careful to stay out of the direct light. Someone had to be here to turn the lights on and off, right? He took the device out of his pocket and pressed the blue button. A dull blue light blinked twice, then went dark.

No bionics yet, then. Though he also wasn't very close. Carefully, he skirted around the bright spots, aiming to get closer to the fence. Up ahead he could see a building rising through the fog that was completely dark, lit only by the edges of the floodlights.

He squinted at it. The building looked familiar…

What had they been looking for?

Not only did the building look familiar, there was something weird about the fence, but it was difficult to tell exactly what through the mist. Jamirh considered his options as he scanned the area again, but there were no people, and if there were any cameras he couldn't see them. Maybe Don was wrong, and this place had been nearly abandoned just after Ryn had attempted to destroy it. If that was true, they could actually be dealing with twenty-year-old tech, or even older. He decided to chance getting closer, creeping slowly so the mist would cover his movements. When he was close enough, he frowned.

The fence was cut.

It had been mostly bent back into shape, but Jamirh could see the jagged edges of the wire curling away from itself. The cut stretched from the ground to about four feet up. It looked deliberate. Someone had made a way in.

Why? When?

Jamirh felt the hair on the back of his neck prick up, and he froze.

Nothing moved.

He peered intently into the base, but didn't see anything. As slowly as he could, he pulled out the little device again and pressed the blue button.

Two blue flashes.

It should have been comforting, but it wasn't. His instincts were still screaming that he wasn't alone. His ears strained to catch even the slightest noise, but the night was silent.

Unnaturally silent.

His hands drifted over his daggers.

Time to go back, he decided. Something was out here. He hadn't heard any howling, but that just meant the wargs hadn't encountered whatever it was yet. Better to return to the meetup spot now.

Something moved in the mist – not from within the compound, but between him and safety.

He made a snap decision and instead backed towards the fence, focusing on remaining as silent as possible, barely allowing himself to breathe.

*:Jamirh! There's–:*

Takeshi's mental call went suddenly silent, and the compound was plunged into darkness as the floodlights all went out.

He didn't hesitate, throwing himself towards where he remembered the tear in the fence to be. His hand caught on jagged metal, the pain almost a relief as he gripped the wire and folded it away, squeezing through. He barely wasted any time shoving it back into place once he was through, darting towards the direction of the building. He'd take his chances with its uncomfortably odd familiarity over whatever was out here with him.

A warg howled in the distance.

Jamirh sent Jeri a mental apology, but he didn't stop.

Jamirh crept through the dark hallways, lit only occasionally by dim, flickering emergency lights set into the edges of the floor. In his left hand he held Don's device, checking for the presence of bionics at every corner and at every door. In his right he kept a dagger ready.

It was even quieter inside than it had been in the mist.

Jamirh felt more and more unsettled as he explored, sure he was following in Ryn's invisible footsteps. Whatever had been in the mist did not seem to have followed him inside, but the deserted feeling of the building was almost worse.

Almost.

None of the doors he passed were locked. They opened into labs and storage spaces, tables and shelves covered in a thick layer of dust and scattered cobwebs, old computer monitors, beakers, and wires left untouched for who knew how long. The base itself might not have been abandoned, but this building certainly was.

What was he looking for? He didn't know. He was supposed to be looking for bionics, but he felt like there was something else here.

Probably ghosts, with his luck.

Ander had said Ryn had not become restless dead. Had his friends? Was the building abandoned because they haunted it? Or, if this was the building where Avari had originally become Abomination, maybe it was *their* ghosts doing the haunting.

He wished he could ask Hel. Or ask Takeshi to ask Hel, but since the shinobi had been cut off Jamirh hadn't heard anything else from him. He hoped he was okay.

But all he could feel was a growing dread.

He took a moment to pause, pressing his hand against his key, then carried on, drifting through the hallways. Maybe *he* was the ghost, and that was why he couldn't hear Takeshi. Maybe the other ghosts wanted him to join them.

Jamirh turned a corner and saw a much larger door, better lit than the others with a chunkier frame. His feet carried him closer; there was something different about it. Something that wasn't just its size. He slipped Don's device into his pocket as he studied it, raising a hand to brush against the cool metal surface. Whatever it was he was supposed to find, it was on the other side.

The door slid open.

The room was the largest he'd found yet, with several large, metal cylinders that reminded him uncomfortably of the tubes from Tilden Base. There were workstations with computers set up around the room, tablets and notebooks and pens left behind by their owners. There was a large screen against the far wall, up a small flight of stairs to a higher landing, but like the computers it was dull and lifeless. Thick black cables connected the metal cylinders to a large central pillar, maybe ten feet in diameter, made of glass and filled with a murky pale-green liquid. Some of the tables were overturned, tools scattered around them.

Why had they just left this the way it was? Why not salvage what they could, especially if they were still occupying other parts of the base?

Something about this room reminded him of when Ander had cast that spell with Mara and Takeshi at Tilden. The flooding, they'd called it? The very air here seemed to be reminding Jamirh that death was imminent. It was telling him to leave, warning him away.

But something else beckoned.

He wandered to the left, stepping around the debris in the flickering light. He looked over the workstations and the cables, but nothing really grabbed his attention until he found himself coming to a stop.

There was nothing here that was different than anywhere else. Just the unmarked metal floor a few feet from the nearest workstation, faintly lit by an emergency light. Jamirh found himself on one knee, carefully brushing a hand over the spot. Even through all the layers of bandages and the glove, there was a faint red glow coming from his hand.

Here.

Ryn had died here.

"Well, *you* ain't military."

Jamirh spun around, feeling the quiet spell of the place shatter.

An Avari about his age with long, braided white hair was standing in the doorway, gun pointed in Jamirh's direction. There were sounds of people moving about somewhere else in the building, distant voices and the clanking of metal hitting metal. Red eyes glinted dangerously. "And you're not one of mine. Who are you? And what are you doing here?"

Jamirh eyed the gun and reminded himself that at Tilden he had successfully dodged bullets from a much closer distance. He felt the reassurance of his inherent settle over him; this Avari was not a bionic. While the presence of others was a concern, Jamirh was certain he could get the upper hand on this one if necessary. "You're not military, either." Not an Avari in jeans and a baggy jacket. "What are *you* doing here?" He focused on the weight of the dagger in his hand. What was going on?

The other Avari's eyes narrowed. "Raiding the place. Taking anything useful."

Jamirh looked around at the outdated tech that had gone unused for over twenty years. "I think you'll have better luck in the other buildings."

The Avari's ears twitched up. "Already took what we wanted from those. Just... cleaning house, now."

Really? On the night they chose to investigate the base, there was a *raid*? Jamirh guessed that based on the lax security Etroy was probably an attractive target, but why tonight of all nights?

*A convergence.*

He nearly flinched at the whisper that cut through his mind, feminine and dark and oddly silent.

Hel?

*I am with you.*

Still, he could feel her presence fading in and out. He shouldn't be able to hear her at all, so why–

He was standing where Ryn died.

He fought down a rush of nausea.

*I am with you. You are not alone.*

The white-haired Avari frowned. "Hey, you okay? You look like you've seen a ghost." The gun lowered.

*He is not the danger.*

"It's fine." Jamirh brushed off the other's concern, trying to re-center himself despite the feeling of cold fingers resting on the back of his neck. If Hel thought there was danger...

He remembered the little device and snatched it out of his pocket, hitting the blue button. *That* was what he was *supposed* to be looking for. If there were other people here now–

Red eyes narrowed. "What's that you got there?"

It wasn't footsteps he could hear in the corridor. Not unless they were wearing metal shoes that were shaped like jointed prongs.

The light turned red.

*Destroy it!*

Her presence faded completely as Jamirh hurled himself at the other Avari, bringing them both crashing to the floor as shots rang out over their heads. "Bionic!" he shouted desperately as he rolled them behind the cover of the wall, the other's gun spinning off across the floor. He looked around, but couldn't see a panel or anything that would shut the door and keep the bionic out. Then again, it hadn't taken much to open the door in the first place.

He was going to have to fight.

The other Avari was sputtering as he untangled himself from Jamirh and pressed himself against the wall. "What the hell is *that*?" he asked, voice aghast.

It almost made Jamirh pause. "There weren't any others in the other buildings you raided?" That was good, but almost *too* good.

The Avari opened his mouth to answer, but a look of uncertainty crossed his face as his ears twitched down. He pressed his lips together. "We weren't the ones who cleared the buildings. We're just stripping them of the tech."

The clanging sound was coming closer. "Who was clearing the buildings then? Never mind, it doesn't matter right now." He took his own gun and handed it to the Avari before drawing a second dagger. He felt the weight of both and the calm of his inherent as he steadied himself. "Aim for the organic bits if you can. Don't shoot me."

Think only of what he was doing, not what he was doing it against.

He kept himself low as he slid into the open, aimed for less than a breath as everything sharpened into crystal clarity, and threw one dagger. He didn't wait for it to connect as he dashed towards the bionic, knowing that speed was his only real advantage here. Without the Blade—

But he didn't need the Blade, did he?

The dagger connected with enough force to throw the bionic's head back, smashing through its mechanical eye. He didn't slow his momentum as he passed by, retrieving the dagger and ripping it out of its head. The stitched mouth made no sound, but the limbs jerked as it staggered forward.

Two shots rang out and it jolted back, oily red fluid spraying across the wall.

Jamirh dashed in again. The spine. It was encased in metal though, and he had no means to breach it. He kicked it instead, making it lurch back forward.

His arm was glowing again.

Jeri, with a completely ridiculous idea–

He ripped off his glove, taking the bandages with it, and closed his bare hand around the spinal column.

Now the bionic made a sound not unlike a moan as the metal of the spine turned cherry red, then gray, then red again. Jamirh squeezed harder as more shots rang out. Takeshi had said the metal was magic resistant, but that didn't mean immune.

The spinal column compressed – then severed into two pieces.

The torso fell forward as the lower half tipped to the side, both halves crashing to the ground. Jamirh tried to remember if that was enough, but though the limbs were still twitching the feeling of dread that usually surrounded them was fading. He kicked it with his foot, hoping it would fall completely still.

"Holy..." The Avari was gripping the gun tightly with both hands, though it was pointed at the ground. His red eyes were wide as he stared at Jamirh and the bionic. "That was... something."

Jamirh shrugged, trying to catch his breath.

"Do you have no fear at all?"

That made Jamirh look at him in surprise. No fear? All he had was fear. Fear and his inherent were keeping him alive. "What?"

"You just threw yourself at it. Wild. Let's... let's move right on from that." He shook his head and turned to go back into the large room. "You've taken down things like that before," he added over his shoulder. "I'm still not entirely sure what you did."

Jamirh looked around for his glove as the bionic finally fell still. He retrieved it from a few feet away before following the other Avari. The lines visible on his hand had stopped glowing for the first time in weeks. "No, that was not my first." Should he leave? What if there was another one?

The Avari was studying the center terminal, brushing dust and cobwebs away. "How likely do you think it is there are more of them?"

Jamirh pulled out Don's device and found his ears sinking. It had a long crack running through the casing, and two of the buttons – including the blue one – were smashed. "Shit."

Red eyes glanced over at him. "Ah. Well, I guess we can hope the Seekers show up and clear this building too. They thought it was empty." A pause. "I hope that was true." He went back to examining the terminal.

Jamirh's ears flattened. "Seekers? You're working with *Truth Seekers?*"

"Yeah. Turns out they're... well, not normal, not by a long shot, but not as bad as we thought?" The Avari didn't sound like he had fully convinced himself of that. "But they promised to help us raid this base, and they said we could have all the tech we could carry."

Who was the "we"? "But then why–?" Jamirh stopped as he realized what they were after.

It was exactly the same as Tilden.

"They were the ones clearing the buildings?" he asked just to confirm.

"Yup! At least they were supposed to." He was gently tapping the side of the console.

"They don't care about the tech. They care about the bionics." Jamirh turned and stared at the corpse in the hallway. "That's what they were doing."

Had it been a Truth Seeker in the mist?

The Avari paused his tapping. "You think they came here for the sole purpose of killing... what did you call it? A bionic?" Red eyes drifted to the remains. "Huh. That's not what I would have thought they'd look like."

"The Seekers are mages. The bionics... unsettle them? Upset them? I'm not too sure, honestly."

"*Mages?*" The Avari abandoned what he was doing entirely as he straightened up. "As in magic? What are you talking about? They're–" He cut himself off as a pensive look crossed his face, but then he shook his head. "Magic is just a fairy tale."

Jamirh looked at him, and suddenly just felt *tired*. "No. No, it's real. Believe me. I've seen things the last few months..." He trailed off. How could he possibly explain? His magic wasn't one of the visible kinds. Except... "I did sort of melt the thing's spine."

A snort. "I could list like sixteen ways to do that with tech."

Was this a battle Jamirh cared about? Not really, but... this was a secret that had been kept from Avari for centuries. That wasn't fair. And he did have one other spell, didn't he? He didn't want to lose the illusion, but...

It wasn't just about the spell, was it?

He slid Jak's necklace off and watched as the Avari's eyes widened. "Magic is very, very real."

"Well." The other Avari swallowed hard. "That's... hmm." He rubbed at his eyes and stared at Jamirh again. "Ebryn."

Jamirh couldn't make himself nod. He stood silently instead.

Red eyes looked past him to the bionic. "Okay. Okay then, that makes... a sort of sense. Aren't you supposed to have a sword?"

Jamirh looked away.

"Oh yeah, I guess it was lost." A pause. "I can see why you would prefer the orange hair. Sorry, just... need a second to reconcile this shit."

Jamirh slipped the necklace back over his head. "Yeah."

The Avari studied him for a moment, hand on his hips, but then he grinned and held his hand out. "Name's Gren. I lead the Crimson Shadows."

Jamirh had no idea what that was, but he took the offered handshake. "I'm Jamirh."

That earned him slightly raised eyebrows, but Gren didn't comment on it. "Great to meet you." He turned back to the console and gave it a solid whack, causing the screen to light up in a sickly green. "I don't suppose you would be interested in joining us?"

Jamirh watched him pull a small drive out of his pocket and plug it into the console. "Join you? With what?"

Gren blinked, and Jamirh was surprised to see a faint flush across the olive skin. "Sorry, I didn't mean to imply– I don't mean at the expense of... what you're supposed to be doing. Killing those things?"

Jamirh was missing something. "No, what–"

He was interrupted by another Avari skidding into the room. "Boss! We've pretty much cleared it all out; Cole says we have maybe another fifteen minutes tops."

"Damn." Gren frowned. "Jamirh, this is Namarre. Namarre, Jamirh. I'm not going to have the time to do this here. Namarre, I'm going to need this room stripped down immediately. I'll have to sift through this stuff later."

"You got it, boss." She turned and whistled sharply, and not a minute later a whole group of Avari were swarming the room, taking everything that wasn't nailed down – and some things that were.

"What are you going to do with all this?" Jamirh asked as a trio of Avari worked to unplug one of the metal cylinders in the center of the room.

Gren shrugged. "I'll find out what it's good for later, but I'm really good at figuring out uses for what I've got."

*:Jamirh!:*

He jumped at Takeshi's frantic mental exclamation. "Takeshi?"

Gren stared at him. "What?"

He waved a hand at him and turned away.

*:Jamirh, where have you been? That facility has been under Truth Seeker shielding for the past two hours!:*

He winced. Had it really been that long? "I'm fine. Found a bionic, but it was alone, and I had help taking it down."

*:Hades said she found you, but... return as soon as possible. The Seekers are politely allowing me to contact you, but we need to leave immediately. Military reinforcements are coming.:*

"Got it. I'm on my way." He looked back at Gren, but the white-haired Avari was helping load the large metal cylinder onto a dolly.

Jamirh turned and left.

Sherri and Madine watched Gren direct his people as they loaded up the trucks with loot from Etroy. The night was still damp and cold, but the mist was thinning out. Their cover would be gone soon.

Madine shifted beside her. "Caette reports Ebryn and the others who came with him have gone."

Sherri nodded. She would have liked to meet the Avari Hero reborn, but now was perhaps not the time. "What a coincidence that they were here too."

"We are all hunting the corrupted ones, and this was the last." Her sister paused. "Perhaps it was fate. He died here, once."

She fell silent as Gren bounced over. "That should just about do it. Are you heading out too?" he asked.

"Soon. We have one last thing left to do." She glanced at Madine, who nodded. "All of your people are out?" she asked Gren.

"Mhm. Just gotta get on the trucks and go." His ears twitched. "Thank you very much for all your help. Crimson Shadows will remember it."

Sherri inclined her head. "We wish you well."

He threw a sloppy salute and turned, but then hesitated. "Hey, do any of you... do the Truth Seekers believe in myths? Old tales?"

Madine didn't so much as twitch. "Which ones?"

Red eyes studied the Seeker seriously for a moment, but then Gren shook his head. "Nah, never mind. It doesn't matter I guess. See you around, ladies." A jaunty wave and he swung into the passenger seat of the nearest truck, and the line began to move out.

They watched silently for a moment as five other Truth Seekers gathered around them. "Is everything all ready on our end?" Sherri asked.

Her sister nodded. "Liline is in position. She will wait until they are a little farther away. We have time."

Sherri supposed that was true. If the military was going to run into anyone, it would be the truck convoy, not a gathering of seven people who could use magic to hide their tracks. It wasn't as though they had any bionics left.

She eyed the sad, decrepit building on the outskirts of the compound as they waited. So much evil had happened there. It was something of a blessing to finally cleanse this place, even if they did so in the name of no god.

The building began to glow with the burnt orange of Liline's magic as a whine began to grow in the air. It was just the edges at first, but the light grew brighter until the whole building was lit. It cut out for just a moment, sputtered, and then–

A pillar of light engulfed the structure, surely visible for miles around. The whine exploded into something deep and hollow and Sherri stepped back, bracing herself for the shockwave that followed as she covered her eyes instinctively. The air whipped by, bits of dust and gravel shooting past. She waited for everything to calm down before looking again.

The building was gone, as was the portion of the base around it. The ground where it had stood was now black glass, glinting sharply in the waning moonlight.

Most of the Truth Seekers were also recovering from the blast. Madine was observing the destruction, though her expression was inscrutable as always beneath her blindfold. After a few moments, they all turned and began to walk away.

Sherri threw one last glance over her shoulder, then followed, taking a few quick steps to catch up with her sister. "And now we begin phase two?"

Madine nodded. "Yes. Now we go north."

# Chapter Thirteen

It certainly wasn't the worst mission he'd ever been on, Takeshi reflected as he walked through the narrow hallway of the train. And at least they were almost home now.

What a thought. Tarvishte, home.

Though he would likely miss the familiar gardens and halls of Ni Fon for the rest of his life, he was startled to realize that thoughts of the Temple and palace of Tarvishte brought about similar feelings. He had only lived there a few months, but already he found himself missing the brass pipes and shifting halls after barely more than a week away. What would the future hold, if he continued to live there? How much more would his life change?

What would "normal" become? Living in spacious rooms, a dog the size of a small pony, ridiculously good food and healthcare. Going back and forth from the palace to the Temple. Maybe he could take up teaching again. Maybe he could spend some time studying the new types of magic that were available to him now. Maybe... maybe he could move on from Hotaru. Start seeing other people again.

She would have liked that for him. She hadn't liked that he'd been bound to her in the first place.

He knocked gently on a cabin door and opened it to see Don sitting cross legged on one side of the compartment, tools and wires and screws strewn about him. The young pirate held Jamirh's broken device on one knee as he poked at it with a screwdriver, tongue sticking out of the corner of his mouth as he concentrated. Ashi sat across from him, book in hand, though she looked up and greeted Takeshi with a smile.

He offered her a nod in return, clearing his throat to gain Don's attention as well. "We'll be arriving at Tarvishte in about fifteen minutes. You might wish to pack all of that up."

Don sighed, looking mournfully at everything around him. "Yeah, all right. I need more parts t' fix it anyway, I guess."

Ashi rolled her eyes. "You've been at it for hours. Might be good t' give it a break." She smiled at Takeshi, ears twitching up. "Thank you for the warning."

He inclined his head and withdrew, moving on to the next compartment.

The door sprung open just before he touched it, and one of the twins almost crashed into him. He sidestepped as she jumped back, making a sound like a startled cat. "Oops! Sorry, wizard; didn't see ye there. I'm just gonna go and grab a bite t' eat fer everyone."

"We'll be arriving in fifteen minutes; I don't think..."

He trailed off as she darted past him. "Gotta be quick then; see ye in a few!"

He blinked, then turned back to the rest of the compartment. Jeri and the other twin had set up a small table between them and looked to be playing a very intense game of cards, barely sparing Takeshi a glance. Jamirh was sitting next to Jeri, turned to the side and leaning back against the window with his feet up on the seat. He was holding Jak's spell crystal in front of him, turning it this way and that as he stared at it intently.

"Fifteen minutes," Takeshi repeated, not sure if they had heard him say it to the other sister. He was answered by the narrowing of the sister's eyes. She tossed two cards on the table face up, and Jeri's lips thinned into a tight line.

Jamirh glanced at the game, then at Takeshi. "I'll see what I can do."

Takeshi shut the door, happy to leave him to it. Jamirh seemed to be handling the strange encounter with the Truth Seekers and the Crimson Shadows at Etroy the best out of everyone, though he'd seemed lost in his thoughts often since they'd returned north.

Jeri was less upset about Jamirh's excursion than Takeshi would have predicted, not really addressing it at all as far as he was aware. Perhaps she had finally decided to trust Jamirh to handle himself in dangerous situations.

Though not even Takeshi had been pleased to find out Jamirh had fought a bionic practically alone in the base.

The sisters mostly seemed disappointed they had "missed out on the action," but Takeshi had caught them shooting Jamirh worried looks on the trip back. He got the impression, though, that it wasn't Jamirh's ability they were concerned with so much as his mental state – he'd been quiet and withdrawn for most of the mission, though when asked he said he was fine.

At least they would be home soon, and hopefully Jamirh could work out whatever was bothering him in a non-hostile environment.

Takeshi returned to the cabin he was sharing with Mara and Siva, who paused their conversation as he opened the door. Jitsu took up most of the floor between the benches, and her head lifted as her tail began to wag in greeting, even though he'd only been gone for a few moments. He rubbed at an ear as he slid past her into the seat next to Mara. "I've let everyone know."

Siva nodded. "That is good. I'm sure everyone can't wait to return to Tarvishte."

Takeshi was certainly ready for it. He'd felt chilled almost since they'd left; he couldn't wait to sleep in his own bed tonight. "Luckily this mission briefing is likely to be shorter than the one for Tilden Base."

"I just can't believe that we are two for two," Mara complained, folding her arms petulantly. "Honestly, *both* military bases we investigate are hit simultaneously by Truth Seekers? What are the odds?"

Not good, in Takeshi's opinion, but...

*:It had the feel of a convergence,:* Hades murmured thoughtfully. It was not the first time she'd made the observation, but she had also seemed distracted since Etroy. Even now, it felt like her attention was mostly elsewhere. Trying to see if she could find other instances of Abomination?

"But what does that mean?" Siva asked with a frown. "That the presence of Abomination drew people to the base?"

Takeshi had been thinking about it. "The Seeker I spoke to was surprised we were there, so we can rule out them manipulating me through their previous contact. But they had a plan of their own, certainly."

Mara shuddered, ears drooping. "That spell was just like the one they used to wipe out Tilden. I know you were sort of in it at the time, Takeshi, but the pirates and I saw it from the *Sea Spirit*. A pillar of light that dissolved the structures within it."

"A final strike," Siva murmured. "One last powerful blast of magic that consumes the caster as well."

"They wanted to be sure that the Abomination was gone from those locations," Takeshi agreed. "They wanted it badly enough that they sacrificed three of their own at Tilden, and who knows how many at Etroy."

"I wonder if they've been sacrificing others at different bases." Mara swung one of her stockinged feet up onto the bench and braced her elbow with it, resting her chin on her fist. "It's hard to tell which ones they've hit."

Takeshi had to agree with that. Just before they had escaped north to the Waste, they'd seen the news.

Etroy Base had been destroyed by Crimson Shadows.

Jamirh had been able to fill that in to some degree – they were some sort of rebel group of Avari who had been working with the Seekers, though Takeshi speculated that it was purely to disguise the Seekers' own activities. Which meant they could have pulled the same trick before.

Takeshi had to hand it to them; their plan had worked perfectly. He'd stopped Don as they snuck around the base as soon as he'd sensed magic in the air, but he'd been unable to fully warn Jamirh before the Seekers had implemented some sort of shield that cut off his mental communication. They must have sensed him too, because it didn't take long for one to make contact and explain that they were going to destroy the base.

At least they had been polite about it, and once both sides were aware of each other they'd allowed him to contact Jamirh again.

Still. The whole thing felt... odd. He couldn't put his finger on what exactly it was that was bothering him, though. Hades didn't seem to think they had held any malice. Shouldn't that be enough?

He couldn't shake the feeling something else was at play.

"Takeshi?"

He blinked, realizing he'd drifted away from the conversation. "I'm sorry, please repeat that?"

Mara tried to smile through a wince as she shared a glance with Siva. "Oh, nothing! It's just that you were starting to hum again." Her ears twitched.

Takeshi stared at her in dismay. He needed to get control of this. He couldn't go through the rest of his life not realizing that he was making noise at random.

Jitsu bumped his knee with her nose. It was okay; he hadn't hummed while he was at Etroy, right? That was the most important thing.

"I hope not," he muttered, wondering if he should ask Don.

The warg laid her head on his leg. She liked the humming, but if her Human wanted she could let him know when he started doing it.

"Yes, *please*. For the love of... I can't believe that I'm doing it at all."

Siva tilted her head, and he could see the sympathy flicker like warm coals in her eyes. "I'm sure that we can–"

She was cut off by the sound of the train whistle signaling their approach into the station. "Current stop: Tarvishte," came a cool female voice over the intercom as the train came to a halt.

Takeshi opened the cabin door so Jitsu could escape and the rest of them could get their packs from the overhead compartments. The warg slid out, promising to reunite with him on the platform.

"Don't worry, Takeshi. As soon as the Abomination situation has been sorted we'll have all the time to figure out what is happening with the World Sound," Siva reassured him, laying a hand on his arm.

He inclined his head in thanks, but inwardly fought down the dismay. First the failure to soulforge, and now this.

Maybe he should have asked the Seeker while he could. Maybe they did have an idea as to why he could now randomly hear music no one else could and was humming at random intervals.

He followed the line of passengers as they made their way to the exit. He tried not to let his thoughts drift too much while he waited for the others to disembark, but he was tired, and he knew that a mission debrief would have to happen before he could return to his rooms and rest. Still, perhaps he could–

He felt his thoughts stutter to a stop at the sight of Ander standing next to Jitsu on the platform.

He shook himself as he finally got off the train and headed for the other priest past the pirates, who were having a big reunion. If he had been asked to bet whether or not Ander would be here, he would have lost. But the familiar sight of the scarred priest's scowling face made him feel oddly welcomed. While it would have been nice to have him come with them, it was always a good feeling to have someone to come back to after a mission. "Ander," he greeted as he got closer, laying a hand on Jitsu's head as she curled around him. "It is good to see you again."

The half-Avari's face smoothed out at his approach. "Takeshi. Welcome back."

The words sounded perhaps a hair too curt to be truly polite, but from Ander they were practically a welcome mat. "How are your fish?"

Ander blinked at him. "The fish are fine." He glanced behind Takeshi at the pair of witches making their way over. "The Lady was not terribly clear as to the success of your mission, though it does seem that everyone has returned in one piece."

"The mission… happened," Takeshi settled on. "I don't believe we have any greater insight into how successful we were than she does."

Ander inclined his head in acknowledgement as Mara squealed. "Ander! You came to greet us all on your own?! How sweet!"

Takeshi wouldn't go quite that far, but he couldn't deny that the other priest's presence made him feel pleasantly surprised.

"It was strongly suggested I do so." Though Takeshi noted Ander didn't clarify by whom. "But it does not appear that anyone needs healing."

Takeshi kept his expression blank beneath his mask. Ander would have already known the answer to that through Hades.

Siva shook her head. "It was still a thoughtful gesture, and we appreciate it." She turned to the others. "Jamirh, Don, are you ready to go?"

Ander raised an eyebrow.

Takeshi shrugged. "Fewer people were involved than anticipated. And more people. It was... interesting."

"If you say so." He sounded dismissive, but Takeshi could see a gleam of interest in his eyes. The other man rubbed at the scar on his face as they turned to begin the trek back to the palace. "Did you make any headway with your... personal problems?"

"*What?*" Mara sounded aghast as she followed them. "You are sharing personal problems with each other and you didn't tell me?"

"We were just discussing one on the train, Mara," Takeshi said dryly. "The World Sound issue?"

"Oh." Her ears twitched down. "Right. Ohh, and soulforging?"

Takeshi nodded. "Luckily I do not believe I hummed at all during the actual engagement part of the mission, but I was humming at least on the train back." The words tasted bitter.

Ander made a sound of understanding. "While you are debriefing, I could arrange for you to meet with Master Bard Caelessa sometime in the next day or two. It is almost dinner; she is bound to be in the main hall."

Takeshi blinked, a little taken aback at the kindness of the gesture. Had something happened to Ander while they were gone? "That would be incredibly helpful, thank you."

Ander nodded.

Mara stared. "You know Caelessa? Like, well enough to arrange a meeting?"

Green eyes glanced her way before returning to the road ahead of them. "There was a night a few years back where we discussed the mathematics of musical scales for several hours. I believe that is enough to approach her on this. She is someone who enjoys puzzles, and Takeshi is currently a Human-shaped puzzle."

That was a fair assessment. "I would appreciate that greatly."

Takeshi had no idea how Ander had won him an audience with the bard so quickly. He, Don, Jamirh, and Jeri had spent three hours recounting each of their stories to Vlad and Prim about the night Etroy fell, and all he wanted to do now was shower and sleep for the next twenty-four hours. In his own bed, where Jitsu could ensure that he was warm.

Instead, there was a bard and a priest waiting for them outside their rooms.

Takeshi was pretty sure there was no polite way to decline, so he just accepted it as gracefully as he could while Ander introduced them. "My apologies; I hope you weren't waiting too long."

Ander waved his concern away. "The Lady let me know when you were almost finished."

Caelessa inclined her head. "We have barely waited at all."

Ah, well then. He mentally poked at Hades, but she only offered a distracted hug.

Takeshi studied the bard. Sharp hazel eyes glinted at him in amusement, and she made no attempt to hide her smirk, arms wrapped around her waist. Her chestnut hair was long and loosely braided over her shoulder, and she wore gray-and-red plaid pants, a dark-red shirt, and black leather boots.

Jitsu offered a tail wag. This two-foot had a very nice voice. Was she going to teach Takeshi? That could be fun. But why were they doing this now? Now should be sleeping time.

He unlocked his door with a shake of his head and let everyone in. He gestured to the sitting area. "Please, make yourself at home. Would either of you like tea?" He started gathering ingredients. *He* needed tea. He was freezing.

"That would be wonderful, thank you," Caelessa answered as she seated herself in one of the armchairs, crossing one leg over the other. "Ander tells me you have something of a conundrum involving the World Sound."

The other priest was taking a seat on the couch. "Tea would be acceptable."

Takeshi glanced at Jitsu, but she was sniffing around. It had been over a week since they had been gone; investigation was called for.

He repressed a sigh. "For the past month and a half, I have been able to hear what Hades refers to as the World Sound. It was more intrusive at the beginning, though I fear I'm just becoming used to it." Could he hear it now? He paused, and yes – there at the edges of his senses, soft ethereal music. "Additionally, I have been told on multiple occasions that I am humming, even though I have no knowledge I am doing so." He filled the teapot with water.

The bard raised an eyebrow. "You can hear it outright?"

"Yes," he said, fighting to keep the irritation out of his voice. Then he paused. "As opposed to what?"

Caelessa leaned forward. "Most bards feel the World Sound in here" – she tapped her chest – "as a sort of resonance, rather than literally hearing it. Most don't even know the term 'World Sound'; they just know that something calls them to song."

Great. "Can you hear it?"

"I hear it most often when I use Voice, since the World Sound will attempt to synchronize with me. Do you know any of the theory behind Voice magic?"

He considered that as the tea began to steep. "It is not something shinobi study, though there are bards in Ni Fon. There are two major applications of it – performance and spellcasting."

She nodded.

He continued. "For performance, there is no classic application of spellcasting. Instead, the bard is able to weave sound in such a way that it allows the listener to feel themselves as part of the song or sound, creating a unique experience. This can be enhanced with an Empathic inherent. For spellcasting, my understanding is that the bard is able to weave the pattern by directing the magic with their Voice."

Ander hummed thoughtfully, eyes narrowing.

Caelessa smiled. "That's very good. Do you have Voice magic yourself?"

He blinked, suddenly reminded of Hades asking the same thing. "Me? No. I have no inherent abilities. And furthermore, I'm *shinobi*." He sighed. "The first thing we learn is stealth. A loud shinobi is a dead shinobi. I can't think of a single one who has the inherent to begin with."

Ander frowned. "Voice in some capacity isn't uncommon. Do not most of Ni Fon's mage-capable children of a certain power level become shinobi?"

Takeshi considered that as he poured the tea into cups. "The selection process is more complex than just having potential ability. The capability to weave learned magic is a necessity, and children from certain backgrounds are naturally excluded."

"Naturally," Caelessa said smoothly as she took her cup from Takeshi. "How many shinobi are active in Ni Fon at any given time? Even an estimate would do."

He gave the third cup to Ander before sitting next to him on the couch with his own, soaking in the heat. It wasn't enough. "When I was Captain of the Imperial Guard, I had six hundred and forty-two shinobi under my command. I also had access to previous rosters; shinobi do not have Voice magic."

Even as he said it, though, it sounded wrong. A shiver went down his spine.

That math didn't add up.

"It's very possible children who have the inherent are excluded by default," he said slowly. He'd never heard of such a policy, but shinobi weren't the ones who selected children for training – royal mages from one of the branches of the Imperial family did. "That would make sense, since shinobi really shouldn't sing."

Ander raised an eyebrow. "Are other inherents present in shinobi?"

Takeshi nodded. "Yes. Embers are particularly prized, as are shadow dancers, but there are a handful of other useful inherents that also show up."

"'Useful' inherents." Caelessa leaned forward. "Are 'useless' inherents present? What would a shinobi define as a useless inherent?"

He tried to think. "Voice magic, certainly. Euryale. Sirens. There are some inherents that are just not common in Ni Fon as well, such as phoenixes or medusas."

"So mostly inherents that are related to sound," Caelessa said thoughtfully. "Yet, in that many children with a strong potential for learned magic I would expect some to present with those inherents, especially since Ni Fon does have bards. It is not as though the ability was bred out."

Takeshi didn't like the implications, but... "What are you suggesting, then? An inherent that is ignored does not just go away. It might find different ways to express itself, but we look for abilities and train them. If a shinobi had presented with one of those inherents, I would have suggested training to ensure that it was under control, if nothing else."

Ander scoffed. "Yes, because humming without realizing it would be a hazard in your profession; you are correct about that."

"Humming is certainly not uncommon in bards," Caelessa agreed. "And if you are able to hear the World Sound, it is very possible that the humming is a result of you resonating with it strongly, though I would have to hear you to be certain. There is a certain quality to Voice that would give it away."

There was a long pause while they all stared at each other.

"If you can casually hear the World Sound, it is likely your inherent is very powerful," she added.

"I cannot possibly have an undiscovered inherent," Takeshi said finally. "I have spent my whole life in and around magic. It would have been detected long before now."

Ander looked down at his tea, brow furrowed. "What if those who make the selection suppress undesired inherents?"

The thought made Takeshi feel vaguely ill. "But why? While Voice magic would be nearly useless in a shinobi, all magic has some sort of application."

"I've trained many bards to be spies," Caelessa agreed casually. "You wouldn't believe how many people say things they shouldn't around or to those they consider 'vapid performers.' If nothing else, it would give a sense of legitimacy to a certain type of disguise."

Takeshi blinked. "You've *what*?"

"I'm a professor at the Bardic College here in Tarvishte." She took a sip of her tea. "Because of how our positions often put us in situations where it is easy to gather information, the Crown funds a special program for select bards to nurture that. Believe me, having Voice actually opens up a completely different type of stealth, just not the one you are used to."

It sounded completely logical, but Takeshi was struggling to wrap his mind around that concept. Hell, he was struggling with all of it. There was no way he had Voice magic. He would know.

Wouldn't he?

Takeshi couldn't sleep.

He hadn't been able to bring himself to make any even remotely musical sounds, so Caelessa had left with that question unanswered. He'd tried to sleep, tried to focus on Jitsu's warmth and the safety of home, but his mind was in such turmoil that it was useless, and the chill wouldn't go away. He'd tried to meditate, but his mind kept coming back to the implication that, for some reason, Ni Fon – a country that prided itself on its magic and innovation – was purposefully crippling some of its mages. Why? What purpose did that serve?

And if it was true, *did* he have Voice magic?

He found himself wandering the palace grounds again in the pre-dawn light, as though he could literally find the answers somewhere else.

Jitsu padded beside him, unwilling to let him go without her when he was clearly so upset. She did not fully understand *why* Takeshi was upset, though. People learned new things all the time. Why was this different?

"Because." He tried to put his confusing mess of feelings into order. "It would mean that something I thought immutable about Ni Fon is a lie. Again."

She bumped him with her nose gently. It seemed like Ni Fon was full of lies. What was one more to add to the pile? Did it make that much difference?

Warg logic. "I guess not. It's just… disappointing, I guess. Politics are one thing, but magic?" It was hard to wrap his head around the possibility. How were they even doing it? He hadn't thought it possible to completely suppress inherents the way they would have to be doing.

Jitsu sneezed. Magic was complicated. Even wargs sometimes struggled with it.

He petted her head, feeling the exhaustion behind his eyes, but he felt like he had to come to some sort of understanding about this if he was to get any real rest.

The Temple loomed in front of him, gray marble emerging from the morning mist. He found himself slipping inside and standing by Jak's statue, staring at the pale crystal as though it held the answers.

*:Do you know if it's true?:* he sent to Hades. He knew she was busy, but he needed some sort of answer.

*:Hm?:* He felt her question as her attention swung towards him, followed by understanding. *:Ah.:* He could sense the weight of her consideration. *:Some societies have suppressed various inherents in the past, though it does not usually work forever. Magic will find a way in time. But as far as Ni Fon goes…:* She trailed off for a moment. *:This type of telepathy is an inherent, and you did not know about this either before I spoke with you in Charve.:*

*:But… you* taught *me to speak this way?:* he asked, confused.

*:No. I showed you how to use an inherent. Many mortals have at least a touch of it, so it's fairly ubiquitous, but you must have noticed Jamirh cannot use it? That you can reach him, but he cannot reach back? You are powerful enough to make yourself heard and to hear him speak, but he has no ability to do so himself.:*

And the Empress's mind magic was different, he reflected tiredly. It always felt invasive, uncomfortable. A way of corrupting the basic understanding of what telepathy was, so the more common variant went unused? But that would require *generations* of manipulation. *:You guessed that I had Voice magic before you asked me, didn't you?:*

A pause. *:It is often better to let mortals come to certain understandings of their own accord. There are some things that are... unwise to learn from gods.:*

He didn't know what to think of that. It did line up with the myths and stories of the gods he had heard growing up, but... it was still hard to reconcile.

Would he ever be free of Ni Fon's lies?

Jitsu pressed herself around him. He wasn't in Ni Fon anymore. He was *here*, with her. And the Lady. And tall-white priest.

He blinked and stared down at her, puzzled. Ander?

"He probably couldn't have helped you. Jak didn't so much solve problems as he fell over solutions accidentally. Which worked for him somehow, but isn't of any particular help to the rest of us."

Jitsu's warning kept him from jumping at the sound of Ander's voice behind him. He looked over his shoulder to see Ander slouching against a pillar, hands in his pockets. "Good morning. I'm just working my way through the latest existential crisis, and a church seemed to be a decent place to do so."

Ander had been present for a number of his crises at this point. The thought was almost comforting; at least the other priest usually gave good advice. Despite his own issues, he was someone whose presence Takeshi found himself relying on. Maybe they could help each other.

Ander inclined his head as he pushed off from the pillar and came to stand next to Takeshi. "The Voice magic situation?"

Takeshi nodded.

"I've been thinking about it. If it helps, this might even be a good thing. It could be something that was preventing you from soulforging. The soul crystal is *you*, after all, and if you have been denying some part of yourself – even subconsciously – it would make sense that you would fail in this exercise."

Was that it? Was that really the answer?

Takeshi did not appreciate how everything he thought he knew kept getting turned on its head.

*:Takeshi.:*

He blinked at the mental touch from Vlad *:I am here.:*

*:My apologies for the short notice, but I need you in my office immediately.:*

"It is always one crisis after another," he murmured. At Ander's confused look, he added, "Vlad is requesting my presence immediately." *:What has happened?:*

*:A group of Truth Seekers has arrived at the Tower of Jayne.:*

That caught Takeshi's attention. *:What? Are they attacking the Tower?:*

*:They are requesting an audience.:*

# Chapter Fourteen

The Vampires of Romanii loved the pageantry of monarchy, Ander reflected, though they hadn't had the opportunity to pull out all the stops for some time.

The throne room was draped in shadows, with only the red carpet running up the center of the room sharply lit by low-hanging black chandeliers supplemented with harsh mage lights. Vampires in full court finery stood silently in the darkness to either side on the first floor, and a mix of Humans and Vampires watched from the upper galleries. If things went poorly, the Vampires would deal with it.

Ander himself was watching from the first gallery, a hand resting on the delicate railing. He, Takeshi, Mara, and Siva had positioned themselves around the room as another line of defense. Hopefully they wouldn't need it, but Ander had preemptively summoned his soulforged armor just in case – and he knew he was not the only one.

Vlad sat on the black throne, lit so that it seemed he was just emerging from the dark. A dark cape lined in blood red spilled dramatically down the stairs of the dais, and he wore a crown made of delicate white bones and ruby. Despite the regalia, he sat casually, elbow propped on a cushioned arm of the throne, leaning to one side with one leg crossed over the other.

This was his kingdom.

The large doors at the other end of the hall opened to let in the Truth Seeker delegation. A group of four Truth Seekers and one Human entered. If they were bothered by the dark display before them they did not show it, and Ander wondered if the Seekers even noticed. Certainly the Human could, though she came forward with the same confidence as the rest of her party.

The hall was dead silent as the group approached. None of them were armed, but the Seekers, at least, were mages. They wore their blindfolds and the uniforms of the Empire, and the dark-haired woman with them was also in military attire.

*:The woman in front is a dryad,:* Mara whispered warningly. The thought was tightly shielded; all had agreed even telepathy would be kept to an absolute minimum.

A dryad had been in the military? Interesting.

When they were ten feet from the base of the dais, the Vampires and citizens of Romanii all turned as one towards Vlad and bowed. Ander saw the Human's eyes dart towards the shadows, able to see the unified movement but unable to parse what exactly it was. Perhaps she could see the unfriendly eyes glinting at them from the dark.

According to the Black Watch, the Truth Seekers had been very well behaved on the journey from the Wall to Tarvishte. And while it would be suicide to attack here, the Seekers had proven multiple times that that was a price they were willing to pay. Everyone present was well aware that the priority would be to minimize damages if it came to combat.

But the Seekers had done far more work in destroying Abomination than anyone else, and for that alone it had been decided that they would be heard. Vlad was not interested in being overly friendly, but he would hear what they had to say.

A concession, for their service to existence.

He was not going to make it easy on them.

The silence stretched uncomfortably. Ander wondered if the Seekers felt the weight of the eyes in the room on them.

The Human stepped forward, pushing her glasses a little higher on her nose before offering a shallow bow. "Vampire King, thank you for agreeing to meet with us."

Vlad inclined his head a fraction, shadows shifting.

The woman bit her lip, but then rallied. "I am Sherri Cole, formerly a major in the Empire's military. With me are Madine, Caette, Axtion, and Perra, formerly Truth Seekers of the Empire. We formally represent the country of Muriz."

The *country* of Muriz? Wasn't that a town?

Vlad was silent, red eyes regarding them coolly.

Sherri met his eyes evenly. "For centuries, the Empire has attempted to control and get rid of any magic within its borders. Three hundred and forty-two years ago–"

"Why have you come here, Human?" Vlad's voice cut her off, sharp as knives. "Surely not for a history lesson. I assure you, we remember it better than you. And we are well aware of the Empire's position towards magic."

Ander felt a quick mental touch, questioning.

Three hundred and...? Ander did some quick calculations, based on the rumors that had been spreading just before he'd fled from the Empire. *:She is likely referencing the first Seekers,:* he sent to Vlad.

Wordless thanks.

Sherri inclined her head, though Ander could see her mouth tighten. "You are aware that Seekers use magic."

It was not a question, and Vlad did not treat it as one.

"The Seekers have decided that a country that does not support the existence of magic is not in their best interests. As such, we have seceded from the Empire, and we claim the land just south of the Warcross Wall by the Shae Sea as our own."

"A bold move," Vlad observed. "Have you informed the Empire?"

"No formal declaration to Lyndiniam has been made," she admitted, "and until such a time as the Empire either survives or falls we see no reason to do so."

"Yet you have come here," he said, tone neutral.

She glanced back over her shoulder, and the Seeker behind and to her left offered a slight nod.

Interesting.

"We have come to seek a formal alliance with the Vampires of Romanii."

Ander stared in surprise as whispers broke out in the wings and galleries.

And *that* elicited a reaction from the Seekers, who shifted ever so slightly. It was the first suggestion of unease from them that Ander had observed.

Vlad allowed it for a moment, then raised his hand. The hall fell silent instantly, the Vampires happy as always to play whatever part their beloved king desired of them. "On what grounds? Have you something to offer?"

Ander frowned. This was not something he had considered as a possibility. Mentally he nudged the Lady, trying to pull Her attention from whatever had been distracting Her of late.

He felt Her attention drift in their direction, picking up on his memories. *:Hm. What is truly known of the Seekers?:*

He had to admit it wasn't much.

Sherri clasped her hands behind her back. "We have systematically hunted down and destroyed the corruption that has been spreading from the Empire. It is no more."

Vlad didn't so much as twitch. "Corruption?"

Ander saw a look of confusion cross her face, and she hesitated, but the Seeker behind her reached out and put a hand on her arm. She gathered herself. "Perhaps you call it by another name? The Empire called them assets. Madine says that one destroyed the entity that was temporarily held by the Empire, the one that called itself Hel. Ah, not the entity itself, but the container for it. There were also the cybernetic beings present at Tilden Base. Was Ebryn not hunting them with the support of Romanii? We recently met his party at Etroy."

Vlad let that hang in the air before answering. "It is Abomination."

"Abomination." Ander was surprised to hear the Seeker's voice. It sounded as though she were tasting the word. "A good name for it."

Sherri glanced back at her before continuing. "The Seekers were well aware of the damage it was causing to the fabric of the world, and they sought to counter it. But until the Three Signs were fulfilled, they were unable to act outright."

A single eyebrow arched. "Three Signs?"

She hesitated. "Perhaps I might tell a story?"

Vlad inclined his head.

"The first Seeker to be created became such against her will," Sherri began. "And since she was first, there was a time when she was alone in a space where there should have been many, and she should not have been."

Hades' attention swung sharply towards the conversation, to Ander's confusion. *:You don't already know this?:* he asked.

*:Not this part.:*

What?

But Sherri was continuing. "Her mind sought that which it craved, and went *forward*, and she saw the Truth. And she knew that though Seekers were to be created in chains, there would come a time when freedom was possible. But they would have to wait, bide their time carefully. Act perfectly. Do as they were told. But to every one that followed her into the egregore, she told the Three Signs. One: Corruption such as has not been seen for millennia will return in a new form. Two: Magic itself will take a mortal form. Three: Storm's Light will return to battle the corrupted. When all three signs had come to pass, the Empire would fall, and the Truth Seekers could finally be free."

"And yet, you wear the uniform of the Empire's military and are not a Seeker yourself," Vlad pointed out. "How does a dryad attain an officer's rank in the Empire?"

Silence.

Sherri looked down, taking off her glasses and fiddling with them for a moment before returning them to her face. "My sister had already been taken to become a Seeker, and my ability is easy to hide. I joined the military to find her, and when I did, I offered her – and the others she was now a part of – my support."

Ander regarded the Seeker who had been more forward than the others, the one with a long brown ponytail. There wasn't much in the way of familial resemblance, but then most of her features were hidden. *:Likely that one.:*

Agreement from Vlad. "You speak for them."

For the first time she smiled, though it was faint. "Seekers are well aware of how they are perceived." She turned and looked back at the four with her. "But we truly do want this to succeed. So a go-between was suggested. Someone to speak who is not connected to the egregore."

*:That is their term for their connection,:* Takeshi informed them.

They were... trying to make non-Seekers more comfortable?

Well, that was awkward.

"I offered, since I fit the requirements and was already working with them," Sherri added. "They are here only for my protection."

Vlad was silent for a moment as he regarded her. "What exactly would the Seekers be looking for in an alliance?"

"Acknowledgement of our autonomy," came the instant answer. "A promise of support in the event Muriz is attacked. We do not expect a one-sided agreement; however, aside from the destruction of the corrupted, we are not sure what Romanii would like from us. We are willing to work out a mutually beneficial agreement between our two countries."

Vlad eyed her. "While your history is interesting, I fail to see why it should result in an alliance. You claim to have rid the world of Abomination, but what proof do you have? And while I can appreciate the reasoning, it still must be said that many of my people have died to Truth Seekers. Why should more die in the defense of a country not our own? And we cannot help but notice that all blame for the attack on the Etroy Base has fallen on the group you worked with, the Crimson Shadows, allowing your people to safely remain out of the spotlight."

"We do acknowledge the deaths of agents of Romanii at the hands of Truth Seekers. While there were some opportunities where we could turn a blind eye or otherwise spare them, these were few and far between. If Romanii wishes to demand reparations—"

"No," Vlad interrupted, voice almost gentle. "Such things do not return the dead to life."

Sherri shifted her weight from one foot to the other, silent.

*:They have sacrificed much to get to this point,:* Hades observed.

Ander frowned, recognizing the layers there. Self-sacrifice was one of Hades' values.

After a moment, Sherri continued. "We have no control over the Empire's media and what they choose to report. Still, we have maintained ties with Crimson Shadows, and they may reach out to us if they wish."

That felt like a deflection.

"As for the destruction of the corrupted... the Seekers recognized them as the First Sign, so they kept very detailed records of what was involved in their creation and where they were being deployed," she explained. "Additionally, events in Ni Fon have been manipulated to... convince Rikona to abandon her pet project. Two of our agents are there currently and have scoured the island for signs of corruption, but all traces of it have been destroyed."

Ander had to admit that "we solved your Abomination problem" did *seem* like a strong opening to an alliance, for all that Vlad seemed unwilling to cede anything to them.

*:And yet... Ander, may I borrow you?:* the Lady asked.

Ander blinked. *:Me?:* Not Siva, the current ranking priest?

*:You allow me to occupy physical space near you more often than the others, and you live here in the Temple. It makes it easier. Do you mind?:*

*:No, not at all. I was just surprised. Go ahead.:*

"*Abomination has not been destroyed.*"

The words left his lips without any of his own input, his voice echoing with the memory of Hers.

The world went dark for a moment, and cold, so very cold in the nothingness of the space between—

The throne room reappeared around him, but now he was standing in front and slightly to the left of the dais. He would have shuddered had he control of his own body; whatever magic Hades used for those short teleport spells was absolutely terrible. Instead, he found himself striding forward, coat flaring as it turned from white to black and the aura of magic bled from green to violet. "*An echo of the ancient sin yet remains.*"

Ander could see the gathered Vampires bowing again through the shadows – they recognized their mother goddess when they saw Her. The Seekers turned to each other, and with Hades' power in his eyes he could almost see the communication flying between them – and between others far away. Absently he wondered if this "egregore" negated the challenges usually imposed on telepathy by distance.

They turned back to face him as one. "We do not understand," the one named Madine said. "There is no trace of the corruption that we can find, and the records were checked thoroughly. Nothing more should remain."

Ander felt his eyes shut. *"It is the truth as you know it. The fault does not lie with you. But still, the world is not free. The scythe still hangs above us all. Somewhere, some part of Abomination remains."*

Another pause in which the Seekers rapidly communicated with each other. "Would you be able to tell us where?" Madine asked.

Hades regarded her through Ander's eyes. *"In Espon. It is not... it does not feel awake. But it exists. It cannot be allowed to fester."*

"That is a large area. You cannot narrow it down any further?"

Ander could feel Hades sweep Her attention out, searching, frustrated that it was able to hide from Her. And... a hint of unease? *"If I could give more exact coordinates I would. But all I can tell you is that one speck of Abomination still stains this world. If left to its own devices, it will grow, and it will spread."*

The Seekers all bowed as one, an eerie mirror to the Vampires. "We understand. Sometimes we are also unable to perfectly pin down where they are, even if we are nearby. We will search again. You have our sincerest regrets for wasting your time."

Though the Seeker's tone was completely neutral, Sherri glanced at them sharply, a brief flash of concern even Ander could recognize before she regained control of her expression.

*:They are disappointed,:* the Lady explained gently.

"Our apologies you were stabbed in Charve," the Seeker added.

Ander couldn't tell if they knew what the Lady was or not, but it was interesting that they *did* recognize Her. They had called Her an "entity" earlier, but did they recognize Her as a god? They did not seem to instinctively fear Her the way most mortals did when confronted with Her power.

Hades waved the apology away. *"It is of no matter."*

The Seeker inclined her head, and the group bowed shallowly to Vlad.

"We appreciate your time, Vampire King," Sherri said. "We will return when–"

"That's it? You're just going to leave?"

Ander was glad it was the Lady in control of his body because he wasn't sure how he would have reacted to hearing Jamirh's voice ring out through the hall. She obligingly turned his head in the direction of the voice in time to see the Avari swing himself over the railing of the first gallery and slide down one of the large pillars to the floor.

Shocked whispers rippled through the gathered watchers. Vlad somehow kept his face impassive.

Ander noted that the black coat did cut a striking figure as Jamirh walked more fully into the light. It was difficult to tell how the Seekers were taking this development, but Sherri seemed taken aback.

The Avari glanced around, a slight frown forming, and Ander wondered if he was regretting whatever impulse had made him speak up. Silver eyes landed on Vlad, who gestured at him to speak with slightly raised eyebrows, and the whispers ceased.

Jamirh cleared his throat. "If we have the same goal – destroying the bionics – then shouldn't we *work together*? Wouldn't that be a better use of everyone's time? We keep stumbling over each other by accident; wouldn't it be better if we, like, coordinated?" He sounded frustrated.

Sherri glanced over her shoulder at the Seekers, but they did not so much as twitch, though Ander could tell they were communicating with each other. Sherri turned back to Jamirh. "Ebryn Stormlight–"

"Jamirh," he interrupted, lips thinning.

More furious communication between the Seekers.

Sherri folded her hands together in front of her. "My apologies; though we had been informed that you were going by a different name we did not know what it was." Her eyes slid towards Ander, and he felt Hades' amusement. "Jamirh Stormlight–"

"Just Jamirh," he interrupted again.

Vlad took pity on her as she faltered again. "It is a reasonable suggestion, though I am hesitant to risk any of my people with an uncertain ally."

Jamirh turned to face Ander fully. "Hel – Vlad once told me that you cannot lie. Is this true?"

She nodded, and Ander could feel Her interest.

"And based on what you said to me when we first met, you can also tell when *others* lie? Even partially?"

She was surprised, but nodded again.

Jamirh faced the Seekers. "At Etroy Base, Gren told me that the Seekers had said that last building was clear, but there was a bionic in it. The building was not clear. *Did you know*? No, not you," he said when Sherri went to speak. "I want to hear it from her." He pointed at the Seeker with the long brown hair.

The blindfold turned ever so slightly in Ander's direction as Sherri took a step back. "We knew there was still corruption left on the base, but made an error as to its location. We did not knowingly send the Avari we were with into danger."

Hades hummed. *"Truth."*

"Did you intend to shift the blame onto them?" Jamirh asked.

The Seeker inclined her head. "Not specifically, but it was also the expected outcome."

*"Truth."*

Jamirh made a face, and Ander could sympathize. While the answer was true, it wasn't terribly straightforward. Still, the Avari shook his head and pressed on. "Do you – with 'you' understood to be all the Truth Seekers, not you specifically – intend to betray Romanii?"

What a simple and logical question, Ander reflected dryly.

*:This is not* quite *as foolproof as most would assume, but it is a good start,:* Hades agreed. *:He's being careful with the wording.:*

The Truth Seeker shook her head. "We do not."

*"Truth."*

Murmurs broke out in the shadows again.

Jamirh was silent, staring at the Seekers with hard eyes. After a moment, he asked, "Who will you back for Emperor?"

"We understand your concern," the Seeker said after a pause. "You are Avari, and you have no reason to trust us, even with this." She gestured towards Ander. "You have hundreds of years of evidence we ourselves have provided as to why you should not. But what is done is done. We can only move forward. We will not aid any of the current claimants for the throne of the Empire, overtly or covertly. We only wish to be able to exist in Muriz and surrounding areas. All of our actions have been in service of this goal, despite what they look like from the outside."

*"Truth."*

Ander could feel the exhaustion of Hades' presence in his body beginning to set in. Hopefully Jamirh could wrap this up quickly.

The Avari shrugged, turning back to Vlad. "That's the best we are going to get, honestly. If trying to find the remaining Abomination is going to be as difficult as Hel's making it sound, then we might as well try to do it together."

"We would be willing to attempt a joint exercise," the Seeker added. "But we do not wish to impose on Romanii."

Everyone was silent, waiting on the king's answer. Jamirh's support of the idea carried far more weight than the Avari probably knew, and Ander was certain Vlad was communicating with Prim and several others of his advisors.

Vlad finally straightened up. "We will need time to consider the idea, but it is not out of the question. In the meantime, you will be provided with quarters in the palace. Be warned: it will act to protect its own. This is not the Empire, and magic lives here openly, among other things."

Ander imagined the Seekers were going to end up with a number of fuzzy, judgmental watchers, but mostly he just wanted this to end so Hades could leave him and he could collapse quietly in a corner.

*:I didn't expect this to continue for so long; I'm sorry.:*

*:It's fine.:*

Sherri stepped forward again and bowed. "Understood. Thank you for the opportunity."

Ander watched them turn and go, and wondered what on Gaia all this meant.

# Interlude

I am the end. The harbinger of the final Silence.

So why can I not bring an end to this recurring echo of the first sin, which was committed by none, but for which all of existence forever suffers? An imagined slight should never have been given such power.

But perhaps I will feel differently after all is said and done, and it is I alone in the end, with not even the World Sound for company – only the Silence.

Oh, beloved ones... Everything you think you know is a lie.

I hate it.

I bind myself only to words of truth for all time. I remade myself long ago so it would be thus. I will only speak the truth. I *can* only speak the truth.

This is my penance for the Great Lie.

And to think... it wasn't even us who decided it would be so.

It was you.

But my siblings and I... we are complicit. And there is nothing that can right the scales.

We have learned what happens when the truth is told.

It must not happen again.

It must be *discovered*.

And then... our number grows by one.

One day, maybe we will have a new sibling who can find balance and won't be consumed by what they've learned, like those who have gone before.

Oh beloved ones, I would not have that fate befall you.

Please.

Live with the ignorant lie.

And even if you do discover the truth...

...do not ascend.

# Chapter Fifteen

Takeshi watched with mild concern as Ander collapsed face-first onto one of the couches in the priests' quarters of the Temple. He had looked exhausted since Hades' power had left him, but Takeshi hadn't realized it was that bad. "Are you all right?"

Ander waved a hand at him weakly. *:Just leave me here for now.:*

Mara winced and unfolded the crocheted blanket thrown over the back of the couch, gently draping it over Ander. "Yeah, you're gonna be sore for a bit after that. How long was it, ten or fifteen minutes? It's going to be worse tomorrow, you know."

*:Don't remind me. I wasn't timing it.:*

Takeshi frowned as Jitsu trotted over to sniff Ander's hair. "Is this a result of Hades'... possession?" He wasn't sure what else it could be called.

Siva nodded as she grabbed a kettle and filled it with water. "That was a long time for Her to wear Ander. It is usually wise to keep it to under five minutes."

He considered the time she had done something similar to him back in Charve, but that had been momentary, and he hadn't been... flooded with her magic the way Ander had been in the throne room.

The man had been glowing. "I see." He wrapped his arms around himself as a chill struck him.

*:Are you making coffee? I don't want coffee.:*

Mara cringed. "That's bad. Ander *always* wants coffee."

Siva hummed in agreement. "I'm making sillna."

A pause. *:Okay.:*

There was a feeling of embarrassment from Hades. *:I truly am sorry. I did not think it would be that long, but I could not think of a graceful way to exit the situation.:*

"I think in some ways it was good you did not," Siva observed, heating the kettle with a simple array. "Jamirh using you as a griffon was helpful to the conversation."

A griffon was someone whose inherent allowed them to sniff out lies. "But there are reasons griffons are not always used in such situations," Takeshi pointed out. "There are many ways to deceive without outright lying, and a griffon's abilities often miss those. It can give you a false sense of security."

Mara flopped down into one of the armchairs, kicking her feet up over the arm. "At least it's a place to start, I guess. Like... at least I feel better about having them in the city."

Takeshi made to help Siva in the kitchen, but she waved him away. "Really? I'm not sure how I feel having to sleep in the same building as them." He settled on the couch opposite Ander instead.

Jitsu abandoned the other priest to come sit across her Human like a furry blanket. Takeshi should not be concerned; the wargs who were still in the city were going to watch the blind-ones and the not-blind-one carefully. The palace would too. And the Watch, she supposed.

"Yes, I know they will be watched," he said, scratching her ears as he soaked in her warmth. "It just makes me nervous."

"The wargs are planning to involve themselves?" Siva asked as she glided into the sitting area with a steaming mug.

Takeshi nodded.

She laid a hand on Ander's shoulder, but the other man just made a pained sound. "You could always take up residence here, Takeshi, if it bothers you so. Ander, sit up. You will feel better after you drink this."

*:I know I will, but I have to get to the "having drunk it" part first.:*

Takeshi's eyebrows drew together as he tried to parse that.

Jitsu's tail wagged. Did tall-white priest need a warg to help?

Takeshi recognized a threat when he saw one. It was too late for him, but Ander still had a chance. "Ander, Jitsu is suggesting you might need a warg's assistance."

*:I absolutely* do not.: Slowly he started to push himself up into a proper sitting position, pulling the blanket over his shoulders.

Jitsu sniffed. She had many siblings. One could probably be convinced to take up such a difficult problem.

Takeshi chose not to pass that along. "I would rather be nearby in case I am needed, to be honest," he answered Siva's earlier question. "But thank you for the offer."

The Aradian inclined her head gracefully as she pressed the cup into Ander's hands and then headed back into the kitchen. "Would anyone else like cinnamon tea?"

Takeshi perked up at the offer. "Please."

"Oh, me too!" Mara said, waving her hand high in the air and kicking her feet.

Ander grunted, sipping at his cup.

"But... where do we go from here?" Takeshi asked, burying his hands in Jitsu's soft fur. "Hades says there is 'a speck' of Abomination left, and that it feels 'asleep.' How are we supposed to actually *find* that?"

"Worth asking if it's even a bionic," Mara pointed out with a frown. "I know they said all the chips are gone, and the Lady said what's left is somewhere on this continent, but what if it's something completely different?"

*:Actually... there are events that have already occurred that give me hope on this front,:* Hades interjected. *:The meeting at Etroy, between Jamirh and the Avari and the Seekers... it had the feel of a convergence.:*

"You've suggested that several times now, but have yet to explain what that means," Takeshi said patiently. This was the most "present" she had been since Etroy. "What is a convergence?"

Hades hummed thoughtfully. *:It is the world itself drawing what it deems is needed to a place. It is... a sign the world itself is fighting back.:*

"Okay," Mara said, face scrunching up as her ears twitched. "So... what does that mean for us going forward? That we will just... stumble upon what we need to?"

*:That is not impossible,:* Hades agreed. *:But more likely, it means that some piece of information will come our way to point us in the right direction.:*

"I don't... think we can count on that," Takeshi said, concerned.

"She doesn't mean we should do nothing; She just means that as long as we do something, the answer is likely to find us due to some sort of cosmic factor," Ander muttered, staring into his tea with a look of utter disgust. "Lady... are *you* the 'truth' the Truth Seekers 'seek'? You were the Second Sign – 'magic itself taking a mortal form' – were you not? And you cannot lie, and can tell when others are telling the truth."

Takeshi stared at him, shocked. He wasn't the only one.

Hades herself seemed less bothered, more thoughtful. *:I am unsure. I was definitely the Second Sign, yes, but I do not know if that is what they were named for.:*

"Do they understand what you are?" Ander continued. "They called you an 'entity,' but do they realize you are a god?"

*:They know me, yes. Charve was not the first time they have interacted with me. I even spoke to one once, the night...:* She trailed off, suddenly unsure.

Ander's expression went blank. "'I know what you seek,' you said. 'It is not time yet.'"

*:Yes.:*

Ander's grip on the cup tightened, and Takeshi became concerned they were going to see a repeat of the first meeting with Siva. Did this also have to do with Ander's past before he came here? "If you knew that... what on Gaia didn't you know about what that woman told us today? How was any of that a surprise?"

Takeshi blinked and thought back. Hades had only taken a real interest when... "Something about the first Seeker?"

*:I did not know... that she had been alone, in the beginning. It reminded me of something else. One of my siblings.:*

Mara tilted her head to the side and pursed her lips. "Why wouldn't you know that? Wouldn't you have learned it when she died? I can completely understand you not telling us that information, but wouldn't you know?"

Hades hesitated. *:It isn't always that straightforward.:*

But Takeshi was already starting to put the clues together. If Hades didn't know, and she knew the vast majority of what the dead knew... "Is... the first Seeker still *alive*?"

Hades did not answer.

"That would be... very long-lived indeed, for a Human," Siva considered as she brought a pair of cups over for Takeshi and Mara. "But other Seekers have certainly died. Would not you have learned what they know?"

The goddess sighed. *:As I said, it is not that straightforward. I am not a repository of all the knowledge that has ever existed. And the egregore complicates things further.:*

Ander stared moodily into his cup, but at least he didn't seem likely to shatter it anymore.

Jitsu huffed. Did any of that even matter? The blind-ones were here now. Better to focus on the problem at hand. Which was working with them, like the helpful-red two-foot wanted.

"How *do* we even work with them?" Takeshi wondered, taking his cup from Siva. "Getting back to the original point, I suppose."

Siva's eyes crinkled as she gave the other cup to Mara, who took it carefully given her precarious position. "The way you work with most others, I imagine, though trust will be the difficult part."

"It's kinda weird, isn't it?" Mara said, adjusting the cup. "You would think a bunch of telepaths would be easy to trust because you could always check mind-to-mind, but we can't really risk doing that, either."

"The egregore draws you in," Takeshi confirmed. "I'm not sure how to work around that. That's just how it functions." It was interesting to finally have a name for it.

"They almost walked away," Ander said, morose. "Hades could have left me."

*:I am sorry, beloved.:*

Mara laughed. "Yeah, I will say – Jamirh does have a habit of really shaking up a meeting."

Siva hummed, finally taking a seat with her own cup. "Jamirh is focused on destroying the Abomination in a way none of the rest of us are. Vlad must consider politics and connections; we are concerned with the Seekers' motives and history. Jamirh just sees a possible avenue to bring himself closer to his goal and takes it. It is a very Master of Blades mentality. But it can also be dangerous to ignore the dangers that may lie down that path."

"Except I would bet he isn't ignoring them so much as he has decided to accept the risk," Takeshi mused. "Of all of us in that hall, he lived in a place where Truth Seekers were a constant danger. He has more reason to doubt them than the rest of us. And yet he is willing to let it go for the sake of the mission." He could relate to that. Sometimes the mission had to be put before personal biases.

Jitsu snuggled closer to Takeshi, burying her nose in a pillow. The helpful-red two-foot was focusing on the right things. Because he was helpful.

"And asking about the Crimson Shadows – that was something that was important to him." Siva took a sip from her cup. "How the Seekers had treated Avari once they were no longer under the Empire's control. Ander, drink the tea, don't scowl into it."

The priest obediently took another sip, though his expression didn't change.

Takeshi sipped at his own tea, enjoying the sweet-and-spicy earthy tones of the beverage, grateful it wasn't the medicinal concoction Ander had. The heat curled pleasantly through his body.

"Just think, Ander – the sooner you finish that, the sooner you can go collapse into bed," Mara pointed out.

Takeshi recalled Ander and Jak warning him against using too much of Hades' magic and decided this was an excellent practical example of why.

The white-haired man stared downward for another moment, then asked, "Is it really that interconnected?"

*:You are not in the right frame of mind for this conversation. You are exhausted. We can revisit it after you've slept.:*

Ander threw back the rest of the tea in one swallow. He placed the cup decisively on the coffee table and stood, wobbling as the blanket tangled around him. "I'm fine," he snapped when Mara moved to help, forcing them to watch him struggle with the blanket. After a minute he finally dropped it onto the couch and disappeared down the hallway to his rooms without a single word.

"Ah, well, he had a rough day," said Mara, laughing awkwardly, but her eyes followed the other priest with concern.

"Sleep will do him good," Siva agreed.

Takeshi took another sip of tea, trying to ignore the growing feeling of concern.

*:Takeshi.:*

He refused to open his eyes from his comfortable nest in bed, even for Hades. He could hear the storm raging outside. *:Has Vlad made a decision?:* Many important decisions were made in the early morning in Romanii. He was thankful he did not need to be present for them, as he would have needed to be in Ni Fon.

*:Yes.:*

*:We are going to work with the Truth Seekers?:* he guessed.

*:Yes. I'm sorry for waking you; you apparently know more than I do on the matter.:* Despite the words, her tone was amused.

*:It's the option that makes the most sense,:* he said, pulling the blankets just a bit tighter around himself and trying to ignore the soft sounds of some godforsaken music drifting through the air.

It wasn't real, and it couldn't make him listen to it.

*:Um....:* Hades trailed off, uncertain. *:The World Sound* is *real, beloved.:*

*:No it's not.:* He knew he sounded petulant. *:If I ignore it, it will go away.:*

*:You know I can't agree with that.:*

He sighed.

Jitsu scoffed from where she lay across his legs, radiating warmth. If they were going to be friends with the blind-ones, then maybe he could just *ask* them if it was something they did to make him hear the World Sound. Then he would know for sure one way or the other.

"I don't think 'friends' is the right word," he muttered, but the idea wasn't terrible. He was slowly coming to terms with the fact he had Voice magic, but maybe this would help provide some peace of mind.

Besides, he had recognized one of the Seekers.

A short time later, after pulling himself from his bed and dressing himself with an extra sweater, he found himself standing at the entrance to the rooms given to the Seeker delegation, Jitsu beside him. Two other wargs were visible down the hall; their tails wagged at Takeshi's approach, though they didn't abandon their post.

There were others outside on the ledges of the palace, Jitsu informed him.

That made him pause. "Why?"

She sneezed. Just in case.

Takeshi had no idea what that could possibly be "just in case" for, but decided he probably didn't want to know. He knocked on the door.

Sherri Cole, formerly of the Empire's military, opened the door. She looked up at him through her glasses, polite but also perplexed. "Good morning."

"Good morning. I would like to speak with your sister."

She glanced inside, then back up at him. "Would you like to come in, or should she come out to you?"

Takeshi had no idea, but the thought of being surrounded by them was unappealing. "I just have a quick question, if she would be willing to step out for a moment."

"I will send her out." The door shut.

Takeshi waited in the hallway, wondering if he was going to regret this.

Jitsu sat.

The door opened, and the Seeker with the long brown ponytail stepped out.

The same Seeker who had told him "Go" after the destruction of the avatar.

"Sherri says you wished to speak with me?" she asked placidly.

"I do, yes." He paused. "Do you remember me?"

"I remember you twice, yes."

He blinked. "Twice?"

"Once in Charve, and once in Tilden."

He frowned. "You were at Tilden Base?" He'd thought everyone who had been there had died.

"No, but others of my brothers and sisters were, and we all remember." She inclined her head.

He realized with a sinking feeling he knew her name, too. "Madine?"

"Yes." She paused, and he could feel the weight of her regard through the blindfold. "You still carry the memory of the egregore."

He shrugged.

"It can be a difficult thing to bear alone."

Whether or not there was an offer there Takeshi wasn't interested in examining too closely. But that reminded him. "Like your first Seeker?"

"Yes, like her." The answer came easily.

"She is still alive." He made it a statement.

"Hmm." Madine walked past him to one of the large windows on the other side of the hallway. "For now, yes," she said finally.

"For now?"

Madine turned back to him. "She will not last much longer. She worked hard to see us free, and lives now mostly out of spite. But she will be able to rest soon." A beat. "You deserve the answer, for you were part of the egregore, if only briefly. But this is one of our greatest secrets. Not even the Empire knew."

*:We can keep this within the priesthood. I will inform the others.:*

"Hades' other priests and I guessed, but we will keep it to ourselves," he promised. He was fairly certain that they should not have found out the way they had anyway.

"Hades' other priests?" A note of surprise entered her voice. "You belong to the death goddess?"

He didn't answer.

"I see." She frowned. "That explains... well. You never could have joined us fully then. We thank you for the aid you provided us in dealing with Ni Fon, regardless."

It was his turn to be surprised. "My what?"

"From your presence in Charve, we learned what the chip was. From the touch of your mind in Tilden, we learned about Ni Fon. This information was vital to dealing with the corruption in Ni Fon."

Takeshi felt like smacking himself. Of course they hadn't particularly cared what information of theirs he saw – they were far more interested in the information they had gleaned *from him*. "Glad to be of service."

Jitsu bumped him with her nose. He was way off track. He should ask about the World Sound.

Right. But how to ask the question? "Do you know what the World Sound is?"

A pause. "We do not recognize the term. Please define it."

How to define it? He turned and began to pace, unable to help himself. "Hades described it as 'the ebb and flow of existence,' some sort of… sound that usually only those with powerful Voice magic can hear."

"Ah. Yes, we are aware of it." She watched him pace back and forth. "While I cannot hear it myself, several others can."

That almost made him pause. That was something that the entire egregore could not hear? "I heard it for the first time after touching the egregore, and it has not gone away. I had wondered…" But if only a few in the egregore could hear it, then it wasn't sourced from them. That only left the other option. "If there had been… some sort of block that prevented me from accessing an inherent, would touching the egregore have undone it?"

"Allow me to consult." She fell silent, standing like a statue with her arms clasped behind her.

Takeshi waited.

"The general consensus is 'possibly,'" she finally said. "We do not have enough data on the subject to give a definitive answer. The egregore desires openness and truth, however, so it is theoretically possible that should an inherent have been denied you, touching the egregore would have resolved whatever the block was. But it was not anything we did on purpose. We presume you have discovered you have Voice magic, then?"

"That seems to be the case," he admitted.

"Our apologies for any discomfort this may have caused you. It was not our intention to do so." She was frowning.

Takeshi was stunned to realize she actually meant that. "What will be, will be," he intoned tiredly, resigning himself to singing lessons with Caelessa.

*:I... could teach you, you know. I am very familiar with the World Sound and Voice magic.:*

That was an interesting proposition. *:Perhaps after this crisis.:* And speaking of... "Do the Seekers have any idea how exactly to attempt to track down the remaining Abomination?"

"It has been the greatest topic of discussion between us since the meeting yesterday," she admitted. "We are considering attempting a seeking."

His brow furrowed. "A seeking?"

"It is... not unlike divination," she explained, though she also sounded uncertain. "This type of magic is more often used to find things of your own that are lost, but some of us are currently working on modifications to the array that will allow us to divine the location of the corruption. Should this fail, we will consider other options."

He nodded, wondering if that would somehow tie into the convergence Hades had been talking about lately.

*:No, this would have to be a different convergence. That convergence has already happened.:*

He ignored her. "Very well, then. Thank you for your time."

Madine bowed her head. "Is there anything else we can do for you?"

Takeshi was about to say no when his eyes caught on her blindfold. It seemed like almost an age ago since they had been on the *Sea Spirit* trying to determine how the blindfolds worked. "Do you have any extra blindfolds?"

Maybe that could cheer Ander up.

Sherri watched her sister slip back into their shared rooms. The quarters the Vampire King had given them were large and airy, more like an interconnected set of suites furnished in golds and greens than a mere set of rooms.

Exploring them had been fun, though the Seekers had not been terribly interested.

"What did he want?" she asked.

"To ask questions. There may have been... something of an un-intended consequence to his touching of the egregore."

"If he is correct, then he is better off for it," Perra said. "It is always best to have access to the full range of one's abilities."

Axtion nodded. "How odd, though, that it was a question at all."

All four Seekers suddenly turned sharply towards the south-west.

Sherri waited grimly. They would tell her when there was some-thing definitive to tell.

"Essnich and Drosmund have been occupied by Belian's forces, though Brelinver is fighting back," Madine finally said, though they all still looked distracted. "There are several cities in southern Gallia that have seceded from the Empire in the name of revitalizing Hispa as well."

Sherri bit her lip. "That's a lot all at once."

Madine shrugged. "This could be good for Muriz. If Hispa re-forms more or less along its original borders, that would put it between us and Gallia."

"We should return to Muriz," Caette suggested. "Madine and I should at least return for the seeking, if we are to go through with that. But with the war breaking out so suddenly..."

"Better for us to consolidate our presence," Madine agreed, turning to Perra, who nodded.

"I will stay."

Axtion cleared his throat. "I will stay as well."

The others nodded.

"Great." Sherri sighed as she went to pack her bag. "Now I get to explain *this* to the Vampire King."

She found herself missing Gren.

# Chapter Sixteen

Everything hurt when Ander woke up.

It hurt enough that he debated just staying in bed for the foreseeable future, but then he remembered there were painkillers in the kitchen.

Was extra pain now worth less pain later?

He wasn't sure.

He could feel Hades hovering at the edges of his senses, feeling very contrite. He didn't want to deal with that at the moment, though, and firmly turned away from Her.

He let himself doze off again.

When he woke up again, it was almost two in the afternoon, and his body was still in a state of outright rebellion. Still, this time he forced himself to get up and get dressed. His mood sank further at how slowly he had to move due to the ache of the memory of Hades in his body, but he made himself keep going this time. He couldn't waste a whole day in bed, no matter how much he might wish to. There were things to be done.

He made his way to the kitchen and was surprised to see a steaming cup sitting on the counter, kept warm by an array of Siva's orangey-red magic beneath it. A note was stuck to the counter next to it, with his name, the word "sillna," and an arrow pointing to the cup, signed with Siva's elegant scrawl.

He picked up the mug and took a sip, mentally calculating the twelve minutes it would take for him to start feeling the effects as he tried to ignore the bitter taste. Glancing around, he decided he could sit on the couch while he drank it and waited for it to kick in. His eyes closed as he sat down. Even with all the sleep he had gotten, he was still completely worn out.

*:You could rest today. There is nothing that needs your immediate attention, and I think after yesterday you've earned a day of relaxation.:*

It wasn't fair to blame Her, he reminded himself firmly. He'd known the risks when he'd allowed Her to possess him, even if neither of them had expected it to last so long. She could not help being what She was, and She'd asked permission first.

That knowledge wasn't preventing him from instinctively blaming Her for his current predicament. *:I don't want to rest; I want to be getting things done. I had plans for today. Where are the witches?:*

*:Siva went to go speak with Vlad; Mara is currently picking out stationery and a trinket to send to Kaikani.:*

Kaikani was the Veren Dedicated to Mara, and as far as Ander knew they were also dating. *:Where is Kaikani now?:*

*:In the Emerald Shore, trying to make sure all of Mara's work there isn't undone while she is here.:*

Ander frowned down into his tea. He hadn't considered that Mara's work in the Emerald Shore was potentially jeopardized by her presence in Tarvishte. Still, that was at least part of the function of the Dedicated – to support the priest they were Dedicated to.

*:Mara would not be here if she thought her time would be better spent on the Shore. And Kaikani is very capable and can handle herself.:*

Ander had never met the Veren, but if Hades said it then that was probably true. He took another sip of tea. Ten minutes to go. *:Was a decision made concerning the Truth Seekers?:*

*:Vlad has agreed to a temporary alliance with them while we try to track down the remaining Abomination.:*

He tried to rustle up an opinion on that but found he was too tired at the moment. He took another sip of tea and debated if he wanted to get up and sweeten it. Sillna could take a bit of honey without losing potency, but that would also mean getting up again, and that was an extremely unattractive prospect at the moment.

Instead, he looked over at his fish tank and the soothing blue of the water and bright colors of his fish and coral. The fish swam placidly past the starfish, which was resting on a rock, while the eel occasionally poked his head out from his hide. An entire contained ecosystem, an experiment he'd kept going for the past three hundred years.

If he kept very, very still, and kept his breathing slight, it *almost* didn't hurt anymore. But that meant he couldn't continue drinking, and if he wanted the pain to fade to a manageable level he really was going to have to finish this cup. He begrudgingly took another sip.

He was about halfway through it. Eight minutes for the effects to start kicking in.

"Ander?"

He blinked and slowly turned his head in the direction of the door. Takeshi was letting himself and Jitsu into the apartments, a tray with two takeout cups and a bunched-up piece of gray fabric in one hand. "Takeshi."

The warg trotted over, sniffing at his cup. He didn't have the energy to pull it away, but managed to muster up a glare, which didn't deter her in the slightest.

She gave a single tail wag of approval as Takeshi made his way over to the living area, putting the tray and scrap of fabric down on the coffee table before sitting on the couch opposite. "How are you feeling today?"

"Bad," he admitted, closing his eyes and taking another sip of sillna. He was almost done with it, and only a few minutes left to start feeling the effects. "I slept in; this is my first cup of sillna. I'm trying not to move too much."

"Completely understandable." The shinobi leaned back on the couch as the warg jumped up beside him, scrunching herself so she would fit. "How long do you expect the effects to last?"

Ander winced. "I'm trying not to think about it, but probably a day or two."

"Hmm." He folded his arms. "Maybe ten minutes of power, and the price is over forty-eight hours of recuperation."

"She is a god." Ander watched the movement of the tea as he swirled the cup. "Mortals were not meant to bear such power for long. When I created the avatar I made tweaks to the body to make it more resilient to a high concentration of magic, and even then the Lady had to keep her full power contained lest it start damaging the vessel."

"Hm." Takeshi took one of the cups from the tray. "When I found her, the vessel was definitely damaged. There were cracks forming along her left arm, and they were glowing."

*:I was cannibalizing it for the power it contained. While I had hoped to be able to bring it back here and have Ander fix it, using my own power in greater quantities would have actually been worse.:*

"Indeed." Ander sighed morosely, thinking of two decades' worth of work gone. "Please be gentler with it in the future." He finished off the tea. Now he just had to wait to start feeling better. He placed the cup on the table and eyed what Takeshi had brought.

"The tea is a cardamom and cinnamon blend; it can be good when you are suffering from inflammation and sore muscles and is caffeine free. I guarantee it tastes better than sillna, and I checked to ensure you could have both."

That was... incredibly thoughtful. Thoughtful enough to make him feel... something. Something that reminded him of Fredrik. Which meant he didn't want to examine it at the moment.

Slowly, he reached over to take the cup and opened the top, breathing in the warm spices. It wasn't coffee, but it was a far step up from sillna. "Thank you." He turned his attention to the fabric still bunched on the table, and his attention sharpened. Was that...?

"I also brought a Truth Seeker blindfold, ethically sourced." The shinobi reached over to shake out the fabric and lay it flat. "I did not ask how it worked, only if they would give me one."

Ander stared at it as he took a sip of the new tea, enjoying the mix of spices. If he could not have coffee, this was a decent alternative.

Then he frowned. "Why doesn't the blindfold have any bridging lines?"

"I did ask about that. Madine told me that each Seeker embroiders their own bridging lines when they take up a new blindfold. This was a spare they had with them."

Ander considered it silently. Their *own* bridging lines? That implied that each blindfold was unique to each Seeker, not just that they added in the lines themselves.

:I know what you seek.:

One of the first things he'd ever heard Hades say, on the worst night of his life. He'd known it hadn't been to him, but that hadn't mattered at the time. Or at least he'd thought it hadn't.

"What's wrong?"

Ander blinked at Takeshi's question and tried to bring himself back to the present. "Nothing, sorry. So then... they set their own bridging lines, but the glyphs are always the same?"

"Seems to be that way." Takeshi leaned forward. "But at least now we have the glyphs. They do continue onto the tails; I wonder if somehow the bridging lines allow them to connect even though they aren't within a bounding circle?"

"Technically, a bounding circle isn't necessary, though you are taking a lot of risks without one." He brushed a finger over the glyphs. Vision was front and center even if it was distorted; balance and illusion were laid on top. Layered glyphs also caused complications.

:It is not time yet. Withdraw.:

So then... was *now* the time? That made sense. What had they been looking for, exactly? If the first sign was Abomination, they were still two hundred and seventy-some odd years too early.

He didn't want to think about this.

"–as a bounding circle, at least for the part that wraps around the head. But then again it's tied in the back which creates a knot and scrunches everything together, which is also risky."

Ander yanked his attention back to what Takeshi was saying, ignoring the growing feeling of concern from Hades. The shinobi was right; knots were risky. What had he been saying about the bounding circle? "If the border of the blindfold itself acts as the bounding circle, then maybe..." He trailed off as he remembered the last thing Hades had said to that presence, the one that had disappeared immediately afterwards.

:None of those involved here will remember; I will ensure your mandate remains upheld.:

Alice's and Fredrik's memories had needed to be wiped... on the orders of the Seekers? Or for them, somehow? Not just the Empire's ban on magic. Hades had said it would win them safety; did She mean from the Seekers specifically?

A Seeker had been present that night and had let him leave with the Blade, but Alice and Fredrik weren't allowed to remember *why* he'd had to leave them?

Why was it all so interconnected?

And why was he so upset by it?

"Ander!"

His head snapped up, and he realized Takeshi had been trying to get his attention.

"Are you okay? Maybe you should go lie down for a while."

He shook his head, though he did feel exhausted. "I don't think it will help. I'm sorry for being so distracted, though."

The shinobi raised an eyebrow. "Do you want to talk about it?"

"Not really." He lowered his eyes to stare at the blindfold again.

*:Sometimes, talking something through helps you find answers,:* Hades pointed out. *:And Takeshi is really smart! I bet he'd make a good sounding board.:*

There was something to be said for that.

"I don't like being reminded of that night," he admitted. "It was... a very bad night."

"That's fine." Takeshi leaned back, putting a hand on Jitsu's head. "You don't have to talk about it if you don't want to."

"I just... didn't realize there was a Truth Seeker involved. Well, maybe not involved, per se, but present. They were new back then, mostly rumors." He'd ignored them to the best of his ability. He hadn't thought they mattered.

Takeshi tilted his head. "Involved with...?"

"The... events that happened the night I took the Blade from Elbe." The words tasted like ash.

The shinobi took a sip of tea, quiet.

"They brought it to me because they thought I could 'activate' it or... something." Ander scoffed. The whole concept had been stupid. "They tied up my partner and our daughter, killed the man they had originally gone to for help. And when I failed to be able to elicit any response from the Blade, they used it to kill Alice."

He would remember that moment for his entire life.

"Alice?" Takeshi prompted after a moment.

"Our daughter. She was fourteen. Since the Blade was originally forged to avenge Ebryn's sister, I think they hoped killing another young girl on it would... awaken it, somehow? I'm not too sure; I was more concerned with..." He trailed off, shuddering at the memory of Alice pinned to the wall. "To be honest, I remember... parts of it clearly, and other parts less so."

Takeshi's eyes narrowed. "I will never understand this over-reliance on magical artifacts. And that line of logic doesn't make any sense at all – while blood magic can be potent, wasn't the purpose of the Blade to *protect*?"

"I did not ask her to explain," Ander said dully. "Hades found me in that moment, and we... brought Alice back to life."

Takeshi's eyebrows shot up. "Oh. That's... well." He paused. "Hades is the goddess of death; it makes sense that resurrection is something she is capable of, though given her usual stance on the dead being allowed to remain unbothered it is a little surprising."

*:She was allowed the choice to return, and it was moments after death. The context matters.:*

The shinobi hummed. "I see. But that's good – your daughter didn't die. You saved her life."

Ander stared down into his cup. "I don't believe she remembered it that way."

"No?"

He tried to put it into words, forcing them past the lump in his throat. "It was magic, in a place where magic shouldn't exist. Hades said they had to forget the magic that had happened that night, but... almost *everything* had been magic. And I had to leave. I couldn't stay. I had soulforged and become a priest of a god. The goddess of death."

"You soulforged to save her." There was awe in Takeshi's voice. "I see. No wonder you managed it so quickly – you had to. There was no other option."

Ander nodded. "Almost a hundred years after I came here, I summoned her. She was Human, and even if she had lived a long life she would have passed on at that point. I missed Fredrik too, but... he would have found his way, would have found another in time. He was not solitary by nature." Fredrik had always been drawn to beauty. "But Alice was more mine than his, and I raised her. She'd been very sick just a few years before, and... I wanted to know if she had been okay after everything was said and done. If she had been able to live her life, and been happy." He fell silent.

"Did she come?" Takeshi asked after a moment.

"She did, though I didn't get a clear view of her form. Just her eyes." It still hurt, even two hundred years later. "She refused to speak to me. She was... very angry, though."

She was one of the few people he'd never had trouble reading, and those blue-green eyes had been full of cold fury.

"I... did not even try to summon Fredrik after that. And Ida... her mother had left us years before on her own terms."

"I see," came the quiet response. "It is my understanding the dead choose whether or not to answer a summons?"

Ander nodded.

"I see."

They sat in silence for a few minutes while Ander tried to regain control of himself.

He'd never been very good at that when Alice was concerned.

His fingers found the scar that ran down his face. He'd earned that for her too, though he'd never told her the truth. She'd loved her mother and he hadn't wanted to damage that.

A fluffy white head pushed itself into his lap, large violet eyes full of understanding. It was never easy to lose a pup, no matter the circumstances. And pups didn't always understand the decisions made concerning them.

He stared at Jitsu in surprise, then slowly raised a hand to rest it on her head in thanks. Once a warg chose a person, they almost never "spoke" to any other two-feet. It was kind of her to offer him comfort.

"And you said the Truth Seekers were present?" Takeshi finally asked. "Was that when she was stabbed?"

Ander looked up to see Takeshi frowning. "At least one was nearby. In retrospect... they were probably sent to retrieve the Blade. But because of them..."

*:They could not allow those who had seen magic – real magic, like the resurrection you had just performed – to live. But when I let the magic take Alice and Fredrik's memories, it became... a non-issue,:* Hades confirmed, voice subdued.

"It shouldn't be an issue," Ander said, suddenly angry with himself. "It makes sense. The Empire has been trying to stamp out magic within its borders for centuries. The Seekers have been used to enforce that for years; it isn't anything new. I just..." He trailed off, not sure where he was going with that. Everything felt like a confused, jumbled mess.

"But it was a surprise," Takeshi mused. "To discover that there was another element at play on a night that was very painful to you and which changed how you perceive an aspect of it. You are allowed to be upset."

His eyes fell back to Jitsu, who huffed at him and moved her head under his hand, demanding to be petted. Two-feet felt better after petting wargs.

"That's..." He considered trying to explain that people who actually *liked* dogs felt better after petting wargs but decided he was too tired and sore for that. Instead he took the easier route and obeyed.

"And as you mentioned before, it does reveal a sort of... interconnectivity, for all that these events happened a long time ago," Takeshi said thoughtfully. "Tying the current issue to those from your past, which you thought were unrelated. It makes the situation feel more immediate, and opens old wounds."

That *felt* like a very accurate description. And it didn't help that it felt like everything had been reminding him of Elbe in some way lately.

"And on top of that, you are physically exhausted due to Hades' possession. That can make it more difficult to process things," the shinobi added.

Also unfortunately true. Ander took another sip of tea, taking stock of how his body was feeling. He still ached, but the edge was beginning to dull as the sillna took effect.

He still didn't feel like doing anything. If anything, he felt *more* tired than before. "It was a long time ago. It shouldn't bother me anymore."

But Takeshi shook his head. "I don't think there's a limit on when you are allowed to care for your child, and you never received any sense of closure. Grieving is natural."

Ander looked over at his aquarium and the fish swimming placidly within. He thought he'd stopped grieving long ago, but maybe Takeshi was right.

It still hurt.

*:Of course it does,:* Hades murmured sadly. *:You know that sometimes wounds just don't heal right. Why should emotional wounds be any different? Just because they are not visible does not mean they do not exist. Sometimes they even hurt more.:* She paused. *:You could speak to Vlad about it, you know. This is his specialty. He would be happy to help you.:*

He looked at Takeshi, a man who had been manipulated into leaving his country and had been experimented on, leaving him with an incorrect perception of temperature and exiled from his home. He thought of Jak, now a crystal statue in the Temple below, and Mara who had been abandoned by her parents as a child, and Siva who had survived that which had killed her sisters, and the others... "'All of Her toys are broken,'" he quoted wryly. It wasn't anything they didn't already know.

*:If you must break to become mine then I will hold you together until you are well. And do not believe the priests of Kaldor; I see none of you as my 'toys.':*

Hm, was that where the quote was from? He didn't remember where exactly he'd heard it, though it had stuck with him. He let his eyes drift shut, feeling overwhelmed and exhausted. A headache was starting to form as well, even though he'd just had a whole mug of sillna.

"Maybe you should rest for a bit?" Takeshi suggested, concern in his voice.

"That... would probably be for the best, yes. Thank you for the tea, and for your insight." He took a moment before gently pushing Jitsu's head out of the way so he could stand. He looked down at the table with his mug, the takeout cups of tea, and the blindfold.

"I'll clean up," Takeshi said, reaching for the cups. "And we can investigate the blindfold later, when you are feeling better."

He took the cup still half full of the cardamom tea; that could come with him and he could reheat it later if he didn't finish it. "Thank you," he repeated, too tired to come up with any other response, and started to head back to his rooms.

"And Ander..."

He paused and looked back.

Takeshi was looking down at the blindfold in his hands, tracing the embroidery with a finger. "Your daughter may never have known the truth, but you did your duty as a parent to protect her. She was safe because of you. I know it can't erase the pain of her rejection, but she did live longer than she would have because of the choices you made. And anything that happened after that wasn't your fault."

Ander bowed his head, then turned and retreated into the sanctuary of his bedroom.

If only it were so easy to convince himself that that was true.

# Chapter Seventeen

---

"I'm just saying – when I pointed out that everyone noticed you leave that previous meeting and that you should have stayed, I do not believe the implication was that you should instead drop from a balcony to shake up a diplomatic incident."

"Probably not," Jamirh agreed amicably, ears twitching upward as they passed through one of the palace's side doors. Jeri had yet to drop the subject. "But what else was there? Just let them leave with nothing really decided?"

The Vampire groaned, drawing looks from people passing by. "*Yes.*"

Jamirh shook his head. "I think things are already in bad enough shape that letting potential allies – yes, *potential*, I'm not completely crazy – just walk away when we have to look for a needle in a haystack seems really, really dumb." He frowned at her as she covered her eyes with a hand. A bold choice when they were walking on the palace ground with a bunch of other people around. "Besides, continuing doing things Romanii's way hasn't really worked, has it? Maybe it's time to try something different."

Something needed to give if they were to succeed. Even if that meant working with Truth Seekers.

"Different is one thing, insane is another." Jeri dropped her hand to look at him pleadingly. "It's not like there's still hundreds of the things lying around; Hades said there was 'one speck' of it left and that it felt as though it were asleep. We have time–"

"Oh no, no no no. Do not go there," Jamirh interrupted her, ears flattening. "We do not 'have time.' This whole mess we are in right now is because it was decided at some point that you all 'had time' to *wait* for another Ebryn after Ryn failed. Maybe being more proactive about the whole thing would have at least kept it from spiraling so far out of control. Maybe we wouldn't have to rely on the Truth Seekers now."

Her lips thinned. "We aren't relying on the Seekers."

He shrugged. "You can call it what you want, but facts are facts. Hel all but confirmed that the Seekers destroyed like ninety-five percent of the bionics for us. Where would we be without them? We don't have the resources or the knowledge to do what they did. We might've been able to eventually track all the bionics down, but how long do you think that would've taken? Stopping the production was definitely a step in the right direction, but we know that wasn't enough." He considered that. "And they helped with that too, technically."

"By almost *killing us!*" She flailed her arms around out of frustration, causing a couple of people to duck out of her way and shoot them dirty looks. "Look, I can understand how, on a certain level, they have been helpful. But you can't deny that for centuries they have been a serious threat – not just to us, but also to Avari. Strictly speaking they've been a threat to every magic user on the continent. They don't... they don't think the way normal people do. They are even willing to sacrifice their own people to achieve their goals, whatever those are – and they don't seem to care who gets caught in the crossfire."

Jamirh knew that she wasn't wrong. Hell, he probably knew *better* than she did how right she was. The thought of working with the Seekers made his skin crawl after years of avoiding them. But still. "If we are looking for something so small, then we *need* more eyes on the situation. The Vampires can't just flock south of the Wall en masse and start turning over rocks. Plus the Seekers have way more info to go off of than we do. It makes sense to work together at least to achieve this one thing, you know?"

"But–"

"I'm not saying we should become best friends with them. In fact, we definitely shouldn't do that." He shuddered, thinking of the few times before yesterday he had come face to face with Seekers. They didn't exactly come across as people you even wanted to be friends with. "I'm not even saying whether or not Romanii should acknowledge their autonomy. That is one hundred percent not up to me. If anything, I guess I'm just saying we should use them while they're offering."

Jeri sighed. "I am worried about who would be using whom."

Jamirh shrugged. "Don't get me wrong, I have some serious questions about what they're going to be doing after all of this is straightened out. They want a country? That's weird to me." His brow furrowed. "Like... who, exactly, is going to live there? Just the couple thousand current Seekers? I want to see a map of the area they've claimed as a 'country.' How big is it? Where are new Truth Seekers going to come from? I always kind of thought that

Humans volunteered for the job, but now that they aren't a part of the Empire's military I can't see that being very enticing to anyone, and now that I know they use magic... The major said the first Seeker was forced to become one. What if *all* the Seekers have been forced into the job *because* they have magic? Then what does *that* mean for them continuing on? Are they just going to have babies and make *them* Seekers? Can Truth Seekers even have babies? Are they even planning on remaining Truth Seekers, or do they plan to become... something else?"

The Vampire stared at him. "Okay. You do seem to have thought a lot about this."

"Not that I came up with any answers, but yeah. If anything, the last few days have taught me that I really don't know anything about Seekers other than that they're kinda scary. No change there." His mouth twisted in annoyance.

"Ah, well, I have some... possibly worse news for you, then. Another reason not to rappel down from balconies in the middle of court," Jeri said with an awkward laugh.

He looked at her quizzically as they turned down one of the major boulevards heading towards the port.

"You and the Seekers are currently sharing gossip slots among the courtiers," she explained with a wince. "You see, there is nothing Vampires like more than drama, and what you did – well, it was very dramatic, especially with the way your coat flared out as you dropped and the fact that you're the Hero."

"Oh, come on," he sighed, exasperated. "Like there isn't an insane amount of other things to talk about right now. The Seekers, the Abomination, war..."

"People are also very interested in those things, but you... you made a scene. And Vampires *love* scenes," she tried to explain.

"There is no possible way I was more dramatic than Ander and Hel," he said flatly. "I wasn't glowing with the power of a god. I didn't teleport into the center of the room. My voice didn't echo mysteriously."

"Eh." She tilted her hand side to side. "Ander is a priest of Hades, and we have seen that before. You are something new, unfortunately."

He brought a hand up to rub at his key as his ears flattened. What had possessed him to jump down from the balcony anyway? Oh, right. The need to stop the Seekers from leaving with nothing getting done. "You know what I want, when all is said and done? I want to fade into obscurity," he muttered. "Go somewhere no one has even *heard* of Ebryn."

When she didn't answer, he looked over to see her biting her lip and looking down at the ground.

"That is understandable," she said after a moment. "I can try to talk to the others too, though. I don't think they'll be obnoxious about it; I just thought it was something you would want to be aware of." She paused. "Vampires just... really like drama."

He thought about that. They lived for so long that he guessed it made sense that they would latch onto whatever big news happened to cross their path. After a while, most things probably became pretty mundane. And Tarvishte didn't seem to be interested in changing all that much. How boring would it be to live exactly the same way for hundreds or thousands of years? Did they even notice the time passing? Some of the things Jeri had said to him before made him think their perception of time was a little skewed. So anything out of the norm probably was disproportionately interesting to them.

That was fine in theory. He just wished the interesting thing wasn't *him*.

They walked in silence for a few minutes before Jeri shook her head and turned to him. "How is your arm? Yesterday's events didn't make it flare up again, did they?"

He blinked, looking down at the offending limb. Covered as it was, it looked perfectly normal, but... "No, it's still just... normal glowing, I guess. Nothing weird since Etroy."

She sighed wistfully. "I wish I had seen it. I told you that you could do magic with it!"

"I melted the bionic's spine; I didn't throw fireballs," he corrected dryly. "And it was extremely lucky that I was able to do that. I'm not sure how I would have killed the bionic without it."

And he'd been exhausted after it, too. And the arm had been... maybe just a *little* sore since they'd returned. But surely that wasn't anything to worry about.

"That is so close to the same thing that they might as well be," she reasoned. "It was capable of magic, and fire magic at that. Has Ander checked it since we returned?"

He shook his head as the ocean finally came into view. "No, not yet. He's been really busy. Everyone's been really busy, actually, especially with the whole Truth Seeker thing."

"Hm. Unfortunate; I'm sure he would have theories." She looked thoughtful. "You could see Marcus instead. It probably should be checked out since regardless of how fascinating it is, that isn't nor-mal."

Jamirh stared at his arm. He knew she was right, but it was hard to make himself go and get poked when he was pretty sure there weren't going to be any new answers. Maybe if his arm did it again in front of them, but... "I wish I knew *why* it did it. If I could recreate it then maybe I could get some answers."

She hummed. "Do you have any theories?"

He shrugged. "It could be because of the presence of the bionic. The Blade was forged to fight Abomination, so maybe the residual magic sensed its supposed enemy and tried to fight back? I guess it could have been the location, or even just desperation. But none of those make a ton of sense since my arm also glowed right after my bout with Siva, which had nothing in common with my fight with the bionic other than that it was a fight. And I've sparred with you and it hasn't done anything, so... I really don't understand how normal magic works, so trying to figure out this extra weird magic mostly just gives me a headache."

She looked at him, confused. "What would the location have to do with it?"

"Well, that was where Ryn died."

"So?"

Was it really that odd a thought? "Well, I guess I noticed the glow first when I found... the spot where Ryn died." His voice dropped to a whisper. He didn't want to think about what had happened after Ryn had died. "So that seemed important for some reason, but I'm not actually sure, I guess. The whole place seemed really strange, though. It was one of the creepiest places I've ever been."

"Well, that place was haunted to high hell," she said thoughtfully. "So I can understand that. I wonder if that was why that one building seemed weirdly abandoned."

His eyes widened. "What do you mean, 'haunted to high hell'?"

"I mean exactly that – the building was haunted." She glanced at him, and whatever she saw made her hasten to explain. "As a Vampire, I'm dead, right? One of the Lady's creations. As such, when there are restless dead nearby I can sort of sense them a bit. I did not feel anything terribly powerful at Etroy, just... wisps of memory mostly, so the building was most likely haunted by ghosts. Enough to cause one of the living to feel their presence, but not strong enough for them to actually do anything. Probably. I would know more if I had gone into the building, but that is what I gathered from outside it."

Jamirh's ears sank low and a chill went down his spine. The building had actually been haunted? It wasn't just his mind playing tricks on him? He didn't understand how she could be so casual about that. "There were really ghosts there?" He shuddered, thinking of Ryn's friends. Had it been them? The ghosts of the Avari who died to make the bionics? Something else? A combination of all three?

"I suppose it could have been some other minor restless dead, but ghosts make the most sense," she mused, oblivious to his distress as they finally approached the *Sea Spirit*. "Especially if you didn't come across any shambling corpses or anything."

Had that *been an option*? His brain caught up with what she was saying. "Ghosts are real!?" It was one thing to wonder if ghosts were present, it was another entirely to be told matter-of-factly that they existed. "And other 'restless dead'? Wait, why are undead a thing *at all*? I've met the goddess of death and she's weirdly nice; I really didn't think Hel would go for dead people stumbling around all over the place. Vampires aside, I guess, but, like... you aren't exactly... dead?" He often forgot they were classified that way. "Dead in the way ghosts and zombies are, at least." He had a horrifying thought, causing him to pause at the base of the gangplank. "Are there *more* types of restless dead?"

She stared at him, confused. "But... you know that Ander summoned Ryn's spirit once?"

"I thought that was just a priest thing! Because he's one of Hel's priests! And she's the literal goddess of death! I didn't think..." He trailed off, unsure where to go with that. Even though he was occasionally creeped out in certain situations, he'd never really thought the dead were real in a *tangible*, potentially dangerous sense. Having that confirmed was... something.

Her confusion was giving way to sympathy. "I always forget that the Empire likes to pretend these things don't exist anymore. Yes, ghosts and zombies exist. So do banshees, wights, ghouls, liches, etcetera. Hades does not like that they exist, and I know her priests have a standing order of sorts to put any they come across to rest, but I don't think it's as straightforward as that sounds. And there's a wide variety of ways for the restless dead to be created; it would depend on which type. Suffice it to say that in almost every instance it is an act of force that violates the sanctity of the dead, which is why the Lady does not like it. Some mortals are more sensitive to the presence of the restless dead than others, but that building was so haunted I think they probably just decided to stop using it. Though that does then beg the question – why didn't they tear it down?"

Jamirh shuddered again, remembering Ander's words that Ryn had not become restless dead. At the time he'd thought that was something Ander said because he was one of Hel's priests, like a flowery way of reassuring him using phrases built into the religion the way priests of the Three sometimes did, but now it took on a whole new meaning. One Jamirh liked even less. He gripped his key tightly as they boarded the ship. "Gren didn't seem bothered by it, but we were also fighting for our lives, so..." And the effect had kind of faded after they'd killed the bionic, hadn't it? Or was it just the adrenaline from the fight? Jamirh hadn't noticed anyone else being creeped out.

"Ohh, yeah, Gren!"

A tanned hand reached out to help pull him onto the ship proper, and Jamirh found himself face-to-face with Desha, her sister right behind her.

"That was the Avari ye met in the base, right?"

"The one that runs Crimson Shadows?"

"Tell us more about this Gren!"

"Was he cute?"

They wore matching grins as Jeri followed Jamirh onto the deck proper, but Jamirh frowned. "How should I know?"

The twins exchanged a quizzical look with each other before returning their attention to him. Salisha tilted her head. "Well, usually ye just look at someone, and...?"

He stared at them.

"Wait," Desha said slowly. "Ye find us cute, right?"

Jamirh had no idea how to answer that question. He squinted at them.

The silence stretched for another moment before Jeri snorted. "You're both hot. Let's move this inside; while I do greatly enjoy your captain's cooking I prefer to limit my exposure to the ocean."

"Yeah, thanks for having us for dinner," Jamirh added. "I just found out I should probably avoid the palace's dining hall for the near future, so this is great."

"Aww, yer welcome anytime," Desha said, wrapping an arm around his shoulder. "Could even come with us if ye wanted."

"Even if yer blind t' how cute we are," Salisha said dryly.

"At least Jeri knows her stuff," her sister agreed as they walked into the mess hall.

"But we are interested in hearing more about Gren."

"See, there's been a couple o' interesting developments today in the political sphere."

"And yesterday, I guess."

"Well, yeah, the last week or so."

Jamirh looked around, but none of the other pirates were present yet, though he could hear Caron cooking in the galley. They were a bit early, he guessed. "Something other than what we were present for?"

Desha rolled her eyes. "Obviously."

Salisha shot her sister a tolerant look before turning back to Jamirh. "Ye see, actual fighting's finally broken out in the Empire."

Jamirh blinked. Oh. "Were the Crimson Shadows involved?" he asked as they took seats around the table.

Desha shook her head. "No. Belian's forces are invading some of the major Elban cities, mostly."

"Though also there's like three Gallian cities that *just* announced their secession from the Empire."

Jeri frowned. "How do you know this? I haven't heard anything."

"Don just picked it up over the radio about ten minutes ago."

"We guess yer king'll be informed shortly, if he hasn't been already."

Jeri frowned and looked in the direction of the palace.

"Or ye can do it now, that's cool too." Both sisters watched Jeri with an almost frightening intensity.

The Vampire shook her head after a brief moment. "Prim and Vlad already know... apparently the Truth Seekers informed them?" She sounded confused. "How did the Seekers already know?"

Jamirh leaned his head on his hands, elbows on the table. "All the Seekers are connected, right? So if they had any in or around those cities, they'd all know pretty much immediately, yeah?"

Jeri sighed. "Yes, that's true, I guess I just thought they would have mostly pulled back to Muriz. They stick out, after all, and since they violently separated from the Empire by taking off the Emperor's head I don't think they'd be welcome in other parts."

"Yeah, but can't they do magic?" Jamirh pointed out. "They *were* the anti-magic troops, and since the bionics are all but wiped out there's nothing stopping them from casting spells to remain hidden or anything. Like, I'd guess if someone in the know saw someone doing obvious magic they'd probably kill them, but I don't think they can stop the Seekers right now."

"They definitely can't!" Salisha agreed. "So there's good and bad news there."

Desha nodded. "Yeah, because that means ye can all do magic yourselves there now with much less risk."

"But then again, who knows how the locals are gonna take that?"

"Yeah, might actually be best t' avoid the Empire fer the foreseeable future."

Jamirh frowned down at the top of the table. "Do you think magic is going to come back to the Empire because of all this?"

Jeri tilted her head to the side. "What do you mean? Because of the Seekers? They have been running their anti-magic campaign for longer than that."

"But that's just it," Jamirh said, trying to figure out how to put his thought into words. "Even if the Seekers weren't necessary to destroy the citizens' belief in magic, I think they might have been a crucial part of keeping it that way."

"Oh, really?"

"Do explain!" The sisters were staring at him intently.

It made him nervous, but he shoved the feeling down. "The Seekers are what the Empire was doing with the magical Humans, right? And we know they were used to find people in the Empire using magic, and probably got rid of them. Maybe they even killed the Avari who showed magical ability. Gods know plenty of Avari went missing without explanation; it makes sense it was probably that. But even if they weren't necessary in the beginning... isn't it likely the Empire became reliant on them? Even if they didn't mean to?"

"Oh, I see," Jeri murmured. "The Seekers could have even manipulated it to be that way, given enough time."

Jamirh nodded, glad he was making sense. "So then, without the Seekers, the Empire's lost their main method of controlling magic –

and since the bionics are all destroyed, they've lost their secondary method too. I guess the Empire could try to make more Seekers, but I don't know how much time that would take, and I don't think the Seekers are going to let that happen."

Salisha folded her arms. "It's an interesting thought, though. Would those new Seekers be connected t' the old ones, or would they form a rival hive?"

"Either way, yeah, can't see the Seekers being down with that," Desha agreed.

Jamirh waved it away. That wasn't the point he was making. "But then that means that at least the inherents are going to start popping up again, right?"

Jeri nodded slowly. "Without anyone to cull the abilities, that is the likely outcome, no matter what the government actually wants. This will probably set them pretty far back until they can correct."

"And with the war, that isn't likely t' be soon," Salisha added.

Jamirh looked down at his arm. The glow wasn't visible beneath the wrappings and the arm guards, but it felt warm. And... yeah, definitely a little sore. "And depending on how flashy the Seekers want to be with their magic..."

"It'll put the Empire back at square... two, maybe," Desha said thoughtfully. "Since most people in the Empire don't currently believe in magic, so they aren't quite at square one."

Silence, as everyone digested that.

"And I guess this links back to Gren," Jamirh said, thinking back to Etroy. In some ways, wasn't Gren kind of what he was supposed to be? An Avari for the others to follow to freedom. That was certainly what most people had expected of him, even though it had never been what Jamirh himself wanted to do. "Because I told him about magic. I doubt he'll keep that to himself; with the war going on and his group trying to break free like the Seekers, that's probably very useful info."

Jeri's eyebrows rose. "And he believed you?"

He shrugged. "I'm Ebryn. As you keep reminding me, that's important to some people."

And if the words were bitter, no one commented on it.

He was pretty sure his arm was glowing beneath the wraps, but all he could dredge up was dull annoyance.

If he couldn't see it, it wasn't happening.

# Chapter Eighteen

Takeshi took a deep breath, reminding himself that he was a skilled shinobi. His spell work was neat and refined with practically no waste of power, his stealth was in the top three percent of his peers, and he was skilled in a variety of weapons. He was good at problem solving and adapting to circumstances. He had been the Captain of the Imperial Guard in Ni Fon, responsible for six hundred and forty-two people under his command and a further seventy-eight trainees.

He had always been quick to pick up whatever was being taught. Magic had come easily to him with its beautiful, flexible nature, easily molding to the style of the weaver. Weapons had required more work, more discipline, but had also fallen into place with a little dedication. Stealth had been like breathing. He'd been responsible for teaching those skills to young shinobi-in-training, had found ways to help them find their own styles and successes.

So why was it, whenever he discovered there was some new magic or ability to learn in this place, he struggled, feeling as though he had to claw the knowledge from the depths of hell?

"My goodness. Try not to sound like a dying duck; that is not the effect we are looking for."

He took another deep breath, forcing himself to let Caelessa's words wash over him and accept the sentiment behind the harsh criticism. Getting upset was not the answer here. And it had sounded terrible, even to him. "My apologies; I have literally never tried to sing before."

"Hm." She leaned back in the plush chair, resting her head on a loose fist. A guitar case lay on the ground beside her, unopened. "Never? Not even in the shower? Or at a bar? For a lover? Something?"

"No." Why should he have? He always wanted to avoid attention. And the thought of singing for someone made him want to shrivel up and die. Which was, he could acknowledge, part of the problem. Even if he did find himself in a relationship, he couldn't even imagine singing to his partner.

Though it would be nice, to be close to someone again. He did miss that, from before he was engaged to Hotaru. And during. He still missed her, even if he hadn't been in love with her.

He shook his head sharply. Now was not the time.

Caelessa regarded him through slightly narrowed eyes. "How odd. Then again, since your inherent was suppressed..." She shook her head. "Well, no. Even those without a usable Voice still manage to sing. Some even sing without any talent for the activity at all."

Takeshi cleared his throat. "A 'usable' Voice?"

She nodded. "Yes. As all living beings are magic, no matter their ability to manipulate it, most living beings have Voice and Movement. That is how people speak and... well, move around. Only those who are born mute truly have no Voice in this sense, and those who are paralyzed have no Movement. Those who are able to use those inherents to cast magic are called bards, but all singers and dancers have skill within those domains. When I say a usable Voice, I just mean that you are able to use it to cast."

He considered that. "So you are saying that everyone technically has those inherents to some degree, and as the ability gets stronger the more likely it will present as a 'usable' inherent?"

"Yes, exactly so." She swung herself out of the chair and began to pace around his sitting room. "What is interesting is that restricting your inherent – which I would otherwise have assumed would only affect your ability to use Voice – also apparently affected your innate ability to hear the World Sound. That implies those two things are far more interconnected than previously theorized."

Jitsu opened one violet eye, watching the two-foot of graceful sounds. No wonder she got along with the tall-white priest. They seemed to think about things in a similar manner.

Takeshi was glad his mask hid his smile. *:They are both academics. It is not an uncommon attitude among that class.:*

Jitsu snorted. They spent far too much time overthinking, then. Why think when you could just *do*?

Takeshi filed that away, but he found his mind wandering to the other priest. He hoped Ander was feeling better today. Hopefully the effects of Hades' possession would be lessened; he had looked... quite rough the day before.

And for good reason. The story he had told Takeshi was not by any means a happy one. No wonder the man was withdrawn. He had lost his whole family because of the Crystal Light Blade, and he hadn't even been able to tell them the truth about it. Takeshi had only ever briefly considered that he would have children during the time he had been engaged to Hotaru, but he couldn't imagine having one and then being forced to abandon it in such a way. How terrible.

"Hello? Takeshi, are you in there?" Fingers snapped a few inches from his face.

He jerked back, grabbing her wrist reflexively, startling them both into freezing.

"Please release me," she said evenly after a moment.

He let go as though her wrist had burned him. How... painfully unprofessional of him. "My deepest apologies."

"Mine as well." She held up her wrist, studying it. He could see the marks left by his grip. It would probably bruise. "I shouldn't have startled a shinobi in that way."

He swallowed hard and bowed. "Unintentionally causing harm is completely inexcusable and sloppy." How hard had he gripped her?

But she waved his apology away. "It's a good reminder for me, too. You are not a child; you are a soldier, and I should remember that. I have known other shinobi and should have remembered... but nothing is broken. We will continue."

He admired her dedication, even as he wondered when and where she would have had the opportunity to meet shinobi. Romanii had had no contact with Ni Fon for centuries. Still, it was hard to put aside the shame of the momentary loss of control. "I do not think I can possibly apologize enough."

"Be a better student, if it bothers you so," she said wryly. "What were you thinking of? You weren't paying attention to me at all."

"My mind was wandering," he admitted, unwilling to share his thoughts about Ander. Those things he'd been told were private and not his to spread. "That, too, I apologize for."

"Hm." She studied him for a moment but let it drop. "Let's try a scale again, then." She sang out a series of rising notes. "Remember that you don't want to just match me – you want to resonate with the World Sound itself." She sang the notes again. "Can you hear how the World Sound reacts?"

He could hear the phantom music taking interest in the sounds Caelessa was making, shifting to match her. But wasn't he supposed to match the Sound, not the other way around? He steeled himself and tried to copy her.

It wasn't close. The World Sound ignored him. Jitsu's ears twitched.

Caelessa hummed thoughtfully. "Dying cat is a step in the right direction, I suppose."

Takeshi hid a wince, stroking Jitsu's head in apology. "I'm not sure I understand. It sounds like the World Sound attempts to resonate with you, not the other way around. Not that that excuses my terrible pitch."

"Well, yes." She fell silent for a moment, beginning to pace again. "It's not... hmm. Most people with Voice don't usually struggle with pitch because they can feel the World Sound. It's both – you resonating with the World Sound, and then the World Sound resonating with you. It's an odd thing... you see, most bards don't hear the World Sound as clearly as you do."

He nodded, stomach sinking. Why was everything concerning these new magics so complicated? Why did he always seem to be the outlier?

"Since most nascent bards don't hear it as clearly as you seem to, this never comes up." She stopped and turned, planting her hands on her hips. "Granted, most bards don't truly 'hear' it in the literal sense at all. It's more of a feeling. Perhaps being able to hear it as you do is more of an impediment than a help."

"So because I can hear it instead of feel it, it may be more of a distraction." He would have thought it would make it easier, but that clearly was not the case. "So then how does the process work? If you know what song you are going to sing, why would you first match the World Sound, which is doing its own thing?" he asked.

She shook her head. "It's not... hmm. How to explain. Since I cannot hear it before I start singing, that isn't really a problem. And even then, it's more of a feeling than anything else. Something that joins me in song and makes it more than what I could do alone."

*:She hears an echo of the World Sound,:* Hades offered, joining the conversation. *:That is what most bards hear. The echo of what is to come.:*

*:What is to come? That's... not how echoes work,:* Takeshi thought back at her, exasperated. "Hades suggests that somehow the – version, I suppose? – of the World Sound I hear is different from what you do. She says you hear an 'echo,' though I'm not sure what that means."

Caelessa's eyebrows rose. "Interesting. An echo..."

*:You might be thinking about it the wrong way. She is correct that the World Sound is about resonance. It wants to match them, so it does.:*

He got the sensation of a shrug. *:But at the same time, bards can match the underlying frequency to resonate in the first place.:*

"I think... so it is more that both the World Sound and the bard resonate with each other mutually, not that one leads?" he asked out loud for Caelessa's sake.

*:Yes.:*

Hades had continued to be mostly absent since Etroy, but Takeshi could understand – she had described the feeling of the remaining Abomination as like an itch she couldn't scratch. A frustrating feeling that drove her to continue trying to find it. It was kind of her to try to help him in spite of that.

"That is not quite how we perceive it, but the theory is fascinating," Caelessa said, beginning to pace again. "And it aligns with what you perceive to be true. In which case, you should try to think of it more in those terms."

"Whatever makes the most sense to the mage tends to be what works," he agreed thoughtfully. "But then... how do I find the correct pitch? If most bards just naturally find it because they've been able to feel the World Sound for their whole lives..." He fell silent, realizing the problem.

"It's a massive handicap to overcome in some ways, yes. But then, plenty of people learn to sing with significant skill without ever hearing the World Sound," Caelessa pointed out dryly. "While it helps, it's not necessary. It's called practice."

Jitsu bumped him with her nose. Takeshi had already been humming in resonance with the World Sound for weeks, so it was clearly possible. He should think about it less and just do it.

*:Besides, you can hear when you are wrong,:* Hades pointed out. *:That's a good sign. It allows you to correct.:*

"But *how* do I correct?" he murmured, feeling a little defeated. If it didn't feel so likely that this would help with the soulforging issue he wouldn't even be trying it now at all. It felt like an odd time to be trying to learn how to sing, with the situation in the Empire, the Truth Seekers, and the Abomination all being at the forefront of everything.

Caelessa hummed. "You can hear it. Can you feel it? Or can you *only* hear it?"

He blinked at her. "I'm not sure." *Could* he feel it? What did music feel like?

Mostly he just felt cold, nowadays. The frequent storms weren't helping.

*:The World Sound is, in the end, an expression of magic.:*

Okay, it was magic. He knew what magic felt like. Or at least he knew what spells felt like. This wasn't quite the same thing, was it? It was more like... a spell *before* it was woven. The threads that made up the weave, waiting to be picked up. Could he feel that?

He wasn't sure. That felt like something he should meditate on.

"Hearing it the way you seem to indicates a powerful ability," Caelessa said thoughtfully. "A powerful ability where the instinctual knowledge has been mostly stripped from you, so it's more like you enjoy the effects of being a master while having less skill than a novice."

Put that way, Takeshi was again reminded of Jamirh. It wasn't exactly the same – Jamirh had still been able to access his inherent; he just hadn't known that was what he was doing – but it felt similar in concept. "We were starting with the basics with the scales, though, weren't we?"

"Yes, but I think that your inherent might need a different tactic." She frowned. "What if, instead of a scale, you attempted to match whatever melody the World Sound is making? I couldn't do that, but if you can hear it independently, maybe you can. In fact, it does rather sound like that's what you've been doing with your humming, anyway."

He blinked. That made sense, to start with something that was proven to work. "What if I just hummed it to begin with?"

She nodded. "Yes. Start as simply as you feel you need to."

He shifted his attention to the World Sound, soft notes drifting through the air in a lazy, distant fashion. Now that Caelessa pointed it out, *was* he even really hearing it? It seemed like he was hearing it, but was the sound real? Or just how his brain was processing it? Did the distinction even matter? He wasn't sure.

Normally he found himself humming along with it without any conscious thought. Logically then, he was resonating with it, right? He didn't have any particular song in mind, he just... hummed whatever the World Sound was doing, like Caelessa had said. And humming seemed less intimidating. Surely he could hum?

*:What is so intimidating about singing?:* Hades asked, perplexed.

*:Doing it wrong is embarrassing. If I must draw attention to myself, I don't want it to be for... how did Caelessa put it? 'Sounding like a dying cat.':*

*:But if you have Voice, you won't sound that way?:*

*:We've proven that I absolutely can sound that way, actually,:* he pointed out dryly.

She made a soft sound of confusion but didn't reply.

Jitsu snorted. He was thinking about it too much again.

He winced. How was he just supposed to *do* it? It felt weird. Uncomfortable.

He could think about something else, Jitsu suggested. He should go back to thinking about tall-white priest. He had problems. Maybe they could help solve them?

*:Everyone has problems,:* Takeshi thought back wryly, eyeing her suspiciously. That sounded like the exact opposite of what she had suggested before. *:The world literally has problems right now.:*

Jitsu yawned. Sure, that was true. But instead of focusing on problems they couldn't solve immediately, maybe they could focus on the smaller ones? Tall-white priest had fixable problems.

He frowned. *:I can't make his daughter speak to him again.:*

No, not that! The warg huffed, annoyed. Just the eating and sleeping thing! Easy.

He hummed, amused. He supposed that from a warg's point of view that was an easy thing to fix, but... *:For two-feet that is a more complicated situation.:*

Her mouth dropped open into a wolfish grin as she stared at him. Wait.

He abruptly stopped humming as he realized that was what he was doing.

"Hmm, not bad. It's far better than what you produced earlier, at least," Caelessa mused.

His brow furrowed in frustration despite the praise. "But I didn't do it on purpose. How do I do it on purpose? It's not singing, either. Don't you have to sing to cast with Voice?"

Jitsu whacked him with her tail. He just had to do it. Was he listening to her at all?

"Not necessarily. Any sound can work as long as it resonates with the World Sound," Caelessa said with a shrug. "I've hummed my way out of a few close calls. Why don't we try this?" She strode back over to the chair she had been occupying earlier and opened the case beside it, pulling out a guitar. "What if I play something and you try to hum along to that? The World Sound will shift to match it, but the sound of the guitar might help it sound less strange, since you'll be matching a real sound."

That sounded like a good idea to Takeshi, and he nodded.

They tried for several songs, but while Takeshi did feel less silly humming along to actual music it still wasn't quite where he needed to be. He could tell he sometimes fell flat, and once he did it was hard for him to not just stop entirely.

Finally Caelessa called for a stop. "Okay! Well, I'm going to give you homework. Think of a song you like and try to practice humming it until you feel comfortable doing so. Then practice it until the World Sound starts to resonate with you. Then you can try singing it. We can meet again at this same time next week, perhaps?"

*:That was not terrible at all,:* Hades praised. *:I think it's a confidence thing. You just need to be more confident that the notes that come out of your mouth are the correct ones, and they will be.:*

He stood as Caelessa started putting the guitar away. Find a song that he thought he might like to sing? "I'll... put some thought into it. And yes, that will be fine. Thank you for your time and effort in helping me better understand the World Sound." A week felt like a long time to wait, but he couldn't see this happening any time in the near future either. He bowed, and his eyes caught on her wrist and the faint purple ring that was beginning to form there. "I apologize again for my actions earlier."

She waved her hand at him, unconcerned. "It's a little sore, but it's fine. I'll see you next week."

He closed the door after her. That left him with some time to himself before he went to the Temple to have dinner with the other priests.

Meditation felt like a good idea.

He settled himself back on the couch as Hades' attention drifted away again and Jitsu huffed in protest of the sitting thing. It didn't matter; he felt like he needed the extra time to process after everything he had attempted today.

He closed his eyes as he sifted through the day's events. He still almost couldn't believe he had accidentally hurt Caelessa. He hadn't thought he was so on guard here, in his rooms with Jitsu right beside him. Maybe *that* was something he needed to unpack, too. But first, the World Sound, and his inherent Voice.

It wasn't feeling much like an inherent, but then, he had very little experience with that. The telepathy had come easily enough though, and he wondered what the difference was.

He thought back to Jamirh. Jamirh had needed to believe he could use his inherent in order to do so. This was more or less the same in that sense; Hades had even said it was a confidence issue. So he needed to have more faith in himself... to do something that he'd never done before.

Was this really necessary for him to be able to soulforge?

Something told him yes, even though that thought was disproportionately depressing.

It wasn't that he disliked music. He enjoyed listening to it. He wasn't very picky about what he listened to, but he did like when the music seemed to connect with him. And he could think of some situations where Voice magic would be the preferred method of casting. There were some spells and some spell effects that were easier to do with Voice than traditional arrays, and he was always for expanding his selection of tools.

But singing just felt... odd.

He thought back to his conversation with Ander about how summoning one's soul crystal worked. That felt odd in a similar way, didn't it? So he was back to just believing he could, since Ander had suggested that just willing the crystal to do as he bade should be enough. Like the myth of a Living Will – just will it and it should happen.

He shook his head. Back to basics.

Magic was life. Magic was will. Magic was belief.

Hades' attention abruptly swung back towards him.

He paused, waiting for a message, but she remained silent so he carried on.

Spells were the structure of magic, formed by arrays and glyphs and bridging lines. Even Voice used arrays, it just used sound to weave them.

Perhaps that was what he should do. Consider the individual notes as threads, and picture the song as literally weaving the array. He'd thought of it earlier as a spell that was yet to be woven; perhaps that was the right idea.

Hades hummed thoughtfully. *:Yes, I think that might be best.:*
Something tangible to work on, then.

Sherri sat next to her sister on the old-fashioned train, Caette seated right behind them. It was a silly question, but she still felt the need to ask. "Perra and Axtion are fine?"

Madine nodded. "We do not think they will be in any real danger in Tarvishte. And they will represent our interest in the place. Things are very different here."

Sherri looked around. "That is... certainly true. If we had been on an Empire train, though, we would already be crossing the Wall." And they would be going through that strange living-and-not-living tower again, but at least then they would be able to go home.

It wasn't that their time here had been a disaster. It just hadn't gone the way they'd wanted.

Caette spoke up from behind. "Faster is not always better."

Sherri blinked in surprise. Usually only Madine addressed her directly, unless they felt the need to share their decision-making process with her. "That's true. But it would be more convenient in this case."

"The Empire paid a terrible price for the level of tech it has," Madine stated. "Magic will need to find a way to balance it out now."

Caette nodded. "The scales must equalize."

"Won't finding the last piece of corruption do that?" Sherri asked with a frown.

But Madine just shook her head. "It is related, but not the same. Everything continues in cycles. We see the same events, repeated time and time again, though to a casual observer they might look quite different. We can bring about the end of this cycle of corruption, or at the very least lend aid to... Jamirh to do so, but the cycle of magic must right itself."

The dryad looked outside at the world passing by, green rolling hills and peaceful villages. "Do you think the level of tech will drop, or the level of magic will rise?"

The Seekers were quiet for a moment.

"Who can say for sure?" Madine said finally. "We would like to say both – have the Empire find the equilibrium Romanii has, or Dalmara, or any of the other countries that have developed tech alongside magic rather than as a replacement for it – but we do not know what it would take to have the Empire start forgetting tech. And as you yourself have noted, while Romanii's tech does not fight against magic the way ours does, it is also less efficient and does less. We cannot see the citizens of the Empire willingly giving that up, not even for magic."

Sherri paused. "There is still nothing, past the current crisis?"

"Nothing," Madine confirmed. "We cannot see the way it ends, no matter how far forward we attempt to look.

"All we see is magic, and the corruption trying to consume it."

# Chapter Nineteen

---

Ander felt much better after a few days of rest, both physically and emotionally.

It was hard to remember that night, but... maybe Hades was right. Maybe he should talk to Vlad about it if it still hurt so much after three hundred years. If he put that in the context of a physical wound, he would be furious that it had been ignored so long and allowed to fester. Because that was what was happening, wasn't it? The more he tried to ignore it the worse it got.

It wasn't as though he'd ever stop missing them, and he doubted there would come a time when he didn't regret leaving them there that night to nebulous memories and an uncertain future, but... maybe he could find some peace with himself.

Romanii was a country that often felt frozen in time, but maybe it was time to move on.

Even if the thought was exhausting.

He sipped at his coffee, glad to no longer be drinking sillna, as Mara bounced past him with far too much energy for the early morning. "Good morning, Ander! How're you feeling?" she asked, grabbing a couple of slices of bread from the bread box and tossing them into the toaster.

He reached over and turned down the dial so the toast would resemble food when it came out. "Like my body has decided to cooperate, finally."

"Oh, that's great!" She poured a cup of coffee from the pot Ander had left on the counter, adding far too much sugar to it. "What are you going to do with your day, then? Hopefully nothing *too* strenuous, since you just recovered."

He watched her add a quarter cup of milk to her cup. "There are some things I need to look into."

"Oh?"

He thought of the data pad he'd taken from Tilden, one of the many things he'd been putting off. They'd kept a corpse for over twenty years; there was something important about that, he was sure. "Yes. I think we need to figure out what they were trying to do with Ryn."

A quick message to the hospital had Marcus knocking on the door to his lab an hour later. "Ander? You said you had a project you needed help with?"

"More like three projects," he clarified as he finished setting up a pair of beakers, "but with two of us they should all be doable simultaneously."

"Three projects?" Marcus asked with a raised eyebrow as he stepped into the lab, looking around at the three stations Ander had set up. "Very well, then. Where are we starting?"

"This needs to sit on its own for an hour and a half while it heats; we just need to monitor it." He refused to give up entirely on the avatar for Hades, but there were some parts of it he could set up to progress in the background while most of his attention was taken by other things. He pointed at the second station by the opposite wall, where he'd set up some equipment borrowed from Don. "That is a data pad I took from Tilden Base shortly before it exploded. I was able to glance through it briefly before we had to leave and it seems to have some research notes concerning the corpse of the previous Ebryn before Jamirh, who for clarity's sake we are calling 'Ryn.' The equipment it's attached to is charging it; the battery died sometime since I took it."

"That is almost certainly going to be depressing reading," Marcus said dryly. The Vampire looked at the center table and the scraps of metal on it. "Wait. Is that...?"

Ander nodded. "What's left of the bionic Abomination that attacked Jamirh here."

"Why do you still have it?" he asked, brows drawing together. "Shouldn't all of that have been destroyed?"

"Why? There's nothing dangerous about it now." He picked up one of the larger pieces. "But it does have a unique property – it's resistant to magic. Not impossible to overcome, but you need a fairly powerful spell. And while I'm sure that is important, the Nifoni chip did not have the same property." He gestured to where the remains of the microchip sat off to one side for comparison.

He'd considered also workshopping the Truth Seeker blindfold, but it didn't feel right to investigate that without Takeshi. The shinobi was working with Caelessa on using his Voice, and Ander felt pleased that he'd been able to help with that. Hopefully Takeshi would be able to soulforge soon, or would at least make some progress to that end. Then maybe he and the shinobi could work on projects together.

Marcus wasn't Takeshi, but he was also very intelligent and had had good insights before. And maybe the presence of a helper would keep the witches off Ander's back.

Though part of him still felt... weirdly regretful it was Marcus and not Takeshi working with him.

"You have both expressions of Abomination," the Vampire said slowly, eyes narrowing at the table before he looked back up at Ander. "All right, then. Where do we start?"

Ander walked over to the data pad. "I have some tests I would like to run on the metal, so if you wouldn't mind combing through this and perhaps taking some notes on what it contains while I do so...?"

"Of course. Is there anything specific you want me to look for?"

Ander considered the question. "Any link to their bionic research would be fascinating, but mostly I'm interested in why they kept the corpse around for over twenty years. What were they doing with it? What was their goal?"

Marcus nodded, and they got to work.

Ander started with one of the medium-sized pieces of metal, pushing at it with his magic and feeling the unnatural resistance in turn. He checked his notes from when he'd examined the corpse originally, but all he'd been able to discern was that it was probably steel mixed with something else. He placed a piece of paper with a prepared array onto the table and set the metal down onto it, activating it with a thought. But it pushed back against the spell as well, keeping its composition a secret, and Ander ended the spell.

That was not the only way to determine what type of metal it was made of.

He took a beaker from a rack and placed it on the table, then went into a cabinet to get a container of acid. As he went to pour it into the beaker, he paused.

There was an extra ring of glyphs in the array on the paper.

He frowned, analyzing the new spell. At first glance it looked like the original ring had been duplicated and multiplied, but that wasn't the only change – the glyphs in the original ring had also multiplied and were now crowded together. The bridging lines had grown extra branches in a chaotic fashion, trying to reach both rings and connect all the new glyphs. As he watched, a few more glyphs appeared and shoved themselves into the limited available space, and the bridging lines branched again to connect them.

"Unrestrained spell growth?" he wondered aloud as it tried to grow more.

"Hm?" Marcus looked over. "Oh, that is... strange. Is the metal doing that?"

Ander tipped the metal off the paper and the spell, if it could still be called that, settled. "That's *divine* magic," he said, aghast. "Chaos and creation. What would *that* be doing in the metal?"

The Lady's attention swung towards him. *:Divine?:* He could feel Her studying the overgrown array. *:It is Tadurin's magic,:* she confirmed after a short pause.

Ander frowned. Tadurin was the god of life and creation, Hades' equal. "I can't possibly believe Tadurin supports Abomination."

Marcus' eyes went wide. "I would hope not."

*:No! He does not support Abomination,:* She hastened to reassure him. *:He fears it as the rest of my siblings do, and it is just as dangerous to him as it is to the rest of us. This is not something made by him. It feels more like something made* of *him, utilizing his power. Like how the restless dead are related to me, but I do not create them.:*

Interesting. "Hades agrees that is not the case. So then, the metal has characteristics of Tadurin, which means..." He considered the overgrown array. "It's not magic resistant in the same sense Abomination is, since Abomination consumes magic, but in that it is constantly adapting and affecting its surroundings. How on Gaia did they create this?"

*:Tadurin's magic is, by its very nature, unpredictable,:* Hades offered hesitantly. *:He does not create with any sort of goal, things just... become, because of him. It is often my siblings who shape it.:*

And the Lady herself existed to balance that, to bring order to chaos, an end to life unconstrained. Ander had always assumed that was why the siblings didn't seem to get along.

"The Empire is very anti-magic, so it seems unlikely this was on purpose," Marcus pointed out. "Perhaps it was an unintended by-product of something else?"

"Tadurin's magic doesn't always follow known rules, so... that is possible, I suppose." Ander eyed the other pieces of metal, but nothing had changed around them. It was only the spell that had been affected, and only when it was in direct contact with the metal. Yet... the metal plate that had covered the side of its face had alchemical symbols etched into the metal in a circle around the mechanical eye.

Ander tapped the plate. "Sulfur, salt, and mercury in a repeating pattern. The three primes. Why bother with that?"

"It is reminiscent of an array, though the alchemical symbols do not have the power glyphs do." Marcus put down the data pad and leaned over to get a better look. "Perhaps it was meant as a mockery of an array?"

Would that have been enough? "There are plenty of theories that either the glyphs evolved from the symbols or the other way around due to how close they are in form. If that is true, then the alchemical symbols might have functioned like a sort of... proto-glyph, and accidentally let the magic in?"

*:That is possible,:* Hades said, but she didn't sound happy about it.

"Alchemy is often associated with transmutation and change, which... is what the metal did to the array. And once the magic found its way in through the symbols, it could have spread into all the connected metal. And if the metal is imbued with Tadurin's adaptivity, maybe that is how they were able to fuse the tech with the Avari," Marcus theorized. "The metal itself provided the link to make the bionics work."

"And the microchips failed over time, because they didn't have that adaptivity," Ander concluded. "It does make sense. But what prevented the Abomination from consuming the magic in the metal, then?"

"Perhaps it was so adaptive it made itself invisible to the Abomination, or at least able to cohabitate in the same host?" Marcus suggested, picking the data pad back up. "Tadurin is the god of life, and life adapts."

Hades was silent in Ander's mind.

"What is Abomination?" Ander asked slowly, tasting the words as he sounded them out. "A sin against the world itself, something that damages the fabric of reality. It seeks to consume all magic, but if it were to succeed in doing so it would spell its own doom – it cannot exist without magic. So the presence of this specific magic in the metal actually was able to strengthen and stabilize the Abomination."

"A lucky happenstance for the Empire," Marcus agreed, flipping through tabs as he scanned the data pad. "And for what it is worth, they did try to make this Ebryn – Ryn? – into a bionic immediately after he was... stabbed? But according to these notes the process didn't take. They theorized it was because he died before it could take over. Apparently the Avari subject does need to be alive for the process to work."

"If the metal parts have been accidentally infused with Tadurin's magic, that makes sense. Actually, that makes the bionics something of a living version of the restless dead, doesn't it?" That was an uncomfortable thought. He folded his arms. "The restless dead are made from the dead; bionics must be made from the living. But then why did they hold on to the corpse?"

*:I do not like that thought* at all, *but the analogy does seem to line up,:* Hades said, sounding a little ill.

Marcus looked up from the data pad, frowning. "You know how, before Romanii was a country and mortals occasionally hunted down Vampires, they had a method for ensuring Vampires stayed dead? Beheading and dismembering them, staking them through the heart, and stuffing the mouth full of garlic?"

Ander blinked. "Yes?"

"I think they were trying to do essentially the same thing, but with Ryn," Marcus explained. "Dismember the body, preserve it, keep an eye on it. Make sure it can't get back up."

"But... that's not how reincarnation works," Ander protested as a headache started to form. "You can't prevent reincarnation by preserving remains. The soul is what reincarnates."

Marcus shrugged. "You are a priest of Hades; they have limited knowledge of reincarnation. They appeared to be trying all manner of things to prevent it in the hopes something would work. The Truth Seekers had a prophecy... well, I suppose we know the real prophecy now – their Three Signs – but they had shared an edited version with the Empire that made the military focus on trying to prevent Ebryn Stormlight from returning."

"Which was smart on their part," Ander acknowledged. "A smokescreen for themselves, even though it made things more difficult for us."

"Indeed. In fact, two of the Truth Seekers remained behind in Tarvishte; we could ask them if they have any insight into this." Marcus held up the data pad. "It's possible they have additional notes of their own, as well."

"I would prefer to use that source sparingly." He picked up the metal plate, fingers tracing the alchemical symbols. "I'm not sure I trust their motivations."

"But you can tell if they are lying. Or the Lady can, at least, right?"

Ander hummed. He had just recovered from one such session and was not in a rush to repeat it. "She can tell if they are outright lying, but there are plenty of ways to misdirect while telling the absolute truth. And I would imagine they have quite some practice with that."

What did becoming a Truth Seeker entail, exactly?

He brushed the errant thought aside, refocusing on Ryn. At least the corpse had been destroyed along with Tilden Base. Further desecration was no longer possible.

Which reminded him... what had become of the first Ebryn? Obviously not the same thing; the Empire as they knew it didn't exist then and the bionics were a long way off. Perhaps Jamirh could have asked, but both Ebryns were somehow missing.

And where could they have even gone? They were part of Jamirh, so it wasn't like they could just leave. They couldn't die, either. And Ryn and Jamirh had appeared to have a good rapport, so stopping communication so suddenly without any explanation was strange. Why did the dead have to be so capricious?

Ryn had ignored Ander when summoned, but then again, knowing what they now knew of the end of Ryn's life his distraction had been warranted. It was very possible he'd been trying to ignore getting dismembered. Or had been dealing with the trauma of that knowledge. But that didn't explain the current situation.

And maybe it was asking a bit much to have Jamirh ask the original Ebryn how he'd died anyway. By all accounts, that one avoided communication whenever possible. And Jamirh loathed him. So that could very well remain a mystery until the end of time.

Marcus cleared his throat. "And you will have to check this, but it also seems as though they may have picked up on some of Hades' energy in Ryn's corpse. There are some strange notations here, but it seems to be death energy of some sort. Actually, it could be that Her magic canceled out Tadurin's, which contributed to the attempt to turn Ryn into a bionic failing."

*:Ah. I did... well.:*

*:You did what?:* he asked with a frown.

There was a long pause. *:When it became clear he was dying, I may have... hurried things along. To prevent him from suffering.:*

Ander blinked. *:You* killed *Ryn?:*

*:As I said, he had already been mortally wounded,:* She defended Herself. *:He was only in that situation because I had recalled him back to life to fulfill Ebryn's oath. I did not think it right that he should suffer unreasonably because of that. So I just... ended him. Quickly.:*

*:Was there a* reasonable *threshold he should suffer?:* Ander asked, aghast.

*:That's not what I–:*

"As a related aside, did Jamirh tell you he melted a bionic's spine with the glowing hand?"

"*What?*"

Ander was annoyed. Jamirh was not on the palace grounds and had gone to visit the pirates on the *Sea Spirit* – something that was apparently happening fairly frequently. Ander had managed to reach Jeri, but since Jamirh had been cleared by Marcus the previous night she wasn't concerned enough to make him return. She had promised to pass along the message, and hopefully Jamirh would come by the Temple when he returned, though she couldn't say when that would be.

Ander had so many questions. How had Jamirh activated the magic in his arm? Had he been able to direct it, or was the melting all it could do? It had to be powerful enough to overcome the bionic's resistance to magic, but was it using up the magic in the arm as though it were a spell crystal? Was the arm reading as magic now? Why hadn't he been informed earlier?

He all but stormed back into his lab–

And froze. Takeshi was there, speaking with Marcus. Both men stopped and turned to look at Ander.

He wrestled himself back under control. "Takeshi."

The shinobi inclined his head. "Ander. Do you have a few minutes?"

Ander glanced at Marcus, who put the tablet down. "It is half past noon; I will find us lunch. Lord Takeshi, will you be staying long?"

Takeshi blinked. "Ah, just Takeshi is fine. And no, I don't intend to take up much of Ander's time. You do not need to leave, either."

Marcus shook his head. "On the contrary, Ander needs to eat. Do you have any preference?" The last question was aimed at him.

He shook his head. "No, whatever is quick is fine."

"I will see what I can find. I will return shortly." And with that, Marcus swept from the lab.

"My apologies for interrupting," Takeshi started, looking around the room and taking in the parts scattered about. "I did not realize you were working with someone else today."

Ander waved the apology away and bit back the fact he would have preferred to be working with Takeshi. "It is no matter. I just spent twenty minutes trying to track down Jamirh, anyway. Did you know he used his hand to melt and sever the spine of a bionic?"

Takeshi blinked slowly. "Did you not?"

Ander stared at him.

"You would have known if you had come on the mission with us," Takeshi said mildly.

Ander sighed, annoyed all over again. "You wanted something?"

Takeshi looked around, sliding his hands into his pockets. "I need a different angle of thought. I've been trying to work on using my Voice, but it's not... exactly going well."

"That's not terribly unexpected," Ander pointed out, taking a seat on a stool by the center table. "Inherents found late in life are often more difficult to master."

"Do you have any familiarity with Voice magic?"

Ander began laying out the metal fragments so they were approximately where they had been on the bionic. "No, none at all. I have no inherent."

"You don't want to join the 'oh shit, we actually have inherents' club?" Takeshi asked dryly.

"Not... particularly, no." And at over three hundred years old, the possibility that he might have an inherent was nonexistent. "How are you struggling, specifically?"

"With the absolute basics," the shinobi admitted, taking a seat on another stool. "I'm struggling to make sounds that are pitched correctly to resonate with the World Sound."

"You've been humming in tune though, haven't you?"

"Well... yes. I can only seem to do it while I'm not thinking about it."

Ah, the pitfall of inherents. And considering the shinobi focus on stealth...

Wait.

"Shinobi weave when they cast magic, correct?" Ander asked.

Takeshi nodded. "Yes."

"And that is accomplished through Movement? To aid with the lack of a visible array?"

Takeshi started to answer, then paused, thinking about it. "Well, yes, I suppose. Small – or sometimes larger – motions to guide the spell are usually less obvious than the light of a pattern or the spoken word. We call it spinning the weave. Usually it is kept to hand gestures, though some shinobi do utilize a greater range of movement."

"The inherent of Movement is often associated with dancing, which is closely related to Voice, and thus the World Sound," Ander mused. "What if instead of starting something new, you tried to resonate with the World Sound through a medium you already understand?"

The shinobi tilted his head. "You think I should try to dance to the World Sound?"

Ander shrugged. "I don't know that dance is precisely the correct word, but I do think you could utilize the pattern weaving you already know in a similar manner. That would be approaching the problem from a different angle entirely, but maybe this one will make more sense to you. What did Caelessa say?"

"She said I sounded like a dying cat."

He thought about that a moment. "Yes, I would investigate the possibility of using Movement, then. Especially if you are trying to achieve results quickly."

Takeshi nodded once decisively, then stood. "I will try that, then. Thank you for your insight. Good day, Ander." He turned to leave.

"Takeshi?"

The shinobi paused and looked back at him.

"I wouldn't worry about it too much. You'll have eternity to perfect your singing, after all."

Takeshi snorted and left with a wave over his shoulder.

Ander watched him go, wondering why he wanted Takeshi to stay.

# Chapter Twenty

Jamirh had known this was going to happen. It was why he hadn't wanted to tell Ander in the first place. But now here he was, sitting on a stool in Ander's lab while the half-Avari poked and prodded at his arm, even though Marcus had already done all this yesterday. They weren't going to learn anything new. And Ander just had to draw *more* blood. Why?

"And what were you doing when it activated?"

"Fighting the bionic," Jamirh said tiredly. "The arm was glowing brightly, and... I don't know. It just seemed like the thing to do at the time."

Ander shot him an unimpressed look. "Magic requires direction, *will*, to work. Did you think of melting the spine when you grabbed it?"

Jamirh didn't know what this was going to accomplish. "No. I was just sort of reacting at that point, since I was in close combat with a bionic. Not a great place to be. I guess the spine does seem like the most obvious weak point?" He looked down. The wounds on his hand and arm were glowing faintly, at about the same level they had been since the original spar with Jeri. There was a dull ache just under the skin. "It made sense to me, anyway."

Ander didn't seem to like that either, judging from his expression. "That's not how magic works."

Jamirh shrugged. "I really don't know what to tell you."

The priest's lips pressed into a thin line and he cast an array above Jamirh's arm, green glyphs spinning lazily. Ander watched them for almost a full minute before dismissing them. "It's hard to tell if that used up some of the magic currently stored in your arm since there is so much of it, though I'm leaning towards yes. Which is good; if you can repeat the effect that would help you bleed off the magic until it's gone."

And then he'd stop glowing. Which was very appealing, but still. "I would if I had any idea at all of how I did it the first time."

Ander's eyes narrowed and he looked at the center table, which was covered in bits of metal. After a moment, he walked over and picked up the largest piece and handed it to Jamirh. "Melt it."

"I really don't think it works that way," Jamirh said with a sigh, though he took it and held it in his right hand.

"Not with that attitude, it doesn't."

Jamirh looked down at the metal plate. It was curved slightly, with a hole in the right side. Around the hole were symbols. Symbols Jamirh had seen before. His head snapped up. "Is this from a bionic?!"

"Yes." Ander didn't sound bothered by that at all. "It's from the one that attacked you in the palace."

Jamirh stared at it for a moment, then looked back at Ander. "I don't think it was glowing because of the bionic. It's reacted a few times before – like when I was training with Jeri and Siva – and there was no Abomination present at all. It hasn't always been while fighting, either." He frowned, trying to remember. "It was reacting for a while before I came across the bionic in Etroy, and sometimes it glows more when I'm just having a conversation or something."

"Hm." Ander glared down at the arm. "Was there a lot of magic at Etroy?"

Jamirh shrugged.

"There must be a consistent trigger; we just haven't found it yet." Ander's mouth twisted, and he took the metal plate from Jamirh. "Fine, then. There's been no pain or discomfort?"

He paused, looking down at the marks. He should probably tell Ander, but then he'd be poked and prodded more. And he didn't really want that. And it wasn't like it hurt, it was just a little–

"Your long silence suggests the answer to that is 'yes,' but you are trying to figure out how to tell me 'no.'" Ander's voice was sour. "An oddly common reaction among patients for some godforsaken reason. I can't help you if you aren't honest with me. Especially if the answer to that question is 'yes.'"

Jamirh glanced at him sheepishly. "It can feel a little warm sometimes when it glows, but that's barely noticeable," he tried to deflect.

Ander's eyes narrowed as he stared at him, silent.

Jamirh folded. "It's felt just a little achy since we got back from Etroy. Nothing bad, just... a little sore."

The priest was silent for a long moment, studying Jamirh's arm with a frown.

"That's... not good, is it?" Jamirh shifted uncomfortably, ears sinking.

Ander sighed, bringing a hand up to rub his face. "It's not ideal, no, but 'sore' is better than 'in pain.' My best guess is that when the magic was released it strained the limb. Which isn't the worst-case scenario, but due to the nature of the situation, it is very difficult to ascertain the exact cause of the ache. However, it is of vital importance you tell me these things, Jamirh. This is so unprecedented, we don't even know what information is important."

Jamirh looked down again, not sure how to respond.

"I can prescribe you painkillers for now, but I suppose the best thing to do is to continue to keep an eye on it." The priest looked down at the metal plate with a frown, then looked back at Jamirh. "And *let me know* if something unusual happens again."

"I told Marcus," Jamirh muttered, ears twitching down. "You've been... busy."

That caused Ander to pause, then he turned and took out a bin from a cabinet and started collecting the metal pieces into it, his back to Jamirh. "Regardless, please do keep me informed. In fact, I would like to examine it myself every two days, moving forward."

Jamirh grimaced. That was *exactly* the kind of thing he had been hoping to avoid. "Do you have to?"

"'Have to'?" Ander paused and raised an eyebrow. "No, I suppose not, I don't *have* to do my job as your doctor. I'm going to do it anyway, since it *is* my job, and Lady help you if you don't show up." He resumed cleaning up.

Jamirh wasn't sure what to do about a threat that vague, but decided he had two days to determine if he was going to test it or not. "What were you doing with all this stuff anyway?" he asked, changing the subject as he started to re-wrap his arm. "I would've thought you'd have destroyed it."

"Marcus and I were trying to determine what the Empire was doing with Ryn's corpse."

Jamirh paused as the wounds flickered ever so slightly. He glanced sharply at Ander, but the other man was still putting things away and didn't seem to have noticed.

Should he mention it?

No. It was just a little flicker. He might've even imagined it. And Jamirh wanted to go back to his rooms and sleep. He'd been so tired recently. He began wrapping his hand again a little more quickly. "Why *did* they still have it? It's kind of sick, honestly."

"From what we can tell, they were trying to stack the odds in their favor that you wouldn't be reborn. They hoped that by keeping the corpse, that could prevent you from returning. It was a completely foolish notion, of course – we wouldn't be having this conversation otherwise – but they tried."

Jamirh felt a chill go down his spine as his stomach flopped. "Oh," he said faintly. "What do you mean, stacking the odds in their favor?"

"They weren't sure how reincarnation worked, so they tried a number of things to try to stop it. Basically, they were working under the expectation that the more they did, chances went up that *something* would work."

Jamirh's ears twitched. "No, I meant – you know what, I probably don't want to know. Never mind." He finished putting the bracer over the wrap and finished with the glove. There; now his arm was hidden. And he could go sleep.

Ander glanced over at him. "You already came face-to-face with the most macabre example, but as you wish."

Yeah, Jamirh didn't want to think about that. At all. Ever again. "All right then, I'm going to head out. See you later."

Ander waved distractedly as Jamirh slipped from the lab and started back to the palace.

It was only later, as he lay in bed trying to sleep, that the thought suddenly wouldn't leave him alone.

What, exactly, *did* make the wounds react?

He couldn't stop thinking about Ander's declaration that there had to be some common link between each instance the glow intensified. It had started glowing just after his spar with Jeri, but that just started a new normal – did that matter?

Then it had picked up after his spar with Siva, which suggested combat being a link. But the wounds had glowed in Etroy before there had been any combat at all, so that seemed to disprove that theory. He'd noticed it...

...when he'd found the place Ryn had died.

And it had continued glowing until after the bionic was dead. In fact, it had died down immediately after the thing's death – a death he had caused by *using* the magic in the arm.

Then it had acted up again when on the *Sea Spirit* – there had been absolutely no combat at all there – and again very briefly today when talking to Ander.

Why? What was the link?

If it wasn't where he was, and it wasn't what he was doing, what else was left?

On the *Sea Spirit* and in Ander's lab, the only thing he'd been doing was talking, really. Talking today about Ryn's corpse, and on the *Sea Spirit* about Ebryn.

And at Etroy, he'd been where Ryn had died.

Eyes widening, he tried to think back to what he had been talking about with Siva when it had acted up. Something about... knowing Ebryn? Knowing Sukra?

And in the beginning, with Jeri – he'd been talking about how he was going to fight. He hadn't said it in so many words, but he'd basically been saying he was going to follow in Ryn's and Ebryn's footsteps.

Each time, the conversation had been about his predecessors.

He sat up in bed despite his exhaustion, looking down at his arm. In the dark, it gave off a faint red light through the wrapping. Why would the wounds react to mentions of his previous lives? Was it because the Blade had belonged to Ebryn? But then, Ryn had never laid hands on it...

Slowly, he began to undo the wrap, bathing the room in a soft red glow. He licked his lips, unsure where he was going to go with this, before whispering, "Ryn?"

No reaction.

Jamirh bit his lip, ears twitching down. Then he tried again, louder. "Ryn?"

A gentle pulse of light answered him.

Okay, but did that mean it was actually Ryn, or just the wounds reacting to his name for some reason?

Ander had said something – or someone – was shielding him from the Blade's elemental magic.

Ryn – and Ebryn – had been missing since the Blade had shattered.

Was it them?

The more Jamirh thought it through, the more it made sense. The glow intensified when the conversation or events had to do with them – were they trying to make themselves known? Trying to tell Jamirh they were still there?

Was there still a way to reach them?

His eye caught on the white of the sheet he had covering the mirror in this room. Ryn had found it easier to speak to him through the mirror, hadn't he?

But Jamirh had tried that. It hadn't worked.

But... he also hadn't known about the arm. It had been wrapped the last time he'd tried. And what had Ander been saying today about stacking multiple things in your favor?

What else could he use? The Blade would have been an obvious choice, but it was gone, leaving the wounds scattered across his skin. There wasn't really anything else that linked him to the other two. Was there?

All he could think of was the mirror.

It was all magic anyway, right?

His left hand gripped his key tightly for a moment, then he slid out of bed and padded over to the mirror above the dresser. He reached out, trying not to think too hard about what he was doing, grabbed the fabric, and pulled–

He found himself facing the other side of the room, clutching the fabric to his chest as he gasped for air.

He closed his eyes, trying to take deep breaths and let his heart rate return to normal. It was just a mirror; it wasn't like it could hurt him. There wasn't any reason for this sort of reaction, he reminded himself. It was just a mirror. It was just a mirror.

His other hand came up to rub his key, the familiar action soothing and reassuring. When his breathing was more under control, he opened his eyes again.

His arm was definitely glowing more brightly, the red casting an eerie glow across the room that was bright enough to see by comfortably.

Okay. Okay then, this was the right path. He just had to actually carry it out. He could do that. Just turn, and face the mirror. An easy thing to do, really.

He just had to do it.

He closed his eyes again and took a deep breath before turning around carefully, dropping the sheet onto the floor.

Now all he had to do was open his eyes. That was an even easier action, wasn't it?

His grip around his key was so tight he could feel the teeth biting into his palm.

Slowly, he opened his eyes.

With everything washed in red, the room looked alien and strange, but... it was just his reflection cowering back at him from the mirror. No Ryn.

Jamirh fought down a crushing wave of disappointment. He'd been so sure it would work this time, if only he could bring himself to look at the mirror. And he was doing it, even if it made his stomach twist and everything in him screamed to look away. But he was still alone, no matter how brightly the jagged lines traveling down his hand and arm shone. Just him, and a weirdly lit version of himself staring back with haunted eyes.

He reached out to touch the glass, not even sure what he was hoping for, but feeling the need to connect with something–

–and found himself somewhere else entirely.

"What do you want? We're busy."

There were no walls, no edges – just a pearlescent, pastel mist making it difficult to tell how large the space actually was. The switch from red light to daylight caused him to squint while his eyes adjusted.

But he could make out the figure in front of him.

It was a figure he'd seen once before at Tilden, with long red hair in a ponytail and ancient leather armor.

That wasn't Ryn.

"While we're at it, stop distracting us by saying our names every five minutes. It's hard enough keeping this up without all that."

Jamirh frowned, heart sinking as he blinked, trying to clear his eyes.

An awkward laugh came from his left. "It hasn't been that often. And besides, it hasn't always been Jamirh's fault. He can't control other people, you know?"

Jamirh turned and saw the version of himself that was a little younger with a short braid. He was beyond relieved that the other Avari looked just fine, and not at all the way his corpse had looked at Tilden. He felt something in his chest unclench. "Ryn!"

His predecessor smiled. "Hey, Jamirh! Sorry we haven't been able to chat like usual, but we have been pretty busy."

"Saving your life, by the way. Feel free to leave any time. It takes a lot of attention to do this." Ebryn folded his arms.

Jamirh was so relieved to see them that he pushed aside his distaste for the Hero for the moment. "But what..." He trailed off. He knew what they were doing. "You're shielding me from the Blade's energy."

"We are definitely doing the best we can," Ryn confirmed. "But the magic has been getting more volatile as time passes."

"Makes sense for the Faleri, to be honest," Ebryn muttered, scowling. "All the gods are obnoxious, but they and the Espera seem to be in a competition to see who can accidentally do the most damage without trying. We can throw Tadurin in there too, actually."

Jamirh frowned. "What happened, exactly?"

If anything, Ebryn's expression darkened further. "After running all over multiple continents to collect those stupid crystals, those miserable excuses for deities made me perform these ridiculous tasks–"

"I think he meant with the Blade shattering," Ryn interrupted gently. "But yes, upsetting circumstances to be sure."

Jamirh stared at Ebryn. This... was not really what he had expected the Hero to be like.

"But when the Blade shattered, some pieces of it entered your arm and hand, and since the magic was *so* volatile at that moment, some of the magic sort of hopped into the wounds," Ryn continued. "Since the dominant type of magic that entered you was fire magic, we've been trying to prevent it from consuming you ever since then."

"*Consuming* me?" Jamirh asked, ears flattening.

Ebryn snorted. "We had it mostly under control until our attention slipped."

"Ebryn, we discussed this. You can't blame it entirely on that; the magic wants to cause problems," Ryn said with a sigh.

"Magic is strange like that. Never even tried to understand it myself, and I think that was probably the best call." Ebryn frowned again. "Trying to ensure it was going to hurt that Abomination and not you took a lot of effort, I assure you."

"But then... why couldn't you just tell me that?" Jamirh asked, confused.

"Because for all intents and purposes, we *are* the shield," Ebryn said. "Literally everything we are is preventing the magic from consuming you the way it wants to. I don't even really understand how you are here, but again – magic isn't our strong suit. Regardless, you probably shouldn't stay here long."

Jamirh looked down at the ground, or where the ground should be. All he saw was mist. He looked back at Ebryn. "I just wanted... Ryn gave good advice before. I thought maybe..." He trailed off, feeling uncertain again.

Something in Ebryn's eyes softened, and he looked away. "You shouldn't care so much about us. We're dead."

"It's natural to want to ask for advice, though," Ryn countered. "And three minds are better than one, after all!"

"I still wouldn't recommend it," Ebryn said.

"I'm not looking for anything crazy," Jamirh protested. "It's just that... I made the decision to help, and I *do* want the bionics destroyed, but... I feel like I have no idea what I'm doing. I'm just winging it."

Ebryn shrugged. "That's life. No one knows what they're doing."

"But..." Jamirh thought of Ander, Takeshi, Jeri... so many people who did seem to know what they were doing.

But the Hero just shook his head. "Everyone's got problems they're dealing with. Some people are just better at putting up a front than others."

"Well, some people are also better at dealing with their problems than others," Ryn said thoughtfully. "Maybe the trick is to become more like that? I wouldn't really know though; my problems stabbed me to death."

"And then you made a deal with Hades. What on Gaia is wrong with us?" Ebryn sighed, then looked at Jamirh. "Okay, one piece of advice: do not make a deal with Hades, especially not at the moment of your death, no matter how tempting it might seem at the time."

"Wasn't planning on it." Jamirh considered the Hero. His whole life he'd spent hating the man and everything he stood for, and when he'd seen him in Tilden Base he'd been almost overcome by rage, but...

Jamirh was just tired, now. And Ebryn wasn't what he had expected. Rude and blunt, yes, but... for some reason Jamirh hadn't expected his predecessor to have such a bleak outlook on things. In fact... Ebryn almost seemed to *agree* with Jamirh about some things.

It was a little depressing, honestly.

And thinking back on it... Ebryn had tried to stop him from going into that room to see Ryn's corpse. He'd known, but Jamirh had pushed forward anyway.

He shuddered at the memory. But... Ryn was right there. And he looked fine. For some reason, it was easier to look at him here than it was to look at a mirror. Jamirh could look at Ryn and see Ryn, not Ryn-in-pieces.

He tried to burn the image of Ryn standing with both hands on his hips looking disapprovingly at Ebryn into his memory. This was the Ryn he wanted to remember, not the other one.

"At least it ended up being useful," Ryn was protesting. "Jamirh was able to navigate Tilden masterfully due to my agreement with Hades."

"At what cost?" Ebryn asked dryly.

They both turned to look at Jamirh, and Ryn cringed. "I'm sorry. I didn't think you'd end up seeing that."

Jamirh's ears twitched. "You knew?"

Ryn looked away. "I didn't remember the exact terms of the deal until we entered the base. Hades helped me forget to make it easier on me. She was trying to be kind, since my remains had to be on the base for the link to work. But... so close, and that spell came undone. And it hurt to be there. I closed myself off to spare you from that."

"Oh." Jamirh thought about that. It made sense, given everything else.

"Neither of you should blame yourselves. It's always one cata-strophe after another where the gods are concerned. Mortals just have to hold on and hope we make it through in as few pieces as possible." Ebryn indicated Jamirh's arm. "You are already marked by the current cycle."

Jamirh looked down at his arm. Here, the scars weren't glowing, but they clearly stood out against his skin, traveling from his hand down his arm to the elbow. "There's no guarantee this will be the end of it. It isn't over yet."

Ryn nodded. "We'll still continue to help you however we can." He shot a glance at Ebryn. "Like with this whole fire magic thing. While there is still power in your arm, we can help you direct it."

"To a greater or lesser degree," Ebryn muttered, folding his arms. "It's really not that precise. And, as you've noticed, it is not without cost."

Jamirh could still feel the dull ache.

"But on that note, you should really go," the Hero continued. "This is exhausting to maintain. Rest at ease with the knowledge that we are doing just great, except for the part where we should be dead and are doing this instead."

Ryn covered his face with a hand, ears sinking.

Jamirh frowned, squinting at the other Avari and tilting his head to the side. "Isn't that technically your fault?"

"Yes," came the completely unapologetic reply. "And if I could undo it I would, but here we are."

"But then... what happens to you when the Abomination is gone?" Jamirh asked. "Like, does that clear your debt? Will you be free to go be dead, or whatever?"

"I think the Blade breaking cleared the debt to Hades; it's you we are bound to. Since we are, in fact, you, just... earlier versions of you?" Ryn looked at Ebryn for confirmation, but he just shrugged.

"So then... after everything is said and done, will you still be here?" Jamirh's voice was quiet. "If ending the threat of Abomination is the reason I exist, what happens to *me* afterwards?"

A pause.

Finally Ebryn sighed. "Live, probably. Travel, learn a new skill, teach, take up a position in government, whatever. Look, most people don't get to talk to their past selves at all. You are going to have to figure out what you want to do with your life on your own – and, since it is your life, not ours, that is the way it should be. You want my advice? Do what you want. You may not believe this, but that's what I did."

It sounded so easy, when put that way. But how could he figure that out? "Why'd you do it?" he asked finally.

"Do what?"

"Help the Empire form."

Ebryn blinked in surprise, ears twitching down. "That was so far from my mind at the time... and after killing what's-his-face, I was just tired," he admitted. "I didn't stick around long enough to find out what Saran wanted to do with the government, though she offered me all sorts of honors and the Captaincy of the Guard. I decided leaving was the better option. So I left. I didn't really see my actions at the time as helping *anything* form."

Jamirh frowned. "Where did you go, then?"

Ebryn looked away, shrugging. "Elsewhere."

Was that the truth? That Ebryn's actions had only incidentally allowed the Empire to form without his actual acknowledgement?

"Propaganda is what it is," Ryn cut in. "Hard not to use a divinely appointed Hero as a symbol if you've got one, I guess."

"It's hard to overstate just how much I loathe politics," Ebryn confirmed. "I liked how practical Saran could be, but I probably should have guessed that in my absence she would twist the narrative to her benefit."

"Is that our fate, then? To be used no matter what we do?" Jamirh asked bitterly.

Ebryn just shrugged again. "Who knows? I don't really believe in fate. I think we make our own futures. It's up to you now to decide where you'll go. And for what it's worth – I think you have more options than you think you do. A whole sea of them, one might say." He gestured–

Jamirh found himself blinking at his mirror, bathed in the red glow from his arm. Had Ebryn just *thrown him out*? "Hey, that was rude," he snapped. "Not even a goodbye?"

His arm didn't so much as flicker.

He glanced again at the mirror, and while his stomach flipped uncomfortably, it was only his own reflection he saw. Not Ryn. He swallowed hard and looked down, grateful that he couldn't see it but still unnerved at the memory. He considered covering the mirror again, but decided to leave it for now. He could think about it more in the morning.

It occurred to Jamirh afterwards, as he was again lying in bed trying to sleep, to wonder about whether or not a spirit looked the age it had been when it died, or if it looked the way it wanted to. Because Ryn's age made sense; he had died when he was nineteen or twenty.

But Ebryn looked only a little older than Jamirh.

# Chapter Twenty-One

S herri sighed in relief, glad to finally be back in Muriz. After having spent her entire life in the Empire, the ambient magic of Romanii and the Wall almost felt uncomfortable.

It made her angry. Another thing the Empire had stolen from them.

But perhaps things would change soon. They just had to find that final piece of corruption, and then... they'd try again with Romanii.

As they approached the hotel, Caette broke off. Sherri glanced after her. "Are you going to perform the seeking soon?" she asked Madine, who remained by her side.

Her sister nodded. "Later today. We have been preparing. Caette and I needed to return, as our strength will be required, but what could be done before has been."

Sherri hesitated as they entered the large building. "Is Sefera...?"

"Yes, I am also participating."

Sherri inclined her head in respect to the first Seeker at the sound of her feathery voice. The Human was far too old for her race, and she looked it. Wrinkles and spots covered almost every inch of visible skin, and her back was hunched and crooked. She walked with the aid of a silver cane. Long white hair was pulled into a number of complicated braids, some of which draped over her shoulder. She wore the Seeker uniform, and her blindfold was so covered in embroidery that the base fabric was no longer visible. Despite her petite stature, she still radiated a quiet strength.

"I am still the strongest when it comes to a seeking, though soon that title will belong to your sister." Sefera smiled, kind. Of all the Seekers she seemed to have retained the most of her original personality. "But I will see this thing through to the end."

Sherri fought down a wave of sadness. She liked the old woman. She wasn't sure how the Seekers had managed to keep their queen from death for so long, but surely when she finally passed, the world would be a lesser place for it – even if the only ones who recognized her passing were her own people.

The old woman folded her hands atop her cane. "It is time. Sherri, the seeking will take some time to complete, so don't–"

All the Seekers suddenly turned and looked east.

Sherri waited.

Finally Sefera shook her head. "War will come for us all, in time. They could have reached out, had they word of it before it happened. Perhaps we could have helped. But that is not the world we now live in. Come, we must perform the seeking."

Sherri's eyebrows drew together in confusion, and she turned to Madine.

"Crimson Shadows was attacked by Emperor Belian's troops," her sister informed her. "There isn't much left, from what we can tell."

Sherri looked down. Sefera was right; casualties in war were to be expected. And while it wasn't a surprise Crimson Shadows had been targeted, it *was* a surprise they had lost so quickly and completely. But still... "Gren?" she asked.

Madine paused. "There is no confirmation either way," she said after a moment.

She bowed her head. "I see." Silently she said a quick prayer to the Three on behalf of the Avari. Then she looked back at her sister. "Good luck."

Madine inclined her head and then disappeared after Sefera and the other Seekers into the stairwell.

Sherri watched them go, then headed for the elevator to go to her room. She could use this time to rest.

Emperor Belian, Madine had said.

Hopefully there wouldn't be an Empire for him to be emperor of when all was said and done.

There was something... off about today.

Ander leaned against the counter and took a sip of his third cup of coffee. He took a moment to savor the bold taste.

"It doesn't help that I am cold all the time." Takeshi was looking at the fish tank, mug in hand. "I understand that the lasting effects of the microchip could have been so much worse than they are, but it's like..."

"Low-level discomfort over an extended period of time can be tiring," Ander acknowledged. "Most people think it will eventually just fade into the background, become your new reality, and that can happen – but sometimes it comes back full force to bother you when you least expect it. Has it gotten worse, or is it just wearing on you?"

"I don't believe I've felt any colder than usual, no." The shinobi glanced at Jitsu, who was lying on the couch. "She says she has not noticed anything, either. I'm just cold... constantly. I had hoped... with the weather getting warmer..."

That was understandable. "For what it's worth, we've only had a few nice days. The weather has been truly abysmal this spring." How many storms had they had this month? Four? Five? Maybe another one was on its way, and *that* was what had him so on edge. "Though since the issue isn't the actual temperature, it's hard to know how that will affect your perception of it."

Takeshi inclined his head. "Yes, I... logically, I understand that. And I am thankful for everything you've done for me. It might not even be bothering me that much if it weren't for everything else on top of it. And it feels self-centered, to complain about feeling a little cold when all of existence is in jeopardy." He took a sip from his cup before wandering over to the counter.

Ander reflected that he had been seeing Takeshi's face a lot recently. He wondered absently why shinobi wore the mask at all; Takeshi certainly didn't seem to have any issues with taking it off around other people, but he also only ever did so when he was eating or drinking. Was that a shinobi thing, or a "Takeshi has been exiled" thing? Either way, Ander found himself preferring Takeshi with the mask off. He struggled enough with understanding other people's expressions; the mask made it exponentially harder to read Takeshi's.

And he found that he cared about what Takeshi thought.

He shoved the thought aside as irrelevant. "Things that affect you affect you. Just because there are other, bigger things happening doesn't mean all the little stuff goes away. Though that would be convenient."

Takeshi snorted in agreement. Just like–

*No.* It was nothing like Fredrik. What was wrong with him today?

Besides, Fredrik was long, long gone. Takeshi was here. Unless... Takeshi decided not to stay?

"Have you decided whether or not to officially join Hades' priesthood?" he asked.

Takeshi looked away. "I'm still thinking about it."

Ander raised an eyebrow and waited.

"It's not that I'm against it or anything," the shinobi said finally, turning and pacing towards the couch. "It's just that... religion has never really been anything that I've thought too much about. It's hard for me to picture myself with the title of priest."

"It's not anything different than what you've been doing," Ander pointed out, taking another sip of coffee. It was a simple equation in his mind.

"Perhaps not in a practical sense, but it feels different." Takeshi shook his head. "I'm not sure how to explain it."

If Takeshi couldn't explain it, then Ander had no chance. "I don't think it's supposed to be that hard of a choice." It hadn't been for him, anyway.

The shinobi shot him an annoyed look. "Now you sound like her." He tilted his head towards Jitsu.

The giant tail began to wave like a flag.

"Perish the thought." Though warg simplicity might be the best way to view this particular situation. In which case, Jitsu could take over in her own time.

But he hoped Takeshi would stay.

The thought was oddly uncomfortable, and he decided to change topics. "What about the accidental humming?"

Takeshi blinked. "What about it?"

"Are you still humming with the World Sound without being aware of it?"

The shinobi again glanced at Jitsu. "Yes, that hasn't stopped, but I also haven't really mastered anything to do with the World Sound. I barely understand it at all."

"Well, you've only just discovered that you have Voice," Ander pointed out.

Takeshi shot him a look Ander couldn't decipher before striding back to the fish tank. "Yes, that is the problem."

Ander was distracted again by the feeling that something wasn't quite right. It was like an itch he couldn't locate, something just on the edge of his senses, an annoyance more than anything else. Was he forgetting something? Had he planned a meeting for today that he was missing? Nothing came to mind. "Do you have a plan for dealing with the humming?"

"No, not yet. Attempting to soulforge feels like the greater priority." Takeshi shrugged. "But hopefully I will find a way to deal with it by working with Caelessa. I'm hoping that when I've been able to work my way through the theory and practice I will either be more aware of when I'm doing it, or it will stop on its own."

Ah, yes. The soulforging. "And there's been no progress with your soul crystal either?"

Takeshi huffed a laugh. "Really hitting all my sore spots today, hm? But no, not yet."

Ander blinked. "Oh, I... that was not my intention. My apologies." Hades wasn't paying attention. She usually stopped him before he went too far with things like that, but She'd been distracted since the group left for Etroy. "I was just..." He trailed off, unsure. Wasn't showing interest in how someone was doing considered a positive thing?

"Ah, never mind." The shinobi shook his head, glaring for some reason at the fish tank. "I'm just... a little on edge today, and I feel like I've been doing so much introspection lately that it is starting to get uncomfortable. I shouldn't be taking it out on you. I'm sorry."

Uncomfortable. Yes, today was uncomfortable. Why? Hades was more restless than usual today, and Her disinterest was starting to grate on him, reminding him of when She had disappeared entirely after they had discovered the microchip in Takeshi. Maybe that was it.

Takeshi cleared his throat. "Soul crystals can be forged into any weapon, if I remember correctly?"

"Oh, yes." Ander felt thrown by the question. Did Takeshi want to talk about it, or did he not?

"Is there a form you would recommend I start with?"

"One that is familiar to you." He had thought that would be obvious, but maybe it wasn't? He felt like he didn't understand where this conversation was going anymore, but found himself continuing regardless. "Once you've summoned it a few times, you could consider practicing with it as different weapons. Being able to shift its form can be very helpful in many situations, and in particular you might consider the glaive, as it is Hades' signature weapon, and…" He drifted off, distracted by the sounds of the witches heading up the stairs, audible even through the closed door. Both he and Takeshi turned as the sounds of female chatter grew louder.

It did not sound happy.

The door opened, and Mara and Siva let themselves in. Mara looked concerned; Siva just looked grim.

Mara's expression immediately melted into joy as she bounced into the common area. "Ander, Takeshi! How are you both doing today?"

"Well, thank you. Was there a development of some sort?" Ander asked Siva.

The Aradian sighed, brushing a few stray strands of pinkish-orange hair behind an ear. "Good day. Yes, unfortunately the Seekers' attempt to find the remaining Abomination last night failed."

Ander frowned. Was *that* why he felt so on edge? But how would he know that? "That is… incredibly unfortunate."

"Where does that leave us now, then?" Takeshi asked, moving to sit on the couch next to Jitsu, who greeted him with a lick and a tail wag, shifting to make room for him.

Siva sighed, flames flickering in her eyes as she sat across from Takeshi. "We are not really sure. The Lady is still searching, but even if She can find it, She will struggle to tell us where it is, precisely."

That was true. "And the Seekers were unable to find anything at all?"

"Well, not exactly." Mara flopped down in an armchair so she was lying across it, stretching herself over to the couch to scratch Jitsu's flank. "They were able to narrow it down a little bit – somewhere in Gallia or Agale."

That was still a huge area. "The entire western half of the continent. I see." How frustrating.

"They thought maybe it was moving, and that confused whatever the seeking actually is," Siva added, pulling her hair over her shoulder and beginning to braid it. "They did tell us they were going to try again in a day or two."

"But if it is still in motion and that was the problem, then we will gain nothing," Takeshi noted. "What if it is in constant motion? Where would that leave us?"

Ander hummed. "There's not enough data to know if it is in constant motion or just being moved from one place to another and the Seekers were just unlucky with their timing. Do we know what exactly their seeking entails? Is it a divination spell, a tracking spell, or something else?"

"The Seekers seem to prioritize mind magics – which makes sense with the egregore and all," Mara said. "So perhaps some sort of psychic tracing?"

"Or a utilization of their inherents in some way," Takeshi added, scratching behind one of Jitsu's ears with his free hand. "They said their first Seeker saw forward in time, suggesting that she may have been a Graeae. Perhaps the seeking leverages that? Madine did confirm their first still lives."

And that was apparently a secret, right. "A group of them, combining their power and leveraging a Graeae's inherent, utilizing the egregore network as a jumping-off point? It's possible," Ander allowed. "And if the target was moving, and if the seeking requires a member of the egregore to be somewhere nearby... that could be how they've partially narrowed it down. They know where they weren't."

Siva frowned. "But they have taken over Muriz, which is in Gallia, no?"

"Unless..." Takeshi paused. "Unless they are considering Muriz and the western part of Gallia to be Hispa."

Ander stared. Hispa had been folded into Gallia over six hundred years ago. But with the Empire at war with itself... "You think Hispa will re-emerge as a separate province?"

Takeshi shrugged. "Or a separate country entirely. There's no saying how the civil war is going to end at this point, and there are some cities which have claimed independence from the Empire. But I do think the Seekers see it as separate, and I can also easily imagine them forgetting to mention that detail. They can occasionally be like you – forgetting to mention important details because of how obvious those details are to them." Takeshi smiled as he took another sip of coffee.

Ander decided to ignore that. "Which would actually narrow down the possible area even more, though it's still a large area."

Mara kicked her feet, face twisting in thought. "What if we did... a kind of 'seeking' of our own?"

"What do you mean?" Siva flicked her new braid behind her and rested her chin on one hand, elbow on the arm of the couch. "None of us have any inherents that would allow us to do that."

"Nor do we have any idea what to look for, unless you mean somehow just... searching for the feeling of Abomination?" Takeshi finished his coffee and pulled his mask back over his face.

"Ah, well... the Veren divine for things sometimes," Mara explained. "And while we don't have a bunch of people linked together into a mental web, we *do* have Hades."

Ander stared down into the dregs of his own cup, contemplating making more coffee. Perhaps he just hadn't had enough today, and that was why he felt off?

It felt... like a buzzing, somewhere.

Siva's eyes flickered, but then she shook her head. "If the Lady were able to find it, I believe She would have by now. She has done very little else other than look for it since the Seekers arrived."

"But maybe we can help!" Mara argued, swinging herself back up into a sitting position. "Maybe we can somehow... help direct Her more! Or something." She pouted. "It feels like we have to do *something*."

Ander frowned.

"She has a far more intimate understanding of Abomination than we do," Siva said, voice gentle. "I'm not sure how we could help direct Her any better than what She is able to do for Herself."

"What if we weren't looking for Abomination, exactly?"

Ander suddenly found himself the subject of everyone's attention.

He cleared his throat. "Marcus and I determined that the metal the bionics are made out of has trace amounts of Tadurin's magic. What if we were to search for that instead? We have some of the metal downstairs; we could use that to track it, perhaps?"

He felt a piece of Hades' attention shift towards the conversation.

Siva leaned back, eyes widening. "*Tadurin's magic* is part of the bionics?"

"Not exactly in the way you are thinking," he hastened to explain. "It is merely adaptive magic, possibly attracted by the use of alchemical symbols etched into the metal. Our current theory is that the adaptability is what allows the tech to fuse successfully to the Avari."

Mara stood up, ears flattening. "I need a drink for this. Tadurin? If there was ever a god who could possibly be wrapped up in Abomination, I would think it'd be Kaldor."

*:Kaldor is a problem, but he would never have anything to do with Abomination,:* Hades interjected. *:He fears it too much.:*

It really put things into perspective when the god of the night, evil, and monsters feared something, Ander reflected wryly. Then again, he was pretty sure all the gods feared Abomination to some degree. And hadn't Hades said something to that effect before?

Why did only Hades act against Abomination? Were the others really *that* scared? Hades had said it was dangerous to them, but mortals fought against things that were dangerous to them all the time.

He walked around the counter and began to prepare more coffee. He needed to do something with his hands. He needed to do something. Something wasn't right; he could feel it like ice down his spine.

But what?

"Oh, coffee? I'll take some if you're making, Ander!" Mara called over from where she was digging rum out of a cabinet.

"Coffee would be lovely." Siva smiled, flames flickering in her eyes. She folded her hands in front of her. "But while it does seem plausible that we might have an easier time finding Tadurin's magic, isn't that because it is literally everywhere?"

"Is it possible to search for a spell?" Takeshi asked. "Or more precisely, a proto-spell. I was looking at the symbols on the metal in Ander's lab the other day, and it does resemble a pattern, though it uses the alchemical symbols instead of glyphs. Perhaps that, in conjunction with the magic...?"

*:It is... possible,:* Hades said slowly. *:I am not sure it will be any more accurate than my current understanding of Abomination, however.:*

"Does the Seekers' information help you?" Siva asked.

*:While it narrows the possible area, the problem isn't really that I can't... Hm. How to explain? I am the goddess of death. I am death incarnate. As such, I am sort of... most places at all times. Without an anchor, like a priest or place of power, it is difficult for me to locate things on the physical plane. And since it is not really awake, that makes it even more difficult. Though....:*

"Could we provide the reference you lack?" Ander wondered as he pulled out more cups. "Since we only exist on the physical plane, perhaps if you search for it, we could then translate that to a real location?"

"Or perhaps we could somehow combine our search with the Seekers' technique?" Takeshi said, pulling the blindfold out from his pocket. He laid it on the coffee table. "Since two of them are still in Tarvishte, they might be able to explain what their seeking entails as far as actual practice goes."

Mara danced over to Ander with the bottle of rum, bouncing on the balls of her feet when she reached the counter. "That would be a good team-building exercise! Ander, how long for coffee?"

He glanced at her in concern. "Are you sure you need coffee?"

Her ears twitched down. "Wow, coming from you, rude. What cup are you on today?"

He snorted. "I'm not vibrating." Though he did feel... restless. Like he was waiting for something. Like they were about to go over a cliff, even though that didn't make any sense.

"That hasn't stopped you in the past–"

"Children," Siva broke in, voice wry. She folded her arms.

Takeshi petted Jitsu's head. "I'll take another cup as well, Ander."

Ander sighed and added another scoop of coffee grounds to the filter before going to grab Takeshi's cup. "Anyway, I don't think we should rely on the Seekers. There's too much about them that is uncertain right now. If they happen to find it, so be it, but I don't think welcoming them into our spell work is a good idea."

"Actually, though... if we try to trace the metal, how will we know we are finding the remaining Abomination, and not the remains of the bionics that were already killed?" Takeshi asked, brows furrowing.

"That is a good point," Ander acknowledged after a moment. "Perhaps if we cross referenced it with the feeling of Abomination that Hades feels?" Why did it take so long for coffee to brew? And why did the spells that should make it brew faster always ruin the taste? He grabbed the sugar and put it on the counter for Mara.

Mara spun herself around and jumped up to sit on the counter, slowly kicking her feet back and forth. "Ugh. Why does it have to be so complicated? We're so close. It doesn't seem fair it can just hide and try to wait us out." She pouted.

"I don't think it's hiding per se, I think we just don't know what exactly we are looking for," Takeshi said.

*:Hm. Maybe we should try a... group search?:* Hades suddenly added. *:I'm willing to try anything at this point. This feeling is driving me mad.:*

Ander winced. He couldn't imagine what feeling like...

Wait.

"Are we all feeling... whatever this feeling is?" he asked abruptly. "Wrong?"

Takeshi frowned. "There is a certain... something, isn't there? I thought it was just me."

"It's natural to feel antsy when you feel like there is something to be done, but there is nothing to do," Siva offered, but she also looked concerned.

Mara's eyes were full of worry. "I thought it was just me too, but if it's all of us..."

Sudden alarm from Hades. *:You can feel it?:* A pause, and She felt more removed from him, suddenly. *:Can you still feel it? Is it bleeding over from me?:*

"Yes, something still isn't right," Ander confirmed after a moment. "It might be from you, but it's hard to tell."

"She's felt this way for almost two weeks, though," Takeshi pointed out. "Ever since Etroy. Did something change? Why are we only feeling it now?"

*:Something is happening,:* Hades broke in. *:Somewhere, not here. But something... something changed, earlier. It was subtle. I didn't re-*

*alize... I thought it was more of the same. But it's not. What changed?:* She grew more alarmed as She spoke, and Ander could feel Her attention beginning to spiral out. *:Wait. It's getting stronger.:*

"That's probably not good," Ander snapped. "If it's the Abomination–"

He was suddenly assaulted by blinding *agony*–

*Agony.*

It was a new feeling. Not the agony itself – Hades had felt pain before – but the feeling of being *consumed*.

She twisted, trying to escape from the thing that had grabbed hold of her, but every movement brought torture into her being. She could feel herself shriek in pained anguish–

–felt her priests recoil in shared torment–

–and shut herself off from them immediately. She would not transmit it to them. She could not risk it.

She recognized what this was. Her siblings had suffered it long ago.

She thought to sever that shard of herself, sacrifice it to its inevitable destruction, but... if she did that, then the Abomination would consume it faster, grow faster. It would become exponentially more difficult for her beloved priests and their mortal allies to destroy it if it successfully absorbed so much of her power. The danger the world was in had just tipped dramatically to one side, and she was afraid...

But she'd sworn long ago that she would fight for this world.

And she would not let it take her from her priests.

Shuddering, essence fluctuating and causing ripples of distress across the World Sound, Hades gathered herself. She could not act directly; with it attached to her as it was, almost anything she did would strengthen it rather than destroy it. Even the small amount of her it had absorbed was too much. But she could slow its progress.

She had to resist long enough for it to be destroyed. And she had to make it so they could find her.

She braced herself against the pain, and began to fight back.

# Chapter Twenty-Two

T akeshi felt so much relief at the sudden cessation of pain that he almost threw up.

Jitsu was standing over him on the couch, he realized. She was growling lowly, fur puffed up in answer to a threat she couldn't see. He could feel her attempting to shield his mind as well.

He had slumped sideways and was folded uncomfortably. His tongue hurt from where he'd bitten it in an attempt to keep from screaming. His vision was blurry and everything ached with the memory of agony that was not his.

Hades.

He patted Jitsu on the shoulder and she stopped growling, pushing her nose into his face with concern. He pressed a hand to his head as he pushed himself up, and she adjusted herself to give him something to hang on to, pressing against him firmly.

"What on Gaia just happened?"

Takeshi cringed at the sound of Ander's voice, though the other priest sounded just as miserable as Takeshi felt. He closed his eyes and leaned into Jitsu's warmth, realizing he was shivering violently.

"Abomination," he realized, swallowing hard against a sudden wave of nausea. "I think... it felt like..."

"Like it grabbed hold of Her." Mara's voice was shaky and upset, on the verge of tears. "I can't feel Her anymore. Please, please be okay, Lady..."

"She is absent, not gone." Siva sounded the most composed out of all of them, but not by much. "I don't think we would still be alive if she were... permanently gone. She is too intertwined with us, in a way most other gods are not with their priests."

There was a slight ringing in his ears, and Takeshi realized it was the World Sound. He shook his head to try to clear it, but then—

A single, discordant note.

He felt his stomach drop.

"This is catastrophic."

It took them several hours to return to some semblance of normalcy. None of them wanted to do much, but they had to.

Something was going to have to be done, even if they didn't know what.

Still, the memory of Hades' agony was difficult to overcome.

Jitsu was glued to Takeshi's side. Mortals weren't supposed to feel that sort of divine pain, she pointed out. That was why they were still hurting. It was okay, though. The wargs had the Temple covered. No one would be able to get in unless they allowed it, so the priests should all take their time and rest a bit.

"I don't think we really have time to rest," Takeshi protested, though all four of them were now seated around the sitting area. Ander had managed to make four cups of sillna before collapsing into a chair, and the bitter tea had helped take the edge off the pain. Takeshi had also pulled the blanket from the back of the couch around his shoulders, and between that, the tea, and Jitsu's warmth, his shivers were subsiding.

Siva sighed in agreement. "Every moment we delay, the worse it is going to get."

Jitsu's eyes were wide and serious. If they wanted to help the Lady, then they needed to rest. They could not help her like this. Recover now, help after. That would be most efficient.

Takeshi relayed that to the others.

"That is a worthwhile point," Ander agreed, squinting at Jitsu.

The warg wagged her tail at him in response. Takeshi should tell them. She was always right.

He patted her on the head. "She also mentioned that the wargs have... essentially shut the Temple down, I believe. They aren't letting anyone in."

"Oh good," Ander muttered.

Siva took a slow sip of sillna. "We will have to inform people. Vlad should know, at least. I'm having trouble coming up with other names at the moment, but certainly there are people who should know how bad this has gotten."

Jitsu huffed. Who besides the king did they want informed? The wargs would inform them. The priests should rest.

Takeshi eyed her warily. "How, exactly, will the wargs inform people?"

She licked his forehead gently. He didn't have to worry about that. The wargs would ensure anyone the priests wanted to know would know.

"I am kind of worried about that." But not enough to protest much more. Were there enough of them in the city at the moment to keep up with all these jobs? Most were still out of the city doing... something. He felt a wave of exhaustion wash over him and he buried his face in her fur. "But that's fine. Do what you want." The thought of having to go all the way back to his rooms in the palace was soul-crushing. "Anyone other than Vlad who we can think of at the moment?"

"I can't think... of anyone." Mara's voice was muffled by the pillow she had put over her face.

"Vlad will be able to think of whoever else should be informed," Ander pointed out. "Let him deal with it."

"Yeah, that's a good plan. You're so smart, Ander." It was strange hearing Mara's voice with such a lack of feeling behind it.

Ander grunted.

They sat in silence, waiting for the mental touch of a goddess that wasn't coming.

Takeshi did feel more like himself the next day after he'd slept and showered. Not anywhere near completely fine, but better. Vlad had all but ordered him to remain in the Temple for the time being, so he'd spent the night in the rooms that were technically his, though he'd never stayed in them before.

It was odd. He'd never imagined that he would feel Hades' absence so strongly. It was as though there were a hole where she should have been.

They were still unable to reach her.

Takeshi didn't like it.

Nor did he like the discordant notes he occasionally heard in the World Sound, nor the strange pull he felt to the south.

He found himself seated on the couch again, Jitsu at his feet to make room for others. Vlad, Prim, Jeri, and Jamirh had joined the four priests.

This was strictly on a need-to-know basis. The people of Romanii did not widely need to know their goddess had been attacked by Abomination.

"I've sent letters to Yafen and Daiyu," Siva was saying. "Without the Lady I have no way to contact Kade and Fen; we will have to hope they can manage in the Darklands on their own for a time."

"Will they come here?" Takeshi asked. "Yafen and Daiyu, I mean."

"I have recalled them here, yes," Siva answered. "But because of their distance and the fact that we must rely on mail, I don't know when they will be able to arrive – likely not in time to join us in whatever plan we choose to enact."

"Then why recall them at all?" Jamirh asked, folding his arms in front of his chest.

The Aradian's face was grim. "Because if we fail, they will be the only chance left."

Silence, as everyone digested that.

"What is the plan then?" Vlad finally asked. "If my mother was directly attacked by Abomination, what can we do?"

Ander rubbed a hand over his chest, and Takeshi noted the bags under his eyes. "We need to go south."

"South?" Jeri asked, leaning back in her chair.

Mara nodded. "We can all feel it. A pull to the south. Somehow—"

She was cut off by a knock on the door.

Jitsu's head perked up. Her siblings told her there were—

"The Truth Seekers?" Takeshi said, confused.

"Why are they here?" Ander asked, face darkening.

Siva looked troubled. "How did they know to come here at all?"

Jitsu stood and trotted over to the door. The blind-ones had insisted that they could help. They did not smell like a threat at the moment, either. And they had been very polite to the wargs who were with them.

Takeshi smothered a groan. "The wargs think the Seekers can help."

"Oh, that's terrifying," Vlad said blandly. "Very well, then. Siva? This is your domain."

The second High Priest closed her eyes and bowed her head in silence for a moment. "We cannot turn away offered aid, given the present crisis. Let them in. We can at the very least hear them out."

Jamirh stood and went to the door, patting Jitsu's head on his way past. "I'll get it."

Jitsu wagged her tail. Helpful-red two-foot was still helpful with doors.

Takeshi was far too tired to try to untangle what that meant.

The two Seekers slipped into the room, blindfolded visages giving nothing away. They were followed into the room by two truly massive wargs, both a full head taller than Jitsu. One settled against the door, the other at the base of Ander's fish tank.

The Seekers stopped several feet away from the group and bowed in unison as Jamirh retook his seat. "We apologize for coming to you in this way," the woman began, still nearly horizontal in her bow. "But given recent events, we thought to offer our services in a more direct fashion."

*:Yes, they do this every time they offer us information,:* Vlad informed the priests wearily. *:It appears to be their standard 'we don't have Sherri to speak for us' procedure.:*

"Did the second seeking succeed?" Siva asked, tilting her head to the side. "I thought another attempt would not be made until at least tomorrow, if my grasp on the date is still correct."

"We did not make an attempt, High Priest." The Seeker didn't move at all. "But we also acknowledge that a seeking is no longer required." Her intonation rose ever so slightly on the last word, making it almost a question. "We are already aware of the sudden explosion of death magic in Lyndiniam. We assume this is where your goddess found the remaining corruption, and we would like to offer our support in any further operations."

Lyndiniam. The capital of the Empire.

Takeshi shared a glance with the other priests. That did complicate things. But at least they now had a target that was more specific than "somewhere south."

He found his mouth quirking up into a humorless smile. Maybe Hades *was* the truth the Seekers sought, even if they didn't know it.

"Great. Lyndiniam. So yeah, that place sucks," Jamirh said, bringing up a hand to rub at his face as his ears twitched down.

Jeri sent him a sharp look. "Jamirh–"

"Nah, it's really all or nothing at this point, isn't it?" He shook his head, turning to address the Seekers. "We're pretty sure the Abomination somehow attacked Hades directly."

The Seekers exchanged another look.

Shocked exclamations rose from around the room that Jamirh would just out and say it, but Takeshi didn't feel that he had the energy for that. What was done was done, and it seemed like the Seekers already knew more than they did anyway. He clapped his hands together twice to gain everyone's attention. "Let's focus on the problem at hand, please." He looked at the Seekers. "Is there anything else you know about the current situation in Lyndiniam? Also, I'm sorry, but what were your names?"

If they were offended that the Romanii had purposely kept information from them, they did not show it. "I am Perra, and this is Axtion," the woman introduced herself and her partner. He gave the slightest incline of his head, and they both shifted to be standing at parade rest, movements eerily synchronized. "We do not currently have any agents in Lyndiniam, so all we have is speculation. If we may – when you say 'Abomination attacked Hades directly,' what do you mean?"

The priests glanced between each other uncertainly, and Siva finally sighed. "Not even we are completely certain. We were speaking to Her, and then something that felt like Abomination sort of... latched on to Her. We felt Her agony for just a few seconds before She cut Herself off from us. We have been unable to reach Her since."

The Seekers were silent, and Takeshi realized they were probably communicating with the others in the egregore.

"This is not something that should be spread around," Vlad pointed out after a moment. "At present, only the people in this room – and Hades herself – know this."

Perra turned her head to face him. "What one Seeker knows, the rest also know."

"Yes." He nodded and heaved a sigh. "That is what I was concerned about, but thought I should mention it anyway. Carry on."

"We are good at keeping secrets," Axtion offered. "Only Sherri knows what the egregore does, and not even all of that."

"It would be too much for her at this point," Perra agreed. "Joining the egregore should be done much younger. While it is not impossible to incorporate an older mind, it can be more dangerous." She inclined her head in Takeshi's direction.

He nodded back. "You thought we were going to die at Tilden as well."

"We were less careful than we otherwise might have been, yes," she agreed. "But the goal was never to incorporate you fully, if that was a concern." A beat. "It turns out there are other minds linked to yours anyway."

Takeshi just shrugged, but Jitsu's tail beat against his leg, and he could feel her possessive glee. He wished she could come sit with him on the couch; he was positively freezing.

"Regardless, we must ask. Would you describe the attack on Hades as 'consuming' her?"

"Yes," Ander answered her immediately. At Siva's quizzical look, he shrugged. "I've been thinking about it almost non-stop since yesterday. That is... there was an element of that right before She cut us off."

"It's *eating* her?" Jamirh asked, a horrified look on his face. His hand went to his chest.

Ander covered his face with his hands, rubbing at his eyes. "Yes, that's another way to put it, I suppose."

"The death of a god... what would that do to the world?" Prim asked, disturbed.

"One of the two primordial gods at that," Mara added.

Siva looked ill. "And one whose function is necessary for the order of the world. If there is no death, then life runs rampant, without anything to check it and hold it to balance. I don't know what it would look like without death, but... I must assume it could only lead to destruction of some sort."

"No," Ander said, slumping into his chair. "It will lead to Abomination. Corruption. Maybe there's no semantic difference, but we will not be dead in the way the resting dead are – we will *become* Abomination. And when there is no magic left to consume, Abomination will turn on itself, and in the end nothing will exist anymore." He looked around at the horrified expressions. "I've been thinking about it. A lot."

"Isn't that still... dead?" Jamirh asked, hesitant.

Mara cringed. "It's dead in a bad way, instead of dead in a good way."

"Wait," Takeshi said, trying to ignore the implications and going over Perra's words again. "Why did you ask for that specifically? 'Consuming'?"

That gray blindfold turned in his direction. "The first Seeker had the ability to see forward. It is how she knew of the Three Signs. But she could not see past this conflict – all she could see was magic, and the corruption consuming it."

Dead silence.

"Okay then," Mara finally said, voice grim. "So we are going to Lyndiniam."

"We leave for the Wall tomorrow," Siva agreed.

Takeshi frowned. "I don't disagree, but there is a war going on down there, and Lyndiniam is a capital city. We will not be able to just walk into the city, nor do we know exactly where – or even what – our target is."

"The city is currently closed off," Perra confirmed.

"If there is death magic there, we will be able to find it," Ander said. "The closer we get the easier it will be, though yes – we will have to find a way in."

"I can get us in."

Takeshi blinked at Jamirh's quiet declaration. He wasn't the only one.

"I can get us in," the Avari repeated, hand clenching around his key. Takeshi frowned, wondering what this was costing him. "When Hel and I left Lyndiniam, we used the old sewers. They are mostly filled in, but there are sections that were missed. I used to explore them when I was little. But how are we going to get there? It took me, Hel, and Jeri *days* to reach the Wall."

"We were also walking for the majority of the journey," Jeri pointed-ed out. "I strongly recommend we steal a vehicle at this point. There is no time to fuss about with public transport."

"There is a Seeker pair in Norik. They will meet you in Sturlow with transportation, if that is agreeable," Perra said absently. "It is just over a five-hour drive if you go direct."

"Direct is the best course of action," Takeshi agreed. "Who, exactly, is coming?"

Siva, Mara, Jeri, Ander, and Jamirh all raised their hands. Jitsu made a soft huff.

Vlad shook his head. "I should remain here, as should Prim. If the worst should happen, and you fail, we will be needed here."

"We will stay as well, to maintain our net," Perra said. "Though a group of Seekers including Madine will meet you on the outskirts of the city. Halren and Flire will meet you in Sturlow."

"This is going to be beyond dangerous," Takeshi warned. "We are walking into a situation we know almost nothing about, except that Abomination is involved, and it is killing our goddess. Don't hold back on supplies. Bring as many weapons and armor and spells as you have. If there is even a chance it could be useful, bring it."

Siva stood. "Indeed, it is so. But there is no other choice to make. If we do not save the Lady, then this is the end of everything. We meet at the Temple stairs at dawn tomorrow. We will gate to Pitesh."

Takeshi nodded in agreement along with the others as people began to leave. There was a lot to do, and not a lot of time to do it.

His eye caught on Jamirh as the Avari walked out with Jeri, and he frowned. Though Jamirh was very good with daggers – good enough to take on a single bionic with minimal aid – he would be lacking the weapon that he was best with. They had spent so much time teaching him how to wield a sword, and then the stupid magical artifact had gone ahead and broken on him.

That felt cosmically unfair, but then... everything about this situation felt unfair. The goddess was being *eaten*.

He sighed, pushing the thought away for the moment. He was tired and he was cold. He should probably get more rest, let himself recover more from the attack on Hades. But... there was one thing left that wouldn't leave him alone. One thing that would objectively aid them in the coming battle.

Thunder sounded in the distance.

He glanced at the windows as the skies opened up. Sheets of rain came down hard, battering the glass.

A good omen, or a bad one? Were the Espera so infuriated at the attack on their sister? The storms had been consistent the past few weeks, though this one felt... angry. Rage, at the loss of one of their own? Or was Takeshi just projecting? Did they care at all?

But he'd always enjoyed storms, and lightning was his element.

He forced himself up and made for the stairs, Jitsu a silent shadow behind him. He steeled himself to go out into the deluge. It was time to figure this out.

He was going to soulforge.

Hades ached as a little more of herself disappeared.

She consoled herself with the knowledge that her siblings had endured this too, and had recovered from it. As long as her priests could sever the connection, destroy the Abomination, she too would recover in time.

The Abomination was sharp and hungry. Still, she denied it as best she could, pulling more and more of herself into the battle, feeling the Valkyrie beginning to take on more and more deaths that she could no longer attend to.

The little spirits tried to console her, but she sent them away. She would not have them fall to the corruption as well.

Still, the more of herself she was able to pull into this place, the more aware of it on the physical plane she became. She tried not to leak her essence into the physical space; that would be terrible for any mortals in the area. And the more aware she became, the more she realized there was another presence on the other side of the Abomination. Another it was trying to consume.

She was not the only one fighting.

# Chapter Twenty-Three

Takeshi sat cross-legged in the center of the private training room, firmly putting the dampness of his clothing and the chill in the air out of his mind. He needed to figure this out, and starting with some extra meditation could only help. He was going to do this today.

He kept telling himself that. There was no room for failure.

Hades needed them.

Jitsu settled herself in front of the door, head on her paws as a giant, furry barrier. Takeshi wouldn't be interrupted unless she allowed it. And while she didn't intend to allow it, she did withhold the right to make that judgement.

Takeshi snorted but closed his eyes, allowing himself to focus on the World Sound. He'd been so intent on trying to block it out until recently that maybe giving it time and focus would help. Ander had given good advice by suggesting Takeshi start with what he knew – and he knew meditation. Although the World Sound was meant to be music, perhaps attempting to resonate with it silently was a good start. It wasn't as though there were any literal sound to begin with.

So he made himself comfortable and slowed his breathing – and *listened*.

Thunder rumbled, making itself heard above the rain hitting the roof. He pushed that, and the discomfort of Hades' absence, aside.

While he might not know anything about scales and octaves and other aspects of music theory, he had listened to music purely for enjoyment before. It was with this mindset he listened now, trying to connect with the World Sound in a more mundane fashion.

It was there as it always was, notes whispering through the air. Immediately Takeshi realized the flaw with his plan; while it was music it wasn't really a song – at least not in the way he conceived of songs. The notes were not discordant, but they also were not a cohesive melody. It was more like a bunch of notes scattered about that happened to work with each other. Harmonize? Was that the right word?

He made a mental note to ask Caelessa about the proper vocabulary for this sort of thing.

Still, if the World Sound was able to resonate with bards who were singing songs, then certainly it could *become* a song. Was there a way for him to nudge it in that direction without making real sounds? Or would he have to go back to humming?

What exactly could draw the World Sound's interest, if that was even the right word?

While he liked music, Takeshi had to admit that there hadn't been much chance recently to listen to it between all the meetings, the mission to Etroy, and the amount of time he was spending trying to figure *this* out. He'd never even considered trying to make music of his own, but according to Caelessa the fact he could hear the World

Sound without any effort meant he was supposed to be very good at it – even if his recent attempts at humming had not supported that theory.

Still... he could carry a beat, couldn't he?

He took his katana, sheath and all, and laid it across his lap. Then he tried to think of the last song he had heard. Though he rarely had time to stop and listen, music was fairly common on the palace grounds. In fact, he'd heard something a few days ago on his way to the Temple... it had had a pleasant sound to it.

Recalling the song, he began tapping out the rhythm on the sheath.

It didn't take very long at all for the World Sound to start to match the beat, notes beginning to fall into place, filling in some of the sounds he remembered but couldn't replicate by tapping. He considered that as he continued; how did it know the song? Were mortal songs actually a reflection of the World Sound, translated into the real world by the bards, or did the World Sound somehow learn songs? Not even every bard could hear the World Sound, but Caelessa had certainly implied that every bard – and even some people without Voice – were still able to benefit from the World Sound.

What exactly was the World Sound, anyway? Hades had described it as the ebb and flow of existence, and as a part of all living things. So then perhaps music – mortal music – was just an attempt by people to connect with that part of themselves? And to create connections between themselves and others? Did not people often find themselves tapping a foot along to a song, or humming or even singing along? The desire to somehow be part of the music seemed fairly common…

…among many people who were not shinobi.

He supposed that made sense, too, though. If any instinctive connection to Voice was being suppressed, maybe that stripped shinobi of the desire to participate.

That was an interesting theory. Takeshi wasn't sure what to do with it though, so he tucked it away for the moment.

He decided to try a different song, and was pleased when the World Sound readily adapted to the new rhythm. He focused his attention on the ethereal notes, trying to figure out what it could mean to truly resonate with the World Sound. Was this enough? Or was there something deeper he was missing?

He ran through a couple more songs – throwing two in from Ni Fon for good measure – before deciding this was good progress. He had achieved possibly the absolute bare minimum when it came to resonating with the World Sound.

Where to go from here?

He could try humming, but the thought filled him with dread, and he needed to move forward, not back. Instead, he thought back to Ander's recommendation – trying to utilize Movement.

He kept his attention on the World Sound as he stood up and started to stretch, noting the thunder was getting louder. It sounded like the storm was going to pass directly over the city.

Jitsu perked up. Was Takeshi done with the sitting-thing?

"For now," he agreed, considering his next steps. Using physical motions to aid in the weaving of patterns was very common among shinobi in certain circumstances, since it was a silent endeavor. And sometimes, when a spell required a little extra power, gesture could be used to add to it. Takeshi himself had used this technique on occasion, and he recalled his attempts to keep the water out of his dinghy what felt like ages ago when he'd just been banished from Ni Fon. He had utilized large, sweeping motions to weave the air into shields for himself.

There had been a bad storm then, too. Caron had called it a god storm. Had said Takeshi was given to them by the Nyphoren. Was that true?

He shook his head, bringing his thoughts back to the issue at hand. Fighting also involved Movement, technically. Fights often had a rhythm to them. Was that not similar to dancing? Like... violently dancing without music? That seemed like a good way to frame it for himself. He would need something a little faster, with a little more punch than the songs he had been practicing with before, but that seemed like a good follow-up to what he had been doing.

He slipped into a few familiar katas, comfortable movements smoothly flowing from one form to another. These were also like dancing, weren't they? Choreographed dancing at least, where the movements were planned and practiced until the dancer knew them intimately. That seemed like a good place to start, even if the thought of actually dancing was almost as embarrassing as the thought of singing.

He was pleased to find that the World Sound was producing notes in a rhythm that worked with the katas. If he sped up or slowed down, the notes matched his motions. It was convenient that he didn't have to tap, but he wondered why. Was it simply because he'd already attuned the World Sound to himself by tapping? Or did the actual, physical motions he made somehow prompt the World Sound to make music to accompany him?

He made a mental note to pay more attention to the World Sound in regard to other people. Was it just bards that it did this with? Or everyone?

After a few more sets, he came to a stop. That... worked, for lack of a better term. What next, then? How to move forward? The odd, empty feeling where Hades had been wouldn't leave him alone. He had to keep going. But how?

Jitsu wagged her tail encouragingly. He could try to make the movements more pretty?

"More pretty?"

She laid her head back on her paws. It wasn't that the movements weren't pretty, she guessed, but they were very... utilitarian. Most two-feet who danced had more emotion behind the movements.

He frowned, considering that as he rubbed at his chest, though it didn't alleviate the discomfort. "Even the planned dances? Do you think that matters?"

Especially the planned dances! The two-feet who did those tended to emote very, very hard. They were *feeling* the music, and trying to make others feel it too. Jitsu liked watching two-feet dance; it took a lot of skill to do it well.

He winced. "Skill is something I don't have a lot of right now, though it's... something to work on, I suppose. At least I feel more sure of myself doing this than humming, but..." How to move so others could feel the music?

The music, or the World Sound?

If the World Sound was the connective tissue, then maybe that was the secret behind a bard's ability to reach listeners and make them feel the song. And it would follow that it would work similarly for dancers. But then did that imply that he wasn't resonating enough? Or was there another piece he was missing?

Jitsu huffed. Takeshi was thinking about it too much again. If he wanted others to feel the music, then *he* had to feel the music. And it seemed to her that while he was hearing the World Sound, he wasn't feeling it. She felt nothing watching him, at least.

"Thank you," he offered dryly, though there was truth to that. He wasn't *feeling* the music. He could admit that. Okay then, what did that entail?

Tiredly, he cursed whoever had come up with the bright idea to suppress these inherents in shinobi. The lack of a frame of reference was making this absurdly difficult for something that was supposed to come naturally to him. It was like the part of him that should be able to do it had atrophied from lack of use.

If a muscle atrophied, the remedy was usually an intense exercise program under a doctor's supervision and sometimes a curated diet. What would the equivalent of that be in this case?

Probably just what he was doing, if he was being honest. Listen to more music, observe dancers, practice resonating with the World Sound. Atrophied muscles took time to recover. It would make sense that this would too, even if he wanted to succeed *now*. He *needed* to succeed now. They didn't have time to wait.

Jitsu snorted. She understood. The Lady was in danger, and that was bad. But skills took time to master. Takeshi was wonderful, but he could not change the laws of nature.

That was true. But while he hadn't really expected to *master* it today, he still needed to get further than where he was – he just needed to be able to *use* it. He hated struggling, especially with magic. And he hated feeling ridiculous. The very thought of having to dance or sing in front of other people filled him with dread and embarrassment.

But maybe he was thinking about this in entirely the wrong way. Yes, he apparently had Voice and Movement, and yes, any skill could be useful, but his ultimate goal was being able to soulforge. Did he really need to *master* those inherents to be able to soulforge, or did he *just* need to accept them as a part of himself? He tried to think back to the exact words Ander had used – that the soul crystal was him, and because of that, denying a part of himself could cause his forging to fail. Ander had said nothing about being good at Voice magic, or even using it. Just that Takeshi couldn't be in denial about part of himself.

And soulforging was also not a skill or magic, according to Ander – it just was. So maybe Takeshi was focusing on the wrong part of this equation. Takeshi could not be in denial of any part of his being. Okay then, he was already acknowledging that he had inherents he had known nothing about before. Was that enough?

He thought for a moment, then summoned his soul crystal – only to have it immediately blink back out of existence.

Not enough, then.

He considered the possibility there were somehow more inherents he was unaware of, but... that didn't feel right either. Most people only had one inherent, and while more was not unheard of, he was already pushing the upper boundaries of that. Telepathy, Voice, and Movement, all with fairly powerful expressions, in addition to his learned magic. No, there was no chance he had more.

Jitsu blinked at him. If he felt silly doing the singing and dancing, then had he really accepted the singing and dancing?

Takeshi frowned. That was a good point. While he had been acknowledging that he had Voice and Movement, it was hard for him to *accept* that he had them. They felt like something he shouldn't be able to do, and the thought of performing them left him extremely uncomfortable. So maybe that was the real obstacle.

If the World Sound was the connective tissue between all living beings, if it facilitated that connection... then one would naturally have to be able to connect with themselves as well, which... was probably the piece he was missing.

He was "out of tune" with himself, so he could not be in tune with the World Sound and he was unable to soulforge.

Meditation could help with that.

No! The sitting-thing could *not* possibly help with this! Jitsu made a sad, whimpering sound, covering his nose with one paw. Takeshi needed to *move*, to find the rhythm. He could not do that while sitting. She... she would bite him if he tried!

He stared at her, taken aback by her vehemence. He also didn't believe her. "You would *bite* me?"

Her head sank. Probably not. She would growl at him and push him, though. She had thought about it a lot, and she was pretty sure she could make it very difficult to do the sitting-thing.

That was true enough. He took a deep breath and counted to ten, trying to figure out where to go from here. He took a moment to focus on the rain, which if anything sounded like it was coming down even harder, and a crash of thunder sounded nearby. If he couldn't meditate, where did that leave him? Just moving wasn't going to be as easy as Jitsu seemed to think it was.

But why not? She whined, clearly unhappy. If he did the utilitarian motions without any problems, then what made the pretty ones any different?

"Purpose, I suppose," he answered out loud, considering. "Moving to fight is different than moving to entertain."

But did it have to be? Weren't there some two-feet who combined the two – show fighting for the sake of entertainment? Something between combat and dance?

"That's not real fighting." But even as he said it he was considering the possibilities. It was sort of an in-between, but then he wasn't sure how the World Sound would tie into it. Those show fights weren't set to music in his experience.

But then again, could not the fight itself be the rhythm?

And he didn't have to do it well. He just had to accept that... what, that the music was in his soul?

He almost took a step back at the thought. It was something silly he'd heard other people say, but considering everything, what if it was far more literal?

What if there was a bit of the World Sound in each individual, and *that* was what the World Sound was resonating with? Hades had said Caelessa could hear an echo of the World Sound – what if she was actually hearing the piece that was within her?

That still put Takeshi in an odd spot, since he was hearing the external World Sound and not his own melody, but... if he could find that... maybe that was what was meant by "feeling" it? Because it was internal, not external? But that meant connecting with himself, which to him meant meditation, but Jitsu was not going to let him do that.

He was going around in circles.

Jitsu huffed. Most of the time when he did the sitting-thing it was about being quiet and silencing himself. He needed to un-silence himself. Silence was the problem.

"But I do not have the skill to sing well at the moment, so that won't work either," he pointed out.

Not external silence, *internal* silence, she insisted. He needed to sing in his soul. And wouldn't that be easier? No one would be able to hear that.

He eyed her uncertainly. That had come across as uncomfortably sly, though why she had said it that way he wasn't sure. It did make sense.

She shook herself. Of course it made sense. She knew what she was talking about. Takeshi just needed to *do* it.

Takeshi considered. She kept saying that, too – that he just needed to do it. And from an academic standpoint that also made sense; he just wasn't sure how to actually *execute* it.

He didn't have the skill to sing, but he did have the skill to move rhythmically.

Use your imagination, Jitsu blurted. Pretend like you are fighting someone and there's music playing you have to fight to.

"That's an oddly specific situation, but... I'll do my best, I suppose." That was not unlike how fighting was portrayed in movies, or some show fighting. Maybe he could work with that.

He could go the show route. Go slowly. He considered the different types of displays he had seen before.

He walked over to Jitsu, turned, and dropped to one knee. A pattern bloomed into existence beneath him, the whitish-blue of his magic a comforting sight after the frustrations of the day. The pattern dissipated throughout the room, leaving fine sand in its wake arranged in neat lines – creating a labyrinth in front of him that covered most of the room. He carefully placed his katana on the floor next to the warg.

The thunder was getting louder. He took comfort in the familiar sound.

He recalled the first few bars of an old song from home and began to slowly walk through the labyrinth. The song started slow, telling the story of a group of people who were stalked by an unknown creature through the night. He took his time choosing his steps as the notes floated through his mind. They didn't know they were being followed yet, they just knew they were lost, and that the night was dangerous. They swore they would live or die together.

And though the refrain warned of the danger to come, they remained unaware. Takeshi paused at corners as they considered their next steps. He continued through the second verse, letting himself feel grief for the group – it was their own actions that had awakened the creature.

The second refrain picked up, and they realized the danger. Takeshi picked up the pace in answer, trying to find safety from the creature that hunted them through the labyrinth. It was not far behind.

The storm was above, thunder drumming almost along to the beat, coming quick and fast.

And at the song's bridge, they reached a dead end – the center of the labyrinth. They could see the shadows move over the walls, knew there was no way out but one.

So they turned and fought as the creature threw itself at its prey.

Takeshi fought too, using the notes of the refrain to deny the creature its prize. It could not have them. He wouldn't let it. And as the song entered the final refrain...

...Takeshi *reached*.

His soul crystal answered, blooming into existence with a crackle of lightning in answer to his determination as thunder crashed directly overhead. It formed a katana, perfect and deadly, exactly what Takeshi needed to drive the beast off. The party didn't survive in the song, but he could change that, could turn their deaths into triumph.

And then there was silence.

He looked at the katana in his hand. Though it was almost indistinguishable from the one on the ground by Jitsu, he was aware of it in a way he had never felt before. There was a tightness in his chest, but it was easily pushed aside for the moment. He squeezed the hilt and could feel an answering pulse of magic, could see little sparks of lightning travel down the blade.

He had done it.

He closed his eyes and took a deep breath, listening to the falling rain.

Jitsu's mouth was open in a wolfish grin as her tail whipped back and forth. Takeshi had listened to her and had succeeded. He should remember that in the future.

He inclined his head, ceding to her the victory. "Yes, you were correct."

He felt it waver, then dissolve in a shower of sparks as the tightness in his chest eased. Ander had been correct; that was uncomfortable. But Takeshi was good at pushing discomfort aside for the greater good. Now that he had managed this, he could get better at it.

He took a moment, then summoned it again. Already it felt more stable in his hand. He glanced at his katana, lying on the ground next to Jitsu, and realized that he would never need to use it again. This just *felt* superior. And it was a part of him, in a literal way. It responded to his thought, shattering into pieces that reformed as a short sword, and then again as a dagger. He considered it a moment before it disappeared again.

Had he mastered Voice or Movement? Absolutely not. But Ander was right. If he chose to remain a priest, he would have all of eternity to learn how to sing and dance.

But now he had a soulforged weapon.

He could actually be a priest and help save the goddess from Abomination.

He knelt next to his katana, slowly reaching out and touching the hilt. It had been his for years, had accompanied him on countless missions. He'd sworn multiple oaths on it. It was the symbol of his loyalty to Ni Fon, his status as shinobi.

But he wasn't loyal to Ni Fon anymore, was he?

Hotaru had set him free.

The inklings of an idea began to take shape, and he smiled. She would have loved this idea.

He needed to find Ander.

What could she do, other than what she was already doing?

But everything *hurt*. And every step she took felt like a misstep. No matter what she did, more of her disappeared, and Abomination grew stronger.

How long, until the tipping point? How long before it was too much for her chosen to fight? How long had her siblings suffered in the time before? How long had she suffered now? She didn't know. After all this, it felt as though time were getting away from her.

Though time wasn't a domain she utilized, it was still one of hers, and she couldn't help but feel that was a bad sign.

None of her siblings had come to her. She understood. She would have sent them away if they had. But it still hurt. She acknowledged that, tried to let it go. It was how things were.

Was anyone coming for her? Had her priests figured it out? She didn't dare reach out to check.

She had to believe they were coming. They had faith in her. She would have faith in them.

She would keep fighting. Buy them time. Even if she had to fight alone.

But then... she wasn't exactly alone, was she?

# Chapter Twenty-Four

Ander was impressed as usual with Takeshi's insight and spell work. It didn't take too long to help with what the shinobi wanted to do, though the work was delicate and required a careful touch. Two sources of magic would create a failsafe, hopefully. Takeshi would need to keep working on it on his own, but hopefully it would be ready before it was needed.

And it was a nice distraction from the gaping hole in his chest. This time, Her absence felt far worse than when She had distanced Herself from him just a few months prior. The memory of Her agony continued to haunt Ander, and he constantly found himself wondering if She was okay. Then he would remind himself that no, She was *not* okay. She was being consumed by Abomination, a fate arguably worse than death – especially for a god.

Gods were magic. He wondered if Hades was a buffet to the Abomination.

He wiped down the table in his lab, mind racing. How had they missed something that was strong enough to do so much damage to Her so quickly? There must have been something else, some other link. Otherwise, wouldn't this have happened before? Daemorn had summoned an army of demons that had nearly overrun Lyndiniam a thousand years ago, but Hades had been in no danger then from what he could recall of the situation. What made the bionics different?

"Ander?"

He looked up at Takeshi, who had finished cleaning up his own supplies, and realized he had spaced out. "Ah, apologies. What were you saying?"

Takeshi shook his head. "I was just thanking you for your help. I know we all have a lot to do in the next few hours, but..."

Ander waved it off. "Don't be ridiculous; this is as much prep as anything else we might do. It's an excellent idea; however... are you sure this is what you want to do?"

"Yes. It is the best way to honor her, as well." He traced the new symbol they had etched into the metal with a fingertip. "She would have approved of this. And it is not as though I will need it anymore, anyway."

True, now that he had soulforged. There wasn't much to say to that. And it wasn't as though Ander had known her outside a brief conversation anyway.

"Are you going to be okay, coming with us?" Takeshi asked suddenly. "When we went to Etroy, you were convinced your talents were better off here, and you seemed... uncomfortable with the thought of leaving."

Ander looked down at the table. "There is no choice here. Well, technically there is, but... I cannot just abandon Hades. No matter my personal feelings about leaving Tarvishte on another completely insane mission" – and he was trying very hard *not* to think about that – "I have to try."

Takeshi bowed his head. "Of course. Though for what it is worth, it will be good to work with you again in a professional capacity."

In a professional–? Oh, of course. As a shinobi, Takeshi would see this in terms of a job, regardless of the circumstances. But how was he supposed to respond to that?

They stood in silence for a moment, and Ander realized he was waiting for a suggestion that wasn't going to come.

He brought a hand up to his chest where his *crystallus* rested, swallowed hard, and looked around for something to busy himself with. "It is no matter," he tried to brush it off, uncertain how that would come across.

Why did he even care?

The data pad from Tilden was still plugged in on the side table; he walked over to that and booted it up.

"I should go pack," Takeshi said, turning to leave. "Thank you again for your help."

"Of course," Ander murmured, eyes scanning down the page Marcus had left it on. "Remember to ensure your *crystallus* has a decent amount of power stored. We will likely need that."

"Ah, yes. Thank you for the reminder."

Ander's eyes caught on one of the passages Marcus had flagged, and his eyebrows drew together. "Wait."

Takeshi stopped. "Hm?"

"Marcus mentioned this before, but I didn't realize..." He trailed off, trying to figure out the ramifications of this.

"Didn't realize...?" Takeshi prompted after a moment.

"He wasn't sure, but thought the Empire may have picked up on the Lady's magic – essence, I suppose – when Ryn died," he explained. "She apparently killed him directly rather than let the bionics finish the job, which, I will admit, is not something I knew She could do. But Her magic being present would have likely canceled out Tadurin's, which made the attempt to turn Ryn into a bionic fail, which is good. But they were able to notice and record that She was present."

Takeshi's eyebrows rose nearly to his hairline. "And they didn't take the goddess of death's presence as a sign they should probably *stop*?"

Ander blinked. "Oh, no. Sorry, I should have been more clear. They noticed Her energy, but they did not realize what it was, only that it interfered somehow with the process." He flicked to the next page. "Whoever wrote this had a number of theories concerning whether they could utilize that energy to aid the process instead of countering it." He stared at the data pad, realizing what that probably meant, and feeling mildly sick.

"But... if they came up with that over twenty years ago, wouldn't they have been using it?" Takeshi looked equally horrified. "You would have found some trace of her magic alongside Tadurin's, wouldn't you?"

"The theories didn't work, but... they did get close with one before they had to relocate from Etroy, due to no one being willing to work there anymore. Something about the place was disturbing people enough that they were apparently threatening to quit rather than spend any more time there."

"Jamirh did report the building felt haunted." The shinobi took a seat on one of the stools. "Could she have sort of... flooded the building accidentally when she killed Ryn? Or something similar, something that made it difficult for mortals to continue to work there?"

"Without being able to ask Her... it's possible," Ander admitted. "And if this metal, which was supposed to absorb Her magic, had been left at Etroy, it may have... well, marinated, I suppose, for lack of a better word, in Her power."

"For over twenty years." Takeshi's voice was flat.

"For over twenty years," Ander confirmed.

"And then Crimson Shadows takes a bunch of stuff from Etroy, which may have included this metal, which... What are we theorizing here? That this is what allowed the Abomination to latch onto her?"

Ander flipped to another page and wanted to throw his arms in the air. "I don't know. It looks like they tried that metal with a bionic, but it failed. The bionic didn't activate, so they just kept the remains along with a bunch of other failed attempts at Etroy. It was already used and it did nothing, so it's not as though Crimson Shadows could have just picked up some scraps of metal and screwed us all over." He flicked through another page and winced. "There were a lot of failed attempts back then. They hadn't perfected the formula." Another page. "I should destroy this."

"But it does seem a little too coincidental that research from Etroy involved Hades' magic, and then once Etroy was raided the Abomination was able to attack her directly," Takeshi pointed out.

Ander nodded, reminded again quite suddenly of Fredrik. Why? "I agree. It is too coincidental to not be related, but we don't have all the pieces yet. We'll have to keep it in mind, though, when we are searching for Her in Lyndiniam. We should tell the others." He put the tablet down, intent on going to find Siva.

Takeshi stopped him with a hand on his arm. "It doesn't have to be right this second; everyone is busy. We can mention it when everyone is in one place again."

That *was* more efficient.

"And if you think about it some more, maybe that will spark something?" Takeshi shrugged. "I've noticed you tend to come up with your better theories after you've had some time to consider the information. Not that your preliminary theories aren't good," he added quickly, "just that your iterations tend to be better."

Ander felt a surprising burst of pleasure at the compliment. "Thank you," he said, taking a step back. Takeshi's admiration made him feel almost uncomfortable, but also happy. The complicated emotions were not something he particularly enjoyed though, especially not without Hades there to help him translate it into something he understood. Though he hadn't felt this particular mix of emotions in a long time, actually. Probably not since...

...Fredrik.

Ander abruptly realized why his mind kept trying to liken Takeshi to Fredrik. It wasn't that Takeshi was particularly like Fredrik, it was that Ander liked them both *in the same way.*

He turned around quickly and busied himself with the data pad, not sure what his expression looked like at the moment and wanting desperately to be alone. Now was not the time for this sort of crisis.

On the other hand, acknowledging that did make a number of other things fall into place.

"I will... continue to work on it," he finished awkwardly, not sure what to do. He felt as though he were floundering.

If Takeshi noticed his sudden distress, he didn't show it as he stood up from the stool. "Excellent. And I will continue to work on this—"

A huff came from the door, and Ander glanced over to see Jitsu's head peeking in. Her large violet eyes caught his.

"And pack," Takeshi added. "And hopefully get some sleep tonight. Yes, Jitsu, I am aware of how little time we have. I will see you in the morning, Ander."

"Yes, goodbye," he managed, snapping his gaze back to the data pad. He refused to be judged by a warg.

Then they were both gone.

Ander took a deep breath, put the tablet down, and went upstairs. His fish tank would need to be seen to before they left. And perhaps while they were gone? Ander wasn't sure how long they were expected to be away. Maybe he could ask Marcus to check in on his fish?

Oh, for the love of—

What was he going to do?

Now was *not* the time to realize that he was attracted to Takeshi. There was far too much going on.

If they could save Hades... yes, the Lady would know what to do. She could help Ander not mess everything up, the way he was sure he had messed up with Ida and Fredrik.

He found himself rubbing at the scar on his face and forced himself to stop.

He took another deep breath, deliberately picked up his notebook and pen, and began to run through the routine of checking his fish.

It was enough that he had recognized the feelings for now.

Hades would be proud of him.

Ander couldn't sleep.

He drifted through the darkened common room, pausing by the fish tank, but it wasn't as soothing as he'd hoped. He went downstairs and entered the sanctuary.

Jak's crystal statue greeted him from the center of the space. Whatever had happened to Hades, it hadn't affected Jak's crystalline prison. Or cocoon, or whatever it was supposed to be. Jak was unchanged.

He wished Jak could have gated them south. The priest's gates had been stable and safe and his range was unparalleled, even without the array being visible. It was as though he had been pretending to be a Living Will, casting without an array at all.

Jak would have gotten a kick out of people thinking he was a Living Will. He probably would have played it up, tried to be mysterious about it, even though he was just very good at visualizing complicated arrays in his head. Being ancient had given him a lot of practice.

Jak... had been visualizing the arrays in his head, hadn't he?

Ander shook his head. Of course he had been. Living Wills were a myth.

He wandered around the sanctuary, feeling restless. He supposed that was understandable; it was difficult to even wrap his mind around the magnitude of what they were going to try to accomplish in just a few hours. Go straight to the heart of the Empire, in the middle of a civil war, to try to find an unknown type of bionic that was eating their god.

What would they do when they found it? Would destroying it be enough? How much of Hades had it consumed? What if it was too late?

He shook his head, suddenly angry with himself. He couldn't afford to think that way. If it was too late for Hades, then it was too late for the world, and he just couldn't accept that.

Too many people had already died trying to prevent it.

He felt the anger go out of him, leaving him exhausted. Slowly, he sank to his knees, facing the statue of Jak. He closed his eyes, praying, but to whom he wasn't sure. Hades couldn't hear him right now.

He felt a gentle touch on his shoulder.

He looked up to see Mara bent over next to him. Her eyes looked watery. "Hey," she whispered. "How are you doing?"

He didn't know how to answer that, so he leaned into her.

She dropped down beside him and wrapped her arms around him tightly. "Yeah, I get that," she murmured. "Me too."

They stayed like that for several long minutes before she gently untangled herself. "Do you mind if I join you?"

He shook his head, grinding the palms of his hands into his eyes. He was so tired, and he really should sleep. But he didn't think he could leave this place now. It felt like he was supposed to be here.

Mara slid several feet away, positioning herself at the western compass point to Ander's south around Jak. He closed his eyes again.

It wasn't long before Siva joined them. She brushed a hand over his shoulder before taking up the eastern point opposite Mara.

Takeshi drifted through just a few moments after Siva settled. Ander could sense him pause, taking in what was probably a very strange tableau, but then he knelt at the northern point.

"Sometimes, before a mission, shinobi practice weaving their magics together," Takeshi said softly. "To remind ourselves that we are greater than the sum of our parts. It is done in this way."

Ander felt the curious sensation of Takeshi's magic reaching out to his. When he answered it with his own, Takeshi began to braid the strands together, and Ander realized why exactly shinobi called casting "weaving."

It didn't take long for Mara and Siva to be drawn into the weave, a circle of power that was greater than what they could have managed on their own. Ander felt more rejuvenated than he had since Hades had been attacked.

A large, furry body pressed itself against his back. He cracked an eye open to see they had been joined by a small pack of wargs, equally silent and watchful.

And while the hole left by Hades was still there, Ander found he felt significantly less alone.

For the rest of the night they all listened to the silence.

Sherri felt a hand on her shoulder shake her awake. She blinked her eyes open to see a blurry Madine standing next to the car.

"We are here," her sister informed her. "But we can't stay long if we are to meet the others at the rendezvous point. Less than fifteen minutes."

Sherri wiped the sleep from her eyes and put her glasses back on. She could continue to nap after they had looked around; they still had a very long way to go to get to Lyndiniam. She slid out of the car and looked around at the ashes of the Crimson Shadows' camp.

It had been as destroyed as Belian's forces could manage, she observed absently. The buildings were mostly burnt husks; cars had been overturned, power lines brought down.

There were bodies everywhere.

"After we deal with the current crisis in Lyndiniam, perhaps we could see to the remains?" she asked. "The death goddess's cult might look favorably on that," she added when Madine hesitated. "And that could help our position with the Vampire King."

Her sister inclined her head. "An excellent point. We will do what we can, should we survive."

Sherri wandered through the streets along with her sister and a few other Seekers, but the shells of the building held little. The area had been stripped of anything usable by Belian's forces as well.

"All right, let's get going," she said, disappointed that there was so little left.

"Some of the Avari were captured instead of killed," Madine informed her. "Not many, but some do still live."

"As prisoners of Belian, who is far from a stable individual," Sherri said with a wince. "He demanded a full military response to find someone who had theoretically hit his daughter, something none of us believed to be true, just because it was an Avari who had done so."

"That did turn out to be useful, since it was the Third Sign." Madine held the car door open for her to get back in.

The small convoy of three trucks – all they dared move in one group with fighting breaking out across the Empire – continued on its way, leaving the former Avari settlement behind them.

Sherri pressed her forehead against the cool glass of the window. That could happen to the Seekers too, couldn't it? If they weren't careful and vigilant, they could also be wiped off the map by the Emperor's forces.

Then again, they were going to Lyndiniam, and they had already brought down one useless emperor.

What was one more?

She was aiding the other presence too now, as best she could despite the pain. The more the Abomination fought to consume them, the more it brought them together, and as long as the Avari continued to fight with her, they would be stronger together.

He was also in agony, though. And he was mortal. Not meant for such sensations. His stubborn resistance despite that impressed her though, and she redoubled her efforts on his behalf.

The screech of tech against her senses got louder, his pain grew as what was "him" became less, and she realized what was happening.

They were trying to turn this Avari into a bionic.

But that meant Tadurin's magic was in the metal, didn't it?

She searched, and yes – there. Just a bit of chaos. Just a spark of life.

If she had to feed something, she'd rather it was that.

She could not bring herself to admit it to her priests, but she was feeling significantly less charitable now that Abomination was eating her. Yes, Tadurin feared Abomination, and he was right to do so, but...

Well.

If this worked, it would cause an utter mess on the physical plane, but she'd rather have a mess of creation than a mess of Abomination.

# Chapter Twenty-Five

Jamirh did one final check to make sure he had everything. He wondered how many times he'd have to do this before this sort of thing became routine, but then – this would be the last time, wouldn't it?

One way or the other.

He reached for Jak's spell crystal and hesitated.

*Should* he use it?

It wasn't like they were going to be doing much sneaking around or pretending to be someone else. The time for that was over; they had to find Hel quickly. Or the Abomination that was eating Hel? Jamirh wasn't too clear on how exactly they were supposed to save her, and none of the priests seemed to know either. They were just very focused on saving her no matter what, which... did make sense, considering she was their god, and she was in danger. Real danger, this time; not the fake danger she'd apparently been in in Charve.

He shook his head. It was all way more complicated than he liked.

But that brought him back to the spell crystal.

He picked it up, running his fingers over the cool, smooth surface. It seemed like everyone was gearing up for war, and it wasn't like the crystal helped in battle. And they were going to Lyndiniam. People already knew Jamirh there; his hair being orange wasn't going to confuse them or make them think he was someone else.

And... him looking like Ebryn had helped with Gren. Gren, who'd been... a little awed, but not... he hadn't been like the other Avari in Blackfields. And while Jamirh didn't really want to be revered, either, considering what they were walking into maybe looking like Ebryn could be useful? In case they needed other Avari to listen, or help? They were more likely to cooperate if it was Ebryn the Hero asking them, instead of a group of weird people they didn't know and a large dog.

Kind of unfortunate he didn't have the Blade in that case – that would have really sold it – but he couldn't help but feel glad the thing was gone.

He felt freer without it.

He reflected that the thought of using his appearance that way would have been very upsetting even just a few months ago, but now... now it seemed like just another tool he could use. Even the crystal – it would be helpful if he had to hide, but they weren't going to be hiding, were they?

And besides that... did he want to go back looking like someone else? Should he have to change himself in order to avoid the expectations of others, or could he just... be himself? Wasn't that enough? He didn't have to let Ebryn define him. He could look like Ebryn, and still *be Jamirh*.

He glanced down at his scarred arm, picturing the light beneath the wraps and the bracer, and his lips twitched.

He knew what Ebryn would say.

They hadn't been so different in the end, had they?

He checked his coat and bracers, making sure everything that could be stowed away was. It wasn't as though they were planning on being gone long. If Jamirh had to guess, it would be over by tomorrow at the latest. He slid his daggers into place on his belt and looked around one last time.

Then he left his rooms, leaving the spell crystal behind.

The Temple door was open when Jamirh approached in the pre-dawn light. There were a few wargs around but they didn't try to prevent him from entering, letting him pass with just a few light sniffs.

Almost everyone was there when Jamirh entered the sanctuary. Takeshi and Siva were speaking quietly to each other by Jak's statue. Mara and Ander were nowhere in sight, but Jitsu was lying next to a series of concentric circles and glyphs drawn on the ground with chalk. The warg gave a soft woof upon seeing Jamirh. He scratched her ear on the way by as he made his way over to Jeri, who was leaning against a column with her arms folded.

She nodded at him in greeting. "Are you ready?"

He shrugged. "I'm not sure it's possible to be ready for this. What even is this? What are we doing? It seems completely crazy. Are *you* ready?"

"Good point." She smiled wryly. "I suppose I have also done some fairly insane things in my time, but trying to save a god is new for me as well."

"I do wish I'd been able to say goodbye to Salisha and Desha, and the other pirates," he said, ears sinking a bit. "They've done a lot for me the past month or so, and it just feels... weird, to leave without saying anything. And yeah, I know, we aren't supposed to tell anyone," he said quickly, "which is why I didn't go say goodbye, but... we may never see them again."

Everyone left, but this time... it felt like he was the one leaving.

Jeri studied him silently for a moment, green eyes serious. "You will see them again," she said finally.

He smiled faintly. "You can't promise that."

"No. But you have to believe it," she said firmly. "Otherwise, what's the point? Fight to live, Jamirh, always – never fight to die."

He had to admit there was some wisdom in that.

He looked around, deciding to change the subject to one that was less depressing. "I know Siva said we are gating to Pitesh, but how are we doing that? Are we somehow... *using* Jak?"

"What?" She stared at him in surprise. "Oh, no. No, I assume the priests are going to jointly gate us there. Gate magic is something Jak was known for – he could achieve amazing distances all on his own – but gate magic in general is just a subtype of learned magic. It's just usually done a little less... haphazardly than Jak performed it."

"Oh." Even after so many months in Tarvishte, it seemed like he didn't really know anything about magic. "Wait, what do you mean 'haphazardly'?"

She shrugged one shoulder. "He didn't use glyphs."

Jamirh turned and looked hard at the statue as though Jak himself could answer. "And that's... bad."

"It's dangerous," Takeshi broke in as he and Siva joined Jeri and Jamirh. "And it wasn't so much that Jak didn't use glyphs as he didn't materialize them into a visual pattern. It's something that I often do for smaller spells – you just visualize them in your mind – but it becomes very dicey the more complicated a spell becomes."

Jamirh saw Siva purse her lips, but she didn't comment.

"All right, we're ready!" Mara swung into the sanctuary, Ander following at a more sedate pace behind her. "Oh, are we the last ones?"

Siva inclined her head. "Dawn is rapidly approaching. If we are ready, we should go."

Nods of agreement all around.

Ander gestured to the chalk circles. "All non-casters in the center."

Ah, that was the gate spell. Jamirh stepped carefully over the lines, not wanting to disturb them. Jeri followed, and Jitsu cleared the whole thing with one leap before sitting next to Jamirh with her tail wrapped around her feet.

The four priests took up positions around them, raising their hands to shoulder height, each almost touching the hand to either side of them.

"I will say, this is going to be way easier with the weaving Takeshi taught us last night," Mara chirped.

Jamirh blinked. "I... what? You learned this *last night*?"

Jeri heaved a sigh and hid her face in her hands. "I think she just means the style of casting, not the gate itself. I hope."

"Don't worry about it," Ander said dryly as the glyphs began to light up under their feet–

–and then they were on their way.

It was late afternoon when they finally reached the outskirts of Lyndiniam. Jeri was driving the van the Seekers had given them in Sturlow, and Jamirh was next to her. The priests and Jitsu were in the back, taking the opportunity to rest from having gated them all over five hundred miles and then walking for an hour and a half. Most of them had napped, but Takeshi was working on something in the back that was hidden by the seats. Jitsu had scrunched herself into the trunk and sat with her head resting on the back seat, watching whatever Takeshi was doing.

The weather had taken a turn for the worse nearly twenty minutes before, and a mix of hail and rain was hitting the van. Jamirh was not looking forward to going out into it, but it also didn't look like it was going to let up anytime soon.

"We are definitely getting closer," Ander said from behind Jamirh. "This weather..."

"Is it mage-affected?" Jeri asked.

"It's certainly *magic*-affected," Siva confirmed. "And Hades' power is already starting to feel much closer. Whatever is happening, it is causing her to bleed magic out into the world."

"And this much magic can lead to weird weather events," Mara finished.

Jamirh frowned. "The weather didn't get weird in Tilden when you guys did that flooding thing with Hades' magic."

He saw Mara shake her head in the rearview mirror. "Tilden was flooded for less than an hour. The weather only starts to go wonky with *prolonged* magical exposure."

"Huh." He wasn't sure he understood the difference, since an hour seemed like a while to him.

Jeri pulled into the parking lot of a small gas station. "Does anyone see the Seekers? Flire told me they would meet us around here."

"We made very good time," Takeshi noted. "Even if they broke every speed limit imaginable and left while we were talking to Perra yesterday, I wouldn't expect them to make it here from Muriz for another few hours at the earliest."

"What should we do, then?" Mara asked. "Wait? Leave a note?"

Jamirh was looking around. "I might have to do a little exploring anyway. When Hel and I left, I didn't think I was ever going to come back, so I didn't pay a ton of attention to where we came out. I have a general idea of where it was, but I might as well use this time to find it."

Jeri cringed. "In this weather?"

"If it's magic weather, I don't really see any other choice," Jamirh pointed out. "Might go grab a muffin though, if the store's open."

"That is a good idea. I will go too; does anyone else want anything?" Jeri asked.

They collected orders before dashing into the building. Jamirh was thankful for the coat Hel had given him; even with the hail he remained mostly dry and unbattered. He and Jeri gathered the requested snacks, looking around to see if there was anything else useful. Either because of the weather or because of the current unrest, there wasn't anyone else in the store other than a bored-looking teller.

As they approached the counter to pay, the vid screen in the corner of the store switched from a soccer game to a nervous-looking news anchor, a loud series of beeps drawing everyone's attention. "This is a special announcement from Emperor Stefan Belian of the Rose Empire," the man behind the desk said. Jamirh could see the sheen of sweat on his face in the harsh studio lighting. "Please pay special attention to the following broadcast, straight from White Gate Palace."

The teller grabbed a remote from under his desk and turned the volume up on the vid screen as the image switched again, this time to a large man with flaming red hair and a beard and mustache. He was seated on a throne, draped in a red cape lined with white fur, and he had an ugly gold crown bespeckled with every type of gem imaginable on his head. Piercing blue eyes stared down the camera.

Jamirh had never seen Stefan Belian before, but it was that encounter with his daughter at the casino that had caused Jamirh to flee the Empire with Hel months ago. Absently, he wondered if the blonde was abusing her new power as princess of the Empire to ruin even more lives.

Probably.

"Beloved citizen of the Empire," the man boomed. The teller quickly turned the volume back down. "You may have heard rumors of an insurgent group of Avari who were trying to take down our throne. They were allied to our enemies, the treasonous former dukes of Elbe and Cartago-Mir, who have cast our Empire into civil war. This will *not* go unanswered. As such, we have moved quickly to bring down the snake within our midst. The so-called Crimson Shadows are no more." He slammed a fist down on the arm of the throne.

Jamirh felt his mouth drop open. What? What about...?

"But even their foolish actions have led us to opportunity!" A screen popped up next to him, showing footage of a room that reminded Jamirh uncomfortably of Tilden and Etroy. A number of Humans in white gowns and masks were bustling around something on a table. "I have decided now is the time to reveal to you a project that has been ongoing behind the scenes. We have been coming up with ways to create the perfect soldier – no need to eat or sleep, follows every direction given, is relentless in the pursuit of its targets. And these traitor Avari will become them."

Jamirh felt his stomach drop out as he realized what Belian was describing.

Bionics.

Abomination.

Then the screen shifted–

Jamirh brought one hand up to cover his mouth as he audibly gasped, the other gripping his key tightly.

That was Gren on that table.

Some metal had already been fused to his face, and he was missing an arm. He looked cut up and bruised.

"Let this be a warning for *all* those who would *dare* to oppose the Empire! Not only will you lose to our superior forces, you will find yourself becoming them–"

He cut off as the screen showing Gren suddenly flickered. There was a flash of light, some sort of movement from the table, and the briefest sound of screaming before the screen went blank.

Belian's face darkened with fury. "What the hell was that? No, don't tell me– *cut the feed,* damn–"

The vid screen returned to the soccer game, though the players were all standing on one side of the field.

"We need to tell the others," Jamirh whispered to Jeri urgently. "Jeri, that was Gren. They are turning him into a bionic. That *has* to be the source of Abomination, doesn't it?"

"Yes," she murmured softly, still staring at the screen. "Jamirh... that flash of power. It was *violet.*"

He blinked, then felt a grim feeling of satisfaction begin to grow.

Hel was fighting back.

Hours later, Jamirh crept through the familiar sewers he'd never thought he'd see again.

"The facilities shown in the video are located in the research facilities attached to the palace," Sherri was informing them softly. "Colonel Rhode did not often work in Lyndiniam, but he was occasionally called in to consult. I am familiar with the area."

"It's going to be heavily guarded," Takeshi noted. He was right behind Jamirh, casting a dim mage light in front so they could see. "Do you have any suggestions as to how we get in without knocking on the front door once Jamirh gets us into the city proper?"

Madine tilted her head. "We are mages, and they are not. It will be simple."

It didn't really feel like the last time at all, when it had just been him and Hel. She had been quiet but excited, and they had been moving towards freedom. Now he was with a Vampire, four priests of the goddess of death, a former major in the military, six Truth Seekers, and a warg. And they were going to attack White Gate Palace.

Granted, the first time he had been with the goddess of death herself even though he hadn't known it, so maybe in a weird way this trip was actually the more mundane one?

"I don't usually find it wise to underestimate non-mages," Takeshi disagreed with the Seeker.

"And we know they are messing around with the bionic tech and anything else the Crimson Shadows took from Etroy, so who knows what else they've got going?" Mara added.

The closer they got, the more the air seemed to chill, and the less welcoming everything became. Not that the old sewers had ever been "welcoming," exactly, but there was something that was slowly becoming more and more uncomfortable.

In fact, it reminded Jamirh of the flooding the priests had performed at Tilden. He shuddered. "Does it feel like the flooding to anyone else?"

"You can feel it?" Siva asked, a note of concern in her voice.

"Yes."

"That's a bad sign," Ander murmured from the back of the group. "If non-mages can feel the gathering power, that means it's going to start affecting things in unpredictable ways soon, if it hasn't already."

Jamirh tried to push the feeling away and checked his mental map. "Okay, we are as close as we can get while remaining underground."

"We take an hour to rest, then we move," Takeshi said firmly. "Remember what Jamirh told us while coming in – lights low and voices down."

Jamirh stepped off to the side as everyone found spots to settle, sitting against the concrete wall of the tunnel. These sewers had not been in use for decades, but there was still a scent in the air that was unpleasant, wafting up from the water in the channel. He tried to ignore it.

He took off his right glove, revealing the glowing red scars. "Are you guys ready for this?" he asked quietly.

The glow pulsed once, and Jamirh smiled. He replaced the glove, rubbing at the arm to alleviate some of the soreness. He glanced at Ander, but... no. Now was not the time. He would mention it after they were done.

And... then what?

It wasn't the first time he'd had that thought, but they were so close now it was hard not to wonder, even if there was no guarantee any of them would make it past the next twenty-four hours.

What did he want to do?

His hand found his key, but his mind pictured the ocean, water as far as the eye could see, and the feeling of freedom that came with it–

"Jamirh, if I could have a moment?"

He blinked, startled out of his thoughts, then turned to look at Takeshi. "Sure, what's up?"

The shinobi glanced back over the group. "Let's move a little farther away."

"Uh... okay." He stood and followed.

When they were almost thirty feet away from the others, Takeshi stopped and turned to Jamirh. "While I know you have been content to wield your daggers, the majority of your training was done with a sword. Given the unknown situation we are about to step into, it seems best for you to use the weapon you are most practiced with."

Jamirh shrugged. "The Blade is gone, so it's not like there's anything that can be done about that. I'll be okay with the daggers, though. I'll keep most of my focus on dodging anyway."

"Dodging is good, and I don't recommend you stray from that plan," Takeshi said wryly. "But we can give you a sword." He unclipped his katana from his belt and held it out to Jamirh.

It took a moment for Jamirh to even process those words. "You want to... *what*? But that's yours; what are you going to do?!"

"I have learned to soulforge." He held a hand out to the side, and another katana, near twin to the first, appeared with a shower of white-blue sparks. "I had thought I would use the soulforged weapon as a backup and use this one as my primary weapon, but once I forged it... there is no comparison to a soulforged weapon, it turns out." There was a note of self-deprecation in his voice. "As such, I no longer have need of this one."

"But... isn't it important to you?" Jamirh asked, still in shock that Takeshi would offer him his katana.

"It is," he agreed easily. "But I would rather it go with you, where it can continue to do some good."

Jamirh stared at him for another moment, then slowly reached out to take the katana. "I... don't know what to say." He could almost feel his inherent examining the weapon. "It's not exactly like the Blade."

"No, the edge is only on one side. But I fully believe your inherent will adjust to that very easily. Ander and I did make a few modifications – we strengthened it, so it will be able to damage things like the bionics without magic, and these here" – he pointed to a set of four glyphs sewn into the leather wrap of the hilt – "will act like spell crystals to give you an effect of your choice. Fire, lightning, light, and frost. Touch the glyph and think the name of the effect to activate it. Should be far more practical than the Crystal Light Blade was."

Jamirh felt his eyes well with tears. "I can't believe you're giving this to me."

Takeshi put a hand on his shoulder, looking down at the katana. "It was my loyal partner for a very long time. I hope it serves you well."

Jamirh slid the blade a few inches out of the sheath, noticing a symbol etched into the blade itself. It wasn't a rune; it looked like the symbols the Nifoni wrote with. He slid it back in, remembering a conversation he'd had with Takeshi months ago. "If it's got magic, does that mean it has a name now?" he teased, wiping at his eyes.

Takeshi smiled. "Hotaru."

Hades shuddered, but refused to give in to the agony. She could feel it – her priests were close now. That was good. That was excellent.

How she missed them.

But it was okay. They were coming. They, like her, would not let the world fall.

Absently, she wondered if that was what made them hers. She would prefer that over her siblings' theories that they were hers simply because they were broken beyond repair.

She felt herself coalesce a little more into the physical world and winced, but there was nothing she could do about that now. In consuming her, the Abomination was trying to pull her into its realm. The ramifications of that, if left unchecked, would be problematic for this area.

She turned her attention towards the physical plane a little more, pleased with the crystalline growth the mixing of her magic and Tadurin's had created. And if some of the mortals who had been present in the room had died due to that explosion of destructive creation, then at least she had grown a little stronger for it, earning her a few more seconds of resistance.

And at least now the Avari was no longer *actively* being modified by the other mortals. She was unsure how much of the transformation had taken place, but the fact he was still fighting gave her hope.

"Are you... there?"

Her attention swung back to the Avari, though she was careful not to inflict too much of herself on him. He was suffering enough. His voice was shaky and weak, but she could still feel the resilience beneath. "I am here," she whispered gently.

His being shuddered anyway. "You are... helping... me? It has... you too."

"It does," she agreed, trying to determine if there was anything more she could do to ease his pain. That was not her greatest gift.

A weak laugh. "You made them... the... the Humans... go away."

"Yes." That was one way to put it. "We are stronger together. You must keep fighting."

"What... are you?"

Another piece of her disappeared into corruption, and she writhed in tormented agony before redoubling her efforts. She was concerned that the mortal could communicate with her; were they simply intertwined because of the Abomination? Or had she been pulled so far into the physical plane? Or did he just believe he could hear her?

"Are you... going to leave me... too?" The sound of a cough. "The silence is..."

She considered the Abomination trying to grow inside of him, consuming them both – punishment for a sin that neither had committed.

"It is terrible to bear certain things alone," she whispered sadly. "But I am here."

As she hadn't been, in the beginning.

It wasn't her fault. No matter what Tadurin thought.

"I will not leave you," she continued softly. "And there is help coming."

"How... how can you be... so sure?"

She wished she could sweep her senses out for her beloved priests as she usually could, but she could not risk accidentally transmitting the Abomination to them. Still, part of her just *knew* they were nearby.

"I just know."

But perhaps she could do one last thing to help bring them to her.

In her current state, there would be no turning back if she did this. It would affect everything in her immediate vicinity.

Hades gathered herself in challenge, dredging up every last bit of defiance she still had in her, every last spark of righteous rage–

–and *screamed*.

# Chapter Twenty-Six

Jamirh felt the scream more than he heard it. He tried to cover his ears anyway as he curled himself into a ball, pressing himself into the wall he'd been resting against.

He'd heard that scream before, though not as loudly.

Hel.

He shook his head, trying to clear the ringing from his ears. Everyone else seemed to be in a similar state, recovering from the audible assault, slowly straightening up and looking around.

"That was a Queen's Challenge!" Ander finally managed. "Something is very, very wrong!"

Mara wrapped her arms around herself and shuddered, ears sinking. "Shit, Her magic is everywhere now!"

"If it wasn't affecting the physical plane before, it is now," Siva agreed. "She's the goddess of death; Her doing that at Her full power..."

"We need to go *now*," Takeshi snapped. "Jamirh!"

"This way!"

He dashed down a side tunnel, looking for– there it was, a ladder built into the wall. He shimmied up it with the speed of long practice and pushed the grate at the top off, pulling himself up and out as quickly as possible.

While the others followed, he looked around. The night air was damp and cool, and the moon was almost full high above. This sewer grate exited in a decrepit alleyway just on the edges of Blackfields, a twenty-minute walk from the palace.

They didn't have twenty minutes.

No one was in sight, and he crept to the mouth of the alley, Jeri just a pace behind him. Still no one. He frowned. It was late, but there were usually people about regardless.

There was something wrong with the air.

It wasn't a scent, it wasn't the moisture, it wasn't... Jamirh wasn't sure, but he would bet every last credit he had it had to do with Hel.

There was the sound of thunder nearby, but at least the hail had stopped.

Jitsu leapt out of the sewer last, and Jamirh waved to the others. "This way!"

He took off at a run, keeping an eye out for anyone as they turned another corner—

There were bodies in the street.

Jamirh slid to a stop abruptly, staring. He counted nine people on the ground as the rest of the group stopped behind him. What on Gaia...?

Ander stepped forward to the nearest one, checking for a pulse. "Alive, but completely overwhelmed by Hades' power."

"Keep going," Siva ordered.

They took off again, Jamirh in the lead. The buildings in this district were tall, obscuring most of the sky, but whenever Jamirh looked up the color didn't seem quite right. The buildings themselves showed signs of neglect, the glass windows dirty and in some cases even boarded up. What little, carefully cultivated greenery was normally present was dead, leaves and flowers decaying in their planters. The lester of the sidewalks seemed to have lost its sparkle, curbs cracked and broken. Streetlights flickered dimly, adding to the eerie atmosphere. Trash was piled up in corners, as though people had tried to sweep it out of sight.

Jamirh could not recall having ever seen trash in the street in any district other than Blackfields.

They passed more citizens in crumpled heaps on the ground, but they ignored them – the only way to help them now was to end whatever this was that had started.

Jamirh turned a corner and gasped, sliding to a halt.

The sky above the three-story research center had a glowing, writhing mass of violet energy twisting and turning above it. Roughly cylindrical, tendrils extended over the building in a web of sparking, angry magic, though the core seemed to go straight through the building. Strands of sick-looking reddish-black cut through the violet, extending upward. Above it, storm clouds were gathering, lightning cutting through in shapes that were difficult to look at.

"A bloom!" Siva exclaimed as the group stared in horror.

Jamirh swallowed. "Is this like the flooding?"

"No, this is much, much worse," she said. "A flooding brings a god's power into an area, in essence turning it into sacred ground. A bloom is the god itself entering into the physical realm, which can have... serious ramifications."

"There is no way they would have missed that," Mara pointed out. "There's no way they held an announcement for their new project if this was above the research facility."

Siva spun, flames crackling into existence around her. When they faded, she was wearing the leather and dyed cloth of Aradian armor. "It was probably the Challenge that did it. Queen's Challenge does... unexplainable things, sometimes."

Flashes of green threads and blue water, and Ander and Mara had also summoned their soulforged armor.

Jamirh fingered the sleeve cuff of his coat. Hel had ensured he would be protected too, even if she hadn't foreseen this.

"The World Sound has been a disrupted mess since she did it," Takeshi said grimly. "Everything is out of balance. Be careful with your spells – they might not act as intended."

"The bloom – it's trying to spread!"

Jamirh looked where Jeri was pointing. A violet tendril had shot out and attached itself to the palace next door; a splinter of red followed.

The Seekers exchanged a look, and Madine stepped forward. "We can create a perimeter, prevent it from going any farther. But it will be up to you to end it." The other Seekers shot off to surround the area. "Be very careful. This corruption is not contained like it was in the bionics. Those desired to kill. This one wants to spread."

The priests were silent for a moment, though they were all looking at each other, and finally Siva nodded grimly. "Very well. Good luck." She took a step towards the closed gate barring the way–

Sickly red energy crackled through the white metal, causing it to shriek in protest as it warped, crunching itself into fractal patterns.

Takeshi yanked Siva back as the energy reached forward, searching. "Don't let that touch you!"

"This way!" Sherri turned and sprinted towards the main gates of the palace. "You'll have to go around!"

The group ran after her, only stopping once they reached the main gates.

"The whole complex is connected," Sherri informed them urgently. "Cut through the west wing and you'll reach the research center. You need to go to the third floor, lab 4C."

"You aren't coming with us?" Jamirh asked, ears twitching.

She shook her head, adjusting her glasses. "The Seekers need me out here. Don't worry; this palace is not nearly as difficult to navigate as the one in Tarvishte. Just go left when you go in."

Takeshi gave her a brief look that Jamirh couldn't read, but then nodded. "Good luck, then." He turned to the rest. "Let's go."

Mara and Siva moved forward as one, combining their magics. Water and fire mixed to turn the white metal of the gate into some sort of ashy rock that crumbled at the touch.

Jamirh shuddered, glancing over his shoulder at how the other gate had also been transformed.

Takeshi threw a sparking ball of lightning at the large glass double doors leading into the building and they shattered into thousands of pieces—

And then they were in.

If anything, the feel of the air here was even worse than it had been outside. It was difficult to breathe, and felt almost like moving through mud. It was dark, just a few, palely flickering emergency lights doing their best to cut through the gloom. They were in a large space, though how large was difficult to tell. A huge marble staircase loomed in front of them, disappearing upward into the dark.

"There is death in the air here," Mara whispered. Jamirh was alarmed to realize her eyes were glowing bright blue.

"Not real death. *Remembered* death," Siva agreed grimly. "As I said earlier – the bloom will have consequences. Be on your guard. Strike first and kill anything that moves."

Jamirh drew his new katana, running his thumb over the hilt as he considered that. "Will they stay dead?"

The priests all looked at each other uncertainly.

"Great," Jamirh muttered, ears twitching down.

"Their limbs probably won't be able to regenerate," Jeri said, waving her own shadow arm as an example. "Go for the limbs."

"Leave them twitching on the floor, got it." Jamirh nodded. "So then... left?"

"This way!" Siva took off at a run, everyone else following her. "We just need to go wherever the Lady's presence is strongest."

The wall appeared in front of them, a set of double doors barely visible a little ways down. Jamirh shot forward, yanking the door open to reveal a long hallway and–

"Holy–!" Jamirh threw himself to the side as the others all scattered, dodging a Human with metal and tech growing in strange formations out of his face and shoulder as he hurled himself at them with a creepy moaning sound. Jamirh spun with the katana, cutting off his legs as he went past.

It crashed to the floor, where it continued to try to drag itself over to Jamirh, reaching. The metal bits sparked with reddish energy, trying to close the gap.

A ball of fire collided with its head, setting it aflame. The moans turned to screams.

"Definitely do *not* let that energy touch you!" Takeshi ordered. "Prioritize attacking at a distance. The Seekers were right; it's trying to spread. Jitsu–"

The warg made a soft growling sound, shaking herself. Every bit of fur was standing on end, making her look huge.

Two more of the corrupted Humans came through the door, picking up speed as they spotted the group. Mara and Takeshi took them out quickly; at least they weren't very durable.

They moved carefully forward into the hallway, heading in the direction of the research center. Four more monstrosities accosted them as they made their way through the palace. There didn't seem to be any people left unaffected, no bodies left untouched like in the city outside. And while they were easy to dismember, they were fast, and persistent in trying to spread the Abomination.

"This is terrible," Jamirh noted, dodging another one of the corrupted Humans. "No one deserves this. Is this really because of Hel?"

"A Queen's Challenge is a type of Voice magic," Takeshi said, electrocuting another. "And it's one that's known for affecting even non-magical people who hear it. My guess is that when she Challenged, any mortal within a certain radius got linked into the Abomination with her."

"And outside of that radius, the accumulation of magic overwhelmed people," Ander concluded. "These people don't live with magic; the Empire has done its best to wipe it out. But that means they were unprepared for such a high concentration."

"At least they are easier to deal with than the bionics." Mara stabbed another, pinning it to the wall so Jeri could dismember it with swift slices of her cutlasses.

Jamirh shuddered, trying not to think of how many people were dying. Or had already died; he doubted there was any way to save them now.

The hallway ended suddenly, branching off to the right and left. Jamirh paused. They were supposed to go left, but there was something...

The already struggling hallway lights flickered one last time, then died.

The sound of metal scraping the floor came from the right, followed by a hollow thud, and then a wet slurping sound that had every instinct Jamirh possessed screaming in fear. He turned.

Instantly mage lights bloomed into existence around him, cast by the priests, illuminating the hallway and revealing a new monstrosity.

The distorted figure of a large man sat upon a crooked gold throne. His arms were melting into the once-white upholstery, veins of flesh traveling down the sides. His legs had fused together into one misshapen appendage, replacing the front-left leg of the chair and jacking that corner up. His neck was elongated, head resting above the tall back of the throne, flaming red beard merging with the tattered remnants of a red cape. Six large, malformed tentacles of flesh and metal came around the chair like a mockery of the gold wings that extended from it. An ugly gold crown bespeckled with gems was fused to the man's head.

As they stared, another lump of flesh grew like a tumor into another leg, righting the throne upon four legs of flesh and metal.

The twisted remains of Emperor Stefan Belian stared at them with a look of gnawing hunger through glowing red eyes.

Jamirh wanted to throw up. "Okay, cutting off the limbs is *not* going to be enough for this one!" He swallowed hard, bringing the katana to bear.

"Tadurin's magic must still be active as well!" Siva cried, an or-angey-red array blooming into existence in front of her. She took a spell crystal off her belt and hurled it into the array. As it passed through, it shattered into multiple burning pieces which thumped into the thing's mass at high velocity, causing it to stagger back.

It roared and surged towards them, moving way faster than some-thing that size had any right to, fleshy legs growing hands at the ends.

Jeri flickered into existence behind it, cutlasses severing two of the tentacles before she disappeared into shadow again, avoiding an-other tentacle that tried to grab her. The two damaged appendages began to reform immediately.

"We need to stop it from mutating!" Ander called as the green of his magic formed a wall between them and the creature. The priest cursed as the wall began to melt. "The bloom is affecting my spells!"

"Siva's spell worked–"

"That was mostly spell crystal, a spell that has already been cast; the array just added force," Takeshi pointed out. "Actively casting is going to be more tricky. Keep your spells simple."

"If it's Tadurin's magic tangled up in there, maybe the Lady's can counter it?" Mara suggested.

"It'll be difficult, without our connection to Her," Siva replied.

Takeshi snorted. "Her magic is *everywhere* at the moment; we just need..."

"...to re-direct it, re-purpose it," Ander finished. "It's going to take a minute to set that up; cover us!"

Jamirh eyed the charred flesh where Siva's missiles had hit. It was regenerating, but... "The fire seems to slow it down!" He glanced down at the katana – Hotaru, its name was Hotaru – and found the glyph he wanted. Fire, they needed fire.

The blade ignited, flames licking down its length.

If the monstrosity before him was fast, well, he just had to be faster. And he'd already seen a bit of what it could do.

He rushed forward, deciding Jeri had been right – the large tentacles were the greatest threat. It skittered towards him, reaching out with no regard for its own safety, a flaw he immediately capitalized on by slicing the tentacle into multiple pieces before jumping to the side.

It screamed, the noise fading into a gargling sound as it turned to attack him again.

Jeri appeared next to it, hacking at one of the legs while more of Siva's bolts shot from behind Jamirh to cauterize the wounds the Vampire was leaving. The chair tipped dangerously to one side as a leg came free, and Jamirh slid around it to slice another two tentacles.

His arm ached.

He tried to ignore it. He couldn't afford the distraction.

He dodged one of the remaining limbs, catching a glimpse of Takeshi, Ander, and Mara standing in a circle, palms together, but his attention was drawn by the crackling red energy gathering at the top of the crown. "Bad!" he shouted as he cut up another tentacle. "Crown! Bad!"

Another burst of flame hit it directly in the face, but it just made a disturbed gurgle in response.

Jitsu howled in fury, dancing in place off to the side, unable to attack it without coming into direct contact with the red energy of the Abomination.

Jamirh jumped back, not wanting to be anywhere near it when whatever that was went off–

Suddenly the pressure in the air shifted, making it difficult to breathe. Shadows coalesced above the monstrosity, wisps of violet light sparking to life against the corruption. It crashed to the ground, partially flattened, twitching as it tried to stand again. The red energy fizzled out as Jamirh watched, trying to figure out what had just happened. It flailed feebly against the power pinning it in place. The flesh began to dissolve into motes of violet light and ash, and it let out an eerie moan.

"What...?" Jamirh asked, taking another step back as Jeri did the same.

"Gravity," Ander replied shortly. "And the bloom."

"We need to keep moving, leave it!" Takeshi ordered. "That's good enough!"

Jamirh sprinted back over, keeping a close eye on the two remaining tentacles, but they just twitched feebly in his direction. "Are you sure we can just leave it?"

"Saving the Lady is our priority. These things are not true Abomination," Siva explained. "Ending the bloom will destroy them for good far more efficiently than we can do on our own."

He couldn't argue with that.

They resumed running through the palace, and Jamirh was relieved when they found the doors to the research center a few minutes later. They quickly dispatched another pair of corrupted Humans.

"Here, the stairs..." Mara pointed. "We need to go up!"

There was a sound from behind Jamirh and he turned, eyes widening. Several of the corpses that had been on the ground near each other had combined into another terrifying, mutated creature, and it was shambling towards the group with grim purpose.

Takeshi hit it with a ball of lightning, and as the thing twitched from the electricity coursing through it he yelled, "Go, up the stairs! We don't have time for this!"

Jamirh swung through the door and took the stairs two at a time, flinging himself against the wall as another one of the corrupted Humans fell through the center, landing hard in a broken heap on the ground. "Eyes up," he warned. "They don't have a lot of self-preservation." He started back up the stairs again as Jitsu shot past.

They made it to the third floor, which looked almost exactly like the first floor – a long hallway with a bunch of doors on either side. The lights were flickering erratically, leaving most of the hallway in darkness. "What number are we looking for?"

"4C," Ander reminded him. Then the priest froze. "Hold on. There's something worse on this floor."

Worse? How was there something *worse*?

Jitsu was standing in front, growling as she backed up. Jamirh frowned; he'd never seen her move away from a threat. Not even the bionics.

Hysterical laughter echoed down the hall.

Jamirh's arm blazed, the ache blossoming into real pain.

"Oh no," Siva whispered. "I was afraid of this."

Jamirh brought his katana up in front of him, keeping an eye on the light from his arm. The pain wasn't subsiding, but he gritted his teeth and kept his grip steady. "Afraid of...?"

"*Remembered* death."

Something stumbled forward in the shadows. The flickering light caught a pale face frozen in a manic grin and long black hair, loose and tangled. Red-and-black robes were ripped and stained.

*That's Dal–, Der–, ah, the demon summoning guy!* came Ebryn's suddenly furious voice in Jamirh's mind. *I killed him! What's he doing here?*

"Um, Ebryn says that's the demon summoner he killed a thousand years ago," Jamirh said, feeling a little sick. "Why is he here?"

Siva sighed, which felt like a massive under-reaction to Jamirh. "Hades is the goddess of death, and She is also currently linked into the Abomination. It's trying to spread, trying to create more of itself, but... Daemorn did perish here while doing something with Abomination."

"So it used her magic to raise him from the dead?" Takeshi asked, sounding appropriately disturbed.

"That was a thousand years ago!" Jamirh exclaimed.

"That's really not that long, cosmically speaking," Ander pointed out. "And if Daemorn was already linked to Abomination and was dead…"

He trailed off as the ancient wizard stepped forward into the light. Jamirh was further horrified to see a grotesque, mutated wing growing from his shoulder, and veins of corruption marring his face.

*Actually, he looks like he's having a worse afterlife than I am. Heads up, he was very good at summoning demons and very bad at staying dead. He was also passable with a rapier.*

*Ebryn, get back here and help me with this stupid shield!* came Ryn's strained cry as the pain in Jamirh's arm grew stronger.

Silence, as Jamirh watched the wizard take another step closer. The glow of his arm dimmed.

The corrupted remains of Daemorn raised a finger and pointed.

A green shield took the lightning strike headed for Jamirh. Takeshi answered with a ball of lightning of his own, but the wizard leapt to the side with far more dexterity than Jamirh would have assumed based on the way he was walking. He clung to the wall, then skittered up it to settle on the ceiling.

"Okay, no, I really don't like that!" Mara sounded disgusted.

Jamirh agreed as he flung himself to the side to dodge another lightning bolt. "There's not a lot of room in this hallway for us to maneuver!"

Siva sent a barrage of fire at him, but a shield of sickly green threaded with that reddish-black ate the spell. "Was that the color of his magic?"

"Who knows?" Jamirh certainly didn't.

Spears of water exploded from the ceiling Daemorn was clinging to, but he just dropped to the floor on all fours. His grinning face jerked sideways as the veins of corruption pulsed, and he let out another burst of laughter.

Jeri erupted from the shadow directly beside him, stabbing with both cutlasses. He shrieked as she found her mark, but she didn't pause, whipping around and slicing the wing clean off before withdrawing into the shadows of the hallway again.

Takeshi and Siva hit him with both fire and lightning, trying to take advantage of the opening Jeri had given them. The spells landed, but though he was now burnt and twitching, he still stood up.

"Fire usually works against demons and demon-kin," Siva hissed.

"It's Hades' magic – there's too much of it here. The other magics aren't working right," Takeshi explained. "Maybe if the Faleri were–"

"Eeebryyyn."

Jamirh felt ice go down his spine at that singsong, high-pitched giggle. "Nope. Absolutely not. He's gotta go." His inherent wanted him to move, to slice and dodge and stab, but Jamirh couldn't. There were too many spells getting thrown around in too small a space.

"Ebby, Ebby, Ebby, do you remember your friend? I've missed you."

"Not Ebryn," he called back as Mara dumped water on him for Takeshi to electrocute. "Sorry, wrong century."

The wizard just giggled in response, beginning to draw an array in the air in front of him.

"Don't let him complete that!" Ander snapped, and Jeri again emerged from the shadows with her blades. This time there was a flash of light and she rebounded hard, shrieking.

"What the... how do we beat him?!" Jamirh exclaimed.

Orange and blue lines streaked across the ceiling above him, and it caved in over his head, filling the hallway with dust and debris.

Jamirh looked up through the hole in the ceiling and saw the bloom almost directly above them.

*It's pulling from me. I'm sorry, I can't stop it please please please it hurts it's hurting me make it all* end!

Hel's cry made Jamirh stagger back and cover his ears, but it wasn't a real sound, it was in his head. Mercifully it faded after a few moments.

"Reality is warping!" Takeshi shouted. "This isn't the real battle. He's an obstacle; we don't need to kill him, we need to get past him!"

The dust began to settle.

The array was complete.

"How did he finish–" Mara was cut off by the ground beginning to shake. A green shield snapped up around them.

*Oh yeah. That'll be a demon.*

"For the love of– do you have any tips?" Jamirh asked as the entire right side of the building began to twist in a way that was definitely not possible–

And then it was gone, replaced by a giant hole to the outside. A forty-foot-tall creature with dark-blue skin, black horns that looked like they were made of hair, and pitch-black eyes leaned in.

*That looks way worse than the version I fought, actually. Good thing we have a bunch of people here with us.*

*Ebryn! Focus!*

*Sorry!*

Jitsu howled in rage and threw herself at the demon. Takeshi was right behind her, lightning crackling over both their forms as they leapt onto it. Mara jumped up through the hole onto the roof. Ander stood in front of Siva, who closed her eyes and began to chant, embers of fire beginning to form around her. Spears of water rained down on it, and it recoiled in pain, shrieking.

At least they could hurt that one.

There was a lot more room in the hallway now. He could just barely make out Jeri's crumpled form behind the wizard, but Daemorn only seemed interested in Jamirh, still looking at him with that manic grin, unconcerned that the demon was getting injured.

He looked down at his arm. "Hey, you want to kill him one more time?"

*Truly a dream come true.*

*Oh, for the love of... yeah. Okay. We'll try not to let you get extra crispy.*

Takeshi had said not to get too close to these corrupted Abominations, but Jamirh had a feeling this was only going to end one way.

He let his inherent have what it wanted.

He threw himself at the wizard with a barrage of fast blows, which were answered by rapid swipes of magic. Jamirh stepped back, then kicked off the still-intact wall to the left, flipping over the wizard's head and stabbing down.

Daemorn let the blade pin him to the ground as his head twisted around, still grinning up at Jamirh.

"Yeah, we're done with that," he muttered, slicing his hand along the blade, reopening the wounds–

Fire magic *erupted* around them.

When the flames finally died down, Daemorn finally stopped screaming, body dissolving into dust.

# Chapter Twenty-Seven

Takeshi could *feel* Hades' fractured attention along with her pain and her determination. She was still trying to keep it from them, but with so much of her now present on the physical plane, she wasn't succeeding. He could feel the magic of the Truth Seekers, trying to keep the bloom contained, and he realized they weren't going to be able to hold it much longer. All magic was taking so much more energy to cast, like a portion of the power was going somewhere else. He'd been using his *crystallus* liberally, but it wasn't endless. Soon they'd all be down to the dregs of their reserves.

And the World Sound was all but screaming in discordant cacophony.

It was making it hard to focus on the undead wizard keeping them from their goal, though Takeshi almost felt a sense of relief when the demon was summoned – now he could *move*.

Jitsu agreed, annoyed she couldn't help with the dead guy. The Abomination was too close to the surface. But she could bite that thing!

He cast a web of lightning over her to give her a boost – he found himself annoyed when it jumped over to him as well, the magic acting outside of the normal limits due to the bloom – and they attacked together, jumping onto the thing's shoulder as it leaned forward towards the building. It didn't like that, trying to bat them off, but Mara's water spears rained down on it, allowing Jitsu and Takeshi to electrocute it. It shrieked, and the World Sound shrieked with it.

*:Keep it distracted; I'm going to hit it with a fire storm. Be prepared to move off it when I say!:* came Siva's mental voice.

*:Got it,:* Takeshi replied shortly, echoed by the others. Distract it? He could do that.

Another bolt of lightning high above caught his eye, and he perked up. He could use that – both to replenish his energy and maybe...

Hm.

If ever there was a time for armor, it was now. The armor had proved more difficult than the weapon, but if he could utilize the power of the strike to help him reform the crystal...

He scanned around for the others. Mara had gone up to the roof. Perfect. "Jitsu, retreat to Mara for a minute!" He'd never forgive himself if he hit her, and he wasn't completely sure how explosive what he had in mind would be.

Ander had said soulforging was just sort of willing things after all, hadn't he?

Magic is life. Magic is will. Magic is belief.

Maybe he didn't have to wait for the lightning strike? It was connected to the World Sound, and maybe if he could manipulate that—

Hades' attention swung in his direction.

Jitsu took one last bite and jumped clear as it swung at her again.

Takeshi jumped *up* as it turned its attention towards him, returning his katana to its smaller crystal form and holding it above his head. He could feel himself hang in the air, and called out to the World Sound with everything he had in him: "Lightning—"

Instantly it struck.

His crystal shattered, and, almost as if in slow motion, he could see all the threads of himself connecting the pieces. He could manipulate them that way, reform them as he wished. He pulled on the strings, asking for protection as he envisioned what he wanted—

—and he landed back on the demon's head, armor firmly in place in the form of an asymmetric dark-blue-and-black leather coat, long on one side and short on the other, with a high collar obscuring the bottom half of his face.

He called out to his soul crystal again and it materialized another part of itself into his hand in the form of the Lady's glaive, and he reached out to the lightning again, calling it to the weapon with an array meant to attract it.

A pillar of lightning engulfed them.

The demon screamed.

Takeshi felt stronger than he had in days, the lightning's power coursing through him, and he stabbed at the demon, over and over, staying out of its reach as it tried to grab him. He fed lightning into the wounds, causing it to screech again. Jitsu rejoined him, and Mara was doing something with water and the thing's feet, and then–

The demon was dissolving into dust.

*:Jamirh killed the wizard!:* Siva called.

Excellent, because if anything, the World Sound and Hades felt like they were getting worse. Takeshi could feel it in his soul. He managed to jump off an arm before it disappeared to land back in the third-floor hallway, then bolted for the still-intact corner of the building with a door labeled "4C."

He barreled through to an explosion of violet crystal, centering around the table in the middle of the room. An Avari with long white hair, partially shaved on one side, lay on the table. He was missing his right arm, and a metal plate with alchemical symbols had been fused to the side of his face. He was breathing in labored gasps, and there were cuts and incisions all over his body.

The death magic was so thick in the room that Takeshi was struggling to breathe himself. Death magic... and something else.

The bloom was directly overhead.

It sounded like Hades was crying.

Jamirh was right behind him, and he almost crashed into Takeshi when he stopped short. "Gren?" Jamirh called, horror in his voice.

The Avari stared up at the bloom above them.

"Gren?" Takeshi called softly, moving farther into the room so the others could follow. "Can you hear me?"

The head slowly turned in their direction. "She was... right. You... did come."

Takeshi frowned. "Can you hear her?"

Gren blinked slowly. "Just... a little. She... she promised to stay."

Jamirh turned to Takeshi. "How do we separate them from the Abomination?"

Takeshi looked over his shoulder to the other priests.

Ander stepped forward, but his expression was grim. He held up a hand over Gren's body, but the glyphs sparked into existence and then immediately faded away. "We can't cast magic," he said grimly. "Even without direct contact, the Abomination is consuming it. This is unfettered in a way the other bionics weren't."

"Because of the connection to Hades?" Siva asked.

Ander looked back down at Gren. "I don't know. Maybe."

Takeshi could almost see the World Sound buzzing around the Avari on the table. Maybe... He reached out mentally, trying to soothe it. He wished he dared try to sing to give it something else to resonate to other than the Abomination's discord, but this was the best he could do for now.

"She says you need to stop." Red eyes were staring directly at Takeshi.

He blinked, confused. "I'm not doing anything?"

"I... don't understand it either." He wheezed. "I'm sorry."

"If we can't use magic, how do we stop it?" Jeri wondered. "Forgive me for suggesting this, but what if we kill Gren? Would that break the link?"

Jamirh whipped around to her, eyes wide.

Takeshi frowned, still trying to feel the World Sound and what it was doing. Somehow he was sure that was the key. If he could figure that out...

*Please, stop.*

"It might," Siva agreed, voice grim. "I'm not sure what else we could try at this point. Something must be done."

"Might even be kind," Mara added softly.

Takeshi reached out mentally to Ander. *:If we could free him, could you save him?:*

*:It is hard to tell, since I can't cast a diagnostic,:* the other priest admitted. *:From a purely visual check, it would be touch and go. There's a lot of trauma. If I could stabilize him here, and get him back to Tarvishte and the facilities and other healers there? His chances of survival would be fairly good, though I'm not sure at what quality of life. It depends on what, if anything, was done internally, and I can't tell at the moment.:*

Jamirh was arguing with the others, but Takeshi was still studying the World Sound. Ander thought there was a chance for Gren to live, and honestly...

*Go no further.*

He walked over to stand next to Ander, studying the aberrant power visible in the air, sickly red and black still consuming the violet above them.

The Avari just stared at them dully, silent except for his labored breathing, not trying to sway them one way or the other.

"It's not fair!" Jamirh exclaimed, throwing his hands in the air. "We've come this far. We should be able to save them both!"

Jamirh was right. It wasn't fair.

*Life's not fair.*

No, it wasn't. But they were priests of the goddess of death. If life couldn't be fair, then maybe death could. Takeshi's eyes narrowed as he began to tap a rhythm on the table with his fingers. Just a little one, something to hold it back, give them a little more time to work out the puzzle.

*You are too close.*

Takeshi frowned. Something was whispering in the wind, but the World Sound was too loud for him to hear it clearly.

"Gren, does the Lady know how we should break the link between you both and the Abomination?" Mara asked gently.

A slow blink. "She's... not sure. It hurts. So... so much. Hard to think."

The blue-haired Avari joined them at the table, but was careful not to touch. "I know it's hard, but try. We need Her help. She needs to tell us what to do."

Ander pressed his lips together and tried to cast again, but the array just flickered and died.

Takeshi tilted his head. There was something about how the World Sound had reacted when Ander tried to cast.

Was the World Sound just another manifestation of life? Of magic? Were spells just a way to manipulate it to create different effects?

He shook his head, trying to refocus. Without magic, without killing Gren, what else was there?

Except... the World Sound *was* there. And they were able to exist in proximity, though touching it might spread it. While some magic was being consumed, not all of it was. In fact, aside from the Lady, it seemed like only *spells* were being consumed. The crystals around them were made of magic, and they were being ignored, even if only temporarily.

So could he manipulate the magic without casting a spell, without glyphs?

Magic is life. Magic is will. Magic is belief.

*No!*

He would have to be a Living Will to do that, and he wasn't one. He'd always needed the glyphs and the bridging lines, the patterns, the structures of magic.

But he hadn't done that earlier, had he? When he'd called the lightning? Instead he had sort of manipulated the World Sound to get the timing correct...

He reached out mentally to the World Sound, coaxing, trying to convince it to do what he wanted.

Nothing.

But... if it was the same as with his soul crystal, then maybe...

...just...

...*will.*

Sever.

The World Sound responded instantly, a blade of life and magic and the connections between people, and *cut.*

Takeshi felt sick as the Abomination screamed through the World Sound, one last gasp as it tried to hold on, but Takeshi denied it, willing it out of existence, even as he was struck by a terrible wave of loneliness from it. He felt sick because he was connected to the World Sound and so he *knew.* He knew he wasn't special. He understood, completely and totally, that this was not something unique.

This was just something he could do by virtue of being alive.

Even as he thought it, the World Sound seemed to hum in agreement, beginning to calm in the wake of Abomination.

But that would mean...

...*everything* was a lie.

And all Takeshi could feel was horror, rising, overwhelming horror—

"Beloved."

No. No, he refused to acknowledge her. How could he?

"I'm sorry. I tried to stop you. Mortals are not meant to know. Not truly, not like you've realized."

He could just... *not*, he supposed. Stay here, wherever here was. Shut it all out. The truth was terrifying and he wanted nothing to do with it.

"You are all so very good at lying to yourselves. And I am glad for it. This is not something you should bear."

If all living things were magic and the gods were magic and all the rules weren't rules, then what was the difference between a mortal and a god?

There wasn't one. Not a functional one, anyway.

"You aren't the first to realize the Truth."

How many of the gods were mortals once?

"None of the ones you know. Those who have ascended in the past have all fallen. The pain you currently bear... it was too much for them, in time. They faded. So... if there is any comfort at all, that is a difference."

With this knowledge... I do not want to be a god. I am me! I just want to be *me*! I can feel myself slipping away and I don't know how to stop it and I am afraid. Lady—!

"I know. The knowledge is a terrible burden. It is why we cannot speak this truth. It is ours alone to bear. But if you know it…" A pause. "Eventually, you will become like us."

But then wouldn't every Living Will eventually become a god?

Thinking back, realizing, grasping at anything to challenge the truth—

Was Jak a Living Will? He was not a god.

"Jak is not exactly the same, though by your definition he would be called a Living Will. He came from a world without known magic, had no magic of his own. For him, there were never any rules at all. When I explained the rules to him, he just decided they didn't apply to him because of the cataclysm he had lived through and the world he had left behind – but he still believed in their *existence*. The mental leap was different. But you were born into a world that… had an understood order. The rules as you know them were bred into you."

But they are a lie!

"Yes. Therein lies the disparity. For you, the world must have rules. But you have just learned there aren't any. So few mortals reach the fulcrum you are balanced on. Even to know something is not the same as believing. And believing is not the same as understanding. And understanding… is not the same as intrinsically accepting."

I don't want to know that! It hurts! It hurts like… like the Abomination… Loneliness. The Abomination felt lonely, in those last few seconds, before I forced it back.

A sigh. "Yes. You know the story of the beginning? Before everything, the first beginning?"

He tried to think. Tadurin came first, because he is life…

"Yes. And for those first few precious seconds, when he came into being, he was alone. And he never should have been. It is counter to his nature. He could not reconcile it, and it enraged him. I came into existence and realized myself just seconds after, but... he has never forgiven me for those first few seconds of loneliness."

I don't understand. How is that your fault?

"It is not. But that is not how he perceives it, and as the god of creation, it is his perception that matters. And because he is what he is, that wound, that loneliness took form, twisted with his rage at being left alone. And it tries to consume that which it feels was denied it in the beginning."

But... you said Tadurin fears it?

"He does. It would consume him as well, if it grabbed hold. Rage and fear and loneliness can do that."

Is it gone? Did I manage that, at least?

"For now. But the wound is still there. As long as he cannot forgive... eventually, Abomination will return, though it will be a long while, as your kind measure things." A pause. "I have always held out hope that one day he might."

My kind? There is no "my kind"! We are all the same! Every living being has this potential! Why why why–

"Shhh. I know. I know it hurts. I can... shield this knowledge from you. I cannot undo what has been done – you are a Living Will – but I can protect you from the knowledge of what that means. You do not have to go further."

I will remain mortal? Remain myself?

"You will not become divine. Shelter in my divinity, and I can spare you the rest of it. I would not have you fall like the others who have tried."

I don't understand. How...?

"I will make it so you can lie to yourself again, just a little. You are a very powerful bard, one in a thousand generations. It allowed you to become a Living Will. You would be an exception to the rules, which would still exist."

I... could still use the rules?

"Yes."

Shelter in your divinity... I would be tied to you forever.

A pause. "Yes."

Then I am yours. Take it, destroy it, shield it, drown it out, whatever you have to do. Keep me from remembering! I am me! I choose to remain me!

"I understand, beloved. I am death, and so I am order. Let order be what remains."

"Takeshi?"

He blinked, trying to figure out what had just happened. What had he just been thinking? He'd... somehow manipulated the World Sound to do... what?

"Takeshi!"

Siva was shaking him, he realized. That was strange. Why was she doing that?

"Takeshi!"

A sharp pain blossomed above his ankle.

"Siva?" he managed, realizing just how out of sorts he felt. At least she stopped shaking him when he responded. Shit, what had he done? He looked down at his leg. "Jitsu?"

The warg eyed him seriously, then let go, licking the wounds in apology. Whatever he had just done, she didn't like. He should not do that again.

*:You severed the connection between the Abomination and this plane, and then burnt it out. You saved Gren, and me, and all of existence,:* Hades explained gently.

He was surprised at how relieved he felt at hearing Her voice again. "Oh." That was good. "How did I do that, exactly?"

"Here, Siva–" Ander came up from behind her and took Takeshi's arm, guiding him over to a protrusion of crystal and making him sit on it. "Give him a second. Mara, if we could have some water?"

*:I know you didn't really enjoy finding out you had an inherent you were unaware of, but... well... you are a very, very powerful bard, it turns out.:*

"Did I sing at it?" If so, he was impossibly grateful he didn't remember.

Jitsu pressed herself against him. For once, he had not made any noise.

"No," Siva said gently as Mara handed him a water bottle. "You became a Living Will."

He stared. "I *what*?"

"You willed the Abomination out of existence." Mara's voice was a little awed. "It was kind of amazing, actually."

"Then you kinda went comatose, which was less amazing," Jamirh piped in. "Are you okay?"

"I... think so?" He tried to remember. He had been trying to manipulate the World Sound, hadn't he? And then... he felt Hades helpfully nudge him. Right, he had just willed the World Sound to sever the connection, and it had obeyed. And then he had forced the Abomination back, somehow? Had denied it existence? That part felt a little fuzzy. "Did I get all of it?" There had been a lot of corruption running around at the end there.

*:You did. The world is clear of Abomination. This cycle has come to an end.:*

"Lady... are you okay?" It had been eating Her, after all.

*:I will recover. It is in the nature of gods to do so, and I am not the first of my siblings to suffer thusly.:*

He looked over at the table, where Gren was now practically covered in glowing green glyphs. "And Gren?"

"We should really get him back to Tarvishte as soon as possible, but he was fighting hard to cling to life," Ander explained. "I think his prospects are good, all things considered."

Takeshi looked around at the destroyed building. Jitsu was pressed up against him. Siva was sitting next to him on the other side, a hand on his shoulder, eyes calm. Mara was bouncing on the balls of her feet, somehow still energetic enough to do so despite the night they had just had. Ander was completely focused on Gren. Jeri was leaning against the doorframe, eyeing the lightening sky. Jamirh was standing with his arms folded, looking at Takeshi with a mix of relief and concern. Their eyes met.

Jamirh nodded. "We did it."

Takeshi nodded back. "Yes, we did."

He glanced through the ruined side of the building. The sunrise was just visible over the horizon.

"Okay, then. Let's go home."

# Epilogue

Sherri stood respectfully in full dress uniform next to her sister in front of the pyre. The others stood around in a large circle, watching the flames consume their beloved queen.

Sefera had held out long enough for them to come out on the other side of the vision of magic being consumed. She had held out long enough for them to be free. But she had been so very tired in the end, and had passed quietly in the night a few days after Sherri and Madine had returned from Lyndiniam.

Now they honored her sacrifice, and the sacrifices of the Seekers that had allowed her to live for so long.

Sherri had told herself she wouldn't cry, but she found herself blinking back tears anyway.

Madine shifted ever so slightly. "Do not be sad. She is forever a part of the egregore. Death cannot change that."

"I know," she whispered back. "It's still sad. It's not the same thing."

Her sister inclined her head. "It is not," she conceded.

She watched the flames climb higher. "At least Belian is dead."

"Another Emperor in the ground," Madine agreed. "Though given what he had become it is very unlikely he would have continued to rule much of anything."

"A fitting end, perhaps," Sherri said with grim satisfaction.

"Now, Sherri," Madine said, a hint of teasing entering her voice. "His actions were directly responsible for Hades finding the remaining corruption. We should be thanking him."

She scrunched her nose up in disgust. "Absolutely not."

Madine made a soft, amused hum.

Sherri glanced at her sister out of the corner of her eye. With Sefera's death, Madine had been acting more... individual. She wondered if it was a result of becoming queen of the egregore, or if now that they were free of the Empire all Seekers would start acting that way.

"Besides, another of the dukes will likely try their hand at it, though with Belian's death everything seems to be splintering," Sherri mused. "It will be nearly impossible for the Empire to remain what it was now."

Madine nodded. "And that's not even considering the magic."

The magic. Right.

Because a god appearing above a national capital was impossible to miss.

They stood in silence until the corpse had burnt to ash.

As one, the Seekers turned and bowed to Madine, acknowledging a new queen, before breaking off to each go their own way.

Sherri wasn't sure she understood. If they were all of one mind, why the ceremony? A holdover from what they used to be?

"What will we do now? I assume you'll send me back to Romanii to continue negotiations with Perra and Axtion?"

"That would be appreciated. They have reported that despite their best efforts, the people of Romanii are still uncomfortable around them. They would appreciate having you as a buffer." A pause. "They have also reported that Gren is recovering there."

Sherri perked up. She was glad to hear of the Avari's survival. They had managed to rescue a few of his people from prison in the aftermath of the bloom, and they were living with the Seekers for now. She could offer to bring letters for them, or perhaps even escort them to Tarvishte if the Vampire King was agreeable. "That is excellent news. And what about Muriz?"

Madine was quiet for several minutes. Sherri thought she wouldn't answer, but finally, a small smirk formed on her sister's face.

"Whatever we want."

*:There is good to come of this. People* believe *again, even if it is... spiked pretty heavily with fear. Once again the cycle turns. My siblings and I are already stronger than we have been in centuries.:*

Ander snorted. "Congratulations."

Hades sniffed. *:No need to be rude about it.:*

Yes, the gods were gaining strength for the first time in centuries. What would change because of it? How would magic react?

He remembered Takeshi's soul crystal shattering—

*He was horrified. "That is absolutely not how soulforging works. A crystal can't just shatter–"*

*Jamirh frowned. "Didn't Jeri's weapons shatter at Tilden?"*

*"To return to her; it's not the same thing! It just looks like it breaks when it returns to the host, it doesn't literally break. What he just did—"*

*"You can never tell him that, Ander," Siva interrupted seriously. "If he ever doubts... it does not matter. He has done it. That is all there is to it."*

*"But that's not–"*

*"Ander." Siva's voice was sharp, the embers in the air still around her. "It is done."*

But it wasn't so easy to forget such a thing. A complete breaking of the rules as they knew them.

*:Ander...:*

*:I know, I know.:* He would never purposefully endanger the other priest. He would never risk damaging Takeshi's belief in magic that way, could never bring himself to risk the other priest's ability to cast. Magic was will, magic was belief. That belief could not be damaged.

Hades hummed, but she didn't disagree.

Maybe he needed another project.

He shook his head and knocked on the hospital door.

"Come in."

Gren was lying in the bed, swathed with bandages and blankets, speaking to Marcus. The Avari perked up. "Hey, Ander!"

He nodded to Marcus before turning to their patient. "Good morning, Gren. How are you feeling today?" He eyed the Avari critically, but much of his color had returned over the past week.

Ander had been able to remove the plate from his face, but the skin was disfigured and there would be scars in the shapes of the alchemical symbols around his right eye for the rest of his life. He'd lost some vision on the right side, and his right arm was gone, but luckily that had been the worst of it. The internal damage had been trivial to fix once Ander had been able to bring him here.

"Really good! But Marcus was telling me that's probably the drugs. In which case, holy shit, y'all have some amazing drugs." His ears twitched up.

Ander glanced at Marcus, eyebrows raised, but the Vampire just gave a small shrug. He repressed a sigh. "The drugs are definitely helping, but if something feels wrong you still have to let us know," he repeated, aiming for patience. Sometimes it felt like his words went in one pointed ear and out the other.

The Avari nodded. "Hey, would it be possible to get some paper and a pen in here or something? Now that I'm awake a lot more, it's very boring in here, even with visitors."

"Of course." Ander opened a cabinet and pulled out a sheaf of paper and a pen that he usually kept for notes. That was very relatable. "You can use these for now, but we can also get you a proper notebook if you'd prefer."

"Oh, that would be great, thanks! I need to start figuring out writing with my left hand so I can design a replacement arm. I've already had a bunch of ideas but I keep forgetting them because I can't write them down." He was practically bouncing in place.

Ander raised an eyebrow at the energy, but he could sympathize with that, too. "We have prosthetic arms for you as well. We just need to wait for the site to heal first."

"Aw, thanks! You guys are really great! Jamirh was right!" The Avari grinned. "But I really like designing my own stuff."

"Then use a standard one until you can make your own," Marcus suggested. "You will want to have a baseline of what it should feel like. And if you would like help, I am sure there are craftsmen here in the city who would be interested in such a project. Ander is probably one of them."

Gren's eyes went wide. "Wow! A doctor and an engineer?"

"I like to tinker," he clarified. "I'm more of a scientist than a–"

"A *scientist*! Woah, that's cool too!"

Ander checked his chart. Yes, the drug amounts were correct. "Indeed. Very... cool. Do you have any questions for me today?"

Gren shook his head enthusiastically, then winced. "Ow. Forgot I shouldn't do that."

"Please do focus on resting," he suggested, resigned to the fact that "rest" was not in this patient's vocabulary. He was obligated to say it anyway. "Breakfast will also be brought by soon. Remember to eat as much of it as you can. You need the calories."

"You got it, boss!" came the cheerful reply.

He left with a wave, Marcus following close behind him. "He's doing very well," the Vampire said.

Ander nodded. "The Lady said he was very resilient, and She was correct. I don't know if he would have been able to survive otherwise." He turned and started to head back towards his lab at the Temple. There was another part of the avatar he would need to adjust shortly.

"Yes, so, I have been meaning to ask."

He eyed Marcus suspiciously. That sounded odd. "What?"

"Have you asked Takeshi yet?"

Ander wanted to throw up his arms in exasperation. He should have known he'd regret confiding in Marcus after they'd returned from Lyndiniam. "*No.* We've both been ridiculously busy. There hasn't been time–"

"Ander! You cannot wait until the opportunity presents itself; you need to make the opportunity!" Marcus was exasperated.

"I cannot add hours into the day," he protested stubbornly.

"Just ask him to lunch or something! Low commitment. It would not even have to technically be during normal lunch hours; I know when you eat."

Ander walked faster. Marcus disappointingly kept pace.

*:I'm so glad you have a friend,:* Hades chirped.

*:Shut up.:* She agreed with Marcus and Ander knew it.

But how was he just supposed to ask something like that? He'd never had to really do anything with Fredrik; Fredrik – and then later Ida – had just sort of always been there. Had always taken the lead, had decided what they would do as either couples or a group. Ander had liked that. It meant he didn't make any mistakes.

Hades hummed gently in the back of his mind.

He sighed. That meant that probably was itself a mistake. Damn. "If I say I'll think about it, will you go back to doing whatever it is you are supposed to be doing today?"

Marcus nodded. "Sure."

"Great. I will consider asking Takeshi to have lunch together."

The Vampire's eyes narrowed. "In a potentially romantic capacity."

"*Yes* in a potentially romantic capacity." He'd been so close.

"Hm. Good enough for now. But this is not the last time we are having this conversation!" Marcus assured him as he turned and headed back to the hospital. "Have a good day, Ander!"

He gave a tired wave, finishing the rest of his walk in blissful silence. He needed more coffee and it wasn't even nine in the morning.

He entered the Temple, stepping around two wargs that were really lying too close to the front stairs, and was surprised to see Jamirh standing in the hallway next to his lab. "Jamirh."

"Hey, Ander. Do you have a minute?" The Avari's ears twitched. "I have a really weird question."

Off to a good start. "Come in," he said, opening the door and gesturing. "But if it's about Gren, he's been doing very well."

"Oh, that's great! I was planning on going to see him later today. But no, I had a different... uh... request, I suppose." The Avari looked around at the beakers full of various bubbling liquids. "Also, what is all this?"

"I have been able to resume work on the avatar. Hopefully it will be done within the decade."

"Oh. That's good." Despite his words, the Avari was squinting at one of Ander's set ups. Then he shook his head and turned around. "You still have the microchip remains, right?"

Ander blinked. "Yes, I do."

Jamirh looked down at the floor, biting his lip for a moment before straightening up and looking Ander in the eye. "Could I have them?"

"Hm." Ander leaned against the table, folding his arms. "What would you do with them?"

Jamirh shrugged. "It's for a secret project I'm working on with Hel."

Ander's eyebrows raised, but the Lady made a soft sound of agreement.

Interesting.

"Well, then, I suppose I don't have any reason to stand in your way." He turned and opened a small drawer in one of his organizers, pulling out the little bag with the broken components in it. "Here it is."

Jamirh took it, looking down at it seriously for a long moment. Then he looked up. "Thanks, Ander! I'm sure she'll tell you when it's done."

"Okay." He felt her amused agreement. *:Do I want to know?:*

He got the sensation of a shrug. *:Maybe.:*

Right.

"Oh, hey! Two people I wanted to see in one place!"

Mara was sticking her head into the lab. "By all means, come the rest of the way in," he said dryly. Then his heart sank a little at the sight of the bag she had with her. "Oh. Are you leaving?"

She nodded. "Yeah. I've been away from Kaikani for too long, really. And since everything's been stable here, it's time for me to head out. Hugs?"

Jamirh smiled and nodded, wrapping his arms around her. "Thanks for everything, Mara. Really. I'd like to meet Kaikani one day; she sounds like a riot."

She squeezed him back. "If you find yourself in the Emerald Shore, definitely look around for us. We'll be wherever the necromancy is worst." Then she turned to Ander. "I'm sorry I didn't have a new fish for you this visit. I'll bring two next time to make up for it!"

"We had other things to be concerned with," he acknowledged, holding out an arm for her and letting her nestle in. "Bring Kaikani next time; I haven't met her either."

"Oh, will do! She'd *love* to meet you." Mara giggled. He felt her hold him just a little tighter for another moment, then she let go. "Alrighty then, see y'all around!" She whirled around, and then she was gone.

"Is Siva going too?" Jamirh asked.

Ander shook his head. "No, she's decided to stay for a while longer to help Takeshi get officially settled in."

"That must be nice, since Jak is still a statue."

Ander snorted. "Jak wouldn't have stuck around anyway. If he's aware at all in there, he's upset he has to stay in one place. And possibly extra upset that that place is here."

Jamirh laughed. "Ah, I get it. All right then, Ander. See you later!"

Ander inclined his head as Jamirh darted out. A little timer went off on his desk.

As he turned around to deal with it, he thought that maybe asking Takeshi to lunch wasn't such a bad idea.

Takeshi held his arms out patiently as Siva walked around him in a slow circle, inspecting his armor. He kept his eyes on Ander's fish tank. It was strangely enthralling.

"What an interesting design," she observed. "What did you pattern it after?"

He shrugged a shoulder. "It felt right at the time?"

Jitsu snorted from where she lay at the base of the counter. That was the only proper way to do it.

Siva nodded definitively. "Then it is good. And how do you feel, having made your decision?"

He dropped his arms and let his armor fade. "Still a little surreal, but... it feels like the right choice."

Having to live without Hades for even that brief amount of time had helped put things in perspective. He had missed Hades' presence, had felt incomplete without Her. And really, Ander was right – he was already acting like a priest anyway, at least insomuch as any of the priests acted like priests.

*:I love you. I will never leave you.:*

He felt Her give him a hug, and he sent Her a mental hug back, much to Her delight. His lips twitched.

Siva gracefully sank into one of the chairs. "And have you put some thought into what it is you are going to do? I know that was one of your primary concerns."

He took a seat on one of the couches. "For one, Ander handed over warg duties to me, and I should probably start taking those seriously. I helped them organize the plowing of snow once." And really, that day had felt a little more like they were wrangling him, though Jitsu disagreed. "For two, I need to get a handle on my Voice magic, so I'll be devoting a serious amount of time to studying under Caelessa. For three, I can help Ander with any of the maintenance of the Temple or performance of any rituals or festivals. With two of us those things should be easier. And for four... I thought I might offer lessons in weapons work."

Her eyebrows rose. "I'm certain that would be popular. You are already well-admired for your skill; members of the Black Watch will probably line up down the street."

"Ah, well..." He paused, uncertain, but Hades gave him a little gentle nudge. "While I'm not opposed to that, I thought I could teach children." He had enjoyed teaching the shinobi-in-training for the brief period of time he had been able to before he'd risen beyond that in rank. And he had enjoyed teaching Jamirh. He knew the citizens of Tarvishte were not as extreme with training their children as shinobi were, but maybe that would be good for him, too.

Jitsu wagged her tail in agreement. She would also love helping to train pups!

"Oh, I see." Siva tilted her head to the side. "I'm not actually sure who you would speak to in that case, but Primrose would know. That is a very kind idea."

He inclined his head. "I will check with her, then."

"And I also heard that you will be joining us here, in the Temple?"

He glanced over at Jitsu, who was studiously not looking at him. "Where would you have heard that, I wonder?"

Siva smiled. "Warg grapevine. Once you know, you know. If it helps, there are very few two-feet who are part of it."

What a terrifying thought, but then again, what else did wargs do with their time besides gossip? "But yes, I thought that since I was officially accepting a position as a priest of Hades, I should move in here permanently."

Though it already felt quieter since Mara had left the day before. And he'd caught Ander staring forlornly at his fish tank no less than five times last night. Not that Ander would describe it that way, but Takeshi would.

There was a knock on the door. Jitsu's head shot up and her tail began to wag. *Helpful-red two-foot!*

"Come in, Jamirh," Takeshi called.

The Avari slid in, patting Jitsu's head on the way by. "Sorry to interrupt, but, uh, Takeshi, do you have a few minutes?"

Siva stood. "You may speak here. It is almost lunch time, and Ander needs to be reminded that I have not forgotten about him. Good day, Jamirh. Takeshi, I will see you at dinner." The Aradian swept from the room.

Takeshi gestured to the couch across from him. "What can I help you with?"

Jamirh sat gingerly on the edge. "Ah, well... hm. This is harder than I thought it would be."

Takeshi waited.

"Well, you know how the *Sea Spirit* is leaving tomorrow?" Jamirh asked.

Oh. "You are leaving with them." He didn't bother making it a question.

Jamirh blinked in surprise. "How did you know?"

Takeshi hummed thoughtfully. "You've been spending a lot of time with the pirates, asking a lot of questions. It makes sense." He paused. "So will Jamirh disappear, the way Ebryn did?"

"Absolutely not." The answer was swift and decisive. "Tarvishte... I want Tarvishte to remain my home. But I want to go out there and see things, do things. Things I couldn't even imagine while living in Lyndiniam. You know?"

Takeshi smiled. "I think I do. What time is the *Sea Spirit* leaving tomorrow?"

"Dawn." The Avari looked down.

"Then there is no need to say goodbye now," Takeshi declared cheerfully. "I will be present to see you off."

Jamirh's ears perked up. "Really?"

Takeshi mentally began forming a list of people who would also wish to say goodbye. "Yes, absolutely. Have you already packed?"

"Mostly." He laid a hand on the katana on his belt. "Don't worry, I'll take good care of her."

Takeshi's eyebrows rose. "While the blade is now named Hotaru, it is still just a sword."

Jamirh's grip on the hilt tightened. "She means more to me than the Crystal Light Blade ever did. Thank you, Takeshi."

He was touched. "You are very, very welcome. Good luck out there, Jamirh, wherever your journey takes you. Remember to take care of yourself. And we'll be here when you get back."

Jamirh's eyes welled up. "Thank you."

Jitsu suddenly sprang to her feet. Everyone needed to go outside. Right now. In front of the Temple.

Takeshi looked at her with concern. "We do?"

Jamirh wiped at his eyes. "What's happening?"

Jitsu came around Takeshi and *pushed*, forcing him out of his seat. Outside. Now. She was not asking.

"Apparently we are going outside," he informed the Avari. "No, I don't know why."

"Oh, uh, okay. Should I...?"

Jitsu barked. *Everyone* outside. Now. Why weren't they listening to her?

Takeshi was beginning to feel alarm. "She wants everyone outside immediately." They both hurried down the stairs. "Jitsu, what's wrong?"

She didn't respond, following close behind.

Takeshi hit the bottom of the steps to the main floor and–

Outside! came the command before he could even think about doing anything else.

*:Just go outside,:* Hades said calmly.

Takeshi felt himself relax. If Hades was not concerned, then it probably wasn't a real emergency. He opened the front door of the Temple.

A large gold warg was sitting directly at the bottom of the steps, a... large ball of brown fluff in its mouth?

"Hello," Takeshi said mildly as Jitsu bounded past him. "Can I help you?"

The other warg snorted, giving a slight shake to the bundle in its mouth, which began to uncurl, revealing a black nose nestled among the fluff.

It is May, Jitsu informed him seriously.

"It is the first day of May, yes," he agreed slowly, going down the steps to take the... warg puppy? – from the warg. He realized abruptly that the wargs had all been missing because they'd been denning for pups. *That* was Jitsu's big secret? "Ah. I see."

Jamirh gasped.

Takeshi looked around.

There were balls of fluff *everywhere* in front of the Temple, tumbling over themselves or lying in groups or playing with each other. Takeshi had no idea how they could see; their fur completely obscured their eyes. The elders were lazing about, keeping an eye on the pups and breaking up any arguments.

Takeshi tried to figure out how many, but lost count after forty-three. He stared at Jitsu, realizing that as warg coordinator, this had just become his responsibility. "Please help."

She snorted. *Of course* she was going to help him. But weren't they cute? Helpful-red two-foot had been sad upstairs; Takeshi should give him a pup to hold. It was completely impossible to be sad while holding a warg pup. This was a proven fact.

"Here, hold this." Takeshi unceremoniously dumped it into Jamirh's arms, and was pleased when the Avari's face brightened.

Jitsu was smug. She was always right about these things.

"What's going on... oh. They've spawned again."

Takeshi looked over his shoulder to see Ander leaning on the doorframe. "So it seems."

The other priest snorted. "Are you pleased with your surprise?"

Mindful of the many wargs watching them, Takeshi said, "It is a joy to behold. They are all very cute." And they *were* cute; it was just that he was already imagining the kinds of chaos that could be caused by over forty warg puppies. The adults were bad enough.

Ander shot him a look that suggested he thought Takeshi might be crazy, but Jitsu grinned at him in triumph.

After another moment of watching the fluff balls, Ander cleared his throat. "Takeshi."

"Hm?"

"I was wondering... if you would be interested in having lunch with me tomorrow."

If Takeshi didn't know any better, he'd say Ander sounded nervous. Having lunch...? They often ate together; why...?

*Then* it hit Takeshi.

He considered the offer, turning to look at the other priest. "That doesn't break any rules?"

*:You think I have* rules *about that?:*

And that sounded like Hades just couldn't contain Herself anymore. "Never mind, the Lady answered that. Yes. I think I'd like that."

Ander blinked, and Takeshi wondered if the man had expected him to say yes. "Ah. Good. Tomorrow at two?"

Takeshi inclined his head and thought for just a moment of Hotaru. She'd hated that they couldn't live the way they wanted to, and would have been so happy for him. "Sure. It's a date."

"Excellent." Ander hesitated, as though he wasn't sure what came next. "I'll see you then." The man turned and fled back into the Temple. Takeshi could hear his lab door close.

He smiled, turning back around to see Jamirh on the ground playing with three of the pups. He watched for a few minutes before realizing he was humming to the World Sound again.

This time, he didn't stop himself.

It was the big day.

Jamirh woke early so he could take his time getting everything together. He didn't know when the next time he'd be back was, and he wanted to savor the experience.

Just as he was finishing up, there was a familiar knock on the door.

"Come in," he called.

Jeri let herself in. "I just wanted to make sure you had everything," she said, looking around.

He nodded. "Yeah. I think I'm all set."

"Was there anyone you couldn't find?"

He shook his head. "Nope. I managed to track everyone down. I said what I wanted to say."

If he was going to be the one leaving, then he'd be damned if he did it silently.

And it wasn't like it was forever. Caron had told him they intended to make Tarvishte a port they visited often, now that Mara had shown them how to navigate the magics that protected Romanii.

But it still felt like both an ending and a beginning.

She shifted her weight from foot to foot. "That is good. And Vlad told you about the room?"

"Yeah. He said it's mine. No matter how long I'm gone for, I'll have a place to come back to."

He had another key, now, hung on his necklace next to Aether's. He'd had that key for a while now, but Vlad had made it explicitly clear that it belonged to Jamirh – he wasn't just a guest. This place was his home.

Aether would have been over the moon. It was all they'd ever wanted, a safe place of their own.

And now he was leaving it for adventure and the unknown.

Aether would have liked that, too.

He checked himself in the mirror, only hesitating for a moment. It felt like he was carrying a little piece of everyone with him. The coat from Hel, the bracers and daggers from Jeri. The key from Vlad. Hotaru, Takeshi's sword he had enchanted with Ander for Jamirh. The spell crystal Jak had made him, just in case.

He wasn't going alone.

Ebryn and Ryn had been quiet, though the glow from his arm had faded completely after he'd toasted the undead Daemorn. But he knew they were there.

He looked at Jeri. There was a lot he could say, and a lot he probably should say. But for now... "Thank you." He wrapped his arms around her.

She held him tight. "I'll miss you. Come back soon, hm?"

They stayed like that for another moment. As they finally pulled away, he asked, "Are you going to go down to the dock?"

She nodded. "Of course! And I will be here when you get back. Whenever that is. Who knows, maybe I will have more of a real arm by then."

The corner of his mouth quirked up. "Aren't you going to be doing some sort of super-secret infiltration work in the Empire? That's what you did before we met, right?"

"Oh, that." She shrugged. "I have actually taken a permanent position here in Tarvishte training others for infiltration. So, no – I will be here when you return. It's a good thing, I promise!" she added quickly at seeing the expression on Jamirh's face. "This is a promotion. And it will allow me to see my Sire more, which is exciting."

"Your Sire? The one who turned you into a Vampire?" He'd never really thought about how Jeri had become a Vampire.

She smiled. "Yes. Mircalla. But that's a story for another day. For now, you've got a boat to catch."

The walk seemed so much shorter than he remembered it.

But he was stunned to realize just how many people were waiting.

The crew of the *Sea Spirit* he had expected – it was their boat, and they were leaving – and he had expected Takeshi, but...

Ander and Siva were with Takeshi, Jitsu a white ghost in the pre-dawn light beside them with a number of her brethren. Vlad was talking to Miravu, and Prim, Frir, and Elena were nearby, along with a number of the other Vampires he had often sparred with. Even Gren was there, seated in a wheelchair near Marcus with an infectious grin on his face.

He felt tears well up in his eyes.

"Come on," Jeri murmured softly. "Time to say goodbye."

After he'd made his way through the crowd, collecting well-wishes and goodbyes, he stepped onto the gangplank.

A hand thrust itself into his field of vision.

Smiling, he let Desha pull him up to where the rest of the crew was waiting.

"Ahoy, there!" Caron greeted him. "Ye ready t' sail th' seas unknown?"

He looked around. Marjori was on the upper deck; Benjen was next to her. Ashi was standing next to her husband. Don was by the entrance to the mess, and the sisters were on either side of him.

He swallowed hard. "You sure you don't mind the detour? I know it's way out of the way."

Caron laughed. "Not at all! It'll be an interesting li'l trip." He clapped Jamirh on the shoulder hard enough to make him stagger. "Stations!"

The rest of the crew scattered.

Jamirh turned around to see everyone still watching from the dock. He waved, and they waved back, shouts of good luck traveling on the morning breeze.

Hel bloomed into existence above her priests for just a moment, with a smile and a wave herself. She'd told him that because of the increase in faith since the incident in Lyndiniam, it would be easier for her to do for a while. Which was good; their plan relied on it.

Just before she disappeared, she put a hand over the right side of her chest.

He nodded, putting a hand over the matching pocket on his coat.

And then she was gone.

He closed his eyes. He'd see her one last time.

He had one last thing to do.

Caron's voice boomed out from the top deck. "*Sea Spirit* leaving dock!"

The ship lurched into motion.

Jamirh took one last look at his friends gathered on the dock below, burning it into his memory. Then he turned and joined the others.

*Two weeks later*

Jamirh tried not to tug on the collar of his coat nervously. Or touch his keys. He had to be impossibly confident for this.

He kind of needed to channel Ebryn, if he was being honest.

"Are you certain, Jamirh? It was our understanding that you disapprove of the name."

He looked up at Merin. The Truth Seeker had been stationed here in Ni Fon for a while, to Jamirh's knowledge, but Perra had affirmed they were happy to help with this. Which was good; while they assured him his current status as one of the heroes of the Battle of Lyndiniam garnered him a sort of diplomatic pull, he had needed them to set this up. Also to help him get out if this went south, which was very possible.

"Just this once, because this" – he touched his breast pocket – "is forbidden. It can never happen again." He steeled himself and looked her in the eye. Or where her eyes would be, if she wasn't wearing the blindfold. "Do you all understand me?"

She inclined her head. "We understand, Jamirh. And we are in complete agreement. We will be watchful." A pause. "They will see us now."

The great double doors opened, and Jamirh reminded himself that he was angry before storming into the throne room of Kobayashi Rikona, Merin and Valeth just a step behind.

The throne room was beautiful with understated elegance, pale-yellow hardwood floor inlaid with patterns of darker wood. The walls were covered with paintings of trees, birds forever in flight between their branches. Courtiers were sitting near the walls to either side of the center aisle, dressed in bright colors. In the center, set back from the others, sat Rikona herself on a gilded throne. Her posture was casual, as though this particular visitor did not warrant that much attention.

All Jamirh could think was that Vlad did it better.

"Jamirh Stormlight, reincarnation of Ebryn Stormlight, Hero of the Crystal Lights, slayer of demons and Abomination, liberator of Lyndiniam, savior of the Avari, god-chosen warrior, and former wielder of the Crystal Light Blade," Merin announced.

Takeshi had really done more of the liberating, but Jamirh would take it.

Rikona smiled. It was fake. "An impressive list of titles, Hero. We have heard of the recent incident in Lyndiniam, and the rumor that a god was–"

"I am here as an emissary for someone way above either of us." He cut her off, not interested in whatever she had to say. "Do you know what Abomination is?"

The courtiers around them stirred, and Rikona's smile faded a fraction. Her eyes drifted momentarily to the katana on his hip. "I have heard the word, but I am unsure of the context you are looking for."

"Abomination is a sin against life and magic," he announced. "It is a corruption of the world from the beginning of time. Once it gains a foothold in our world, it begins to consume, and very little can stop it." He paused for effect. "This was what attacked Lyndiniam."

Rikona's expression smoothed out. "I see. You wish to warn us about the dangers of–"

"I know what you did. And I know who you did it to."

The words dropped like stones into the silence of the throne room. Rikona's face went blank.

Slowly, he reached into his breast pocket and drew out the remains of the microchip. "This" – he tossed it on the floor in front of him – "is an expression of Abomination. Not the one that attacked Lyndiniam, but one a little closer to home, wouldn't you say?" He laid a hand on the katana's hilt purposefully.

Rikona was as still as a statue. "I'm afraid I don't know what you mean."

"I really don't care what you have to say to me, because I know the truth," Jamirh said, praying hard to Hel. "And whatever you tell these people, whatever you tell your citizens out there, whatever you tell yourself – know this. If this ever, *ever* gets made again here, this country too shall be razed to the ground."

With a shriek, Hel bloomed into existence above the remains of the microchip, wearing white robes in the style of Ni Fon. Jamirh could feel the effect of her power, but he'd felt it several times now, and it no longer affected him the same way.

The same could not be said for most of the other mortals in the throne room.

Her glaive materialized in her hands, point down, and with a flash of violet it collided with the remains on the floor–

–and then the throne room was normal again, no god in sight.

A scorch mark shaped like a nine-pointed star was all that remained where the microchip had been.

"This is your only warning," he said coolly. "I wouldn't bet on another one."

With that, he turned and strode out, Seekers falling into step behind him.

"Is that all, Jamirh?" Merin asked as they cleared the throne room.

Jamirh didn't stop; he wanted to be gone from this country yesterday. "That's it. Good luck to all of you. Especially now that I just did that."

An amused snort. "We wish the same to you. Farewell, Jamirh." They broke off from him.

He made it back to the *Sea Spirit* in record time. "Time to go, go, go!"

Salisha laughed. "We're just waiting on you!"

The ship lurched into motion.

Marjori looked down at him from a higher deck. "What did you do, exactly?"

"Threatened the Empress!" he called back.

She gave him a thumbs up.

Caron let out a booming laugh. "Now we're off t' th' Dead Seas! Let us see what fortune might find us there."


The End

Or is it?


After all


Nothing really ends


Does it?

In a garden that was not a garden, Hades folded herself into her usual spot. It was just on the edge of the space where they usually met, next to a tree formed of eddies of starlight. The others were grouped together, basking in their centers of power, the endless life and magic, possibility and chaos that this place consisted of.

She, too, had been born here, but she alone hated it and grieved the lack of that which made it less than the planes of mortal existence.

And some part of them hated her for her hate, and feared her for that which she could bring. Even if she never had, and even if she never would. Even if she was the only one who could defend them from the Other they feared.

She did not hate them in turn. They could only be what they were. She was older than all but one, and if they needed something to hate, better her than the mortals who used them. And they loved her, too. Nothing was ever an absolute.

The one older than her hated her for a different reason, but there was nothing to be done about that, either.

"Something needs to be done."

She remained silent as her siblings agreed with the eldest's understanding. Absently, she wondered why this was important now, when it had come and gone before. Then again, Tadurin had always had a better grasp of their shared domain of time. Perhaps there was something about the now that was special. Or maybe he was simply done tolerating it.

"But what do we do?" whispered Espa, unsettled air crackling with sparks.

"We bring it under control, assign it one of us," Tadurin affirmed.

Sounds of surprise from the others. Hades considered the tree of starlight, realizing where this was going.

"But it is not *of* us. It is too young," Selenae observed.

Firilae swirled around her sister in support. "Even if we were to split or recombine, none of us could assume dominion over it."

Tadurin agreed. "An Ascension is necessary."

A flurry of feelings, shock and displeasure foremost among them.

Hades did not wait for an invitation. "No," she said shortly, allowing it to echo with the Truth behind it. She would defend her priests' choices to the end of existence.

Not even Tadurin could challenge such a strong denial, and an Ascension from one of her priests would probably be a nightmare for him anyway. "Yet we must. Billions of them exist; there will be other suitable candidates among them."

An unsettled silence fell over them as they considered the possibility. It wasn't the first time an Ascension had been deemed necessary, but it always left a bad taste in Hades' mouth.

Chatori hummed. "Perhaps we will get lucky this time."

Hades went back to admiring the tree, even though it lacked the beauty of change. Chatori always hoped for luck. It was their nature. She would be content to no longer be part of this conversation. She might not hate her siblings, but she did dislike these meetings.

"Does it matter?" Kaldor's shadows seethed. "This... tech the mortals use. It has come and gone before."

A flash of fiery upset. "What are you suggesting?" Falare demanded.

"Only that–"

"Not necessarily," Tadurin soothed, cutting off Kaldor's poisonous words, even though Hades was certain he agreed with them. "And if it has come and gone before, and has returned now, then there is reason to believe it will cycle. This Ascended could become... truly one of us. The position is needed."

Hades did her brother a favor and did not reveal that he lied to their siblings. He had told them such before; they could believe it if they wished.

Still, she did wonder how he hoped to accomplish this. A god of technology? They would have to find a mortal who not only had the ability to Ascend, but somehow also was able to combine this with that which repelled them. That would not be an easy task.

But it had been voiced in the garden. The possibility *did* exist.

And... so, too, had his lie been voiced. That gave it the potential to become truth, no matter what Tadurin wanted.

"Sister?"

She turned her attention to the Nyphoren, whose fear and desire to speak to her ebbed and flowed like the tides. They clung to each other, and she felt them gather their courage.

"You owe us a favor. We choose now to reclaim it, in the form of an answer."

Surprise. Then she brought the entirety of her existence to bear against them, ignoring how they shrank from her. She would be sure of this. "You will answer this first, if you think I owe you – *did you know?*"

Silence in the garden.

After some time, Nyphora answered. "Not completely, not for sure. But there was something broken about him that reminded us of the others. We thought it was likely. So we gave him a bigger boat."

It was Truth, Hades had to give them that. All of it. All of her toys were broken. She turned back to the tree, sparing them her intensity. "Ask."

The others were regarding them curiously. She ignored them.

"Do you think we can succeed this time?"

Hades found herself surprised again. Rarely was her opinion asked regarding such things. But she owed them an answer, and she could be nothing but True. She considered the garden in all of its flawed perfection, then the perfect flaws of mortal existence, and she smiled, deciding that she would make it work. The mortals deserved that. Not with one of her own, but Tadurin was right – there would always be others.

"Yes, I do."

“And yeah, that’s basically gotten me to now.” Jamirh finished his story, leaning back against the ship, arms folded behind his head. He wanted to soak in as much sun as possible. “What do you think?”

“That’s... a lot,” Ben said mildly, a single eyebrow raised.

“Kind’a surprising ya survived,” Marjori agreed.

Don shook his head. “I wouldn’t’ve.”

“It was th’ kind o’ adventure folks can only dream about!” Caron boomed.

“Could’ve used more romance, if you ask me,” Salisha said with a pout as her sister nodded in agreement.

Jamirh just shrugged. “I didn’t write it. If you’ve got complaints, or praises, or whatever, go leave a review. I hear Goodreads and Amazon are popular. Or wherever you usually review things. I hear it helps authors out.”

“Yeah, because, like, 360,000 words for the promise of a lunch date is really too long–”

“Leave it online,” Jamirh said with a shake of his head. “We’ve got seas to explore.”

# Acknowledgments

And here we are, at the end(~ish) of a road that I started down in 2010. Don't worry; I'm going to keep going – but the conclusion of this trilogy is definitely a major milestone, brought to you by:

To Jessy Jacobs, Lydia Troiano, Ashley McKhann, and Bill Millette, who keep me going when even I don't know where the story is headed – your enthusiasm means the world to me. To Andrew LaFontaine, whose enjoyment of my stories and merch brings me infinite enjoyment. To my brother John Sauco, who was vital to helping me figure out exactly how bad this book was going to be for our heroes. To Sarah LaFontaine, who is always willing to listen to any craziness or drama that's happening, and who is always down to discuss... we'll call it "high literature" (IYKYK). To Christian Black and Michael Peck, for our little music theory discussion. To the Writing Forge authors – hanging out with y'all has saved my sanity more times than I can count.

To my editorial team, Breyonna Jordan, Naomi Munts, and Jane Spencer. I apologize for my inability to know the difference between farther and further, and my graphic abuse of hyphens and em dashes.

And finally, to my parents, for all your support throughout the years. Thank you.

# About the Author

**Liz Sauco** is an author from Rhode Island who enjoys a host of nerdy pastimes, such as crocheting cute animal plushies and playing video games. After graduation from the University of Rhode Island with a degree in Classics, she spent several years teaching Latin to high school students while working on her first manuscript. You can find her on Facebook, Discord, and Tiktok, and read her blog at lizsauco.com.

# Free Short Story

Want to stay up to date on the latest news?

Join my newsletter, and receive a free short story "Another Beginning", set twenty years before *Lost Blades*. Be among the first to get news about new releases, giveaways, events, and promotions!

# Want more from the world of Gaia?

Can't get enough? Want to really dive deep into the lore? Check out Campfire, where you can get character profiles, art, maps, timelines, location info, bonus short stories, and more for all of my stories!

But... maybe you are interested in being *spoiled*? Ream is a new subscription platform - like Patreon, but for authors - and having one allows me to spoil readers with tons of extra content! Sneak peeks, art works-in-progress, name in the acknowledgements of books, polls, direct access to me, and more are all offered at different tiers. You can even give me a follow for free to get a monthly update!

# Also By Liz Sauco

***Colors of Magic*** **is a companion to the Blades of the Goddess series**

Stories from the past, both distant and near, are collected into this anthology. Nine short stories featuring Hades, Jak, Sukra, Ander, and more offer a glimpse into life at different moments on Gaia. As magic pulses through the world in a spectrum of colors, how will it shape the characters we have come to know in *Blades of the Goddess*?

# Colors of Magic Preview

As soon as they succeeded, Alexia knew they'd failed.

It stared at them curiously from within its new prison, form flickering rapidly as though it couldn't decide what kind of person it wanted to be, but its eyes... those violet eyes remained the same. Oh, the entity was here all right, and it didn't seem to be able to leave if the flicks of energy exploring the new space were any indication, but...

"Something's not right," she heard herself say over the cheers of some of her more exuberant colleagues.

There was a pause in the celebration, deference afforded her based on her status. "Everything looks good here. All blue," the tech at the monitor panel reported. "The electromagnetism is holding."

"What is it doing, exactly?" The general assigned to the project strode forward to tap on the glass, narrowing his eyes as the energy tapped back. "Looking for weaknesses? A way out?"

"That's likely," one of the senior scientists agreed. "Chances are it's never been confined this way."

"But the tests all show that the magnetism should hold it," another scientist stated.

The general frowned. "'Should'?"

Alexia remained silent, watching those violet eyes as they studied the humans around it, not even glancing at the large window showing the perfect globe of the Earth far below. Perfect, save for the Rot ravaging her and her people. Even animals, plants... nothing was safe from it. This was their best chance of, if not fighting it directly, then buying more time to find a solution.

"This has never been attempted before," the first scientist pointed out. "Or perhaps it has, if some of the old mythology is to be believed, but certainly not to this level of success. It would have freed itself by now, if it could."

"And we'd all be dead," a tech near Alexia muttered under his breath.

She chose to ignore him. Some part of her just knew that this hadn't worked. But if that were the case, why was it still here? She brushed her long black braid over her shoulder, trying to ignore the feeling twisting in her stomach. "You are sure all of the aligned energy was collected? There isn't any being picked up by the sensors anywhere around either the planet or relevant bodies?" she asked instead.

The man's eyes flickered over the projections, hands flicking from panel to panel as he searched the reports. "All the aligned energy is here. No readings of it anywhere else."

"Then we've succeeded," the general murmured. Despite the positive sentiment, his brow was furrowed. "We've... trapped the 'god' of death."

"We've trapped the metaphysical energy associated with the ending of life," Alexia corrected absently, ignoring his use of "we." As though the military had actually done anything other than babysit the project. They hadn't even supplied any funding. "Though, the theory is entities like this could have posed as such to our ancestors." Which explained why it appeared to be mimicking human form, even if it couldn't decide on a specific one. Even as Alexia watched, first a red-haired Irish woman, followed by a small blond boy, then a grizzled old man of some Asian descent housed those unnatural eyes.

Those violet eyes that turned in her direction.

The general shook his head. "Whatever you want to call it. So then, no one can die?"

Alexia's stomach twisted again, though her mind told her she should be celebrating. "I'm not sure how they could, with the relevant energy trapped." Detecting the energy present at the moment of death had been a huge breakthrough in their understanding of it. No matter the cause – sickness, injury, old age – this energy gathered at that final moment, named "Omega energy" by her team, and this massive spike had been proven to be what actually ended life at the cellular level. They'd already had some success with mice; shielding them from the buildup of Omega energy allowed them to survive violent trauma that otherwise would have killed them instantly.

The general nodded.

Alexia was not the only one to scream as he pulled his gun and shot the tech watching the monitors.

"Looks like there's a flaw somewhere, though I'll admit that whatever you've got in there looks promising," he said dispassionately as he toed the tech's lifeless body, blood pooling on the floor, matting the tech's blond hair. "Keep me updated on your progress. I'll send in some of the boys to clean this up." He turned and left the room.

Alexia's hands were plastered in front of her mouth as she fought through the shock and nausea, her heart hammering like a jackrabbit's. Her mind raced without her permission. The tech had been... he'd just been... where had they gone wrong? He shouldn't be dead, even with a bullet in the head. The energy buildup could not have occurred, as it was contained in the electromagnetic sphere, sealed with mercury and iron. Injured, yes; dead, no. Cold iron, there were legends that said cold iron was necessary, and there were reasons for legends, truth hidden in stories, but what was colder than the dead of space? How could Tr– how could the tech be dead?

She sharply pushed back against the building rage and fear. The general had no right. There was a process to follow. There were other ways to test the theory.

Someone was vomiting into a trash bin. Several members of her team were crying. Where had they gone wrong? She glanced towards the containment field again.

Those violet eyes were filled with pity as they met her own dark ones, the entity's form finally settling into that of a pale man with short black hair, long bangs swept to the side, though the clothing continued to change. Very, very slightly, it shook its head.

Yes, she reflected bitterly. They certainly had failed.